CLOUDS END

C L O U D S
E N D

SEAN STEWART

A C E   B O O K S ,   N E W   Y O R K

CLOUDS END

An Ace Book
Published by The Berkley Publishing Group
200 Madison Avenue, New York, NY 10016

The Putnam Berkley World Wide Web site address is
http://www.berkley.com

Book design by Fritz Metsch
Cover art by Tara McGovern

First Edition: August 1996

LIBRARY OF CONGRESS CATALOGING-IN-PUBLICATION DATA
Stewart, Sean, 1965–
    Clouds end / Sean Stewart.—1st ed.
        p.   cm.
    ISBN 0-441-00347-8 (hc).—ISBN 0-441-00332-X (tr)
    I. Title.
  PR9199.3.S794C56   1996
  813'.54—dc20   95-43833   CIP

Printed in the United States of America

10 9 8 7 6 5 4 3 2 1

CLOUDS END

PART ONE
The Sea Loop

CHAPTER 1: OUT OF THE MIST

Shandy, fourth Witness of Clouds End, watched from the west window of her tower as the sun drowned and twilight came lapping over her island.

The last boats were sliding in. Crews emptied their holds into waiting fish barrels and tied up for the night. They checked every knot twice, glancing eastward at the dirty rack of clouds building above the Mist. A mean wind kicked up whitecaps and swung boats against the creaking dock.

A new island had been born one day's sail to the east, crusting around a story in the Mist-time like a pearl forming around a grain of sand. Shandy's daughter Shale had been the first to see it, out sailing with Rope and Foam, but Shandy had felt it happening for days. As Witness of Clouds End it was her duty to learn the new island's story.

But still she closed her eyes and waited, scared to open herself to the Mist on a night when its powers were so fiercely surging.

Duty, Witness.

Duty.

She emptied herself, and was filled up with the world, filled up with stone and sea and fire. After all these years it was still a horrible feeling, like drowning; the world filling up your heart, your lungs. Her blood shook as she opened to the speaking night.

If you are tired, the darkness whispered, come to me. I will show you a great secret under the pine's dim branches. I will show you bare ground and a hollow place between waiting roots. Come find out what the grass has already learned.

Shandy had better things to do than listen to that dark voice. What says the wind? she asked.

And the wind said, This is a story of the Mist-time and the real world, where all things are true, and few things are what they seem. This story is a One Twist Ring: a tale of two empires that is also the tale of two women.

Two women? Shandy said.

And the wind said, Brook.

The next morning dawned windy and clear.

It was Brook's turn to mind the children of Clouds End. Her band of tiny scavengers swarmed across the rocks and sand, shouting at each new piece of salvage the night's storm had thrown up. Waves slapped against the point and then foamed across Crabspit Beach. The breeze tugged at Brook's brown hair, still wet from her morning swim, and swirled deeper, into her heart.

Only yesterday Shale had seen a brand new island forming at the edge of the Mist. Seen it with her own eyes! Because she was quick and strong and fearless, a clever sailor in her own right who got to crew with Rope and Foam whenever she wanted to.

. . . While Brook was stuck minding the children. Again.

Brook had always known in her heart that something magical and strange waited for her, out in the Mist. But it was hard to be patient, to sit at home and sew, or play games with the children, knowing that Shale, who hadn't a thimbleful of magic in her, was out in the world having adventures.

The breeze whispered in Brook like a secret. She had always felt a destiny waiting for her in the Mist.

A flock of gulls soared overhead, screeching and fighting.

Shriek, shriek, soar and scream! Yellow feet and beady black eyes; around her the batter of white wings. Below, the old sea, crawling and crawling.

Aiee! Fire crept along the muscles of Jo's wings. Hungers jumped in her belly like little fish: hey! hey!

Finally, an island underwing. Grey stone, green moss. Shores of barnacled rock, or gritty sand. An elm-shadowed pond at its heart.

A shoal of human children went darting and drifting across the shingle. A young woman moved among them, her dress blue as stream-water, her rippled brown hair bound in islander braids.

Jo cocked her head and screamed, falling down the long sky. A swoop, a gliding arc, a chestful of wind cupped between her wings—and then her webbed feet touched at last the solid rock.

Brook had always felt a destiny waiting for her in the Mist.

She broke apart her little sister's braid. "There's a story swimming by these days. It came in very close last night. I felt the wave of it. I felt the island rocking."

Finch looked over her shoulder. "You're trying to scare me. This isn't The Island That Went Back, you know."

"A Hero was passing. Hurrying by."

"You heard a Hero?"

"Fires. Lots of fires." Brook wove her sister's hair into two square knots, to dangle fetchingly beneath Finch's ears. "Like boats burning on the water."

Gulls swirled overhead.

Finch squirmed, curious in spite of herself. "Fires! If it was a Hero, then, it would be Sere. If it was." She squinted narrowly at her big sister. "If you heard anything at all."

Gulls swirled down, all white breasts and grey backs, drifting onto Crabspit Beach or standing importantly amidst the seaweed at the water's edge.

And then, as Brook watched, the largest gull stretched and blurred, its body oozing like hot wax, changing shape.

With a yell, Brook jumped to her feet and grabbed Finch by the arm.

The children turned to look where Brook was staring.

"Brook!" little Toad wailed. From between her legs he stared at the Mist-creature on the beach. Its white back rippled like blown water.

"What is it?"

"Will it sting?"

"I want my daddy!"

"B-r-o-o-k!" Toad wailed again.

"Hush now. Don't be frightened," Brook said, remembering her duty. The children were panicky, staring at her, trying not to cry. "Finch! Take them back to the village. Tell Shandy there's a Mist-thing on the beach."

"B-but, what about you?"

"Do what I tell you!"

Finch nodded, herding the children up the Ridge path. Again and again she looked back, hoping her big sister would follow, but Brook did not come.

A stink of crab, yes? Hey?

Rattle him, rattle him! Yaw! Split split split!

Aiee! Mine!

Aiee! Hssss! Hss!

Gull voices spat and screamed, and the sea ate the sense from them as Jo fell back to earth. Their harsh tongue broke apart, its meaning splintered by the rush of wave on rock, the hiss of foam, the stone's deep voice, the great humming silence of the sky.

She was alone.

And oh, the terrible emptiness of this moment as her body spilled and ran, hungry for a shape. The terrible sucking need. The world in its madness pulled on her from every side. The stone spoke his hardness through her skin; she was drugged by the smell of salt water and wet sand.

The wind poured through her like a river.

Alone, shape-shifting, she was surrounded by the voices of the world: the stone's old, dark, clean thoughts; the shrieking gulls; the sly wind; the ceaseless waves.

Is it time yet? the Seventh Wave said.

for flood.

a cleansing.

the stone understands.

and we are (I am) restless.

and we are the strength of cold fathoms.

and we are the keepers of the voiceless dark.

Not yet.

not this season. not this time.

we (I) do not yet dream the High Dance.

I (we) sing the Wave: and the stillness under.

So the waves argued, bold and mild and murderous by turns, every seventh one their deeper, truer tongue. How well Jo knew them.

With ferocious will she pulled herself together, shutting out the roaring world. She had to be human, she remembered that. But it was hard to craft a body from memories the Mist had confused. Hard to make a woman from wind and waves, from the stone beneath and the indifferent sky above.

She needed someone to shape on.

She *listened.*

Listened into the knot of children, their panic and their wide eyes and their trust; listened for the young woman minding them. Yes: that was a woman the villagers would trust.

She wound herself around the young woman's voice, pulling together sea and stone, cloud and sky—knotting the elements into human form. And then Jo reached out to the person behind the voice, and took that pattern for her own.

Brook. Brook was their name.

Brook trembled, twisting a bracelet of blue shells around her wrist. Magic crawled and shivered in her like a fever. To watch the Mist-creature take shape before her was terrifying: precious: secret.

All her life she had treasured the moment when things called to her from out of the Mist, strange and heavy with meaning. But never had she felt the magic as she did now, alive and bitter in her blood. Something inside her had broken, some dike against madness. This was the terrible magic, the Mist that had swallowed Rope's father on a sunny day fifteen years before.

Mist poured from the gull's body. Its tiny head grew; its round eyes narrowed and silvered. Its beak re-formed into a strong hooked nose. Its head-feathers unravelled into hair, a drifting mass of white spider-web. It stirred, hissing like a gull, and stared at Brook with inhuman eyes.

As the gull-woman held Brook's gaze her pale flesh tanned. Her white hair thickened into four brown braids, looped behind her neck. Bones erupted from her wrist and hardened into a bracelet of blue shells. Her body rippled and shrank, melting down like a candle before Brook's eyes, changing into a young woman in a dress of blue-dyed sailcloth and eelskin boots.

"A twin," Brook whispered: for it was herself she saw.

She was going to die.

Gently, Brook stepped forward. She had to kill the twin before it killed her.

"Don't be afraid," she said.

She had to get ten strides closer.

Eight.

"I won't hurt you."

The twin was on a spit of rock with the sea behind it and a sharp drop to the right. It was Brook, Brook in every detail: the woman she saw reflected in Teardrop Pond every day. No one would know it wasn't her. No one would be able to tell.

But she would be gone.

Six strides.

An empty crab shell splintered under her heel.

The twin frowned and fluttered. It yawped, a bird's cry from a woman's mouth. It blinked and coughed.

Brook's heart was hammering and her throat cramped when she tried to speak.

"I won't hurt you."

Another step. "We don't get many strangers here."

Four strides.

"There will be jerries when the boats come back. Smoked eel and pickled gulls' eggs. We always offer travellers the best of our catch."

Three strides.

The twin stepped back. Its skin bleached to gull's-belly white. Its brown eyes turned gleaming silver, like fish scales.

Trying not to look like me, Brook thought. Trying not to scare me.

Gulls screamed overhead.

Two strides.

Brook lunged forward. The twin flung itself to the right, into the sky, but its white wings were gone. Betrayed by its human body, it fell badly and slammed its head against the rock.

Brook scrambled after it, slipping on the slick stone. She saw a sharp-edged shell and dove for it. Ripping it out of the cold grey sand, she turned, hoping to slash out the monster's throat.

The twin's silver gaze slid into her like a steel hook. She felt herself jerk, her hands twisting at her sides. Sobbing, she fell to her knees, transfixed.

The twin touched its salt-white cheek. Its fingers came away spotted with blood. "Aiyee! Hurts." And then looking at Brook, it said, "You hurt me."

The moment was slipping from Brook like the tide, the sand shifting and draining out from underneath her; her anger dwindling into fear.

She had been twinned.

She was going to die and no one would know. She would never have a baby and she would never sail to Double Eagle or the Harp, and the Brook who made love to Rope at last would not be her.

And she saw that in the Mist this destiny had always been awaiting her.

Jo twinned Brook, and took much knowing from her.

She was on Clouds End. Shandy was Witness, Stone was Trader. Her best friend, Shale, had long legs and a short temper and you could crack oyster shells with her sharp laughter.

Rope was her love. He was steady as an anchor and he had sailor's hands, so tough you could blunt a bone needle on his calluses. Though he was only twenty-one, he had a boat of his own—he was that reliable—and he would marry her one day.

Or rather, Jo thought pleasurably, he will marry me.

Deeper still she reached into Brook, drinking her like water. She had been in the Mist so long, lost in Sere or the Gull Warrior, that she had forgotten how good it felt to escape the magic's fever-grip; to sink into a real life as if skinny-dipping in a shady pool.

(Oh and being Brook ten years old on the beach before dawn, playing the pretend game of what Clouds End would be like if she were dead. Thinking, What secrets the waves must tell the shore, if only you could hear them!)

Fear started in Jo, splashing and rippling. She had forgotten how deep a life could be. Now Brook was running into her like water, filling her up, clogging her lungs and heart.

(And seven years old, the day her parents drowned, pulling her mother's shawl around her shoulders while Trickfoot's Witness looked at her with teary eyes, and the Trader told her about the boat ride to Clouds End, where she and Finch were to be fostered.

The shawl still rich with her mother's smells.)

Brook closed over Jo like the sea.

She filled Jo up until she ran through her heart and spilled from her eyes, and their currents mixed into a single stream.

Jo felt a knot cinch tight around her life, binding her to Brook. Brook the fool, she thought angrily. Brook the girl still young enough to long for magic in her life. Shale had a traveller's heart, and Rope a sailor's eye, but what did Brook have? A pocket full of stories?

Brook the foster-child. Brook the idiot who sent the kids away but stayed because she wanted to see the magic all by herself. Wanted to feel the touch of the Mist.

Fool, fool, fool! Jo raged, weeping. Brook she loved just a little bit too much to kill.

Yet.

CHAPTER 2: THE WITNESS

The haunt no longer looked like Brook. She was tall, with salt-white skin and hair. Her narrow silver eyes were set far apart on either side of a strong arched nose.

Trudging behind her, Brook felt empty. Gone.

She had been twinned. If the stories were true, she was as good as dead, destined to vanish into the Mist. She'd had her moment of bravery and let it slip away. Now she broke around the haunt, like water against white stone. "You are one of the people of the air, aren't you?"

"That's right." As Jo strode up the path she wiped the blood from her cheek and licked her fingers. The scratches faded, leaving only whiteness.

Sun! Sun on face! Ooh, that tickles! Mind your step! said the wildflowers bobbing beside their feet. They squeaked when Jo trod on them.

Up the Ridge path and across the east meadow. Then they were at the village, thirty small stone houses. They passed old Stick, whittling on his stoop. Long years of sun and wind had left his skin tough and creased as turtle-leather. Don't look, Brook thought desperately. Stay away. As if one glance from the haunt could splinter him to pieces.

"Brook! Your sister blew through here with kids flapping in front of her like jib sails in a storm." Stick looked up, and slowly considered Brook's guest. He peeled off another switch of bark.

"Shouldn't be surprised if there's dirty weather coming."

Purple clouds now bruised the eastern sky. The wind was freshening, kicking up whitecaps off Crabspit Point. Villagers called to one another. The door to the Witness's house banged open and Finch came out, dragging Shandy by the sleeve.

"Great flock of gulls just came in. Never a good sign." Stick studied his old knife, its blade seated in its third whalebone haft and worn thin with many sharpenings. "My grandfather came to Clouds End before it was one year calved from the Mist, you know. A lot of queer catch swimming out of the East, back then. We learned to be careful." Stick paused and spat. He looked at Brook. "We learned to take care of our own."

Shandy walked up to meet Brook and the haunt. "Don't you make a fine pair!" (And Jo felt Brook's memories ghost through her. Shandy the Witness, like an old boat weathered but sound. Her stubby fingers stained with liver spots and traces of dye, her hair driftwood grey. Her eyes shrewd in a face worn to wrinkles.)

Brook stood behind the haunt like her shadow, as cold in the spring sunshine.

Shandy squinted up into the rising wind. "Storm coming. So, Brook. Just had to top Shale's new island, eh?"

Villagers were watching them from every window. When they caught Brook's eyes they looked away as if she were already dead.

Jo said, "I come to warn you of a great danger."

Shandy grunted. "We're obliged."

They walked back to the Witness House, where Shandy's husband, Moss, was waiting. Shandy invited Jo inside to talk. Brook she told to wait on the porch. "So everyone can see we're looking after you," Moss said, after his wife and the haunt had gone inside.

Every night for as long as Brook could remember she had seen Moss and Shandy sitting in the two old net chairs hung from hooks in the porch beams, facing west to watch the sunset. Now she sat in Shandy's chair, swinging slowly back and forth. She was deeply grateful for the older man's company, his stories or his big comfortable silence.

As the afternoon passed, her foster-mother, Otter, came by with a plate of honey cakes, which she and Brook ate while Moss went inside to check on Shandy and Jo.

The eastern skies bruised more badly. Otter left to start dinner. Boats ran back into the bay. Rope's came in soon after the tide turned. Shale leapt from the deck to the dock and turned the painter a quick couple of hitches through the docking ring. Foam ambled after, and then Rope, last as always to leave his ship.

Brook watched them from Shandy's porch. There were tears on her face.

Shale came first, racing up the meadow path and into the village. Someone must have told her the news.

"Are you all right?" Shale demanded.

"I always run like there's something coming after me," Brook said, trying to smile. "But you always run like you're hunting something down."

"Is she inside with Mom?"

"Yes."

Foam and Rope were now hurrying toward them.

"You shouldn't stay here. It isn't safe to be near me, Brook said."

"Oh, shut up."

A moment later Rope and Foam joined them. Foam sat with his back to a post and his lanky arms around his knees. Rope sat in Moss's chair. He reached for Brook's hand. She wanted to take some comfort from him but her fingers and hands were wood, her whole body like driftwood abandoned on an empty beach. Unfeeling.

Down at the harbor the docks groaned. Boats creaked and bumped. Up at the center of the island, the elms around Teardrop Pond began to murmur darkly about the rising wind. Driving westward, the darkness of a great storm front raced over the sea toward Clouds End. Gulls swirled along its leading edge, glints of white fire lit by the westering sun.

"It will get dark early," Rope said.

Foam frowned at a small tear in one of his elaborately braided cuffs. "Time to get out my needle." In a village where most men

would cheerfully have worn walrus pelts, Foam was cursed with a
sense of style.

"Get with carriage what you can't with cargo, eh?" Shale's
shark-tooth earring danced as she paced restlessly along the ve-
randah. She stopped in front of the hanging chairs and wiped a
tear off Brook's cheek. "Come on, Bug! You aren't dead yet."

"I used to wish I were Shandy's daughter instead of you. I used
to imagine I was the Witness, seeing magic things."

Shale grimaced. "Your face would cloud up with this Mysterious
Look I always hated. The one that said, 'I am a deep person,
thinking deep, secret thoughts.' "

Foam grinned. "We all know that one."

"Sometimes I would pretend I had died," Brook said, "and I
could wander anywhere on the island without being seen, and
listen to what people said about me." She sat silent for a moment,
twisting her bracelet of blue shells around her wrist. "Well that's
me now. I'm the walking dead."

Shale swore and kicked her. Not very hard.

Women's voices murmured from the room behind them as
Shandy and Jo kept talking. Jo's voice clear, rising and falling like
the wind. Shandy's blunt and to the point.

"Come on, Brook. This isn't the time for self-pity. It doesn't
help."

"That's our friend Shale," Foam murmured. "Always a kind
word or a friendly smile." Shale favored him with a look that could
gut fish.

"Though I admit you would have made a better Witness's
daughter," she said. "I always got Mom's stories mixed up, and
the incense made me sneeze."

Brook laughed in spite of herself. "When I'm Witness I'll make
you Trader, then. First woman Trader in the Eastern Islands."

Shale nodded. "A fair bargain."

"Is there nothing in your hold for me?" Rope said, scratching
his beard in a thoughtful way. He was heavy-muscled and still
thickening; the sailcloth shirt his mother had made him only last

summer was already tight across his shoulders and around his broad, hairy wrists.

Shale grinned. "Oh, I'll let you be my first mate, I suppose."

Foam said, "I think Brook has an idea about Rope's first mate."

Shale laughed, watching Rope and Brook blush. "Better. See—you're not dead yet." She examined her eelskin boots, sticking two fingers through a hole in one toe.

"Was it terrible?" she said.

Brook looked at the darkening sea. "You know how it is when you climb the bluff to watch the sun set? It goes down and everything gets very dark, until it's so dark you can't see the edge of the cliff. But you still feel it there. You still feel the drop." Her shell bracelet, turning, clicked and whispered.

Foam said, "It's hard to untie a knot made of Mist."

Shale's fingers tightened on the haft of her knife. "So you cut it."

"How would you try?" Foam said. "Wait until the haunt lies sleeping—in your mother's house—and cut her throat with a scaling knife? Watch her blood go spilling across your mother's floor after having offered her traveller's welcome? I don't think so."

"It doesn't have to be in the house."

"Then where?" Rope said. "A haunt's death brings down a haunt's curse anywhere on the island."

"On the sea, then," Shale said. "She said she had a warning."

Brook nodded. "A message to send to Delta. She says Sere is bringing his fire to the first island. I heard that much before they went inside."

"So give her a boat and a crew, get a day's sail away . . ." Shale sliced her knife across an imaginary throat. "Dump the body overboard. Scuttle the ship within swimming distance of home and drown your bad luck with it."

"What if Sere really is burning through the Mist?" Brook looked away from Shale's angry eyes. "She twinned me, yes. If the stories are true, she'll try to kill me some day, or throw me into the Mist. But that doesn't make everything she says a lie." Brook's fingers wound tightly into the lines of the net chair. "She is a little in me now. I think her fear of Sere is real. I can feel his fever."

From under raised eyebrows Foam said, "Now, would this be that distant, Mysterious Look you were talking about, Shale?"

Quickly Brook shook her head. "No, I'd be much grander about it. Believe me, I've never felt less distant and mysterious in my life. I feel like a bug on the bottom of someone's boot."

"What about sailing off?" Rope suggested. "Not forever, Shale. A few weeks. Long enough to let the haunt go and leave Brook alone. We could go over to the Harp, or back to Trickfoot and visit some of Brook's kin."

"Or sail out to the new island," Foam suggested quickly, for about the thirtieth time in the last day.

"No, no, and no," Rope growled, exasperated. "For Fathom's sake, will you shut up about the new island? It's too new, it's too dangerous, and it's too near the Mist. Shandy will send someone over when the time is right."

Foam grinned and shrugged. "You can't blame the fisherman for casting his line."

Shale's short bangs fluttered in the rising wind. "I want to go out there as much as you do, Foam. But is the Mist the best place to go if you're running from a haunt?"

"I don't think I can run from her," Brook said. "We're a Sheet-Bend story now, she and I: a little rope and a big one knotted up together. The knot can't be slipped. It has to be untied."

Shale flicked her dagger. "Or cut."

As Witness, it was Shandy's duty to give the haunt supper and offer her a bed for the night. Her daughter Shale she sent to stay with Brook at the Trader's house. When she had seen the haunt to her room and her own family to their beds, Shandy returned to her tower and sat before her brazier for long hours, deep in thought.

Outside, the bad luck that had been building for days around her island had broken into a fierce squall. The wind battered her house with flying rain. Down at the harbor, wood roared as ships slammed against the dock.

In her hands the Witness cupped a burning cone of incense. A bittersweet scent stole from between her fingers.

In the room below, her two halves slept. Moss, her husband and her anchor: for thirty years her line to all that was human. And Jo. Jo who was all Shandy might have been, if she hadn't loved her parents and her family and the small doings of her village, but listened instead to the wind's wild voice.

Jo had chosen that freedom, and become one of the people of the air. She had turned away from the world of men—or perhaps men had driven her out, afraid of her strange gifts. There had been no Moss for her, no anchor line. She had given herself up to the wind and the world.

The storm blew harder, rattling at the shuttered windows. Shandy shook her head. Why, why did the haunt have to pick Brook? For thirteen long years Shandy and Stone the Trader, with Otter his wife, had taken such care to bring Brook back into the sunlight. She had more of the Mist in her than was healthy. For years they had feared their fosterling would leave them; would sink into herself and walk into the Mist. But Shale and Rope held her, and her love for her sister, Finch, and Otter her foster-mother, and patient Stone.

Until the stupid girl had gotten herself twinned by a haunt. Well. If stories were easy, they wouldn't be told in knots.

Fear almost kept Shandy from going down the stairs.

Duty. She had to know the haunt's thoughts. She had to brave the wind.

She crept downstairs in the dark, skirting the table and the stove, and eased herself onto the low stool beside Jo's cot. Incense like scorched honey trickled down her throat.

She didn't want to die.

Duty, Witness.

Shandy stared at Jo. The room was dark, but the haunt's white skin shone pale as the moon burning through a bank of cloud. Her breath had a strange uneven rhythm, ragged and gusting like the storm outside. It took a long time for Shandy to match it. Slowly, slowly she fell into the creaking house, the spattering rain; the restless, raging, wild-hearted wind. Incense crawled and buzzed in her blood, and she drowned in the haunt's dreaming.

A flock of gulls carved circles on the wind, swooping and screaming around a young woman. It was Brook. Blood welled in streams from her palms. The mob of gulls thickened, obscuring her. When a big wind came up and blew them away she was gone.

Shandy despaired.

A single gull preened upon the rock and laughed. "Witness! I am shocked! What courtesy is this, to peek at other people's dreams?"

"Is this nothing but a joke to you?"

Jo hissed and clacked her bill. "The spy who peeps through the window can't complain at what she sees!" Her gull's body stretched and blurred. "You think you are so clever, you aging island witches. Peering and blinking at the world like moles, impressed that you can see at all. You thought you could come sneaking and prying into me!"

Jo shifted, taking the shape of a white-skinned woman with narrow silver eyes. "Creeping into my sleep like a crab in the ooze. I heard you and I caught you. Don't pretend you should be offended! I came to tell the sea's people of Sere's great advance; fine thanks this is for my warning. Perhaps you islanders deserve the gift the Fire will make you."

"I'm sorry," Shandy said. "Sorry to have tried it, and sorrier still to be caught."

"Aaiee! At least you are honest! Yaw."

"What did you expect me to do? Nothing? After you spelled one of my people?"

Jo shrugged and grinned. Brook's features floated into her face.

Shandy said, "You will give back everything you take from her."

"I did not come to cause trouble. I came to give warning, and seek help."

"What help do you need that an aging island witch can give?"

"Company." Jo shook her arms into wings, changing back into

a bird. "Sere works the world through human hands, and human hands must stop him. I need a guide to take me to Delta, and perhaps beyond."

"Why? Go! You can ride the wind faster than we can sail the water. Take your warning to the first island yourself."

The gull hissed and screamed. "Yaw! And what good would that do, aaaie? They hate haunts no less there, and have no Sight to show them what I say is true." Jo flapped down onto the rock. "Have pity, Witness. I dare not make such a trip. A gull does not remember the purposes of men. I would fly to Delta and forget why I went."

"Mm. And who would you have me send?"

Jo preened and cocked her head. "Brook! Why not? We are easy together. Send Brook! I would take care of her."

"No doubt," Shandy said. "No. No ship will sail from Clouds End if you are on it."

"What isn't offered will be taken!"

"You will give back everything you take from her, Jo."

Jo screeched, flinging herself into the sky. "Don't presume to threaten me! Haunts get what they want, Witness. Remember that! I am of the air!" She yawped and circled over Shandy's head. Her wings roared like a crackling fire, like a rushing wind. "So you want to touch the air? Then hold your ear up and tell me what you hear!"

And now the world was a storm of sound, a thousand voices crying out at once; stone sea sand bird's banter, the emptiness of the terrible sky. The crushing noise was driving Shandy mad. She shouted but her words were broken and whirled away.

And then she was sitting by Jo's bed.

The storm had broken.

In the deafening silence Shandy thought she heard the sound of unhappy laughter, faint as memory.

The cot was empty.

The haunt was gone.

CHAPTER 3: SAGE CREEK

The next morning the squall was gone. The sea still remembered the wild night; the swell ran heavily against Crabspit Point, and boat-bells clanked down at the harbor as ships rocked at anchor. But above the waves, the air hung heavy with fog.

It was a strange, still, expectant mist, Stone thought as he walked up from the boathouse in the darkness just before dawn. The meadow path he knew so well in daylight was gone; the one he walked seemed steeper and rougher, studded with unfamiliar roots and rocks. Tripping, he swore and stumbled through a pocket of fog. Its clammy touch on his face was cold as a ghost's kiss and unwholesome. He realized he was bracing himself for something dreamlike and dreadful. As if at any moment an omen might step out of the dripping darkness: the spirit of a drowned man, or some cursed traveller, knotted in a story bigger and more terrible than himself.

Dawn had yet to break when the Trader came to Shandy's house. She almost didn't hear his knock, it was so uncertain—and that wasn't like Stone either.

But when she pulled the door open and peered out into the deep blue before dawn, there he stood on her stoop, with one hand pulling at his long beard. "Regrets, Witness. I shouldn't have come so soon—"

"True," Shandy said, yawning. "But she's your fosterling, eh?"

Stone ducked under the lintel and came inside, nodding to

Moss, who was already awake and bustling over the oil cooking lamp in the corner of the room. Though Stone was only thirty-seven, his face was seamed by sun and wind, and his forked braid was shot with hanks of white. He breathed the dim, homey smells of Shandy's house: beeswax and cut planking, old dry cloth and apple vinegar, scorching butter and fresh-steeped peppermint tea from the breakfast Moss was making.

He glanced at the guest bedroom.

"Already gone," Shandy said. "As for our daughters, Nanny is still asleep and Shale stayed with you, of course."

"Knife drawn and pacing half the night, it seemed. Otter finally had to yell at her to lie down and be still so the rest of us could pretend to sleep in peace and quiet."

"How many times have we heard those two whispering in the corner of a room, eh?"

Stone said, "Not enough times yet."

"No. Not yet." Shandy got herself a mug of tea and sweetened it with honey. "Sometimes I think it isn't me that gets frailer as the years go by, but the world. More ripped sails, more warped wood. More friends lost. Everything is taken, sooner or later, by the Mist, or the sea."

Stone sat at the table. "It was good for Brook to have Shale there."

Shandy grunted. "And good for me to get Shale out of the house! What net would we be thrashing in if the Witness's daughter had taken a poke at our haunt? As she looked very keen to do."

"I had that urge myself."

Shandy laid a finger across her lips. "She could be anywhere, Trader. A wren in the eaves, a spider hanging from a lamp . . ."

Stone dropped a clatter of filleting knives onto Shandy's table and took out his polishing stone. Delicate with years of practice, his huge hands set to work on the blade of the longest knife, wearing away its rust in patient, perfect circles. "Even if the girls had been quiet, there was no sleep under my pillow. Otter finally tossed me out of bed, so I went down to the boathouse. Caulked a seam in the steambox and sharpened the flensing scythes."

Burly Moss tossed mushrooms into a skillet. They hissed and snoozed as he added a fat drip of oil. "Sometimes a man thinks better with his fingers than his head."

Witness and Trader, the two guardians of Clouds End shared for a moment the heaviness of their choices.

Shandy sipped her peppermint tea. "We can't let Brook stay."

The polishing stone stilled in Stone's hand.

"The haunt twinned her," Shandy said. "She won't give the girl up. We can't risk keeping her here."

"She deserves better."

"Do you let all hands founder to save one man? Deserve? Of course she deserves better. Nobody asked for this wave. But we must ride it the best way we can."

The polishing stone resumed its patient circling. "Daughter, and dear as daughter lost to me within the year." The knife-blade gleamed, long since clean; in its clear surface Stone saw his daughter Blossom's pale, drowned face.

"These are hard things." Reaching across the table, Shandy clasped his big hand with her small one. "You took her into your family and gave her a home. She will always remember that. I don't say we should give up. Last night the haunt told me there was a battle of Heroes in the Mist: Sere against the Gull Warrior. I believe her. Time and again this last moon I've touched visions of Sere's fire closing around Delta."

"And we are to save the first island, who can't save our own girl?"

"Stop it! She's mine too, Stone. She's mine too. And yes, curse it, we're going to send her to Delta. Because that's all this aging island witch can think to do."

Stone looked away.

"I want to send Brook to Delta with a warning." Shandy took another sip of her tea. "There they must have Witnesses greater than I. There perhaps the knot that binds her to the haunt can be ravelled."

Stone grunted.

"I'm not giving Brook up for dead! She's not helpless. She has her wits about her. She can handle people when she puts her mind to it. It's what she does best."

"Haunts aren't people," Stone said.

"They were once. They can be."

Stone shrugged and chose another knife to polish, a small-toothed one with a handle carved from narwhal's tusk. Silently he wore away the flakes of rust. "Who would go with her?"

Moss yawned. "Rope and Foam and Shale, of course." He tossed a handful of scallops in with the mushrooms. "Neither Rope nor Shale will let you send Brook off without going too. You might as well use that crew as any."

Stone flipped the knife over to polish the other side. "To sail to Delta? Rope is a fine sailor for a young man, but for such a journey you need a skipper with more experience."

Moss poked at his scallops. "Of course the Trader knows best about the sea. But remember, Rope has the newest boat. Young boats and young bodies are best in dirty weather."

Shandy nodded. "For once my great shambling husband is right. Those who hear the magic need anchors. Rope and our Shale are Brook's. To send her away without people to hold her to the world would be as good as giving her to the haunt. I'm willing to risk my daughter to keep that from happening. At least you can risk Rope's boat."

Stone frowned. He tested the knife's edge against his thumbnail, grunted, and took out a sharkskin cloth to buff the blade.

Dawn had come. Pale sunshine slanted through Shandy's shutters, winking off the steel. Stone saw his face mirrored there, tired and careworn. "The tools stay clean and sharp. But I get older, and my joints rust."

Shady smiled. "We are of the sea, not the stone. Say rather that the mountains' people are dull for a thousand years, while we are sharpened right to the nub."

Stone laughed and stuck the knives back in their oiled leather sheaths. "Very well. Brook sails to Delta aboard Rope's ship. Fathom help us all."

Shandy's decision blew a squall of activity through the village. Rope and Foam hurried to check their gear and tackle, looking for rot in lines and shrouds and stays, and checking every stitch of every sail. Foam's father, Sharp, paddled around the ship in his little dinghy, fussing with the caulking. Stone and the other men of the village stocked her with dried fish and oil and barrels of water, along with a few pearlweirds to use for trade when their supplies ran out later, among the inner islands.

Rope's mother, Sweetpea, baked for dear life, her thick arms floured up to her elbows; as if potato cakes and salted biscuits could protect her son from shoal and storm and the Mist that had taken his father.

Shandy pressed an eelskin pouch of simples into Shale's hand, along with a fuseware jar of her best Cut, Bruise and Sting liniment. "I make the best salve in the islands because of you," she remarked, giving her daughter a quick hug. "No other Witness can have a daughter with so many elbows and knees." Then Shandy tied a Witness Knot around Brook's wrist as a message to the Witnesses of Delta, and sent her to pack her things.

Once done packing, Brook had meant to join in outfitting Rope's ship, but wherever she offered to help, villagers smiled and looked away and told her not to mind, that it would be better for her to rest up for the trip.

She was cursed.

Oh, they didn't mean it badly, but she had been twinned. Even Otter, her foster-mother, who loved her like one of her own, was tactfully careful to keep herself between Brook and her eldest, Swallow, who was pregnant.

There was nothing for Brook to do but choke down her bitterness and take herself away. After all, they were right: her story was knotted to a haunt's tale now. She had no business getting the people she loved tangled up in that.

Even her goodbye to Finch was brief. Brook hugged her little sister tightly, rocking her from side to side. Finch stiffened and Brook drew away, hurt.

Finch stared at the floor, ashamed.

"Because I was twinned," Brook said.

Finch shuddered, and her mouth twisted down as it always did when she cried, making her look even younger than her twelve years. "I'm sorry. I'm so sorry. I'm no sister to you at all."

Brook kissed her forehead. "I love you, Finchling. I'm not like Shale, you know. I hate leaving Clouds End. But there's something wrong in the Mist, terribly wrong. I can't let anything happen to Otter or Pebble or Sweetpea, or most of all you."

Finch's tears were wet on her sister's neck. "You're all the family I have. Please come back."

Brook nodded, and held her close, and cried.

Then she sent Finch away to help Otter, and slipped out of the village to say goodbye to Clouds End itself.

Whatever happened after they set sail, Brook would never return to this island the same person she had left. She needed to take leave of the bone-colored rock and the scraggly trees and the brook that was her namesake: the places that held her childhood.

She walked up the meadow behind the village, following the course of Sage Creek. A dragonfly cut hard, colored lines through the air with crystal wings. Was Jo watching her even now, hidden behind a gull's white breast, or a squirrel's black eyes?

If she took my place, no one would ever know.

Like cold water, a shiver ran down Brook's back, half fear and half rebellion. "This is my home!" she shouted.

No one answered.

Up here the stream was a sweep of silver; she could see the pale rock through the water, speckled like a trout's belly with flakes of pink mica. She had found her name here while cooling her feet in Sage Creek. Admiring its flow from pond to shallows, and the courage of its leap over the bluffs. It was quick and slow, strong and weak, always changing, always faithful. She hoped she could live up to it.

The morning fog had burned away. Now the sun rubbed her back as she scrambled up the bluffs. Shale would have made short work of them, of course. Brook wondered how much of her life she had spent dreaming up adventures for Shale to have. This trip to Delta looked to be her best trick yet.

Brook's shell bracelet rattled and clacked against the rock and her braid was coming undone by the time she pulled herself, sweaty and triumphant, over the last outcrop, to lie gasping at the head of the falls.

Heaving herself to her feet, she followed the creek back into the woods. Sunlight spattered down like rain between the leaves. She took off her boots and played pirates, quiet-walking on cool green moss that squished between her toes. Leaves murmured and birdsong hung in the drowsy air.

At Teardrop Pond, Brook found a sunny rock and looked down into water green with thoughts of limb and leaf. On impulse she peeled off her clothes and waded in.

"Uuiooo!" Water pressed smooth and cold around her, as if she had been dunked in mint tea. She paddled furiously until she was warm, blowing and gasping like a seal. Her braid floated behind her like a snake. Spring was everywhere.

She let her feet touch the oozy bottom of mud and boulders and waterlogged leaves. She circled the pond, alert to its life. She peered at balls of floating cottonwood fluff, inspected the cunning spider webs with a predator's respect, and probed a papery wasps' nest left over from last summer.

So she drifted at the heart of Clouds End, at home.

She loved it. No matter what else happened, she loved the rocks and the water and the vast, mysterious world. She loved being alive.

And she would die before she let the haunt steal her home and life away.

They launched just after noon. Rope, Foam, Brook, and Shale waved from the deck of Rope's boat. Villagers waved back from the quay.

"Bring back lots of silk!" Finch cried to her sister.

"New seeds," Sweetpea suggested, fanning herself with one large hand.

"Wheat flour!" "Tomatoes!" "Cider!" "New sailcloth!" "A goat!" . . .

At last Rope held up his hands. "All we have to trade is a small cargo of pearlweirds and eelskins. Fuseware and sailcloth is all I can promise."

"To Delta for sailcloth?" Foam's father called in disgust.

Old Stick shook his head. "Sailcloth and adventure! Us Clouds Enders are made for it! Why, I recollect my grandfather, who was—"

" 'the first man as ever set foot on Clouds End proper,' " the rest of the villagers chanted.

Like a haughty tortoise, old Stick peered, blinking, at his fellow villagers. "The first and *best* man to set foot here, that builded half your homes for you, you might remember. He always said that every life was an adventure, when you lived two docks down from the sunrise."

Standing on deck, Brook shivered. "Being twinned is enough adventure for me," she said quietly.

Shale shrugged. "Even a haunt is just another wave. You have to ride it out, same as anything else."

"Every year you sound more like your mother."

"I do not!"

"Who's handling the sheets?" Rope called, untying his painter and shoving off. Shale uncleated the foresail sheet.

As they set sail the others had eyes only for the open sea, but Brook stood at the mainmast, looking back at Clouds End: liver-spotted rocks and moss, smelly fish-barrels and dock-posts armored with barnacles, the long meadow sloping up to the bluff, Sage Creek a silver thread spinning endlessly out from Teardrop Pond. Old Stick and little Pebble, Sweetpea, and Swallow (seven moons now—she'd have her baby before Brook got back) . . . Finch.

Stick might die. Others would be born. The fire Shandy had felt burning through the Mist might sweep over Clouds End, taking it away like The Island That Went Back.

Fierce love welled up in Brook. This was the place she was going to save. She wouldn't fail it.

The crowd clapped and cheered as Rope's boat sidled away from the dock. "Be good!" Shandy called. "And be careful!"

"And be lucky!" old Stick added. "I recollect my grandfather once said that a lucky man . . ."

The rest of his story was lost in luffing canvas. Rope's mainsail pushed out north and east, a grey wing straining into the Mist. Lordly white clouds towered overhead, looking down on Rope's boat, a brown and grey water skater crawling over the deep.

And far above the tiny ship, white breast lost against the clouds, a single gull circled and watched.

Watched and circled.

CHAPTER 4: SHALE'S ISLAND

They ran before an easterly breeze, scoring an arrow of foam upon a sea so blue it seemed the sky had drowned in it. Clouds End dwindled behind them, while the new island Shale had first spotted two days before grew out of the east before their prow.

Rope looked around his ship and raised his eyebrows at Foam. "Well? Do you think she's ready?"

His best friend grimaced, rubbing one long-fingered, big-knuckled hand through his thinning hair. "She's the newest craft on the island. Why else do you think we were sent?—Or are you casting doubts on the soundness of my knotwork, eh?" Foam leaned out over the starboard rail to examine the braid he had worked into Rope's hull with chisel and lacquer and dye, the best charm to hold a ship together through Mist and rain. He pursed his lips and scowled, squinting, in a perfect imitation of his father. "I'm a man of craft, I am, so you just worry about your business and I'll worry about mine!" He wiped his hands on an imaginary apron, and squirted a thin spit into the sea.

Rope laughed.

"Don't worry about the ship," Foam said, dropping back into his normal voice. "It's surviving forty days on a tiny boat with Shale that will be the problem!" He shivered as Shale glanced back at him, grinning. "She and Brook were always tight as limpets. A more terrifying pair of little girls it was never my misfortune to mind."

Foam was actually a few years older than the rest of them, but as Shale unkindly said, it rarely showed. Rope himself admired Foam's good faith and subtle mind. But it was true there weren't many on Clouds End who saw more to Foam than jokes and riddles and funny stories.

Foam said, "You feel steadier now, don't you? Now that we're out on the sea."

"You know me too well."

"You know the touch of this ship better than the feel of Brook's long hair in your fingers." Foam waved at the distant horizons. Already the nearest islands had shrunk to no more than stepping stones in the ocean's endless blue immensity. "No cover to creep behind out here. Not even for a haunt."

Rope's hands rested lightly on the wheel, feeling every subtle shift and pressure on the rudder. So much of his life rested in that touch. His eyes could tell him a thousand things about the daylight world; but sailing he lived most deeply in his hands, feeling his way through the blind and secret country below the waves. "The Mist took my dad on a sunny day."

"I remember."

"Not a cloud. The sea as flat as glass." Rope shook his head. "I was so angry at him for leaving us, the bastard. I never forgot that. What I did forget was the fear." He tapped his chest. "The way it sits up here, like a stone under your ribs, so you can barely breathe. That I had forgotten."

"Until the haunt came."

Rope looked at Brook astern. "Until the haunt came. And isn't that a bold way for a young man to feel?"

"Well now, if it's a bold deed you're looking for . . ." Foam threw up his hands as if to display a grand design. "Just think! Here you have been blessed with the chance to explore an island fresh from the Mist. To seek out its name and its story! Perhaps even spy a Hero-dropping! A spare pin from the Singer's braid, say, or a white feather molted by the Gull Warrior!"

Rope groaned.

"This wave will only pass once!" Foam argued. "I want my

grandchildren to be able to say, 'My grandfather Foam came over not one week after Twelve Hiccups came into the world!' "

"The land is probably still spreading from around the story. It may be weeks before the island finds its final shape. Even then the Mist will be rolling across it almost every day. Not to mention that there may be a haunt on our trail."

Shale pushed herself away from the mainmast. "Rope, you're so old they should give you grandchildren."

A rare, slow anger began to smolder in Rope's chest. He was so tired of saying No, so tired of pointing out risks. So tired of Foam and Shale needling him for his stodginess.

A big gull circled lazily overhead, screeching its derision until he could almost hear its scornful laughter. Free to soar the air, it laughed at good old dependable Rope. Laughed at his dullness. His wearisome old man's caution.

So his father had gone into the Mist. Why should Rope let him loiter all these years after, like a ghost in the shrouds? In more than a year of sailing, Rope's new boat hadn't even found her name.

But he had seen the new island too, after Shale had told him where to look. Its mystery could be part of his story, if he only dared to claim it.

"All right," he said.

The gull screamed once, mockingly, and peeled away.

"What?" Foam and Shale looked at him in surprise.

"We'll do it." Rope laughed and raised his arms wide. "If the wind stays fair, we can be there by tomorrow morning."

"Wonders and miracles!" Foam looked curiously at his captain. "What made you change your mind?"

"Swap's Breeze is blowing. I don't want to be left out." Rope looked fondly around the decks, feeling his ship roll beneath his boots, hearing the creak of her timbers. "You know, I think this will be the trip she finally gets her name."

"If you go by the new island, your boat will find her name by sunset tomorrow. Or be lost," Brook said.

Shale stirred. "I hate it when you're like that."

"It's typical," Shale said later that evening as they ate their first supper on board. "I find a new island and nobody cares. You get twinned by a sea gull, and we're off to Delta!" She rummaged in a fuseware jar for some pickled mushrooms.

Rope had finished laying strips of seaweed and salted fish between two potato cakes. "Do you believe what the haunt said, that Sere was fighting the Gull Warrior?"

"That's the whole reason we're going to Delta," Shale answered in a fine spray of mushroom. She swallowed. "To warn them. Mom said she thought the first island was in danger." She pointed to a band of blue knotwork braided around Brook's wrist. "That's why she put a Witness Knot on Brook, so the Witness of Delta would know to take our warning seriously."

"Shandy is sending us to Delta to make sure I won't be on Clouds End when Jo kills me." Brook fingered the Witness Knot. "I don't blame her. It's what I would do, if I were Witness. Better to lose one woman than a whole village. And after all, it isn't like there's any family to offend."

"That's so like you. You never believe that anyone acts with honor," Shale said. "No. Everything is always about you. Always about people cutting you out."

"Hey now," Rope murmured, covering Brook's stiff hand with his own.

"No, really," Shale said. "Why see loyalty when you could see treason? Why see good will when malice is so much more interesting?"

"The thing I like about old friends," Foam remarked, "is that you can heave all the fair words overboard and go straight for the kill." He inspected a pickled gull's egg and popped it into his mouth. "Delicious. But as for the argument, is it not possible that both things are true? Maybe Shandy did mean to send Brook off the island until she is no longer spliced to this haunt. And maybe the Witness really is worried that Sere is burning through the Mist. What could be more sensible than sending Brook to Delta? At best, Brook frees herself from the haunt, and warns the first island of Sere's threat. At worst, Brook dies at sea." He paused to swallow a sip of water. "Along with her three closest friends."

Silence brooded abovedeck.

"My mother is no spider-minded murderess," Shale said.

Foam nodded. "She would have to have a cold heart indeed, to send Brook to her death with her own daughter on board." He glanced at Brook and shivered. "Hmm! Scary wicked bad!"

"All right! All right!" Brook threw her hands in the air. "Everyone loves me! Everyone needs me! They won't let me near their children now because they don't want me to catch cold!"

Foam nodded. "*Much* better." He picked up another pickled egg and delicately belched. "Otter made these, didn't she? Lovely."

Shale sighed. "Yes, all right Brook, people are scared. Maybe everything you say is true, but other things are true too. Why not think about the good parts? How many people have a chance to make a trip like this in their whole lives? Tomorrow we'll put the first human footprints on an island just birthed from the Mist. If Rope is still willing."

"Sail into the Mist," Brook murmured. "What a splendid idea. I'm fairly seething with good luck."

Rope's hand stilled on her ankle. "We won't let anything take you."

"You may not have much of a—"

"We won't let anything take you," Rope said.

Sea and ship talked in slaps and mutters at the water line.

Together but not speaking they watched the sun set, somber as an embering fire, majestic and a little sad. When the last flames guttered in the western sky and were lost beneath the rolling dusk-blue sea, they all felt as if a part of their old lives had flickered and gone out, never to be rekindled.

The next morning Swap's Breeze came up at dawn, blowing away sleep and filling every heart on board with wonder as Shale's island crept out of the Mist.

Its contours seemed to shift and waver before them. Behind the

beach, gleaming like beads of dew, boulders rose toward a loom-
ing cloud. Beyond this cloud was the Mist, grey and featureless.
Shale's island lay at the edge of the world and nothing lay behind
it, not even darkness.

No one looked up into the sky above their boat to see what
might be circling there.

A gull's cry blew into Shale's heart. "I want to get off this damn
boat," she growled.

Rope shook his head and stamped on the deck, grinning. All
night he had been afraid that dawn would bring disappointment,
but the magic was real, and he was a part of it.

Brook leaned against him, needing his steadiness. "We should
go back."

"Back!" Foam cried.

"It makes me feel . . . Can't you hear it? We should go back."

Shale grunted. "Nobody's making any sense." Her straight
black hair fluttered in the breeze, tangling around her shark's
tooth. "There are too many people on this damn boat."

"We're almost there, Brook. It won't hurt just to take a look."
Rope fought to control his frustration. "Wind's quartering." The
sails luffed, sliding out of trim. Rope squinted at the waiting sea.
"It smells like singed pine needles."

Shale shook her head. "I can make out some colors, but they
feel bent."

"Spring," Brook said. "Spring and cinnamon." Magic passed
through her, pure and unpredictable as birdsong. "The wind in
the reeds. So lonely."

"Or scorched leaves burning," Rope said.

"A spire of cloud reaching down to touch a spire of stone,"
Foam said. "Two islands, one in the sea, one in the sky, reflections
reaching to one another."

Rope grunted and spun the tiller, swinging the ship around. "I
can't come this far and no farther. It's my story too."

"The cloud-color drips onto the rocks," Shale said.

"*Island, island, island,*" Foam said. "That's what this place
shouts at you. It's more like home than home is."

Shale shook her head, laughing in wonder. "No. It's like every place that isn't home. Every place new and exciting."

Foam laughed. "Let's call it Shale's Adventure, then, and make you famous forever!"

But Brook said, "Not yet. The story isn't over yet. The island isn't finished. It has not yet found its name." The Witness Knot around her wrist was a chain shackling her to Clouds End. "Shandy sent us to Delta. That's our business and we should be about it. This island is no part of that."

"It's part of the story!" Foam said. "We have to know what Sere is up to. Shandy would want us to learn anything the island could tell us about what is happening in the Mist."

"Heroes deal with Heroes. Our business is with the real world."

Silence washed over the deck for the space of five heartbeats. "I'm sorry you didn't see it first." Shale said. "But I've waited all my life for an adventure to happen to me. I won't turn it down now. Foam! Help me with the dinghy."

When the others shipped out for the island, Brook went with them.

Rope left the others as soon as he could. He knew he ought to stay by the dinghy, ought to return to his ship. He shouldn't have left Brook alone. They were supposed to stay together.

He was tired of caution.

The island was alive with voices of wind and wing and fire. The sea wove mighty songs against the Mist. The air smelled of scorched herbs. There were no paths and the ways he took closed behind him as he walked.

It was farther to the island's peak than he expected. He plodded on, always climbing, until the muscles in his legs ached. A gull flapped heavily overhead. It screamed three times and disappeared behind an outcrop of crimson rock. The sky above was cream, no longer clear. He caught a rank smell and shouted, startling a beast with a topaz pelt from a stand of silver birches. He fled under a canopy of vines, stumbled and fell. The ground rippled heavily beneath him.

Rope struggled to his feet. He was in a clearing walled with honeysuckle; hundreds of humming bees drowsed in the liquid air. A carpet of moss crept to the lip of a small black pool.

Jo stood on the other side.

Honeyed sunlight dripped on her ivory skin. Her narrow silver eyes were still and sad, looking at him. She was naked except for a bracelet of blue shells she turned slowly around one wrist. The honeysuckle smell made it hard to breathe. Somehow the odor seemed to come from her, from her white skin. Her hair floated before her face like wisps of cloud. Diamonds beaded on her shoulders and sparkled in the snow-white hair at the bottom of her belly. Pale as a drowned woman, her reflection glowed in the black pond.

"It is lonely here," she said.

Rope's heart raced. Bees. Bees crawled across her white flesh. They used their wings to balance, scrambling clumsily along her shoulders, her arms.

Jo reached behind her head and shook out her long white hair. A cloud of bees rose humming into the air, circled and landed on the honeysuckle, on Jo's shoulders, on her hands and on the tips of her breasts. "So lonely. I thought this was what I wanted. But the wind blows everything away."

Alone. He was alone with her.

His eyes met hers and he thought, She could twin me. Twin me, kill me, have it all. Brook, the ship, the human contact. No one would ever know.

Shells clicked and clattered as Jo turned the bracelet around her wrist.

And he was lost in the Mist-time, with no paths to follow, surrounded by honeysuckle and drowsing bees. He was alone with her. There was no place to run. These things he thought in the space of one long look, while Jo's shells clattered and clicked.

"Well met!" he said. "I . . . We thought you'd left."

"I had."

"We're very grateful. For your warning." Rope took a deep breath and walked a couple of steps toward her. "We fear haunts. You know that. Haunts and Mist."

"Where is Brook?"

"I left her beside a stream." Rope frowned as a swell passed through the moss below his feet. The island was rocking like a boat at anchor.

Jo stood quite still on the other side of the pond. The air smelled of honeysuckle and sex and milk. Bees clambered and buzzed. "I am hungry."

They were terribly alone. Rope looked around the clearing. "Not much here."

"Perhaps in the pond," Jo said, not looking at the black water, not looking away from his face. "I thought I saw a fish—here."

"We lack a net." Rope walked around beside her, wondering if she would kill him. He smiled and rolled up his tunic sleeve. "Ever tickled for fish?"

She laughed and shook her head.

Rope laughed with her. "You have to wiggle your fingers a certain way; so." He let his arm hang limp and wriggled his hands, using a trout pattern. He was good at it. He was pleased with the craft in his body.

Her pale fingers slid down his arm, cool and soft as blossoms. She lifted his hand and placed it on her breast. She trembled, looking at him, and her silver eyes widened. The smell of honeysuckle rippled out from her, damp with warm rain.

"Make love to me."

"I want to."

Her blossom skin made his fingers tingle.

"We are very near the Mist, here," he said. "My father sailed out one morning into a day clear with sunshine and never came back. I don't want to go where he went."

"Haunts get what they want," Jo told him. "You came here when all sense would have kept you sailing for Delta. You came here alone to me."

"It was Foam, he . . . we had to, to find out about Sere . . ."

Tears stood in Jo's eyes like drops of dew. "I won't make you want me. I ask only what anyone might ask. I ask to be loved. I am tired of freedom." Desire crawled under Rope's thoughts like the blood beneath his skin.

He took his hand off her breast.

Jo kicked at the black pond, shattering their reflections. "Twins. Haunts. Idiots! *In the Mist everything is true.*" Bitterly she stared at him. "One day life will slit you open like an oyster." She screeched, an inhuman sound. "What could I have seen in you?"

She dove into the black pool. There was no splash; the water closed smoothly behind her, swallowing her white feet. After many heartbeats a swarm of bees bubbled to the surface.

Jo's reflection still floated on the black water.

Rope touched the reflection's white cheek. It was cool and petal-smooth. He drew back his hand without rippling the water. His fingers were wet.

He reached out again, more firmly this time. He stroked her cheek and her neck. Reached further under the water to touch her breasts.

From beneath a hidden rock an ancient trout rose and struck his hand. Rope jerked his fingers away, swearing. A ripple started in the pond, breaking Jo's nude body into confusion.

Bees hummed and drowsed.

A water skater tested the black surface, growing bolder as the ripple died.

The wave was gone.

Shale stayed by the shoreline, hopping from rock to rock. Foam followed her, stooping to pop strange flotsam into a bag at his side. They stopped to study a tidal pool. A gemmed crab sidled by Foam's foot. "To each barnacle the crab is an island," Foam mused. "An island within an island. Shale, have you ever stopped to consider that the world is an island? Yes, that's it, sticking out of the sky just as Clouds End juts from the water. And the sound

of the wind blowing through the trees is the sound of water breaking over the rocks." He frowned. "No, wait. We're still in the air.
Which means . . . which means we must be *fish*," he cried. "And
perhaps the Mist is a net the sky's people throw down to us air-
dwellers from time to time, dragging us off like poor Rope's father,
to be, to be . . ."

"Eaten."

"Mm. I suppose."

Softly Shale chanted the verse that began all her mother's stories. "The Mist churns into sea, the sea hardens into stone, then
islands, then land. The land leaps into mountains and the mountains fade into clouds and Mist; for change is the way of the world."
She stood looking back across the water. "Every step I take seems
like the first in a journey whose end I cannot imagine."

Foam grinned back at Shale. "You are beginning to sound like
Brook."

Shale laughed and started down the beach. "She's much better
at it."

Foam tarried, admiring the way Shale hopped from boulder to
boulder. Never graceful, always sure. He ambled after her, studying the great cloud that bulked behind the island, swallowing its
summit. Gleams of muted light shot through it, and suddenly he
remembered the haunt's warning about a fire growing in the Mist.

But of course this was only the sun, he told himself. Only the
sun.

They were at the edge of the Mist. They should be scared. The
Mist from which twins came. The Mist that had taken Rope's father.

"Where's Rope?"

Shale started. Behind them, the beach was empty save for the
smell of burning herbs and a single gull's cry. "And Brook.
Weren't we supposed to stay together?"

They looked at one another with growing fear.

"Shale." Foam stared at the great cloud of Mist boiling above
the island's heart. Where before they had seen gleams and glimmers, a shape was beginning to emerge. Jerking and dancing,

taller than the tallest tree, a puppet-shape with limbs of flame ate through the Mist: a body of flat and bending fire.

"Sere," Shale whispered.

One of Sere's arms was still within the Mist, and one shivering leg. A stench of burning came from him, and a terrible hunger.

Like a flame leaping in a breeze, his huge flat hand stabbed out to touch the crown of a mighty tree standing just beyond the line of Mist. Its head exploded into flame. A moment later Sere pulled the fire into himself, gobbling down the blazing tree as if swallowing a candle.

The Mist boiled up behind him, stirred by a thousand wings. Sere's head snapped around, his long curving eyes streaming fire as he stared back at a dim figure bulking in the Mist—a glimpse of white and a sea bird's scream.

So rich the island was with magic, that even Shale could understand Sere when he spoke in a cruel, hissing voice, like the sound of dry leaves burning.

I told you she was mine, he said. I am in her now.

Shale swore, dizzy with fear and furious with herself. The island was alive. The world she knew was weak as rotting sailcloth here, and the Mist-time was pushing through. Sere and the Gull Warrior might be only moments away from sweeping across them all.

What madness had made her leave her best friend alone, in the Mist, with a haunt stalking her?

"We've been spelled," she said. "Foam, we have to find Brook and Rope." Her eyes searched the endless jumble of boulders above the beach. "Fathom drown me and all my line." The haunt had called them here. They had been mad to come.

CHAPTER 5: SERE

From a shelf in the topmost room of her tower Shandy pulled a black fuseware jar glittering with mica. She grunted and tapped a dark brown ball of incense into the palm of her hand. It was flaky and oily at once, a wad of old leaves gummed with resin.

She missed her daughter. Shale the sharp-faced, all elbows and knees, with a shark-tooth earring swinging by her cheek as she scrambled through the day.

Shandy prayed for the safety of her travellers, feeling as helpless now as she had twenty years before with Shale at her breast, wondering how so small a thing as a baby could so easily hold her deepest hopes and most terrible fears.

What kind of mother could have sent her daughter to the lonely sea?

Duty, Witness.

She blew into her battered copper brazier until her cheeks were red. Then she crumbled incense over the coals. The gummy flakes did not flame, but after many heartbeats they began to smolder, throwing off ropes of thin black smoke.

Shandy, Witness of Clouds End, inhaled the bitter gift of incense, waiting to hear what the wind would tell her. What the emberlight would reveal.

There is a place, the ember said, a place of
    joy,

of jump lick crackling,
of
wind dance wavering,
a place of fierce desires
fiercely gratified;
of boundless cleansing.

Shandy shivered. It was rare to hear a Hero speak directly, but there was no mistaking Sere's crackling voice, his yellow tongue that shook with hungry laughter.

What does the Fire say?

Tell the haunt she can't run from me! I am in her now.

A creek flowed down from the new island's heart. Brook had named it Stick's Stream. "Us Clouds Enders," she whispered. "We're made for adventure."

At first she had been hurt that Rope would leave her on her own, but then the world seemed to whisper, Let him go. Something special waited for her, something magical, and it wouldn't do to risk marriage and children: to risk becoming the ordinary woman she and Shale had sworn they would never be.

She sat on a big stone in the center of the channel, watching bits of fire-red fern come whirling up, bob briefly against her rock, and then vanish, pulled on by the greedy sea. Water foamed endlessly under her feet. Sunlight broke into glints on the stream's back.

The water had many voices: a splash and chatter it spoke with the stones, a deeper, cooler conversation with its banks and its bed; the drifting, solemn talk it held with the clouds.

Brook barely noticed when the breeze began to blow, adding a restless note to the water's song. Now the birches waved farewell and the white clouds sailed on toward Delta, leaving her behind, and the grasses whispered, and a new voice called to her.

At first this voice was so faint she could barely hear it. A skittish, rushing, sighing voice. As it spoke, the tiny glinting fishes in Stick's Stream flicked away like frightened gems. A wave of white stones rolled down the streambed.

"Mountains leap into cloud and the clouds drift at last into Mist; for change is the way of the world. . . ." And the voice laughed like the wind kicking up a pile of autumn leaves. The broken sunlight pulled together, riding the stream's wavering back like a shadow of light. It was this brightness that had spoken to Brook. A reflection, she knew, but she could not bring herself to lift her eyes and look at what cast it.

The Witness Knot Shandy had tied around Brook's wrist bucked and writhed like a sail left up in a squall. "Are you Jo?"

"Me?" A gust of laughter. "The haunt is here with you, islander, but she is the least of your problems. You sit at the edge of the Mist! Such places are dangerous, even for me."

The sky darkened and the air shook as with the beating of great wings. Burning feathers danced roughly in the angry wind. "Jo has been pulled into the story of this island," the voice said. "A story of Sere and the Gull Warrior. The Warrior thinks he has won. But you know what happens when you cut fire to pieces, don't you?"

Fear jumped in Brook, and a vision poured through her: torches, thousands of torches weaving through the Mist. Searching.

"The sea's people think little of Sere. But a Hero's reach is long. You have desires, and your haunt has them too: and so here you have come to kindle on his fingertips. He does not want her to bring her warning to the islanders. He would not have her smother a spark he has waited so long to light."

"I don't understand," Brook said.

The throb and rumble faded slowly away, and the lightshadow wavered once more upon the surface of Stick's Stream. Now it was clearly a woman's form, with glass hands and mirror eyes and a braid of black hair as dark as the bottom of the sea. "Let me tell you a story," it said.

Brook tried to speak but found herself mute, and by this she knew it was the Singer who had found her, for no tongue might speak while the Singer told a tale.

The Singer laughed with a sound like the wind in burning branches, and began.

This is a story of the Smoke, where the heat burns but the Spark is hidden.

In the dark time before time, the forest people were imprisoned within the trunk of a great bronzewood tree. They did not know the warmth of the sun or the beauty of the sky, and the birdsong they heard was dulled and without grace.

They clamored mightily to be set free. So great were their lamentations that at last they heard a sound like the wind in the branches, and a voice of a thousand breezes said, "Why do you shriek and mutter so?"

And the people cried, "Set us free! We are prisoned in darkness and we long to feel the wind upon our faces!"

The voice considered, and at last it said, "I will set you free, but know this: I send my people over every part of the earth, and they never know a home. They may wander the frozen deserts for a hundred years, or whistle along the mountaintops, or speak with only the waves. Do you still crave your freedom?"

And the people within the tree were greatly dejected, and their leader said, "This tree is all we know. We do not wish to wander foreign lands. There must be an easier way than this."

But the Singer said (for it was I), "That is all the freedom I have to give."

Then the people redoubled their cries, and beat against the walls of their wooden prison, and finally Fathom bellowed to them with the voice of a thousand waves crashing onto shore, saying, "What do you want?"

And the people cried out, desiring to be set free. "But this tree is all we know," the leader said, "and greatly as we hunger for freedom, we will not leave it."

"Very well," the Hero said. "I will release you, and from the body of this tree I will make a ship, and teach you to sail within it. But when I am angered, or playful, or bored, I may drown you beneath cold waters."

And then the people were bitterly afraid. They argued fiercely, but at last their leader said, "Many thanks for your generous offer, but the conditions you propose are too unpredictable. We prefer our dangers to be less arbitrary."

And Fathom shrugged, saying "That is all the freedom I had to give."

Now those inside the tree flung themselves about in a frenzy of despair. Their laments rose up to the heavens, and rumbled down into the center of the earth, and there was terrible strife.

Finally they roused Sere. "What in the name of the Seven Humiliations is all this racket?"

"Help us, O help us! We are imprisoned in this tree. We have no liberty!"

"Neither do stones."

"We have no light!"

"Neither do moles."

"We are starving!"

"Hunh! . . . Poor blighters." Sere sighed; for he knows a thing or two about hunger. "Very well. I will set you free—"

"And we don't want to leave our tree," the leader added quickly.

"Don't push me. I will give you light, and food, and liberty, and keep you near your precious tree. But beware!" The people groaned. "Beware, for you will have taken the Spark that casts shadows: you will have learned freedom."

"That's it?"

"That's it."

"Done!" the leader cried.

"Being is hard work," Sere warned. "Sometimes you will wish to be free of that too."

But the people rejoiced, and lifted their voices in praise of Sere the Liberator. And the third time they chanted his name, the Tree was riven by a bolt of lightning, and they stumbled out from their ancient prison and into the world.

Yet behind them the lightning smoldered, and a tiny spark fled deep into the heart of the wood, taking with it a host of shadows, waiting only for a breath of wind to wake to fiery life.

"And that breath of wind has come. The Spark burns in the breast of the Emperor of the forest people," the Singer said. "And here you sit, while the fire closes around you like a noose."

And Brook leaned forward, reaching over the water. "Please. Please help us. What are we to do?"

But the Singer laughed like the wind from a great burning. "It is neither my place nor my time to say more in the world of men. But I am not done with this story; of that you may be sure. The best stories begin and end at home, and I tell only the best."

And then a stray gust of wind rocked Brook forward, and she touched the water, and the Singer's glinting shadow broke into fragments and went whirling downstream.

"Brook!"

She jerked her hand back from the cold water.

"Brook! Come on!" Rope stood on the bank, chest heaving. He held out his arms and swung her to shore. "We've got to get back to the ship! Look!"

Daylight was dying swiftly around them. Like a volcano, the island's heart belched forth slow waves of heavy Mist. Whipcracks of flame made their shadows jump. Chopping wingbeats pounded the air. A gust of wind blew the Mist aside like a curtain, and Brook screamed. Sere danced over the island, impossibly tall, a grinning, jerking puppet of flame. As they watched, a sudden arc of whiteness flashed from the Mist, and Sere's right arm dropped to the ground with a roaring crash. Trees and ferns exploded into fire around it. Weaving and bobbing, Sere stooped suddenly, grabbed his arm with his other hand, and gobbled it up.

Brook felt sick. The wind swirled again and Mist closed around Sere and the Gull Warrior.

Another burning feather twisted into the stream and hissed out its life. "Jo is trapped in there," Brook said. And despite everything the haunt had done to her, she found herself hoping that somehow Jo would escape. The thought of Sere devouring her twin left a terrible hollow in her.

"Come on!" Rope pulled her away and they staggered downstream.

Mist boiled from the island's heart and spread far to the west. It brooded over them, smearing the sun with a film of bloody vapor. Wind thundered and flame burst behind them, making Brook stumble. She was gasping and her heart had lost its rhythm. Her muscles felt like stones and her spit tasted of blood.

A web of something like damp grey string reached for them, and Rope reached to brush it away.

"No!" Brook screamed, feeling the magic in it, but it was too late.

Rope staggered as a shock took him. His blood crackled, and energy poured through him as if he were a cloud full of lightning. The grey string snapped and curled around his hands. It was blowing into him, whistling through his palms and rushing into his heart.

Now it was a pulsing, twisting silver-blue web. Unreality poured from it like heat from a stove door; the blue limbs became solid, elastic, possessed of tremulous strength. Rope felt the creature fluttering like a giant moth around his hand; its glow subsided; it lay still.

"Spit!" Rope yelled. He jerked his hands back as if from a flame, but the string wound itself around his wrist and held on tight, refusing to be shaken off.

A wave of panic washed through him, then ebbed as the creature rubbed itself back and forth, sliding through the black hair on his forearm. Somehow he was sure that whatever it was, the net of Mist-stuff meant him no harm.

"I'm all right. Keep running!" Rope cried. "We're almost at the shore. We've got to get back to the boat before the Mist rolls over us!"

As they staggered out onto the shingle they saw Foam and Shale before them, madly trying to shove the dinghy into the water. Rope swore. "Tide's out!" He sprinted over the sand.

Mist flowed down the slope behind them, witching the rocks as it came.

A single white gull struggled out of the grey fog. Flames sparked along its wings. It swooped wildly overhead and then crashed to the ground beside the dinghy.

"Spit!" Rope gasped. The gull was beginning to blur. "It's her."

Foam and Shale whirled. They saw the haunt curled on the sand behind them, trembling with exhaustion. She shook her wings into arms; her tiny head flattened; her sleek feathers unravelled into a drift of white hair.

Quick as thought, Shale leapt to pin Jo's throat beneath her elbow and fumbled for the knife at her side.

Jo twisted under Shale to look for Brook. "Help me," she called weakly.

"Help!" Shale spat, shoving her elbow down until the haunt jerked and gasped. "Since when do haunts need help?"

"He's in there. He's in there!" Jo screamed, looking only at Brook. "Don't let him take me!"

Faint with exhaustion, Brook stared back at the haunt. Angry red welts striped Jo's face. Her arms and hands were smudged with soot, and her fingertips were red where the skin had burned away. Like a shadow Brook stood above her, dark and trembling. Around her wrist she felt the Witness Knot, taut with magic like a straining sail.

Behind Shale and Jo, Foam yanked on the dinghy, glancing back at the fire.

Come, Jo, the Fire hissed. Take the Spark and learn what the ember knows!

Jo shuddered as desire crept like smoke through her veins. Desire to shed her heavy flesh and be free, to throw all care into the flames and burn herself away.

Have you come to hear the end of my story? The Fire licked his red lips with his shaking yellow tongue.

I promised you a place of jump-lick-crackling, remember? Of wind dance wavering. You are almost there now, Jo. Only come behind the Mist and I will cleanse you with your own desire. Ah, you flinch. Does my touch sting? You will find you crave it more the fiercer it burns. I have kindled—

No!

I have kindled something in you. . . .

No! Jo held desperately to the sound of the sea, the touch of sand, the human voices shouting overhead. She could not let herself give in to the Fire. She did not want to be devoured.

"Please," she begged of Brook. "Take me with you. Don't leave me."

"Not to sound impatient," Foam snapped, "but when the Mist and fire roll over us, the haunt won't be the only one in trouble."

"I know, I know!" Brook hovered in an agony of doubt, looking at the others for guidance. Angrily Shale shook her head. Foam shrugged and threw himself back against the dinghy; her nose was almost in the water.

Brook touched the Witness Knot around her wrist. Calmness flowed from it like a cool stream. For an instant she saw her life, with its great tragedies and small joys, its accidents and chance encounters: all part of a grand interweaving of a thousand thousand threads, a moving knot of stories, making a braid whose design she could feel, but never understand.

"We will take you," she said.

Swearing, Shale rolled off Jo and ran to the dinghy. Jo rose, silver eyes glittering.

The haunt was back.

They pulled like madmen for the ship and hoisted the sails while sparks rained hissing around them.

And then like a blessing a sea breeze came up, pushing them on toward Delta, away from the Mist and the Fire.

———

When they were safely away, Rope breathed in and breathed out and stared at the world's plain blue sky. He had done what his father never could: touched the Mist and come back. Not before senselessly risking his ship and crew, of course.

"Salamander," Foam said, pronouncing the word with grave care.

Rope frowned. "Eh?"

Foam stared around the ship. The deck was singed and the sails were peppered with pinhole burns. "The name of this boat. A salamander lives half in the water, half in the air. But in the Mist-time, in stories, a salamander is a creature that walks through fire."

Rope stroked his beard. "Very well," he said at last. "*Salamander* she is."

"*Salamander*. That's good." Shale looked at Brook on the fore-deck. "You were right. We had no business going to the island."

Foam nodded. "Delta's our job from now on."

Remembering, Rope carefully rolled up his sleeve. The tendril of Mist was still there, clinging to his arm. "Hey, net-thing. What are you?"

"Part of your story," Jo said.

In their furious haste to get underway, they had shoved the haunt down the steps to the hold and told her to stay out of the way. Now she had come back on deck. Still streaked with soot, her white hair snapped and coiled in the sea breeze. "You made it. You have called it into being, given it a part of yourself. You have let its tiny story gel, like a living pearlweird. Be honored. Few humans are granted such an opportunity."

The islanders peered at the Mist-creature like children investigating a wasp's nest.

"It's . . ."

"It's . . ."

"It's a bit of turquoise string, is what it is," Shale said.

Foam reeled. "Turquoise string!" He clapped his hands to his forehead. "Who would have believed it! Turquoise string!" He turned on Rope. "Your one chance to play the hero and you give us turquoise string! I should have created a jewelled anklet, to grace a dancing foot. Or perhaps a harp with five strings, each of which played music for a different sense. Or then again, perhaps a fish whistle, to charm mackerel into our hold."

"Bugger yourself," Rope said genially. He was terribly pleased that it had been he, staid old reliable Rope, who had given life to this tendril of Mist. He gazed fondly at the tiny turquoise wriggle creeping around his fingers. "What better for a simple fisherman than a decent little net?"

Brook fingered the knot Shandy had tied around her wrist. "I met the Singer," she said.

Foam looked up from the Mist-thing around Rope's hand and gave a low whistle. "Are you su—"

"She had a voice like the wind, and when she told her story I couldn't speak. I know what I saw."

"She is right," Jo said unexpectedly. "I felt the Singer there."

Rope looked at Brook in wonder. "What did she say?"

Brook frowned, touching the knot, trying to remember. "She told a story about the forest people. How Sere freed them from darkness. But the end of the story was that a spark lingered somewhere. Within them, I guess. And she said this spark has been fanned to life."

"Aha!" Foam cried. "The fire Sere is bringing to Delta!"

Rope frowned, touching the wheel to keep their sails full. "But does that mean a real fire is burning on the mainland? If so, how could that hurt an island?"

"But it's the forest people who are carrying the spark. Maybe they mean to burn Delta down," Shale said.

Rope's frown deepened. "But why? What could woodlanders want from the sea?"

Jo's face was grim. "The people of the air are drawn from every place," she said slowly. "From sea and desert, wood and plain and mountain. All are of the air, and yet colored by their birthplace. In the islands we are shunned: praised to our faces and cursed behind our backs.

"But in the forest, now, there is a different role for some of those the magic touches, neither Witness nor wanderer. They may be Bronze. A Bronze listens not to the world, but to the hearts of men. And the one who is strongest, the Bronze with greatest guile and stealth and ruthlessness, this one becomes Emperor."

"Marvelous," Foam muttered. "A people ruled by ruthless haunts."

"However you may hate us, there is an honesty in the voices of wind and wave that is lacking in the hearts of men. Bronzes live by twisting others. I think you will find a Bronze burning at the heart of Sere's fire."

Shale stood scowling with the mainsail sheet still wrapped around her hand. She looked curiously at Jo. "So where did you come from?" she asked. "Which people, I mean."

Jo stared back at her with a look, part sad, part dreamy, part defiant. It was so exactly one of Brook's expressions that it took Shale's breath away. "Me? Why, I am one of you. I too was once of the sea."

"Funny name for an islander," Foam said. "What's a Jo?"

"A Jo isn't anything," the haunt said. "The name I bore in the world of men has long since been lost in the Mist."

"You made up your name?" Rope asked, faintly scandalized.

"I chose not to be named after a kind of crab or a piece of fishing tackle, if that's what you mean."

And Shale said, "How old are you?"

"How old . . . ? I am older than . . ." Jo faltered. She seemed suddenly smaller, and weary; her face was smeared with soot, and showed red where the fire had come too close. "I do not know," she said.

All her mystery had gone. It seemed to the islanders then that they saw her for the first time: not a spell-weaver but only a woman, a woman who once had lived on an island very much like their own. Who perhaps had been tended, and taught to gut fish, and braided knots in a sister's hair.

Shale nodded, leaning on the forward rail and looking out over the sea. "How long have you been travelling?"

"I do not remember. But it seems like a very long time since I was home."

Shale nodded again, staring west. "Going to Delta!" she breathed. "I always wanted to go. Of course they tell you that a girl can't expect to, that even the Trader goes only as far as the fostering islands. Harp or Trickfoot." She gripped the gunwale and rocked her weight onto her toes. "But I always knew that I was meant to journey. That I had been given the gift to *go*."

Foam sighed. "We're going to Delta as fast as we can," he said. "I just hope someone has a gift for getting us back."

CHAPTER 6: THE STORM

Rope's crew drove themselves hard over the following weeks, passing Three Elbows and Stump, Sharp Feather and Driftwood, Beachwood with its white sands, and Telltale, where the people were such terrible liars. By then they were well beyond the fostering islands, into waters never sailed by any man born on Clouds End.

At first the islanders were deeply suspicious of Jo, watching her every move and making doubly sure she never spent time alone with Brook. But as the days passed, drawing them beyond Ringwold and Terrace, Tansy and Bitterwood and the Midline Cluster, where the dolphin trainers lived, their vigilance dwindled. The islanders treated the haunt like a bad wound: first as a threat, then as a nuisance, and finally as a fact of life.

Meanwhile the islands came closer together, the wind blew more fitfully, and the late spring days grew ever hotter. Life on board became more and more cramped. Rope pored over his charts, studying them for insights or correcting their mistakes. Other times he played with Net, the little Mist-thing living in his sleeve like a pet mouse.

Foam tinkered with the bag of oddments he had collected on Shale's island. He kept his fingers busy to calm his heart, for as the days turned into weeks he began to feel something for Shale he had never felt before. It caught him when she talked of travelling, or pulled their sails taut, or stood on the foredeck at dawn, eyes sparkling, looking forward into the new day. Sometimes after supper they would all sit together on the tiny foredeck to watch the day gutter and go out, and he would be painfully aware of Shale, long and warm and tremendously alive, lying there, just next to him, just touching. His elbow would brush, very lightly, against her leg, moving with the gentle roll of the waves, and he would be whelmed with her nearness.

He wanted what Rope had with Brook.

One morning early in the voyage, something shook Rope as he lay pillowed on the foredeck. Swell must be coming abeam, he thought sleepily.

The shaking grew stronger. Groaning, he opened one glassy eye. A slim pink light was in the eastern sky. Brook's fingers were in his chest hairs. She tweaked them.

"Hey! Ummggh. 'S not even dawn yet."

Brook's fingers tickled their way down his short ribs toward his belly. "The others will be asleep for hours."

"Good idea." Rope struggled upright and peered from gummy eyes.

"*Salamander* is right." Brook was alert, dressed and smug. "There is something lizardlike about you when you first wake up. A heavy, brainless look that says, 'I'd kill you. If I could move.' "

Rope replied with a ponderous flick of his tongue.

Brook said, "You are beautiful, you know."

Rope blinked.

Brook grinned, stroking his bearded jaw. "You'll be a wonderful lover some day." Then she lunged forward and knocked him over on his back. "You look so helpless!" She planted her fists in his stomach and bounced up and down a few times.

"Groooo!" he moaned. "You'll squeeze the water out of me."

"Take care of it, then." Brook squashed him extra flat, then leapt up to wander the deck. She dawdled at the transom, watching the East blush. The light broadened. Trees became visible atop a nearby island, taking off their blankets of shade. Brook sniffed the pine-scented morning air.

Rope peered at her suspiciously. "You look smug."

"Who, me?"

"Hmm." The deck creaked beneath his feet as he walked over to the hinged gate on the starboard rail. He slid his feet into the leather shitstraps bolted to the deck and unlatched the gate behind him, thinking for the thousandth time how undignified he looked squatting bum-first over the edge of his ship. Brook had modestly turned away.

The cabin doors creaked. Great, he thought. The crew chooses now of all times to come on deck. Blushing, he hiked up his tunic and hunkered down.

The leather footstraps gave way.

Rope yelled and clutched at the rail, but it was too late. His tunic billowed up around his ears as he tumbled helplessly over the side and crashed into the sea below.

"Somebody cut the straps!" he spluttered, coughing out a mouthful of salt water.

The other islanders were leaning over the rails. "By the Singer's perky breasts!" Foam said, "Isn't it a little early for a swim?"

"If this was your idea, Foam you louse, I'll pack you in a pickle jar and heave you overboard, you leech-infested crab-catcher!"

Brook stood beside Foam, sniggering. Both of them turned to look at Shale, who lay helplessly across the rail, whooping with laughter.

Rope caught his breath. "I should have known."

For revenge he set Shale the task of sewing up every little pin-hole burn in their sails. He watched with satisfaction as her thimble-finger turned slowly blue with bruises.

Brook spent her days amusing Shale by telling stories and allowing herself to be thrashed at every game they knew and a few she made up. "It's that or have her murder us all out of sheer boredom," she said, and Rope had to agree.

Jo, of course, could always take wing and soar over to a nearby island when she needed a change of scene. The islanders admitted they would do they same if they had the chance, but they still resented her for it.

And around the *Salamander*'s tiny world stretched the sea, its very vastness making their prison more unbearable. In the wide light of day every rock, every island, every cloud and circling bird was made plain to the end of vision. A sail luffing gently as they came around, the wash fanning out behind their stern, an osprey crying overhead—each thing had its form and sound and movement. Clear, sure, particular: this was the islanders' world, the world of the sea that made them and shaped them and would call them home again.

They sailed while the new moon waxed, aged, and withered. When it came again, it brought a season of killing heat. One day after lunch Brook and Jo went into the stuffy cabin to hide from the sun.

Coming out of the bright spring day, the cabin seemed murky and uncomfortably intimate. Sunlight slid in pale bars through the shuttered doors. Silver-eyed Jo sat on one bunk, thin fingers setting out the cords Rope had given her for knot practice. "Bowline . . ." She made room for Brook.

"Once around and up through the hole . . ." Brook prompted.

"Behind the tree and down the hole again. I remember." Jo held up her knot. "Will it pass?"

"My standards."

"And Rope's?"

Brook laughed. "Has he been drilling you?"

"Mercilessly."

Brook smiled. She looked with pleasure at Jo, admiring her beauty. The haunt was not graceful, but she was aware of her body, its movements and form.

The haunt made a comic face. "The bowline is the only knot I can remember."

Brook leaned forward beside Jo, almost touching her. She sorted through the bits of cut line until she found two pieces of the same thickness. "Then I shall teach you another."

"Ecstasy! What is it, and what is it for?"

"Reef knot. For joining ropes of the same size. Also the knot we use to tie our bootstrings," Brook added, putting one foot up on the locker to demonstrate. Her tunic slid up her leg, two hands above her knee. She felt Jo watching her.

"I see."

Brook unlaced her boots and tucked them under her bunk. She smoothed out her tunic and wiggled her toes. "The reef knot is very simple."

"It should appeal to our sailors."

"Right over left, then left over right," Brook said, demonstrating. Jo's hair hung loose and fine as spider web, drifting around her shoulders. She smelled of cool flowers. "Or the other way around. Why do you say that? Do you think us simple?"

"Not you."

The light coming through the shutters barred them both in stripes of light and darkness. "Good knot," Brook said.

"Good teacher."

Again Jo looked steadily at Brook, and again Brook looked away. She remembered the hollowness she had felt within Jo the day she found her on the beach. Sitting there in the cabin, alone with her, Brook felt Jo's emptiness like a riptide, dragging her out to sea. Jo was powerful. She had let herself become more than human. She could go anywhere, dare anything, be anyone . . . because she was nothing inside.

Something in Brook longed for that freedom. She could almost touch the sky-wide emptiness. But she was held back, entangled by Rope and Shale, Finch and Shandy, Otter and Stone: her friends and family and life on Clouds End.

Beside her, the haunt's long white fingers plaited line, weaving a knot between two cords, binding them together. Brook shivered in the stifling heat. She saw herself in Jo's empty eyes, and she was afraid. "Good. Good reef. Here's another one you'll need." Brook picked out two pieces of line, one thick and the other much thinner. "This is a sheet bend. For joining two strands of different size. Use the stronger piece to make the loop."

Jo shifted closer. Cloth rustled against cloth as their legs touched. They bent over the knot. Strands of white hair slid over brown.

"There. See?"

Brook felt a pause, as when a boat trembles on the top of a wave, about to sweep down into the dark sea.

Reaching for the knot, Jo touched her hand. A wildness dilated through Brook; weakness and strength, a confusion in her blood. Jo held the touch until Brook was forced to turn her head, to face Jo's hooking nose, her silver eyes. They were alight, mocking, tender. She was very beautiful.

Jo smiled and dropped her eyes to study her sheet bend. "A thousand thanks! Now I can help out. I hate to be a burden."

"You are not a burden," Brook said. "You are the voyage. You are Sere's prey and a thread in the Singer's braid. It is we who are merely sailing in your wake."

Jo fingered her handiwork, two cords locked together, one great and one small. "Either way. The future will take care of itself."

"The future," Brook said dryly, "will take care of all of us."

Two days later they were becalmed. The sea glistened like oiled glass under a hot white sky. Brook stood by the transom, fighting to breathe. The sea, the sky, the remorseless sun—they were so big, so inhuman. The world cared nothing about her.

Planks creaked as Jo came aft. "Thinking, I see. Bad habit. Ruins your skin and makes you bald."

Brook's eyebrows rose. "Tell that to Foam. It would comfort him to know why he is losing his hair."

Shale swam around the bow and waved up at Brook. "Taking a dip to cool off!" she called. And keeping an eye on Jo, no doubt. Brook felt a little shiver of gratitude.

"This heat is unbearable."

"Melt into it." Jo stretched languorously. "The secret to weather is not to mind it. The more you mind it, the more it hurts."

"You aren't gulping like a fish," Brook said crossly.

A tired fly circled Jo's head.

Gulping like a fish, Jo snapped the luckless fly out of midair and swallowed it. She grinned. "Think of it as a new experience. It will broaden you."

Brook said, "You like to scare people."

"Haunts aren't given many other choices," Jo snapped. She looked away, embarrassed.

"Hey!" Shale yelled. "Hey, you! Foam!"

Foam roused himself from the shady spot beside the cabin. "Me?"

"Yeah, you. Help me back into the boat."

He squinted out into the glaring sea. Shale's head and naked brown shoulders showed above the hull. He gulped. "Are you sure you don't want me to get Brook? Or Jo?"

Shale shook her head impatiently. "They're playing at Tool and Wit astern. Just glance over. If the haunt hasn't got her fingers around our girl's throat, help me up."

Foam put out his hand. "Rope is eavesdropping from his hammock, pretending to sleep. Up you come, then." Not for an instant did he let his gaze stray from her eyes.

Shale clambered up to stand nude and dripping on the deck, her straight black hair plastered to her cheeks. "Thanks. Say, remember how Rope looked when I loosened the shitstraps?"

"You have nice eyes," Foam remarked. "Sort of a pale grey-green. Quite unusual."

"I can't stand the idea of putting my tunic back on in this heat."

"With goldish flecks near the center." Sea-green eyes alight with life.

"I'll dry off first." Shale lay belly down on the foredeck. "Oh, Foam?"

"Yes?"

"You can stop nodding now."

"Right," he said briskly. "Just so . . . You know, Shaley-fish, you turned out all right."

"Oh! Well." Surprised, Shale jiggled her ear to get the water out. She felt pleased, but now, suddenly, rather embarrassed about having come aboard naked. "Don't call me that."

Foam grinned hugely. For the first time in many days, all was right with his world.

"Have you ever listened to the sea?" Brook asked. "I mean really listened. Not just to the wavetops, or an inlet, but to the whole thing?"

Around Jo the waves murmured, and high overhead the world-riding wind offered her its cold companionship. "No."

"Why not?"

"I would drip through the planks and float away." Jo looked back over the ocean, to the east. "My people know not to listen too closely. Do you know the story of Holdfast?"

Brook shook her head.

"Holdfast was a mighty haunt, very talented. It was said he could follow the conversation of one ripple down the length of a stream. He married a forest woman when he was still young. One summer he determined to understand the speech of the great peak above his home. As he listened to the mountain his skin became as hard as stone. He stayed this way for many days.

"Now it so chanced that a fire—Sere's fire—began to devour the woods around his cabin. Holdfast suddenly realized that his wife and child must be in great danger. Without thinking he sprang up to save them." Jo paused, looking out over the lifeless sea.

"And?"

"He shattered into a thousand pieces."

Brook imagined it: the statue stirring, splintering, spraying into shards of rock.

Jo shrugged. "Haunts never die. But sooner or later we are caught in the web of the world. Overwhelmed." She glanced at Brook. "What sort of story is that?"

"A sheet bend. A mortal caught up by Heroes, or the world—that's a Sheet-Bend story. There are many of them."

"How many have happy endings?"

Brook said, "How will this one end? This sheet bend you have made between us?"

Jo did not answer.

"The ocean broods," she said, some time later. "The sky, the sun, the haze—none of them are speaking. All are silent. Waiting." Jo glanced around at the *Salamander*, tiny in the immensity of the sea. "I hope we are ready for whatever they are waiting for."

The day died slowly but the fever-heat lingered. Brook and Foam slouched in the shadow of the cabin roof. Shale, dressed once more, lolled aft. Rope stood frowning at his charts. Net reared on his wrist, turning an ominous purple. "Spit!" Rope muttered.

"What?" Foam murmured. The boat was trying to rock him to sleep. "Why d'you swear?"

"Swell."

Shale looked up. "Hey! The boat's rocking. Why is there a swell in this calm? It was flat as flat when I was swimming."

Foam's eyes widened. "And why is it coming from the west?" He scrambled to his feet.

"That's what I'm hoping the charts will tell me," Rope said.

A cat's-paw batted the masthead pennant, then vanished.

Rope looked up sharply. "Gale," he murmured. The islanders glanced at one another.

"It's there," Jo whispered. "I can hear it coming."

Rope stood for a long moment, staring at the western horizon. Feeling the sea turn uneasily beneath his boat.

His voice crackled with tension. "We may not have much time. Get the mainsail down! We'll keep the jib up as long as we can. Shale, you help Foam. Brook and Jo, tie down anything that moves."

Rope lashed himself to the wheel as his crew jumped to work.

"At least I get a chance to use my knots," Jo muttered.

Oiled broadcloth snapped as Brook shook out a tarp. "Over there with that. No, over the barrel."

"Move it!" Rope snapped.

Tense and unsmiling, Brook met the haunt's eyes. "We islanders fear the sea."

The ocean ran heavier with every wave. Each new roller threw the *Salamander* to the top of a higher hill, then pushed her down into a deeper green valley. Rope hove to as Foam and Shale worked furiously to strip the mainsail.

"Topsail?" Foam yelled.

"Let it go! Get your gear!"

"Look!" Shale cried. A black line came racing across the green waves and a roaring wind bore down on them. "Fathom," she whispered.

"Here it comes!" Rope yelled, and then all words were blown away by the storm.

The gale spun the *Salamander* sideways, and heavy rollers caught her square abeam. A great sea crashed over the decks. Sails cracked explosively overhead.

The big wind hit just as Foam was fumbling to lash himself to the mast. The whirling boom clubbed him into the side of the cabin so hard it made him sick.

Then the first wave buried him, beating his head against the cabin again, rushing up his nose and into his lungs. He yelled, retching salt water as the retreating wave tried to suck him into the sea. He grabbed for a cleat on the cabin roof and hung on as the *Salamander* swooped down the next great trough. A wall of white spray exploded over the bow.

The whole storm was ringing in his head. He couldn't tell the thunder from the savage wind, the driving rain, the salt water that burned his eyes, his nose, his lungs.

Going away.

He was going away. Annihilated by the fury of the sea, he had no thoughts, no fancies, no memories, no ideas. He was a length of rope, a piece of wood. The sky was a purple bruise. The air was drowning and stank of salt. It was suddenly cold. A curtain of white swept toward him from the storm: hail beating into the black water.

A hand yanked around his waist. Shale crouched behind him,

trying to tie a line around his middle. Something was wrong with her left hand; one stiff finger refused to curl. She screamed at him, but the wind tore her words to pieces and threw them overboard.

She wrenched the rope around his waist. The hail was almost on them now. She grabbed his shoulders and turned him around, leaning in until their faces touched. "Get under cover!" she screamed.

She dove back for the mast, staggering as the *Salamander* pitched to port. A tiny spark was rekindled in Foam. He struggled to wake up, to reach the mast, but he couldn't unclench his fingers from around the cleat.

He screamed. A ball of hail cracked against his wrist and he jerked madly until his fingers opened. He scrabbled back to where Shale held a corner of the mainsail over her head. And then he too was beneath the tarp, propping it up with one hand, clutching Shale's arm with the other. He clung to her like a drowning man to a spar, needing something human to hold, something alive in the midst of the storm's vast, mindless hate.

White fury took them.

When the storm hit, Jo was belowdeck with Brook, putting on her slicker. The gale's first blast hurled her to the cabin sole. Thunder ripped back the sky. Wood screamed around her and the lines sang and snapped.

Fear rushed up her throat like bile. She was trapped in a wooden egg, soon to be crushed between the sea and sky. The world was howling through her. She could think of nothing but staying human. If she gave in to the storm it would tear her into nothingness.

But what would happen if she was listening to her twin when Brook drowned?

Then the hail descended, battering against the cabin roof. Jo howled like the storm itself. She was trapped in a peal of thunder, a moving pocket of hate. She was going to die. Her thin cage of flesh would fill with water and she would drown, trapped in it, and the cruel wind would shriek with joy.

Unless . . .

She could join it. She could let herself billow up into freedom. She too could sing for joy, could blast through the shrouds and ride the wild lightning.

Beside her Brook sobbed and screamed, but Jo heard only the waves, and the wind, and the sea.

Nothing Is, That Resists Me Forever.
 Even the fishes, that I give life, I give in
  turn as life to others.
 Even the trees I bleach their bones.
 Even men sink, when they can swim no longer.
 Even the fire, I drown with cool fathoms.
 Even the sand, I pound into rock.
 Even the Mist, I churn into the world.

All Is Change, And I Am That Change.
 When the blue sky is black with clouds, I
  am that darkness.
 When the drought fails, and the rain comes, I
  am that life.
 When the heavens open and the flood descends, I am
  that death also.
 When the waters break, and the child is born, I am
  there.
 When the newborn dies, and sorrow leaks from human
  eyes, I am those tears.
 I am the world, and I am the movement of the world.
  I water the desert, I eat the mountains, I dance
  with the moon!

The *Salamander* crested a giant wave and hung, skewing wildly. Then the murderous sea drove her over. With shattering impact she dropped flat on her wooden belly and lay dead in the water. Another wave caught her in the bow, and a boiling wall of fury smashed down the cabin doors. It hurled itself on Brook and Jo, driving them against the aft bulkhead.

The ship lurched, then shuddered, making way again. Brook

struggled to her feet in water up to her knees. They were in terrible danger of losing their freeboard. They would have to close the hatchway as fast as possible and start bailing. The wave had drowned the cabin lamp; she and Jo were in total darkness. She retched, coughing salt water through her nose. Hail screamed and skipped off the companionway. The world was pounding hail and groaning wood and choking blackness.

She spent an eternity there, pressed against the aft bulkhead of the cabin, staring into the darkness. She couldn't go abovedeck in the hailstorm. But each time the ship heeled on her side, Brook had to fight a mad urge to dash upward. Anything, anything but dying trapped belowdeck, holding her breath until the sea strangled her. She remembered Blossom's bloated body, drowned last summer and washed up on the Talon, water running from her mouth. Crabs had eaten her lips and eyes.

Brook reached into the darkness for Jo. It was impossible to hear anything above the fury of the storm. The haunt could be dead already, knocked out by a big wave and drowned. She could be wedged under the starboard bunk or drifting face down against the companionway with her long white hair floating like seaweed in the black water.

Or she could be drowning right now, screaming for help, trapped and gurgling under a trunk or a piece of wreckage. Crying with horror, Brook thrashed around the tiny cabin with the water up to her waist, gasping at every touch until she found Jo's arm and grabbed it.

The haunt's flesh squished beneath Brook's fingers like a jellyfish and she screamed. She gagged and clamped her jaws until she could breathe. "Jo! We need you here, Jo." She could barely hear herself shout.

Jo's arm quivered and firmed. "That's it! That's it," Brook cried. "Come back. Come back to us. Keep coming. Storm's almost over," she lied frantically. "As soon as the hail lets up we'll go topside."

At last she felt the haunt's hand fumble for her own.

———

Up top, water bubbled across the foredeck and streamed down the mast. The hail had given way to lashing rain. Salt water battered Shale from every direction. The straining storm jib was driving the ship onto her starboard side; the mastheads and yards circled as if waving for help. All around them huge mounds of black water heaped and vanished, swallowed by the deep.

Shale raged back at the storm. She wanted to hurt it, kill it. Her hands itched to pull a line or take the wheel, to fight back. Delta, she thought furiously. The mainland. The Northern Desert and Lianna's jungles, the western grasslands and the strange mountain cities of the stone people who lived forever and trod upon the clouds. "You won't stop me!" she screamed. "Not Sere, not Fathom, not anyone!"

The wind howled her curse away.

The *Salamander's* prow burrowed into the heart of another giant wave. A huge sea raced over her foredeck, hurling the dinghy up into the air. Either the cleats or the ropes holding the small boat gave way and it tumbled aft, caving in part of the cabin roof. It clipped Shale, hammering her against the mast, then smashed through the starboard rail and disappeared.

Salt water filled her mouth as she tried to scream. Her lifeline bit into her waist as she was swept helplessly aft and battered by the passing waves. She banged against the cabin and felt something drive into her shoulder, a splinter or a nail. Salt burned in a dozen cuts and she coughed seawater from her lungs, choking with fury. "Not yet, you *bastards!*"

She was weak and shaking when Foam pulled her back. Pain raked her shoulder, her ribs, her hands. He reached out to hold her, but she panicked and shook him off. It was a death-grip. She couldn't let Foam freeze onto her now. She was still strong enough to live; she couldn't let herself be dragged down by his weakness. She knew she hurt him when she struck his hand away but she had to do it. It was all she could do to save herself.

Through the storm Rope stood at the helm like a straining statue, willing his rudder to bite. Willing his ship to go on.

It was dark, endlessly dark. The world was one great roaring. He did not know if the others were alive or dead. He was alone. Wind and salt closed his burning eyes and he steered by touch. His right thigh trembled from bracing against the gale and his shoulders felt like burning jelly. The sea was taking him as it had taken Brook's parents, as it had taken Blossom. As it always took the men of the islands, one by one.

He was alone. Alone and utterly insignificant. The storm wrestled with him through the helm. Whether he rested now or later, the end would be the same. No one would ever know if he let the wheel spin free, if he fell against the mast and let the gale drive them back the way they had come: blowing past Telltale and the Snout, Tansy and Four Tops and Pinehaven, Giant's Tomb, Trickfoot, the Harp, Double-Eagle, past Clouds End, into the east, into the Mist.

A hundred times he gave them up for dead. And a hundred times he forced himself to go on a little longer.

At last a pale, sickly light announced the coming of a dawn drenched in spray and driving rain and offering no hope. The ravening wind made the masts quiver; made the lines whip and hum.

There was an explosive crack. Where the topsail had been, furious streamers knotted themselves around the stays and shrouds. The *Salamander* fell off a cliff of water. The next wave, racing up with unfair speed, caught her amidships and threw her on her beam ends. Like a dead thing she lay down, tilting at almost 60 degrees. The crew dangled from the mast, kicking madly as the sea chased them up the deck, wondering if it would stop, or if they would founder at last.

A lifetime later the storm began to blow itself out. Clouds splintered and went spinning to the east. The crew of the *Salamander* was battered and beaten, stiff with cold and sleeplessness and hunger.

Shale swore weakly at the sea.

"Reef the mainsail." Rope's voice was cracked and hoarse. His face and beard were caked with salt. He did not turn to look at his crew; his body had frozen into place, locked together with the wheel. Open or closed, his eyes saw only seething ocean. His right leg twitched and trembled.

"What?" Shale said stupidly.

"The mainsail," he whispered. "Reef and set the mainsail."

Numb with disbelief, Shale and Foam clambered over the tilted deck, creeping along spars, trusting only to balance, too tired to be wary. Now that it seemed they might survive the storm, they no longer cared; they had long since used up the last of their fear. They took crazy risks before a sea more terrible than they had ever seen, merely because it was less terrible than it had been before the dawn.

The mainsail flapped dead to wind, luffing hysterically. With Brook and Jo helping, they managed to reef and set it to Rope's directions. It filled with a bang like a clap of thunder.

The *Salamander* began to drag sideways through the water. Again and again foaming seas swept the deck, kicking at their feet. They started up the side of a towering wave. "Hard a lee!" Rope screamed, wrenching furiously at the wheel. His rudder bit and the *Salamander's* head turned through the wind.

He timed it perfectly. Just as they reached the top of the wave, wind rushed into the sail from the starboard side. The ship staggered up, shaking her head like a wild horse, and heeled to port.

An ocean poured from her decks; she bled like a great animal from many wounds. Clothes and rope and food and smashed dishes were belched out on the flood. A set of winter sailing gear, a present to Shale from her father, drifted by with its arms spread out, face-down like a drowned sailor.

"Give it back!" Shale yelled.

But Rope said, "Let it go, Shale. You know what the sea demands."

"Everything," Brook said. "Sooner or later."

PART TWO
The War Loop

Jo's Line

CHAPTER 7: HAZEL TWIST

The three islands of Delta that Hazel Twist had spent so much effort on winning seemed tiny to him now, their houses and harbors and muttering inhabitants like flotsam, resting for an instant on three small rocks before being swept away by the next wave.

The sea, the sea: a vast, blind, groping animal curled around Delta. It was too great, that formless green-blue ocean; Twist's woodlander eyes could not meet its empty stare for long. And so he stood before the eastern window of his commandeered quarters and studied his prize without self-congratulation.

Delta was his. Directly below his windows the cobbled streets of the Foot curved steeply down to the waterline. Wind-seamed sailors and longshoremen with brawny chests dawdled in the streets, trying not to look at the soldiers before his door. Down at the docks half the berths were empty now, marking Deltans who had fled during the first skirmishes, or slunk away while Twist's men were taking the wealthy houses on the landward side of the Foot.

This close to land, the sea moved uneasily. Hard light glinted from its surface and made his eyes smart, as if an army in blue-grey-green had encircled him, visible only when the sun glanced from its steel. Hazel Twist did not like the sea. Its barren emptiness appalled him. Only days after their conquest a mighty storm had fallen on Delta with a fury and a naked power he had never imagined. But to take the rest of the islands he would have to cross that water.

He needed islanders, he decided. Islanders with whom he could negotiate, who could teach his men to sail across open ocean. But Delta was old and prosperous; most of her people had never had to leave sight of land. And of course Deltans would not be inclined to aid him, now that he had taken their city.

He would think of something. The price of disappointing the Emperor was high.

Returning to his desk, Hazel Twist rubbed his eyes until they no longer stung, and picked up his quill. The touch of it, slim between his fingers, gave him the same assurance a soldier feels when he grasps the hilt of his favorite weapon.

My dearest Blue:

My love returns to you, yet one more time, prisoned in this clumsy cage of ink and paper. Too well I know that summer will be over before you receive this letter.

> *My thoughts cross the wilds*
> *In the blinking of an eye*
> *While on the ground a summer's march*
> *of chartless, pathless, leafmeal lies*

Loneliness blew through Twist like wind in the branches of a willow tree.

He must be careful; his letter would certainly be opened and a copy given to the Emperor. Twist frowned. The Emperor would know that he knew the letter would be opened; any critique of Imperial policy would be considered a deliberate insult, and no Bronze bore insult well.

Hazel Twist wanted above all things to abandon this invasion and return to his family and his bower. He had to be discreet.

Things go well with us—if a war can go well. When last I wrote we were camped in the grasslands, and hoped to stay. I thought the Fire unlikely to reach there, and I was reluctant to leave all forest behind. We all felt naked and uneasy beneath the peering sky.

But the Emperor has many shadows to cast. He cannot allow himself to accede to his troops' nostalgia. He ordered us on, demanding certain protection from the Fire before we called a halt to our quest. The safety of the clans, he said, must harden us to endure the blank northern skies.

But now at last we have come where the Fire can never reach: We have come to the sea.

I cannot convey to you the desolation of the open sea. Its people are scattered across a thousand islands that dwindle into the endless East. Many of these islands are wooded, and there my hopes lie.

As the Arbor is to us, so the city of Delta is to the sea's people. It straddles three islands at the mouth of the great river called the Vein. I took my men far upstream; using wood from the river valley, we made a fleet of rafts such as they use in your mother's country. How apt, that the forest should be used to surround the sea! When the rafts were ready, we floated down upon Delta.

Victory was simple and complete. They are a people without skill in war. My men landed while I parleyed. A few locals struggled when it became clear they had been displaced, but they were not trained soldiers, and our sprayers dismayed them. The contest was over almost before it had begun.

In short, the capital is ours.

(Twist swore mildly as another glob of ink dribbled from his quill.)

In general, their civilization is less rich than ours, and less beautiful. As you can see, their inks and papers are very crude. They have little sense for art or design, lacking all subtlety. There are, of course, exceptions to this observation. They wear leathers of an exceedingly fine and supple grain, which they harvest from eels! They love knotwork and embroidery, and make clever jewelry from shells and ivory. They wear their hair long, split into two or more braids and fastened with knots and ivory pins; a good thought, as it draws one's gaze from their faces, which are etched by the wind and dyed by the sun. Above all, they build beautiful ships, exquisitely ornamented and intricately constructed. I am sure we would be quite helpless if we tried to sail one.

There is a small band of islanders who have actively opposed the occupation. They are led by a man named Seven, whom I believe from his astonishing martial skills to be Bronze Switch's famous islander pupil. An anomaly among his people, he is a true warrior, but he lacks finesse and poses little threat. While they may be able to intercept our clumsy rafts on the open sea, his men have no pitch bombs; we will burn their beautiful ships beneath them.

In time, of course, they may develop answering weapons. I will suggest to the Emperor that we try to co-exist with this people. Many islands here are empty or sparsely inhabited. The islanders choose not to live on the ones that are most heavily wooded; they prefer land they can garden. If we move quickly to tell them about the Fire, and thus explain our urgency, we may be able to negotiate our way to amity. I would far rather learn the lore of wind and water from the islanders than from the cruel sea. Only a week ago we were swept by a storm whose fury was inconceivable to those bred beneath forgiving leaves.

Some have said that the Emperor has taken the Spark; that he is driven by a need for conquest. I do not believe it. He has the best interests of our people at heart. I am sure he will proceed judiciously.

After all, the islanders would be children at diplomacy. They lack subtlety: easily deceived, oddly transparent. The endless sea, an emptiness studded with unambiguous islands, has shaped them to corresponding simplicity. Such clarity has its charm, but in the end one longs for the sinuous sophistication of life growing through a maze of branches . . .

vine-slender singing dapple-yellow quicksmile secret-under-leaf
graceful beauty laughing wise woman
heart-keeper
friend wife
lover
The lost linnet sings sadness into the cool green air:
"Behind the blossom, the sweetest fruit
waits."

I miss you, Willow Blue.
Your husband,

Hazel Twist

He folded the letter carefully, sealed it with wax and addressed it in his intricate hand.

There was a knock on the door.

"Come in." Hazel Twist dried his pen. The Deltan ink clotted with annoying speed, like blood.

His lieutenant entered and snapped off a quick bow. Spear was a definitive Ash: upright, energetic, straightforward. "Sorry to interrupt, sir. New arrivals."

"Very good." Twist rose and swung the shutters closed against the glinting eastern light. The room dimmed.

"She limped in this morning. Five staves, I would say—maybe a little longer. Badger and his fellows met them at the dock. The captain was giving a great rush of orders about boat repairs. Badger kept nodding and smiling long enough to tie her up. By the time they realized we weren't Deltans it was too late. No fighting, but two of the crew had mouths on 'em."

"I trust Badger's sensibilities escaped unscathed."

Spear grinned. "Oh, he'll recover. But if he'd done the things they told him to, we'd be burying him tomorrow. Or sending him back to the Arbor as a curiosity."

Spear's sense of humor tended to the crude, but he was bright enough, and a loyal soldier. Ashes always were.

"We need one of these islanders to work with us," Twist said. "They know the wind. They know the sea."

Spear nodded uncomfortably. "There are those two Thorns the Emperor sent along."

"Spare us! Useless as well as distasteful. No. Suppose we torment this captain. He agrees to tell us what he knows. How can we know he speaks the truth?"

Spear shrugged.

Age had flecked Twist's black hair with white, and would have given his fine features an air of quiet certainty, were it not for his curious Hazel eyes. They shifted with the light, neither green nor grey nor blue. Now and then, even those who knew him best would catch a secret expression, as if Twist saw things differently, but either from courtesy or caution kept his own counsel.

"We can't sail. We don't know the region. Our islander might direct us onto the rocks, or into the trackless sea."

"We could make him steer the ship."

"If you were asked to lead an islander raid to the Arbor, would you hesitate to misguide them at the cost of your life? Of course not."

"Thank you, sir."

"The sea's people are not soldiers, but they are no cowards either."

"Why would an islander help us?"

"That is the question." For a long time Twist pondered, while Spear stood attentive and undoubting before his desk. At last the commander stirred. "I have some ideas. Bring the islanders to me."

"Yes, sir."

"And make sure we have provisions. Good, but simple."

"Yes, sir." Spear snapped off another quick bow, and hustled from the room. A simple soul, Twist thought. Just as well. Clever subordinates were notoriously problematic.

Something the Emperor knew as well as he. Would the Arbor be safe for Hazel Twist if this campaign ended successfully? Very possibly not. It would be wise for Blue to leave the capital; she might be too tempting a hostage for a Bronze jealous of his general's success. Twist broke the seal on his letter home, and began with great patience to draft another. This time he would extol the coolness of Willow's rivers and the beauty of its autumn, and he would suggest she take the children back there for a season.

He dipped his pen and began to write.

Eight soldiers escorted the crew of the *Salamander* into Twist's office.

"Hang a lamprey on your balls and pull hard," Shale said to her guard as she stalked into the room. Days had been long and rations short since the storm. Her tunic sleeves were badly ripped and she still bore an ugly red scab on her shoulder where she had taken a nail during the gale. A fading bruise made her scowl all the more ferocious, and her right cheek was raked with scratches. Her shark-tooth earring was a white hook between matted black hair and skin burned brown.

"What fools do you have down at the docks?" Rope said. "They didn't even let us get the docking floats out before marching us up here. Whatever you want from us, a sprung ship won't do you any good."

Dressed in deep green leathers, their captor awaited them, staring out the eastern window. He was very small, like most of the soldiers they had seen. He glanced at one of their guards. "See to it."

"Yes, sir."

Foam came next. His hands were stiff and swollen and his head ached as it had every day since the gale, but he alone among the islanders preserved an air of elegance. His braid had been carefully tended, and in the dawn watches while the others struggled to wake, Foam had been up early, dangling his legs over the stern as he patched his torn clothing with quick needlework.

His throat was cramped with terror and he couldn't keep from glancing at the spear-points levelled at their backs. Was he a coward, or were the others just hiding their fear? His eyes darted over their faces. No, Rope was thinking of his ship, Shale was furious, Jo was almost mocking. Brook—Brook was scheming, trying to think her way out. He recognized that meek, distant, defiant look. It was he, only he, that felt sick with fear for their lives. His life.

And so he kept talking, talking, as he always had, as if talking would somehow help, as it never had on Clouds End. As if the woodlanders would hear only his words, and not the thinness in his voice. "I would have taken you all for boys, but surely even woodlanders don't let their children play with nasty, sharp weapons."

"We all know how the caged bird sings," Ash Spear said.

Jo came last of all. She was no longer a white-haired haunt with silver eyes, but a stocky island woman with a fading bruise on her left cheek.

The woodlander captain looked them over. "Hungry?"

"Starving," Rope said. "We lost most of our supplies in the gale."

"You sailed through that alive?" The woodlander glanced at the shuttered eastern window. "I would not have believed it. Spear, bring in whatever we've been eating. See there is enough for my guests."

"Guests!"

"No irony intended, young woman." The woodlander nodded to Shale. "I would prefer guests to prisoners." He crossed the room to sit on the edge of his desk. "My name is Hazel Twist. Yours are?" They told him, and Rope asked him what woodlanders were doing on the first island. Twist held up his hand as Ash Spear returned with a tray of food. "In good time. First, please break your fast with me." He picked up a pickled gull's egg and ate it slowly, frowning. "Damn fishy taste, this has. Still, it's all one to my belly." He poured cold water into a fuseware cup. "My orders are to find a place for our people to live."

Foam popped down a potato cake, licking his fingers. "Tired of trees, are you?"

"That is not your concern. The Emperor believes we can no longer live in the forest. But we can live here." Twist scooped up a handful of pickled mushrooms and ate them like nuts. "I don't like the smell here. All wet sand and salt water. I miss the smell of home. But orders are orders. We have an army, and you don't. If I wanted to, I could take the entire archipelago."

"Try it," Shale said.

"I could. I do not wish to. I'm a simple man, Shale. I like to do things the easy way. Your people know things about wind and rain it would take us a hundred years to learn. Your ships are better, your sailors are better. I'd rather have you as friends than enemies."

Foam nodded, washing down a strip of salted fish with a drink of water. "Did your mother teach you to make friends by sacking large cities, or was that your own idea?"

"Quit that, son. You are in no position to chafe me. I had my orders. Now I am giving you a choice. Show me which islands we can have, and how to get there. Teach us a little wind-wisdom. In return, I call off the troops."

Rope shook his head. "Commander, this can't work. As soon as you try to move off Delta our ships will scatter you."

"How? Trained soldiers are more than a match for fishermen, however valiant, and we have many weapons. We can rain fire on your beautiful ships and burn them underneath you."

Rope did not answer.

Brook said, "How can we know you will keep your promise?"

"You can't." Twist did not smile. "But I will."

"Prisoners secured and under guard," Spear reported later that night. He lingered in the doorway. "Will they accept your offer, do you think?"

Twist peered up from a pile of dispatches on his desk. "And betray the islands? Of course not. Not yet."

Spear cocked his head. "But then . . . I don't understand."

Twist licked his fingertips and used them to clean off the nib of his pen. "It's very simple, Spear. Our first interview was only to suggest that I might deal honorably with them."

"That's why you carved the Simple Man mask."

"You were not convinced?"

"Well, everyone knows that you're not . . . You're more . . ." Spear blushed, fumbling to a halt.

"Less direct," Twist suggested. "Quite. But these islanders do not know me. If fortune smiles on us, they see me as a gruff and aging captain who longs for his home port. Not wholly a lie, as I'm sure you will agree."

"It made sense, the way you put it."

"You gratify me. But no man decides such things on sense. A shadow, even the shadow of so great a thing as war, is still not palpable enough to make a man sell me the secrets of his way of life. If they came to me now, I should ignore them. They would be trying to trick me. Only when they know in their hearts that the consequences of silence will be far worse than those of speaking, will they give us anything of worth.

"Now we allow them to learn a little more by 'chance.' Some talk between their guards might do. The sentries should not begin their play until late, and they should whisper, as if eager not to be overheard." Twist frowned. "But remind the guards to speak clearly; the islanders' hearing is worse than ours."

"What if the prisoners fall asleep?"

Twist shrugged. "No doubt some will. But with such a decision to make, they will quarrel. Someone will be too angry, or nervous, or upset to sleep. The guards should talk about the Emperor." Twist paused. "We pass into delicate realms here, Spear. But it's for the good of the clans, eh?"

Spear nodded. "Of course, sir."

"This conversation will be about the bloodthirst of the Arbor. You know, soldiers' talk: 'It's easy to want killing if you don't have to do it, . . . I'd say he's got the Spark,' and so on . . . To discourage those who would challenge him, our Emperor has cultivated a reputation for ferocity. That reputation need be exaggerated only a little to seem like madness to these peaceful islanders.

"Tomorrow, take one of the men with a fair dose of the sea in his features—Elm Creek would do—and toss him in with the prisoners. He will say that the Emperor is mad, that I am the only thing standing between the archipelago and red havoc. I have already earned my master's displeasure for refusing to indulge in certain atrocities. Only the rapid success of my scheme will prevent the Emperor from recalling me and sending out someone more bloodthirsty."

Slowly, Spear said, "You want them to believe the story you

told them, but to imagine they discovered it themselves. You are not a simple man, Hazel Twist."

Spear's commander shrugged, looking over his latest letter to the Emperor. "Nature rarely puts a straight track between the trees."

Spear coughed, nodded, cleared his throat. "Is it true?"

"About the Emperor?" Twist looked up. "Of course not. Let me say something to you here, Spear, and I want to emphasize it very clearly." He held Spear's eyes with his own. "The Emperor desires only the good of the clans. The Emperor is the sanest of men. The Emperor acts only for his people. Any other assertion is the screeching of owls and the braying of asses." And then, his eyes half-hooded, he turned away from his subordinate. "And the Emperor, quite reasonably, nurses a stringent distaste for slanderers. Do you understand me, Spear?"

"I hope so, sir."

"I hope so, too. Now, I really must get back to this letter. Fetch me my tambra before you retire, would you? I will play before sleeping tonight."

Spear bowed and retired from the room, leaving Hazel Twist alone in the pale, sea-stained light of the late afternoon.

Even after darkness finally fell, the night brought no relief for the islanders, penned in the sleeping chambers of what a few days before had been a wealthy merchant's house.

Brook lay sweating on the left side of the merchant's overstuffed bed. The cuts she had suffered in the storm itched fiercely. Shale lay next to her. When Brook's leg touched her, she growled and rolled away.

Foam's shaky voice came out of the darkness across the room. "Now's the time to turn into a breeze, Jo!"

"Breeze be drowned," Shale said moodily. "Blow us out of here."

"How?" Jo said. "There are too many guards to daunt one by one."

"You drew us onto the island, haunt. Had we sailed straight from Clouds End, we might have been here soon enough to warn the Deltans."

"Don't blame me for your own desires. Sere was pulling us all into the Mist."

"Even if Jo did get us away, that wouldn't unravel the knot Hazel Twist has tied for us," Brook said. "Maybe we should give Twist what he wants."

"Don't be gutless. Give up the islands without a fight?"

"Who is the coward, Shale? The woman willing to risk her people's hate to save their lives, or the one willing to let thousands die to save her own pride?"

"Softly there, Brook," Rope said. "Shale is no coward. She just hates to give up."

"No, she's selfish. It's different." Soldier's cries, and the wink and flare of passing torches filled a long moment of silence. Brook said, "I expected more from the Witness's daughter."

Shale sprang, catching Brook around the neck and throwing her back on the bed. In the darkness Rope and Foam scrambled to their feet.

"Throttle your friends while your enemies hold you prisoner," Jo said. The haunt's voice was bright and hard as steel. "You make me laugh, you heroes. Sent to save the islands, and you lie in bed squabbling like suspicious lovers. You humans are just what I remembered."

"She had no—" Shale's sentence was bitten off as Rope jerked her off Brook, none too gently. "She had no right! To call me a coward for not betraying the islands!"

"You called me traitor first." Brook rubbed her throat. "This isn't like seeing who will walk into the leech pond first, Shale. What we do next has to be for the good of everyone. And maybe the cost of saving the islands is to be hated by our people."

"That won't be hard," Jo remarked. "The people of the sea find it easy to hate what they don't understand."

"I think Brook could do without you on her side," Foam observed.

"What's to stop Twist from taking what he wants?" Brook said. "Do you see something hidden from me, or are you speaking only with your heart?"

"Brook may be right," Rope said unhappily.

Brook looked at him. "If I told you to help Twist, you would do it, wouldn't you? And feel like a traitor for it."

"Is that what we should do?"

The hot night lay on Brook like an animal.

It would be simpler to resist. Let someone else make the sacrifice of treason. She shook her head, marvelling. Here she was, willing to risk thousands of lives to avoid angering her friends. Cowardice. Cowardice masked as loyalty. She wondered what Shandy would do.

A breeze slid across the windowsill, listening to their quarrel. Shadows jerked across the ceiling as a torchbearer passed along the street below.

Two soldiers muttered beneath their window. ". . . night." "Heard . . . news?" ". . . peror." "Orders . . . arm . . . every man . . . islands!" ". . . lost it!"

Brook lifted her head off the bed and shook Shale's shoulder until her friend grunted and stared back at her, eyes narrow with anger.

"I find your comments on the Emperor . . . intriguing."

Brook cupped a hand around her ear and gestured to the window.

"Chopping's a fair topic for the woodsman."

"Like it or not, those are the orders."

"Rope. Foam. Listen," Brook said.

"They're only islanders, after all."

"And a babe that miscarries is not yet a child. But pruning is for trees, not for people. I cannot call it civilized."

"The Emperor's wishes are civilized by axiom."

"Lopping off their arms?"

"No man likes it, but Palm is already cinders and I hear that Vine is burning. Which pigeon here will complain to the hawk? There are Thorns in the city, don't forget."

"I heard the emperor had taken the Spark and now I believe it. I don't envy these sea-born bastards, I tell you."

"And I cannot love them. I am on watch here in a moment. Nothing to do but sit at the bottom of the stairs all night, lose a little more money to Cherry Gall."

"You aren't playing with his dice, surely?"

Laughter. Farewells. A lone torch went bobbing down the street, jerking its catch of shadows behind.

Brook said, "Now you see what we have to do." She looked at the others, their faces half-visible in the faint light of stars and torches: Rope frowning, Shale scowling.

Foam blinked. "What was that about the Spark?"

"The Emperor is mad. We have to go along with Twist. The risks are too horrible if we don't."

"No," Jo said. Her voice was cool as the dawn wind. No longer in the guise of an island woman, her steel eyes glinted in the starlight. "We must go to the Arbor."

"What? Oh, certainly," Foam said. "Dance there, I should imagine. Disguised as a group of village idiots banded together for protection. You can be chief lunatic."

"Foam is right, for once. You must be . . . Mind you, it would be a journey to make songs about," Shale added thoughtfully.

Jo's voice was low and assured as a distant river. "The Emperor is mad. His own army knows it. We must pull the weed out by its roots. As long as he holds power, any deal you make with the people of the forest will be caulking a bad join at best. Did you not hear? He has taken the Spark. The hungry fire is in him." She stared at Brook. "It is better to have peace than war. But this Emperor is Sere's shadow now. It is folly to believe war can be avoided."

"I am no traitor," Brook said.

She touched the Witness Knot around her wrist as if the right choice lay buried in its windings. "There was a Spark in the story the Singer told about the forest people." Her meeting with the Hero seemed as distant as a dream. "But that Spark had more to do with freedom, with giving up."

"The Emperor desires the islands," Jo said. "That is clear, whatever the Singer's story may mean. You know as well as I not to trust what you hear in the Mist."

"We know not to trust haunts either," Shale said.

"After all, Bug, I'm sure it's all true," Foam said. "But I suspect it isn't what it appears to be."

Brook could not follow the windings of the Witness Knot. And she felt, more deeply than she ever had, how lost every person was in life. The past foundered like a ship seen through long fathoms, sunk beyond all hope of salvage; the future was only clouds. Between them, life—one long breath, one breaking wave made from equal parts of luck and guesswork, of tea and lamplight and laughter and heartbreak and peppermint and tears, and hope and hope and hope—that nameless faith raised like a candle against the storm of things.

"I don't know what to do," she said. "But if my friends believe that going to the Arbor is better than helping Hazel Twist, I will do that, and be glad."

Foam whistled. "B-but . . . The Arbor! People of the sea aren't meant to stray so far from the waves."

"People of the forest shouldn't be landing troops in Delta either," Rope said. "Perhaps this is a time for strange journeys."

"Think of it as an adventure," Shale said.

"So was the storm. I swore off adventures last week." Foam spun out questions with nervous fingers. "How are we to find the Arbor? And what are we to do when we get there?"

Jo said, "I will guide you."

"Oh, great."

"Which way is the mainland?" Brook asked.

Rope picked his way through the dark room to the window. "See the Ship? The transom star should be to the west, over the mainland."

"But I can see lights over there, and buildings."

"That's the Sock. Delta is a triangle of three islands, remember. We are on the Foot. The country of the forest people lies to the south and west." There was a tug on Rope's fingers; Net had crept down from his sleeve. "We have passed through the Mist, through Sere's fire and Fathom's wrath. I think we were meant to go." Net gripped him fiercely, twisting this way and that, his strands glowing luminous silver.

A faint gust of wind swirled by Brook into the night and she shivered. "Magic," she said. Net whirled in the breeze and then fell still.

Shale said, "Where's Jo?"

"Spit! She's changed again," Foam said.

"She will be back," Brook said. "She has uses for us yet."

"She did say she would guide us," Shale said.

"Scouting," Rope said. "Marking the number of guards and their posts. That sort of thing."

"I hope so. I didn't much like the sound of what those soldiers were saying." Foam made a sarcastic flourish. "Come! See the dancing toes of Rope and Foam, armless wonders who sail using only their feet! Salamanders regrow lost limbs, you know. Tragically—"

"Shut up, Foam. Do you think this is helping?"

Tramping footsteps climbed the stairs. "Prisoners fall out," a rough voice called. "Commander's orders."

"Helping? I'm too busy being terrified to worry about helping."

The door flew open. "You don't let people get a lot of sleep," Rope said.

Halfway down the stairs, unseen, Commander Twist said, "Bring them."

A clump of guards stood to attention in front of the house. "Two will be enough. These people are not warriors." Twist pointed at two men, who stepped forward.

The other sentries clustered around the doorway. "Duties, Commander?"

Twist hesitated. "No further duties. Take the night off. We have earned a little rest, I think."

"Thank you, sir!"

The soldiers watched Twist leave with the prisoners. "The old man's been tipping back a bit too much brandy," one murmured. The others laughed quietly.

Twist led, followed by a slender guard, tall for one of the forest people. Then came the islanders. Then the second guard.

The night air was stifling, a hank of hot damp cloth pressed against their faces. Soldiers laughed in the streets. Deltans crept from doorway to doorway, vanishing before the guards' torches like roaches running from the light. Jo, Jo, Brook thought bitterly. You couldn't have picked a worse time to leave. She wished desperately for a breath of wind. The stars ran at their edges in the humid night.

"The docks," Twist said.

"Sir?"

"The docks, take us to the docks! Can't you hear?"

"Yes, sir."

"There's someone on the next island I think our guests should meet."

Shale glared. "What does that mean, you eel-sucking old man?"

The front guard said, "Careful, poppet. Them Thorns now are real pricks."

The other guard laughed unpleasantly.

"What's a Thorn?" Rope asked.

The rear guard shoved him in the back and sent him sprawling. "Shut up."

Twist turned to the guard. Hesitated. Looked at Rope. "Your questions will be answered soon enough."

"Hey, Gall!" a rough voice called from the darkness. "This sea gull shit giving you trouble?"

The rear guard grinned and kicked Rope to his feet. "Ah damn! I stepped in it." A round of chuckles swept the street. Rope struggled to catch up with the others, limping and grasping the back of his thigh.

Off-duty soldiers began to follow them. Rope felt their contemptuous eyes. Too many, too many. Maybe later they could escape, maybe in the boat. They'd have to use a boat to get to the Sock. These people didn't know the sea. They could be tricked, unbalanced, capsized. Outswum.

"Hey, Gall! Don't use them all up! Save some for us."

"Ah, hunt your own. These are mine, on commander's orders."

"And mine!"

"Tell me, can you shit in midstride?" Shale asked the taller guard. "There must be some use for walking assholes."

"Sing, little bird. Sing while you can."

Twist was grimly silent.

Images bobbed in the jerking torchlight: a leer or a scowl or a smooth, pale face; a disembodied hand, fingers curled around a knife.

A soldier fell in next to them. "How about it, Gall?" he whispered. "Give us a taste?" Before Gall could reply, the newcomer snaked his foot around to trip Shale. She stumbled, whirled, and kicked him hard in the shin. He swore and lunged at her, breaking into the knot of islanders. The mob swirled closer.

"You! Gall! Stop this!" Twist demanded, voice quavering. Gall grabbed the soldier from behind, pinning his arms. Shale seized her chance and kicked him in the balls.

Then several screams burst out at once. Bodies bent like grass flattened by the wind.

Cherry Gall's eyes widened in wonder. "Sh-sh-sh-shit!"

Where seconds before there had been a cluster of forest soldiers, four corpses lay in the street. A fifth man crawled slowly backwards on his hands and knees. His elbow stuck out the wrong way from his arm.

Hazel Twist knelt in a ring of dead men, shrieking thinly into the pavement. A red-cloaked figure knelt over him, holding a sword under his throat. With his other hand he held Twist's arm high up behind his back. The stranger's wrists were cabled with muscle. Blood dripped from his fingers. "If anyone moves, he dies." The hand locked around Twist's wrist moved, almost imperceptibly. Twist twitched and screamed.

Torches choked and flickered in the sudden silence.

"Seven." Cherry Gall could not look away from the dead bodies that lay like jetsam scattered on the cobbled street. "You must be Seven."

Other islanders had come up behind the cloaked man, armed with clubs and axes.

"Now we can talk." He shifted his grip on Twist's arm, who shrieked again.

"I am not Twist!"

The commander's head began to jerk and flow, sliding away from the sword-blade like quicksilver. For an endless moment everyone watched Twist dissolve, melting under his astonished captor, shrinking, curling into a ball of white feathers. Then there was only a gull, beating its way into the sky.

"Jo!" Rope breathed.

The mob sprayed into violence.

"Islanders, to me!" the swordsman yelled. Shale darted forward, dragging Foam along.

The forest soldiers pulled out clumsy tubes and squirted jets of evil-smelling blue spray into the humid air. The islanders clutched their eyes or staggered backwards, shrieking. Their leader blocked a deadly stream with his cloak and lunged for the nearest woodlander.

Shale and Foam followed the fleeing islanders, dodging and twisting. A point burned in the middle of Shale's back, waiting for a spear to find her. Shouted orders and the shrieks of the dying warred in the darkness.

Then they were at the shore. They jumped into the first boat they could find and shipped oars, thrashing the water white. No one lit the running lamps. They hit other boats twice. Swearing and creaking, a fleet of shadows pulled out into the bay. Then Delta was behind them.

Their wake was a trail of silver. Shadowy boats on every side slid over the gently rolling sea, long oars out like water skater's legs.

Foam grunted, pulling hard. "Shale?"

"*Ung!* Yeah?"

He took two more strokes, getting his breath. "Where *ung!* are the others?"

"You *ung!* didn't see them?"

"No."

Shale's aching arms flexed, pulling her oars into a smooth, dipping slash. Oarlocks creaked and strained. She pulled her oars clear. Salt water trailed dripping from her blades into the sea. "I don't know." She pulled another stroke. "We'll just have to find them later."

Foam rowed. "How much later?"

But there was no way to answer that question. Foam knew it and Shale knew it too. They were rowing away from all answers, pulling with every stroke into a deepening night where the dark sea and the distant stars reflected in it were the only certain things.

CHAPTER 8: ROPE, BISCUITS, PEPPER

Rope gasped as pain shot through his thigh. Someone tripped him and he hit the pavement hard. Blue vapor sprayed overhead.

Cherry Gall shrieked and fell on him. Blood spurted from his severed throat and hit Rope in the face, tasting of salt and meat. Rope's head and legs burned where the blue mist touched them. Gagging, he hid under the corpse.

Metal bit bone, and steel clattered against steel. Rope's cheek ground against paving stones slimed with blood. Net writhed beneath his ribs. Someone tripped over Gall's body and Rope bit his lip to keep from crying out.

Running footsteps echoed from every cobble. The shouts fell back toward the water. Orders were given. Farther up the hill someone beat a gong.

Rope spat out Gall's blood and rubbed his face on his tunic. The blue vapor had faded with the shouting. He pitched Cherry Gall off his back and took the dead man's sword. Soldiers ran by without looking at him.

"Brook?"

She sat only a few paces away, hugging herself and rocking back and forth. He crawled over to her.

A huge gull landed on the cobbles beside them, hissing and clacking. It hopped away, heading for the nearest alley. They followed, crawling around corpses, then staggering down to one of the smaller docks.

Clumsy with fear, they untied a small launch and set sail for the mainland. Behind them, Delta's night was stitched with fires as torchbearing soldiers raced through the streets.

Around the angry city the black sea curled, deaf to gongs and orders, deep as the night. It bore them far out into the gulf, until only the rustling sail remained, the creaking boom, the hiss of cut water from beneath their bow. The moon's sail bellied out, running low along the far horizon. A narrow path of shaking silver light ran across the dark water to it, glimmering, glimmering. Wholly inconstant.

Like babes in a cradle, they lay in their boat, hidden from all eyes save those of moon and stars, and rocked into darkness by the tireless sea.

Rope woke when they ran aground.

The smell of salt water and dim forest mingled in the morning air. Net had crawled up his arm as he slept and now reared up on his right shoulder, swaying, grey and tremulous as a spider web. The boat tilted, pushed by the swell. Brook lay slumped across the forward thwart, still sleeping.

There was no sign of Jo.

The sun was not yet up. Grey light the color of driftwood lay over the world. The Sock, Delta's southernmost island, was a dark smudge behind them. Small rollers pushed their stolen boat along the beach of a wide, shallow bay. Coarse grey sand ground beneath her hull. She had scarlet gunwales, Rope saw, and leaning over the side he read her name: *Eel*.

It was low tide. The sea had drawn back from the cold beach as if wanting no part of it. Farther up, beyond the high-water mark, a jumble of grey boulders littered with bits of shattered shell lay at the base of a short cliff. Sword ferns and twisted black roots sprouted from the bluff. At its top stood a line of forbidding trees: drooping red cedars like woodlander sentinels, guarding the mainland against invasion.

Brook opened one eye. Her right cheek was swollen by an ugly purple bruise, and clumps of her hair had fallen out where the blue spray had touched her. "I feel like a wrecked ship," she said.

Slowly Rope tried standing up. His legs trembled. Even his fingers ached as he took down the sail.

Brook gasped. "What happened to you?"

"I got kicked around. I've felt worse. I think."

"But the blood!"

Rope touched his face. Something cracked like dried mud on his cheeks and mouth. He stroked his scabbed beard and his fingers came away red. "I don't think it's mine. Not much of it, anyway."

"Your hair is falling out."

"It was those sprayers. Your braid isn't doing so well either." Rope eased himself over the gunwale, grimacing as cold seawater flooded into his boots. The blue spray must have eaten through them. "We're alive, aren't we?" He spied a large gull on the beach, shifting from one grey form to another. A whisper of fear entered him through his shoulder, where Net sat. "Jo's here."

Two of Brook's braids had split. They dangled raggedly about her shoulders. She touched them. "I must be very ugly."

"You sound like Foam." Rope cupped cold seawater in his hands and splashed it over his face and beard. Red dribbles rained from his jaw. When he finished washing the blood away, he took Brook's hands in his. "You look beautiful."

Brook squeezed his hands, hard. "I hope they're all right. Foam and Shale."

She clambered from the boat.

Jo was waiting on the beach. Her smooth white flesh was unmarked, but her silver eyes had dulled almost to grey.

"Grab this." Brook handed her the painter and turned to Rope. "Should we pull up the boat, or scuttle it to cover our tracks?"

"Scuttle it! How would we find Foam and Shale without a boat?"

Jo said, "How would we find them with one?"

The dread that had been building in Rope since he woke went suddenly hard and painful, like a stone in his chest. "Can't you turn into a breeze or something?"

Jo was wearing one of Brook's deep blue tunics. Her white hair floated around her shoulders. "And do what? Look in every house in Delta? What if I cannot find them? What if they are on the Foot or the Sock, or not on Delta at all? They may be in Twist's prison, or they may have escaped with the cloaked islander."

Grey waves crawled across the beach. Jo turned a bracelet of blue shells around her wrist. Her long nails clicked and clattered. Rope remembered her on Shale's island, callous at his father's death. "I am tired of your excuses. And your orders."

"Rope—" Brook followed him out of the water.

"If it wasn't for you, pretending to be Twist," Rope told the haunt, "we would never have lost Foam and Shale."

"If it wasn't for me, you would still be locked up. No, that isn't right. If it wasn't for me, you would still be back on your little lump of dirt, going out day after weary day for another hold of smelt or sea bass or oolichan and wearing the smell home at night as the badge of your manhood."

The stony anger in Rope's chest was growing, gouging his heart and lungs, making it hard to breathe. His big hands balled into fists.

Jo's features blurred. Where moments before a white-haired haunt had stood, Rope now faced an islander with broad shoulders and a bloodied beard. Big callused hands. "Try it," Jo whispered. "Come learn what Brook already knows."

"Stop this," Brook said.

"We wouldn't be fighting if Jo hadn't—"

Brook slapped Rope, hard. "Shut up! Shut up!"

Rope grabbed her wrist. It seemed thin as a bird's bone in his strong hand. Her skin turned white around his fingers. "Don't hit me," he said.

"Don't make me."

They had spent better mornings together than this one.

The sun was well up before they decided what to do with the boat. They had to get rid of the dinghy so none of Twist's patrols could find it and figure out where they had entered the forest. But the cursed boat was too heavy to drag up the shore and hide in the bushes. They had a sword, but didn't dare hack at the hull until they holed her, for fear of making too much noise. For a moment Rope had thought Jo could turn to fire and burn the *Eel* to ashes, but of course that would have made too much smoke.

In the end he ran up the sail and got Jo to turn into a breeze, blowing the boat back onto the sea.

Rope and Brook sat on the boulders behind the beach and watched their empty dinghy head for the middle of the bay.

"There goes our last chance to warn the other islands," Rope said.

"Other islanders already know about the invasion. Remember the cloaked man."

Rope nodded. "True. But shouldn't we rouse our own people, instead of taking up this mad quest into the heart of the forest?"

"Maybe. But that would only spin the war out, not stop it. Besides, there is one other reason for going to the Arbor."

"Hm?"

Brook looked out into the empty sea. "She wills it. And haunts—"

"—get what they want."

They had gathered a small pile of clams and mussels. Rope eyed them without enthusiasm. A deep bruise made his thigh throb and tremble. His back and wrist ached badly. "We shouldn't leave Foam and Shale."

"We have a job to do. We have our duty. If they are dead, there's nothing we can do to help them. If they are well, we'll meet again on Clouds End—if we stop the woodlanders. And to stop the woodlanders, we have to stop the Emperor."

Rope tapped the Witness Knot around Brook's wrist. "Those are your duties. Mine are to my ship and crew. My ship's banging against some dock on Delta, in the hands of idiots who don't know a sheet from a halyard. And my crew—" With a wet crunch Rope splintered a blueback shell with the butt of Gall's sword and scraped up the clam within. "What did they do to deserve this?"

Softly, Brook said, "They were my friends."

He wondered if Foam and Shale had eaten yet that morning. One day, Jo had said, life will slit you open like an oyster.

Brook fingered a clam. "Three moons to the Arbor, Jo said."

"You really think Twist will send trackers after us?"

"We are more than escaped prisoners. We are islanders in league with a haunt. He has to know more about us."

"I'd like to know how much she says is true. About needing humans near her to stay human."

"That's true, I think." Across the bay, Jo was blowing their dinghy ever farther from land, out into the heart of the great wild sea. "Sometimes the world rushes over you and it seems so big, so big. And you are only a character in someone else's story. A rag of Mist blown into shape by the wind. And then it's time to put the kettle on the fire, or sew a button on, and that's no story but your own," Brook said. "But Jo—Jo has no need for buttons. She left the kettle behind, and chose the steam instead."

Rope sighed. "Then I guess it's up to us to hold her purpose steady until she has dealt with the Emperor."

"If driving this haunt to the Arbor is what it takes to save Clouds End, then by Fathom, drive her I will." Brook laughed without smiling. "Isn't it funny? We used to think she was using us."

Jo returned well before noon, and they started walking west along the shoreline, making for a creek she had spotted from the air.

"So how will you find the Arbor?" Rope asked.

"Twist marched an army through these forests. The birds saw them pass, the deer ran from them and the grass was trampled under their feet. The trees will be talking about it for months, if not years."

Brook and Rope, laboring behind the haunt, glanced at one another. Rope shook his head. "Shale will kill us for stealing her adventure."

They drank long and deep when they came to the creek's mouth, and ate another meal of shellfish. Rope looked up the stream. "Not bad. I was afraid it would be too choked to follow. You can barely move for the undergrowth on some of the islands around Clouds End."

"Those islands are but newly out of the Mist. Their woods are young." Jo led them along the stream and into the forest. Little grew on the ground save moss and ferns. "Here the trees are older, and greater."

"Soft ground for aching feet!"

"And tonight soft ground for aching everything," Brook added. "My whole body is one big bruise. I hope it doesn't get too cold."

"We will survive," Jo said. "We won't be warm, but spring here is giving way to summer."

"The oolichan will be running at home," Rope said.

"And Sparrow's baby will be coming any day."

With every step the stream's sounds changed. Echoes splashed off a rock in its midst, or widened with the current, or were swallowed up by a bank of tall, silent ferns.

Rope said, "How quiet it is."

Instantly his voice died, as if the forest did not care for the speech of men.

"Secrets," Brook said. "There could be anything, back a few steps from the path, and you would never know it. A deer, a house. A corpse."

"Or a spy."

Jo laughed. "What seems quiet to you is full of a thousand noises. Believe me, everything in the forest knows we are coming: you two shamble like deformed bears. Now try to be quiet! I must listen."

A long . . . warm . . . day, the cedars sighed. Both warm and long.

Lovely, the maples replied. The sunshine made their veins stand out, vivid green in leaves like golden glass.

The wind yawned.

Up above, muffled by the canopy of leaves, the sky was addressing some long, abstract thought to the philosophical clouds. The trees murmured on about the likelihood of sun and rain. Ferns bowed as the travellers passed, offering to tell Jo the dew's strange secrets.

The haunt let herself flow into the whispering woods, spinning out her senses in ever-thinner spider strands, tacking herself to leaf and tip, blossom and bole.

It was only as they walked through a dusty copse of pines that she realized the whole forest spoke of death. Beneath every friendly greeting, beneath every guess hazarded about the chance of rain, lay a deadly struggle for light and water and earth.

And below that was something else, something *wrong* in the wood. She could feel the strain of it, cracking within the forest core. Somewhere a splinter of fire burned and would not heal. Fear flowed from it. Fear not of death, but of madness.

Very far away. Very faint. A fear of madness, blooming like poppies on a fresh grave.

"Jo? Jo?"

"Wh—?"

"Come back!"

"Wh . . ." Jo opened her eyes. Blinked.

Startled, Brook and Rope saw that the haunt's face had taken on a greenish tinge. Her eyes were the color of an oak leaf held up to the sun.

"Is something wrong?"

"I'll . . . I'm fine. I got lost," Jo said. "Easy to do, you know—get lost, walking in the woods."

"Don't wander now," Brook said, shaking the haunt lightly by the shoulder. "It's a long way to the Emperor yet."

In the early evening, sore and weary, they made their camp at the base of a great cedar tree.

Rope stared up at it in awe. "This must be taller than all of Clouds End!" The cedar's riven trunk opened like the mouth of a cave into a great hollow space with charred walls. "Has it been hit by lightning?"

Jo shook her head. "All red cedars have split trunks. Someone has made camp here before us. See the ash pit in this corner?"

"I wonder if any forest soldiers will be heading here as night comes on."

"Oh, thanks, Brook."

The islanders gathered firewood while Jo went to hunt for dinner. The light was failing by the time she returned. At first Brook mistook her for a wisp of fog, coiling between the cedars. Net reared in greeting.

Jo tossed a bundle at Rope's feet; it landed with a soft thud on the hard-packed dirt, seeping blood from a line of punctures on its side. "Rabbit," Jo said, flexing her fingers as if to ease a cramp.

The meat was a long time cooking and hardly worth the wait. Rope chewed grimly. "I was hoping hunger would make it delicious."

"Maybe tomorrow," Brook ventured.

Rope spat out a piece of gristle and wiped his greasy fingers on a fern. "Fish is so much cleaner."

"It bleeds less, anyway." Jo poked the fire with a green switch; a shower of red sparks whirled up into the blackness. "You should be grateful the dinner was drained before you got it." The islanders winced and she grinned at them. "So then, what shall we do?"

"I could tell a story," Rope said, clearing his throat. "A very simple one."

"I have ears," Brook said.

"And I," Jo put in.

"Well, all right." Rope glanced at Brook. "This is a story of strange journeys, and stout companions, and the advantages of being prepared."

The moon was not yet up. Darkness lapped like black water around their campfire. Insects creaked in the night and leaves whispered. Reflected flames danced in their eyes. The sound of wood burning was like the sound of the sea.

Rope settled himself, took a deep breath, and began:

"This is a story of the Mist-time, where everything is real, and nothing is what it seems to be. It is a Figure of Eight story."

Brook leaned over to Jo. "Looks like it sounds. A figure of eight knot keeps a rope from pulling through a block."

Jo nodded.

Bottom Loop

Eh, yes. Well, nineteen or maybe eighteen generations ago, there was a famous explorer named Chart.

(Brook grinned, leaning against the rough-barked cedar.)

He had sailed far to the west, into the upper reaches of the Vein, where he befriended the people of the grasslands and met the Su-Tan, the spirit hawks that drift over the endless plains. He had sailed far to the north, where the sea threw up floating mountains of ice and snow-weirds tried to trick his ship into foundering. He had sailed south to the dense, hot, violent country that Lianna calls her own. And he had even travelled east, skirting the edge of the Mist, which in those days was much closer to the mainland than Clouds End is now.

He had seen many fabulous sights on these voyages, and acquired great wealth, and people began to call Chart of Delta the Greatest Explorer of All Time. He was improbably tall and absurdly thin. Whenever anyone asked him about his exploits, he said, "You need three things to be successful. Extra rope. Lots of biscuits. Plenty of pepper."

Was that it? people wondered. Was that all there was to being the Greatest Explorer of All Time?

At last Chart's fame caught Fathom's ear. Now Fathom is as rash as any Hero, and more jealous than most. "Hah!" he said. "Greatest of All Time? I'd like to see him prove it!" And faster than a fish can strike a fly, he was off to test Chart's mettle.

He blew in to Delta that very night, spurring gouts of hail from a storm-cloud and arriving between a stroke of lightning and its peal of thunder.

He knocked four times on Chart's door, or maybe three, and each knock was like the sound of a whale leaping onto a longboat. The door opened after the fourth, or possibly third, knock, and Chart looked out into the wild night. He was improbably tall. He was incongruously thin. He had long mustaches that drooped like wet string and he'd caught a bit of a sniffle. He examined Fathom without enthusiasm. "Gud ebening," he said.

Fathom strode in with a breeze at his back, blowing maps through Chart's house like dried leaves. "I'll get right to the point," he said. "Are you the Greatest Explorer of All Time?"

Chart shrugged. "Hard to say. Peeble say I'mb de Greates'— *snffff!*—but dere may be udders I habn't herb uv."

"What about the Navigator, who pilots his celestial ship between the stars?"

Chart shrugged. "Oh, I dink I'm probably bedder dan himb, anyway."

"Really!" The Navigator was Fathom's son-in-law whom he'd hurled into the sky so hard the midship lamp broke, which is why the Ship only has stars forward and aft. "And why do you say that?"

"He sails de same course ebery year, and he nebber got back home. No boyage is wort' spit unless you can dell udder peeble about it."

"Really!" Fathom said, seething inside. "How interesting! And tell me, what is your secret, O most potent of adventurers?"

"Egstra rope. Lots ub biscuits. Plenty ub pepper."

"I'll give you all the rope and pepper and biscuits you can possibly imagine if you agree to go exploring for me."

Chart grunted. "Where?"

"The Mist!" Fathom says. "Explore the Mist, and your fame is assured."

"And if I don't want to go?"

Fathom just grinned in that dangerous way only Heroes can grin.

"Thot so," Chart sighed. He stroked his weedy mustache. "Gonna take a lot ub rope," he warned.

"As much as you can imagine."

"Gonna take a load ub biscuits . . ."

"As many as you like."

"Gonna take a deal ub pepper . . ."

"All the pepper you could desire."

"All right," says Chart. "I'll do it."

(The darkness washed a little closer to the islanders as their fire dimmed to embers. Everybody felt better for having had something hot to eat, though Brook wished she could get the taste of rabbit out of her mouth. "I need a drink of water," she said, creeping over to the stream.

It tasted of leaves and quiet earth. She followed the red glow of the firepit back.)

Top Loop

Famous as he was, even Chart had trouble getting a crew together to go into the Mist. He had to promise four or maybe three thousand times that there would be more rope, biscuits, and pepper than anyone could possibly imagine.

At last the big day came. Chart had a brand new boat to make the trip, and he named it *Figure of Eight*. "This here boat won't get carried away by the Mist," he said. "I don't aim to get flung about like a loose jib sheet." All of which sounded pretty good.

But before Chart was even out of the harbor, the Deltan crowds were shaking their heads in dismay: he had forgotten to take up his anchor! For every length the ship covered, another few loops of rope dribbled over the transom and into the sea. Everybody felt embarrassed on Chart's behalf, and they quickly left the port so he wouldn't feel ashamed when he had to come back.

Oddly enough, when the Deltans went to work the next morning, the anchor was still there. A length of rope—the lightest, thinnest, strongest rope Chart could find—led far away into the east.

When the sailors noticed, Chart just said, "Yep. That fella sure gave us plenty of rope." And then he didn't exactly smile, not being given to the habit, but he sighed a cheerful sigh, and his frown had a sort of twinkle to it.

Well, it was a long way from Delta to the Mist, but the weather was fine, and the fish were plentiful, and the crew stayed in good spirits, as long as they didn't think about what lay ahead.

It took four or maybe three moons for the *Figure of Eight* to reach the edge of the Mist, and when the crew finally saw it, shimmering and shining, gleaming and glowing, blacking and whiting and boiling up like a silvered thunderstorm before them, they got scared.

"We can't go in there!" one cried. "What if we meet the Muck, what eats ships whole?"

"What if we fall off Swap's Log!" said one with a shiver that made his earrings jingle.

"Or maybe fetch up on The Island That Went Back," a third sailor moaned.

"I'm the captain, and I order you to trust me," Chart said; and each time he saw a frightened sailor he would lean over, and wink, and mutter, "Rope! Biscuits! Pepper!"

Well, into the Mist they went.

They saw a cloud give birth to a bright blue island.

They dove for pieces of sunken rainbow off the coast of Fire Island, and almost sank when a shooting star crashed through the deck like a cannonball.

They saw Sere lose a race with Time, leaving feetprints of fire on the cloud's surface for as far as the eye could see.

And of course the old *Figure of Eight* went through a few changes of its own. For a while it had a hull of beaten gold, thin as a dragonfly's wing, and rigging all of spider's web. Then the ship took the shape of a walrus with a giant heron on its back, spreading its wings for sails. They saw many marvels, and had many adventures, and before long you couldn't say they were all quite sane. But Chart kept them as steady as he knew how, and tried to write his experiences in the log every day, regular, before he went to bed.

Finally they'd had enough. They were ready to feel the rock beneath their feet, and plunge into honest water, and tell their stories to the people back at home. Everyone was pleased the day Chart came out of his wheelhouse and said he was ready to turn for home.

But just as the crew gave a great cheer, the Mist under them bubbled up black and crimson. Then the lookout spotted an enormous tentacle, far alee, writhing on the surface of the waves. "The Muck!" she yelled. "The Muck! We're doomed!"

But Chart started shouting like a crazy man. "Biscuits!" he yelled. "Crumble biscuits overboard!"

Nobody moved a muscle. Chart was frantic. "Didn't I take you to the utter South? Didn't I lead you past the Ice Islands of the North? Didn't I get you back down the Vein with your blood still inside?" he screamed.

The Muck's threshing tentacles bore·down on the *Figure of Eight*.

"So CRUMBLE BISCUITS!!!" Chart roared, heaving a grand load of dry biscuit overboard.

Crazy as it seemed, every sailor on that ship started crumbling biscuits as if feeding Sere. The air was thick with crumbs; hair was white with flour. The deck looked like a bakery. And now everyone could see the nearest tentacles, black and livid red, groping for the ship.

Then the lookout saw the first gull. Just circling there, screaming, nearly too fat to fly on ship's biscuit. Pretty soon another came swooping down out of the misty sky. And another, coming from abeam. Two more gulls from the transom, one flying out onto the bowsprit, several flapping down from the rigging, a whole flock from the starboard rail. There were gulls everywhere: gulls bubbling out of the water, gulls bursting from the ship's lockers, gulls tangled in sailors' hair. All fighting and clacking and screaming at one another to get those pieces of biscuit.

And the closer they got, the thicker they got, trapped in a whirl of wings. A vast white swordsman formed from the birds, spoiling for a fight: the Gull Warrior, the Hero of the islands.

Now, conveniently enough, there was a big red and black slimy smelly oozy horrible tentacled genuine four- or maybe three-times life-size monster there for him to battle.

And battle they did.

The fight raged for seven days and six nights.

"Watch out!" Chart cried, as a severed tentacle crashed onto the foredeck.

"Take care, lads," he roared, as the Muck squeezed one of the Warrior's limbs right off, dissolving it into a storm of wheeling birds. "The Gull's been disarmed!"

But on the seventh day, the Muck finally decided the *Figure of Eight* wasn't worth the effort, and slithered off to engulf a small, sparsely populated island.

"We did it! We did it! We're alive!" the sailors cried. And then they turned as one to the captain, and said, "Surely you are the Greatest, Most Resourceful, Most Extraordinary Explorer of All Time! How can we ever thank you?"

Chart wrinkled his nose. "Scrape the gullshit off my boat," he said.

So they cleaned up the *Figure of Eight*, now well convinced that Chart could deal with any danger.

But Chart wasn't happy. "No wind!" he grumbled. "For the last four days (and three nights), there's been not a breath of wind." To make matters worse, the ship smelled terribly of gull droppings, and Chart would dearly have loved for a breeze to blow the stench away.

No breeze came, and the ship lay in irons for a month of deadly calm.

"Tentacle, tentacle, tentacle," the crew grumbled. "That's all we've et for weeks. Tentacle stew, tentacle pie, creamed tentacle in brine with tentacle fritters on the side. Ugh! We want to go home!"

Finally Chart set them to pulling at the rope still attached to the anchor in Delta harbor. "It will be a long haul if we have to drag ourselves home, but what choice do we have? Oh, and one other thing. Bring up those extra barrels of pepper."

And so, during the long, weary days while the crew pulled the *Figure of Eight* back toward Delta, Chart sat tinkering with an odd contraption made from rope and a pulley and three ship's hatchets, one for each pepper barrel.

Thirty days later, or maybe twenty-five, who should Chart see but his employer, walking down the bowsprit and jumping onto the foredeck. Now Fathom stood twice the height of a normal man, and his eyes were storm-cloud blue, and lightnings played around his head. His cheeks were all puffed up, and he didn't say anything, just smirked. Finally he looked up at the sky and muttered a few words, very fast and breathy: "You-seem-to-be-stuck-Greatest-Explorer-of-All-Time."

Chart looked up and saw his mainsail pennant leap straight into the air. "A bit of calm," he said. "But I'm about to leave it behind."

"Ha!" Fathom snorted, and the boat heeled wildly in a sudden wind. She steadied as Fathom sucked the air back in. He looked around at the frightened sailors, and the dirty ship, and Chart. A mean grin spread over his face, like the shadow of a storm spreading out black across the water. "*Fwuuuuuuh!* And-how-do-you-intend-to-do-that?"

Chart stroked his weedy mustache and looked up at Fathom with an appraising eye. "Why, you're going to help me, neighbor!" He nodded as Fathom's eyes bulged. "Yep," he continued, "I figure you're too stupid not to."

"HAH!!!" Fathom snorted, and immediately the sails surged out. Chart yanked on his rope, which pulled through a pulley on a bracket, which jerked three other ropes, which yanked the braces out from under three ship's hatchets. And Fathom, realizing he'd filled the sails with air despite himself, sucked in as hard as he could: *fwuuuuuuhhh!* But what he sucked up was ounces, gallons, *barrels*, of fine ground pepper.

His heroic eyes watered. His heroic nose ran. His cheeks fluttered and his brow sweated lightnings. "Grab hold!" Chart cried, and his crew hung on for dear life as Fathom spun his head around, wheeped, heaved, and delivered himself of a sneeze heard round the world.

Well, every people has stories about that sneeze. The grasslanders say that the sky is on a hinge, and that once it swung down sideways and blew them halfway up the mountains at the end of the world. The people of the forest found every tree, shoot, and sapling within three days of the shore swept into the air and stacked as firewood. Back in Delta, the wind hit so hard that it spun the triangle of islands around so that the Foot became Spearpoint. And above all, the sneeze blew Chart's boat clean out of the Mist and back to Delta.

That ship flew so hard and so high that every person on board should have been killed, smashed to splinters on one of the Outer Islands, only Chart had the *Figure of Eight* built flat-bottomed, so she hit the water just in front of Telltale and skipped like a stone over the tallest hill on it. She bounced five more times, clearing islands on three bounces, before she came skidding back into Delta harbor and tore out her hull on the dockside reef.

Well, the townsfolk poured out to greet them. They shouted Three Cheers for the crew and Three Cheers for the *Figure of Eight*. They cheered the rope, the biscuits, the pepper, and themselves. They cheered three cheers for Captain Chart!

But all that gloomy man could do was complain. "Why'd you move the islands around?" he growled. "That new reef tore the bottom out of my boat!"

Which proved that the Greatest Explorer of All Time was a true ship's captain, and an islander to the bone.

Jo clapped softly. Brook had already fallen asleep, but a grin remained on her face.

They bundled up for the night, Rope with his arm around Brook, Jo with an arm around Rope to ward off the cold.

As he lay on the hard ground, trying to sleep, Rope drank in the strangeness of their journey. He was in a story. This—this was so different from ordinary life.

This mattered.

Earth beneath his head, darkness beyond the embering fire, leaves murmuring in the night . . . the press (he couldn't ignore it) of Jo's breasts against his back; the touch of her leg.

He closed his eyes and drowned in sleep.

Later, much later, Jo was still awake, drawing warmth from Rope's broad back, staring down the night with secret silver eyes.

She hissed at a touch on her arm.

It was Net, slinking spider-soft over Rope's shoulder and onto hers. Through his feathery touch, she could feel Rope's sleeping

core. He was open to her, slumbering there, on the other side of
the mesh, warm and human: an anchor to hold her to the ground,
if she chose to use him.

She shivered as Net slid from her shoulder. A palp touched her
breast, lightly, through the cloth. Retracted. Reached out again.

She fell asleep during his delicate examination.

CHAPTER 9: THE FOREST

A scream woke them.

Jo sat bolt upright with her heart hammering in her chest. The fire was a dim red glow inside the cedar. Darkness pressed against her from outside.

The scream was suddenly bitten off.

"What was that?" Brook hissed.

"Shhh!" Jo's whole being was in her ears. Night sounds filled the silence the cry had left behind. Trees murmured of rain and wind. A weasel dove into the creek. An owl hooted and Brook grabbed Jo's hand.

A thin breeze slid by, whispering dark secrets. Jo tried to hear its tale, but fear scattered her thoughts. "Too many trees! I can't hear anything over the trees." She squeezed Brook's hand. "But before the scream died, I thought I heard a man."

"A woodlander."

"Perhaps."

Rope had woken. "One of Hazel Twist's trackers?"

"Not anymore. Something killed him. But there's nothing out there now. Nothing but trees and wind."

Rope scrabbled to all fours, groping for Cherry Gall's sword. Net writhed and darkened, poised like a web of shadow on his shoulder. Around their camp the trees muttered darkly to one another.

Rope sighed, reaching for the tinder. His whole body ached. "I don't think we will sleep again tonight."

But care and weariness proved him wrong. Like a spring tide, sleep overran them all long before dawn.

Jo woke gasping from a deep green dream. Creepers and vines and coiling roots had grown over her, sending their pliant fingers around her throat.

The night was over and the fire was cold. Their first full day in the forest had begun. Jo breathed deeply of the woodlane air, letting her dread ebb. Lumps of shadow gradually became logs, trees, ferns. She reached down to rub her leg. Two, no, three spider bites on her left foot, none on her right.

Her hand stilled as she remembered the scream.

Rope and Brook lay together across the cedar's gaping mouth. Their acid-eaten hair was tousled and dirty. Net nestled around Rope's wrist; Brook was curled up with her face toward the fire. Jo hugged herself and shivered. Squatting on her haunches, she thought about how far she had come since fleeing the Mist, and how much farther they had yet to go. And at the end of their trek . . . ?

She had never met a Bronze. They scared her. She had twinned Brook deeply, and made copies of Twist and Rope. Even that had been a mistake, confusing the pattern of her human self, threading too many lines through the design. She must not do it again.

So what could a Bronze be like? The haunt who could maintain himself while listening ever to the hearts of men must have a center beaten from steel. She could not imagine it.

With a grunt she rose to her feet. No point worrying about that yet. The scream was a more pressing riddle.

Time to hunt.

What shape? Eagle? Hawk? But keen eyes could be baffled by leafscreen . . . A nose would be best. A slinking, a skulking, a red-tailed black-paw. Warm fur to keep out the cold, clever feet to tread the rabbit tracks, ears to prick and a nose to sniff.

She foxed herself.

Ahh. Better. So much easier to trot along the forest floor, slinking by the dew-tipped ferns. The stream: a long drink of water and a quick cleaning. Now, sniff out the world's news.

Deer spoor and ashes and the smell of humans. Jo shuddered. It's only Brook and Rope, she told herself. But the human reek made her tail twitch. She bounded upstream, searching for a dead-fall bridge.

The campfire smell was fading. Better. Mouse holes and grouse . . . Not so long since the eggs had hatched. Jo's pink tongue lolled for a moment, and her eyes gleamed. Fuzzy little snacks in the bushes hid. Farther off, the smell of meat.

Human meat. Curious, Jo thought. Of course, that would be it. The scream. She paused. She had almost forgotten the scream. She would have to be more careful.

A hare burst from beneath a bush in front of her. Her legs pounced of their own accord but he was an instant faster, bounding wildly before her, over log and under leaf. Jo flashed along the forest floor, burning with the thrill of the chase. It would be good to feed.

Sunlight slid between the branches of a great maple and fell on the corpse huddled at its base. Flies hopped and circled around the bloody mash that had once been the left side of the woodlander's face. His spine and ribs had been snapped like kindling. His sword lay by his side, undrawn.

The day grew warmer and the smell stronger. Pecking at the exposed meat, a murder of crows flapped up as a red vixen charged into the clearing and chased them into the sky. They screeched indignantly as she nosed over the body.

When she was full she trotted away, pausing to sniff at a strange thing that lay on the moss some distance from the corpse. It was a tube with a sack of skin at its base. An evil smell leaked from it, like liquid fire. She growled and backed away, then turned and trotted through the forest, following the distant scent of ash.

"Jo! What did you find?" Brook's thin shoulders were tense. Rope stood before the cedar, gripping his stolen sword.

The haunt shook her head and frowned. Some memory nagged at the back of her mind, but it was covered in fox-thoughts and she could not recapture it. "Nothing," she said at last. "Trees."

"Come look at this. Please." Brook pointed back into the fire pit. "I had some very strange dreams last night, after the scream. In one of them, someone was trying to get in here. Then when I woke up . . ."

It was full morning. Even in the dim forest, the light was broad enough to show four footprints, huge and inhuman, clearly marked in the soft grey ash of the fire pit. "Look at the toes!" Brook murmured. "Like talons."

Jo stirred. "Or roots." She looked around at the towering trees, remembering their secret talk of death. "I too had strange dreams last night."

"Something is out there," Rope said. "Some monster killed that woodlander last night."

Jo listened to the wind murmur its secrets to the trees. She felt a thousand eyes watching them. A thousand ears pricked with their every footfall. "Then let us hope the forest is kinder to the sea's people than it is to its own."

All morning they hobbled beside the stream. Twisted, sinister cedars swayed above thickets of evil-scented elder. Striped spiders the size of Brook's thumb hung thick before their faces and tangled in their hair. Rope took to clearing away the webs with a piece of deadfall. Even so, they walked shuddering through bales of silk and gathered many bites: hard aching bruises with a red blister at the center.

"At least on a boat there might be something to see," Rope griped. "Here it's just trees, trees, trees. What I wouldn't give for a real view! My eyes are cramped. What kind of people could live here?"

"Secret," Jo said. "Pale and hidden and quiet as mushrooms. The forest knows no straight lines and thinks always of death. It does not strike but strangles."

"Great," Rope muttered. "I'm so looking forward to meeting its Emperor."

All their lives Rope and Brook had known the vast, empty world of the sea. Wind and surf made ceaseless songs from the rhythmic rush of water onto rock; the air was open and cut with salt. Rolling waves marched on and on beyond the range of human sight. Every island, every ship, every sound or smell was sharp and tiny and particular, clearly placed against an immense backdrop of wind and water. At night floating stars drifted on the sky, to be devoured by clouds that rose silent as pike from below the horizon.

The forest was a different world, close, dim, and secretive. Red cedars sighed and maples murmured in a language the islanders could not understand. Wind, light, sky—everything was muted by the trees, everything was dimmed. In the universal murk each sliver of sunshine was a surprise, touching moss to green fire, or glinting from diamonds of dew in a spider's web. And then a branch would sway as if pushed by an unseen hand, and throw its shadow over them.

Often their hurts forced them to halt, but soon fear of Twist's trackers or the memory of the scream would drive them on. As they walked, Brook and Rope often wondered about Foam and Shale. Had they survived that night on Delta? Did they flee with Red Cloak? Or were they locked in some woodlander prison, paying the price for their friends' escape?

Rope grumbled continuously but would never suggest stopping. Brook would answer for a while, then fall silent. Finally she would ask for a halt, resenting the others for making her ask for the rest, and despising her own weakness.

Just as they were stopping for lunch on their third day's march, it began to rain. Jo offered to turn her hands to fire to dry out firewood, but Brook and Rope quickly declined. "The less you touch on Sere the better," Brook said. The haunt shrugged and left to go hunting while the islanders foraged for dry tinder. Even when they got the fire going, it gulped like an old man on his deathbed.

"Ow!" Caught in a billow of black smoke, Rope coughed and scrambled out of the wind's way. "All this for another filthy rabbit, no doubt."

"Ugh!"

"What I wouldn't do for a nice fillet of bass!"

"Rock bass."

"Caught off the Talon—"

"Sizzling in oil," Brook said dreamily. "Otter's way, sprinkled lightly with dill." They looked at one another, stomachs growling. Rain dripped gloomily from the branches overhead. "This is not a good idea," Brook said.

Rope nodded. "We must make do with what we have."

"No use thinking about grilled bass—"

"Or pickled mushrooms—"

"Or Shandy's plum wine!" Brook sighed.

The fire hawked and shuddered. Hastily Rope flung several more strips of cedar bark on the dull embers and blew them into brightness, covering himself in a cloud of ash.

Brook passed over a handful of soggy tinder. "You—*cwuh!*—look like a roasted ra—*ack!*—coon. The grey in your hair—so distinguished! I shall swoon!"

She swooned gracefully on top of him, and opened her eyes to find him worrying her tunic, teeth buried in her collar. "Oh, you beast!"

He held her in his arms and growled, kissing her neck.

"This is nice." Brook laughed, blinking as raindrops sprinkled on her upturned face.

Rope smiled and kissed her lips.

"Very nice."

He met her eyes again, still smiling, still silent. He held her with one hand and caressed her with the other. His fingers slid down her arm and up her back, stopping at last to caress the nape of her neck. Dirty and wet and tired, he held her beside the smoking campfire, and his smell mingled with the smell of wood smoke and damp earth and green things in the drizzle.

She kissed him back until she was breathless. "It should rain more often."

Still smiling, he stroked her arm again and then moved his hand up to touch her breast. He held it firmly through the damp cloth of her tunic, not hiding his face in her neck or coyly closing his eyes. Still looking at her, still smiling. They were far from Clouds End, in a secret place where the rules were different. They were no longer children. They had sailed to Delta and trekked across the mainland like adventurers in a story, like Chart or Swap.

He moved his hand around her breast in a slow, firm circle and she gasped. It was the confidence of that touch; and his pleasure; and the way he looked at her, forcing her to admit that he was touching her breasts, that he wanted her. Brook felt her face flush. "Jo could be here any minute!" she whispered.

His smile broadened and he kissed her again, squeezing her breast, running his hands around it and up to her neck and finally down to stroke between her legs, cupping his hand around her mound, still looking into her eyes, still smiling. Her skin kindled where his hand passed.

A rustle in the bushes made Brook scramble to her feet, flushed and breathless.

"You got it lit!" Jo called, stepping back into the clearing.

"What?"

"The fire." Rope grinned, throwing on another strip of cedar. "We got the fire lit."

Jo's hands were hidden behind her back. "Our lucky day!" she said. "Guess what I caught?"

Rope and Brook looked at her, then looked at one another. "Rabbit," they chorused.

"How did you know?"

"Just lucky."

Brook's face was burning with embarrassment and her stomach snarled vile things at her as she looked at Jo's rabbit. Then, suddenly, inspiration struck. She jumped up and scouted around their campsite, glad to have something to do, trying not to think about Rope's touch. "Shale would kill me for not thinking of this," she muttered. "Walking by the creek all day." She scrabbled in the mucky loam. "Come on, come on . . . Aha!" she cried, plucking forth a long, pink, wriggling worm.

"FISH!" Rope shouted.

Brook looked back, grinning ecstatically. "Fish! If we could catch a few fish every day," she explained to Jo, "we could keep you from shifting so often. It's no use getting to the Arbor with an owl instead of a haunt."

"And we could eat decent food for once!" Rope paused, considering. "But worms are not enough. We need rods, hooks, line."

"We could tickle for them."

Rope flexed his fingers. "I'd rather not." He could not help looking at Jo. He had offered to fish this way for her before, back on Shale's island. And she had offered him something in return. He had been right to refuse her, of course. And yet . . .

And yet, looking at her now, narrow face wound about with silver hair, he felt a stab of guilty desire.

Brook saw the look that passed between Rope and Jo. Jo was beautiful, she realized. Jo could take Rope away from her.

Jo shrugged. "Very well. Lead on. What catches fish, anyway? Eagles? Otters?"

"Um." Brook glanced at Rope for encouragement. "We are grateful for everything you've done for us. We really are. But we don't want you to shift. We'd like to try to catch some of the food ourselves."

Jo looked dubiously at the little stream beside their camp. "Good luck."

Poles were easily fashioned from available branches. In a stroke of genius Rope thought to use Net for the line. "He'll hold the hook and grab at any fish that strikes," Rope boasted. The women watched, bemused, as he trained Net to grip a hook he made from the rabbit's splintered collarbone.

Brook studied their tackle without much hope. "This is the clumsiest fishing rod in the history of the world. It will never work."

Rope's confidence was sublime. "It will work! And do you know why it will work?"

"Rope," Jo asked, "why will it work?"

"Because fish are very, very stupid."

They lost the first two worms on nibbles. "Good sign!" Rope muttered. "They're in there. Net will come through." He threaded another worm, and cast. "They like a little drizzle, just like this. Makes 'em hungry. Oh, I seen 'em in there. Big, fat, silver-bellied trout. Golden bass. Carp, oozing through the muck below."

The line bucked suddenly downward.

"Got one!"

"Get him, get him!"

"Is he hooked?"

"It's a MONSTER!"

Jo rolled her eyes heavenward and licked rabbit juice from her fingers.

Rope stared at the water in a frenzy of concentration, steely-eyed, alert to every twitch and vibration of his slender rod. It was Man against Fish in a sprinkle of rain.

Then the trout took a fatal turn into an eddy, and with one flick of his powerful wrists, Rope sent the doomed fish skipping onto a broad stone by the bank, where Net wrestled it into gasping surrender and then slithered smugly away. Brook ended the trout's agony with a clanging sword stroke.

"Ooh," Jo said, wincing at the knot left in the sword's blade. "They're not really made to swing at granite," she suggested.

Rope surveyed his catch. "Well. Brook. There's not much left of it, is there?"

"You meant to eat the head?"

"Head! Your cut went through at the hips."

"The whole fish wasn't as long as your hand!"

"Mock not!" Rope warned. "It was a good fish, and a valiant fish."

"It was a tiny fish," Brook said. "A teeny tiny eensy little fish."

Jo sauntered over. "Is honor satisfied? Will you take some real food now?"

Hunger growled savagely in Brook's stomach. "I'd say honor was—Ulp!"

"Terribly sorry," Rope said, removing his elbow from her side.

"Oof! Uh, thanks, Jo," Brook said glumly, staring at the tiny bisected trout. "If we're still hungry after we eat all this, we can always catch more."

It was a hungry afternoon and a weary evening, but that night the sky cleared, and the waning moon drummed down a magic light through the leafscreen, wild and holy and awash in spirits.

Somewhere in the darkness a mad owl screamed her kill, and Brook's heart jumped. She felt the sight shudder through her. The forest made mock of the owl by daylight. The crows shrieked crude comments and the mice mimicked her, turning their furry heads about, holding their little eyes wide open and blinking stupidly while their fellows laughed.

Things were different when darkness fell. Then the owl floated from her branch—soft as snow, as quiet, drifting. Seeking vengeance. Then the mouse who had been so bold by day trembled at every rustle in the leaf mold, scurrying from root to root, dread thumping from his tiny heart. Suddenly a mad scream would explode behind him and turn his blood to ice while talons like nails hammered through his jerking back.

Jo's silver eyes glittered in the moonlight. Rope had already settled for the night, snoozing inside the split trunk of another great red cedar.

An owl's shadow fell across Brook's mood. If a night like this brought the Mist before her eyes and made the world sing huge within her heart, what must it be like for Jo? It was big, too big to contain. Brook fought back, cramping herself down to human size. We are not meant to hear the secret songs, she thought. Our stories are not the stories of wind and sun; we hear those at our peril.

With a shock like an unexpected touch, Brook felt her story waiting for her, out in the Mist.

And she thought about how foolish she had been, holding herself apart from Rope and Clouds End, savoring her sight like her most precious secret. But the magic was deadly to her. The Mist had rolled over them, hunting for Jo. The Mist had taken Rope's father. It was not kind and it was not human. She feared it.

Magic is like water, Brook thought. We only swim so long before we drown.

Jo stirred by the campfire. "I think I shall watch tonight, and see if our long-toed guests return. And Brook, think about trees!"

Brook blinked. "Trees?"

"Mm. I was dreaming of them two nights ago when the long-toes came. Listen to the wood. Hear what the cedar says."

Rope snored softly by the fire. Brook shrugged. "If I can stay awake, I'll try."

So she lay beside Rope in the cedar's split trunk, drifting between sleep and waking, staring into the woody darkness. She felt life surging through the cedar's roots and running like blood into every vein, and knew the tree to be a living power far greater than she.

Fear seeped into her like rain into the ground. What if she were to lose her way and sink into the wood forever?

When finally she slipped into sleep, she dreamt that Jo was crawling through a hedge into a secret room. And it seemed this room was inside a tree, near the topmost branches, and it swayed from side to side in the wind.

At its heart a golden spark cast a host of shadows.

●

CHAPTER 10: ASH AND IVY

Shouts woke Brook, and the stench of acid. She twisted away from the cedar's mouth.

"Bind me, will you!" Jo stood with her arms outspread across the opened trunk. Where her fingertips touched, its bark was black and bubbling; her body writhed rivulets of blue vapor like that which had hissed from the woodlander's evil weapons.

"Mercy!" called a high, sweet voice from within the great cedar. "Please! The vapor is torment!" A second voice, much deeper, groaned in pain.

The islanders scrambled together and Rope reached to take Brook's hand. "Good hunting for Jo."

The haunt's skin sizzled and spat as she stepped back from the cedar's mouth, thickening into flesh. "If you lie to me, or turn to flee, I will not be merciful."

"Anything, but take away the sting!"

Jo retreated, condensing to womanhood.

Two figures crept out into the moonlight, smooth-limbed, deep-eyed, and clad in living leaves. The woman was no taller than Brook, but her huge companion towered over Rope. They smelled like moss.

"Wood spirits," Rope murmured. Net tingled around his wrist, glowing luminous green.

The wind rustled in the woman's hair like a breeze through a tangle of vines. "We are grateful for your mercy. My friend is hurt."

"Do not waste your sympathy," the man said. He was tall and stiff-backed, but his walk was broken with pain. If the woman's voice was a flute, his was the wind moaning over a hollow stump.

"I am Ivy." The woman bowed, body dipping like grass before a breeze. "This is Ash, my companion. Forgive him. The pain makes him ill-tempered."

"What are you?" Jo asked.

Ivy's laugh was like a trill of birdsong. It made Brook shudder. "We are the forest. Just as you, of the exiled air, may take a tree's shape to better understand its speech, so the wood may take the form of men." Ivy gestured to herself and Ash with a hand as graceful as a willow wand. "Such are we."

"The forest wished to bind me? I find that hard to believe."

"We are trapped," Ash said. He lowered himself painfully to the ground. "We cannot return to the wood. Men and trees have grown too far apart. The forest people burn with disease. As I now burn." He thrust a long hand toward them, turning it to catch the firelight. The exposed flesh was pitted and blackening. "The forest and its people have sundered and the crossing is barred to us. We are dropped leaves, broken branches."

"They meant to use me as a bridge," Jo said. "Tie me to the trees so they could return from being human."

Around them the forest sighed and muttered in its sleep. Brook's bracelet clicked in the long silence. "We are people of the sea, Rope and I. We know what it is to be far from home."

Clinging gently to Ash, Ivy shook her head as he tried to back into the cedar. "You left a fire, and Ash stopped by it."

"I was cold." His voice was like the wind passing through a bed of reeds on a cloudy day. Sprinkles of rain, sadness in the air. He drew his arms in around his body with a creaking, rustling sound, and inched a little closer to the fire. "Cold . . ."

Ivy shrugged. "I believe we can still cross back if we can reach the Arbor, the heart of the wood. But that journey is long and Ash is hurt."

"I am getting better."

"Of course you are!" Ivy said, loudly and with great cheer. "But you must not tax yourself." She turned back to Jo. "May we travel with you for a time? The company would do him good." She looked at Brook. "Empty stomachs make weak legs. We can find you food. We could show you swifter ways. Will you have us?"

"A strange proposal, after what you tried to do to me," Jo said.

Brook laid her hand on Jo's arm. "I'd rather have them where we can see them."

Brook's mind was racing. If they took Ash and Ivy on as guides they could travel far faster, and Jo would need to hunt less often. The less time she spent as hawk or wolf or otter, the more chance there was she would stay human, and remember her woman's purpose in the Arbor.

Rope held silent, seeing that Brook had some reason for wanting Ash and Ivy along.

Brook said, "I am tired of suspicion." She squeezed Jo's hand, cool once more and soft as flower petals. "Let us try. We will part at the first sign of trouble, I swear to you."

Jo hesitated. "Very well," she said to the wood spirits, "but our joining can be easily sundered. Take no liberties."

Ivy bowed, reaching out to wind her supple fingers around Brook's wrist. "Our gratitude will be no less than your compassion."

Ivy's complexion was a rich, warm brown, with berry-red cheeks. Her leaves were dark green and glossy. Ash's were paler, like paper; they whispered as he walked, striding with a stiff, proud gait.

Ivy was fluid and lively, always darting off the path for berries. "Ugh!" Rope said, watching her shin up a seemingly unclimbable tree. "Like Shale when we were little. It makes you tired just to watch."

Ash made a queer sound almost like laughter. He was a massive man, two heads taller than Rope, with muscles like knotted roots. But the black pits in his head and hands grew deeper every day.

The wood spirits were excellent guides. They left the little stream the islanders had followed from the coast and made more directly for the Arbor. Two days later, they crossed a track just wide enough for three men to walk abreast. "Twist's road north," Jo said.

Rope blinked. "Why would anyone choose this as their road? It meanders all over the place."

"You are too blind to see the bog on our left?" Ash said. "Too deaf to hear the stream to our right?"

"Forgive Ash!" Ivy said, stroking his shoulder. "It is the pain."

"I will be rude if I wish. I do not need your apologies."

Jo said, "Then perhaps you do not need our company."

After a moment, Ash took one giant stride into the forest.

"It will be cold tonight," Ivy called to him.

"Why must you always . . ." A grimace of pain tightened Ash's face. "Very well," he whispered. He returned, but for the rest of the day he did not speak.

Each night Ivy sped about the camp, bringing in rosemary and fennel, or scavenging for mushrooms. She cooked, she cleaned, she told stories—always touching someone's hand or shoulder with her cool, clinging fingers. Ash became ever sicker and more morose, sitting and staring into the fire as if a great secret lay hidden behind its flames.

One evening as they foraged for raspberries, Brook asked Ivy about Ash's injury.

"The scars, you mean? We met a woodlander the first time we approached your camp. He fired his sprayer before we could get away. I was behind Ash, but the cloud caught him in the face."

"The scream," Brook murmured.

"Ash killed him," Ivy said. "Ash is very strong, you know. Very strong."

"Perhaps," Brook said. "But something in him is broken. He hangs from the forest like a broken branch." She looked curiously at Ivy. "But you seem very well."

Ivy glanced sideways. Brook was shocked by the look of cunning on her pleasant face. "I am not too proud to drink the rain, nor too meek to fight for sunshine," Ivy said. "Like your haunt."

Brook picked raspberries. "What do you mean by that?"

Ivy laughed. "Have you not seen the smiles she gives him? The way he thirsts for her tales of magic as dry roots thirst for water?"

"Who, Rope?" Brook remembered the desire that had hung between Rope and Jo the morning they caught the tiny trout. "I don't believe you," she said, finding that she did.

(And another, more secret jealousy stabbed Brook's heart. Jo was hers. Her twin, her secret. Rope had no right to her.)

Brook stood, hands still, tangled in a web of emotions, while Ivy chatted on. "Oh, I don't say they have betrayed you yet. But your man longs to journey and your haunt longs for a home. Each has what the other wants. 'Fire creeps to wood; wood warms to flame,' the woodlanders say."

Greedily Ivy gulped down a handful of berries. "There is another thing about your haunt. Why do you think we came the night she caught us?" She squeezed Brook's hand. "We did not come that night on a whim, Brook. We came because she drew us there."

At first it was all they could do to keep up with their guides, but as they approached midsummer, Ash grew weaker. He walked beside them, dour and silent, while Ivy flashed ahead and behind and off to either side.

"You don't seem worried about the wood spirits anymore," Rope murmured to Jo one day as they walked behind the others.

Jo shrugged. "Ash lacks the will to bind me, and Ivy the desire. Every day they stay with us they become more human. As do I," she added thoughtfully. "As do I."

They had two encounters with bears, one (much worse) with a skunk, and one with deserters from Twist's army. When Ash grabbed their leader's sword and broke it in half with his bare hands, the bandits ran yelling back into the woods.

"We must be getting close to civilization," Brook said dryly.

Ivy nodded. "We are not yet at the outskirts, but we are nearing them." She looked sympathetically at Ash, who dropped the sword fragments wearily to the ground. "Poor fellow. If only we could go a little faster!"

As the days passed, Ash grew ever grimmer and more morose.

Ivy became ever more human. She made herself a shirt after the woodlander style, and then wistfully asked to borrow Brook's belt. Brook smiled and knotted it around her waist. They all began to bathe more regularly, and Ivy scrubbed their clothes to rid them of wood smoke. She washed herself carefully as well; each day her skin grew lighter, and a few more leaves washed away. Of the spirit they had trapped in a cedar's heart, soon only Ivy's long, twining hair remained.

Brook smiled and put her arm around Ivy's slender shoulders. "Soon we shall have you looking like a proper woodlander."

Rope knew Brook too well to miss the falseness in her voice.

They began meeting woodlanders, and the paths multiplied. ("Not that any of them are straight," Rope grumbled.)

It got very dry as they entered the outskirts of the forest people's territory. As summer waxed in the forest they walked on through weeks of drought, passing tattoo artists, tanners, nutters, wicker-workers (dangling clever birdcages from poles yoked across their shoulders), carpenters, trappers, spider-wranglers, fruit-sellers, moss-gatherers, apothecaries, dentists, potters, candle-makers, beekeepers (whom they gave a wide berth), falconers, grafters, perfumers, fruit-pickers, and topiaries.

They saw a young woman treated for a fit by a man who gave her an infusion of skullcap and mint. He carried a white bag at his waist and had three berries tattooed upon his forehead, one red, one gold-green, and one black. They learned to be careful when passing sawyers; these always travelled in pairs, each carry-ing one end of a gap-toothed saw twice as long as Rope was tall. They were exceedingly superstitious, and Rope barely managed to avoid a fight after he brushed by accident against the back of a sawyer's blade.

And then there were the many grim young men, each bearing an ironwood shovel on his back and a red-flame tattoo upon his forehead. "Warders," Ivy explained. "When the forest burns they man the front lines. Many die every year. Summer is their least favorite season."

Each evening they passed at least one stall by the side of the path where puppeteers put on strange shadow plays of the forest people's mythic past. Only the storytellers were allowed to see the sacred puppets, but a lamp threw their shadows on a paper screen for the audience to watch, while one of the troupe's jongleurs hammered eerie, chiming accompaniments on his gleaming stel and the other pounded out fierce, unsteady rhythms on hooting hand-drums.

As they approached the capital, the drought showed in the woodlanders' faces, which became pinched, tense, and suspicious. Even Ivy seemed nervy, and they filled their waterskins to the brim every time they got a chance.

Now that they had reached civilized lands, food was scarce. Animals were few and wily; berries had been picked by countless fingers before them. As a result, they went hungrier than they had since the first days out of Delta. Ivy grew ever less interested in foraging. Chunks of edible white lichen were all she bothered to bring to their meals. Rope eyed these with disgust. "Oh, wonderful. Trees. After months of sleeping on their roots, now we have to eat their boils."

Ivy shrugged. "If you want better, I must take more time."

She looked at Brook, who grimly shook her head. "We've already taken too long. Every hour we waste, Twist gets closer to Clouds End. Perhaps Foam and Shale spend another hour in prison."

Rope groaned, but he could not disagree.

They met the herbalist in a cedar wood only a fortnight from the Arbor. It was early in the morning and Ivy was foraging far up the path. They heard snatches of her song winding between the trees. Suddenly her trills turned to shrieks. For an instant the travellers froze, and then Rope was racing down the path with the others behind him.

They came upon her suddenly, cringing between two cedars. A bramble cord was tied around her arm; where it touched, her leaves were withered and black. A round-faced hairless man held the other end of the cord. "Mind the creature," he said politely.

Hunger had cut deep folds in the stranger's fleshy face. A gold-green berry was tattooed upon his forehead. On his feet were sandals made of cedar bark. His leggings were of birch, and came in two pieces, one for the shins, the second for the thighs; each was fastened behind the leg with wooden pins. Around his waist and privates he wore a girdle of leaves. His stomach and chest were bare; rings of loose skin spoke of recent starvation. On his head he wore a sloped hat: sides of cedar bark set in a brim of ivy. The fourth finger on his right hand was disfigured by a bramble ring, its thorns bedded in scabs.

Ivy whined like an animal in pain.

"Let go of her!" Rope demanded.

"Terribly sorry! Is it yours?"

"What do you m—"

"Yes it is," Jo said, striding up to join them.

The stranger blushed. "How embarrassing," he gasped. "I saw it running loose . . . It never occurred to me." He fumbled with his bramble leash and slipped it off Ivy's arm. "There: unbound. I assure you, I would not have bothered, only I am in desperate need of a sprig of Maid's Ease." He looked at them with sudden hope. "You wouldn't happen to know where I could find some, would you? I wouldn't trouble you, only every moment I search is time away from my suffering wife, Rowan Berry."

Rope looked at Ash. "Can you find the Maid's Ease he needs?" Ash nodded and stepped into the forest. "We will help you," Rope said. "Follow me."

"Two of them!" the pudgy man exclaimed, eyeing Ash. "I can see from your control of two such formidable spirits that you are people of discernment, of education. Of experience."

"Rope!" Brook grabbed his arm. "We shouldn't be wasting time."

"Do you think Shandy would ignore someone in need?"

Ivy snickered.

"Generous, exceedingly generous of you!" the stranger said as they began to follow Ash into the wood. "Have you ever done something you knew was wrong?"

"I suppose if I really thought something wrong, I would try not to do it," Rope said, wondering what he was getting into.

"Would you? Would you? It is not an easy matter. Not a trifle. If she had an understanding of alchemy, then perhaps the scheme would have more merit; she would have a chance to detect the drug. But how could she?

"Some will say, Is it fair? Is it honorable? A herbalist of the stature of Pine Quill, using his—for I do have some stature, you know. I was once well-known. I worked in the Arboratory; Garden's certificate hangs on my wall at home. They said I would do great things! Great things . . ."

The cruel dawn showed his wasting muscles, his sagging skin. "I have since learned I am not destined for greatness . . . But I forget myself! Pine Quill, at your command! Pardon me for not taking your hands. The search for Maid's Ease is not easy. It is a tender plant. A wild plant. It must be approached with caution. With deference. It feels the suffering of all flesh—hence its curative powers! But it cannot abide the animal touch. At the scent of meat it slips its roots and floats away; it is found only in bodies of water, and through a secretive device always floats along the bottom. To track it, you must eat nothing but soil. No part of your flesh can come in contact with the ground; its roots will taste your sweat." He pointed at his garments of bark and grass. "You see I have taken the proper precautions. I keep upon my person a wad of mint to flavor my breath. Ah!" Reminded, he extracted several leaves of mint from a small grass pouch at his waist and chewed them with great deliberation. "I have observed the proprieties. Though my end is ignoble, I come in humility.

"It is five days since I have seen my wife and children. They depend on me for their food, for their livelihood. For their protection." His round face was grim. "The woods are full of desperate men from the vanished southern provinces, now turned to banditry. Twice already they have assailed our cottage. Only a combustion of foul smokes hurled through the window kept them at bay. Are you married?"

Rope shook his head.

"An enviable state. I recommend it. My wife is an admirable

woman. A saint! She is full of spirit, of ambition! She is impatient, it is true, and beats me some days, but it is I who drive her to it, with my penury and my faithlessness! She was invited to a dance at the Palace on one occasion, and was remarked on by Bronze Cut as a very gallant and spirited woman. And this paragon, this superb spirit, lowered herself to my level! Think of it! I revere her condescension. She was widowed when we met; her husband was a captain in the army, I believe, who gave way to drugs and gambling. He was court-martialled for negligence and died a broken man. He beat her near the end, but he was handsome. She reproaches me with him, but I am glad she does. Glad! I want her to believe she was happy once."

Pine Quill paused. Two spots of scarlet burned in his sagging cheeks, and each breath rattled in his chest. "Look at me, friend. Can you look me in the eye and honestly say that I am not a filthy beast?"

Dawn's first golden finger slid through the woods and rested on the herbalist's face like an accusation. "Believe me, I do not seek forgiveness. I am beyond it. But I need an audience of some understanding, with some ability to make moral distinctions, to whom I can communicate the depth of my calumny."

He paced on before them, following Ash. Caught in his bark sandals, bits of grass and twigs left a confused trail on the ground. "Rowan Berry is at home, a woman I prize more than life itself. She is there this very minute, perhaps facing bandits, perhaps faint with hunger, perhaps in terrible pain. She was in terrible pain when I left her.

"Aha! You think you understand why I need the Maid's Ease, to soothe her pain. But you are wrong—there's the wonder of it! I will use the Maid's Ease, when I find it, in a philtre I will give another woman, half my wife's age and possessed of not one quarter of her intellect. What will the philtre be? A love potion! And why? Because I desire her! Is it not astonishing!" Quill shook his head. "Here am I, pursuing the daughter of my nearest neighbors, a worthless slip with no opinion on any topic greater than the weather. And why?" His shoulders sagged, his head sank. He whispered: "I do not know. A spark burns in me that casts a host of shadows.

"You may ask why I need the Maid's Ease. The answer is simple. I brewed my potion according to my best recipes, making adjustments for elevation, quality of water, unavailable ingredients, and so on. I did my best. But there were, after all, adjustments to make; I could not afford to try it on Lily, you see." His voice broke; he fought to control it before he could go on. "Here is the final perfidy. I gave the mixture to my wife! It was brewed incorrectly, it contains an unknown additive—I do not know. I left her, that high-spirited woman, convulsed upon our cot while our children cried in fear. I cannot give the philtre to Lily as it is."

"Fathom," Brook whispered.

"Exactly! It is monstrous. Inconceivable. And yet I did it, am doing it even at this moment, knowing it to be wrong."

He sat down abruptly, so that his grass and bark clothing squeaked and whispered. "Is there some deficiency in my moral makeup? I have lain awake these last five nights, watching the moon die and praying that I am a monster. I know I am. But to think that I am not alone, that others can also do what they know to be wrong—that is more than I could bear."

He shivered with horror. When he looked up, the strain of a ghastly obsession was carved in his face. "But what about our soldiers, who kill for pay? What about the bandits who want to ravish, who may be raping my wife even as we speak? Surely they know what they do . . . Or have they too discovered that we are evil?"

He stopped, staring at the ground. Slowly he pulled out another mint leaf and began to chew.

"Rope, this is far enough. I will not help this thing. His heart has spoiled." Brook turned back for the path they had left.

Pine Quill nodded. "Absolutely. Consider the philtre itself. Who could rejoice in the love I hope to gain? Brutal, enforced, springing neither from Lily's natural affections nor toward my better qualities. I had some once, you know. Rowan Berry spotted them. She was the guardian of my secret worthiness. Unhappy sentinel, struck down by treachery! Can there be a crueler irony to the farce than this: racked with pain, my estimable wife cannot help but love me utterly, helplessly, in spite of what I did to her! Evil spreads out from me like a disease. Perhaps you will be the next infected. Who can say?" He turned to Rope. "So you see, your answer is terribly important. Could you do something you knew was wrong?"

Quill knelt on the ground, looking up as if to challenge the scourge. His breath rattled in his chest. There were black stains around his mouth.

"You are a man," Jo said. "Nothing more. You seek to excuse the flame of your desire by making it cast a great shadow of guilt, but you are only a man. Every day the Singer tells a thousand such stories about your kind."

A cold breeze swirled by the herbalist; he grabbed for his hat.

"The conceit of it!" Jo said. "You are ugly, yes. But you are no monster."

For the first time the herbalist was speechless, clutching his hat. The fire dimmed in his eyes.

Rope shook his head. "We will find your Maid's Ease," he said, grabbing Pine Quill by the shoulder.

"What!" Brook said. "Haven't you been listening? Why would you mend such a rotted net?"

Rope ignored her. "I'll meet you back on the path. Ash, please help me."

The great grey spirit nodded. He turned to gaze at Quill, who staggered weakly to his feet, grabbing at a fern and scrubbing violently where Rope had touched his skin. "Follow me," Ash said.

The men struck deeper into the forest, leaving Ivy and Jo and Brook behind. "What madmen these woodlanders are," Brook whispered. She tried not to imagine what wickedness the forest's kindred might have cut into Shale and Foam over the long summer.

Ivy smirked. "Is Rope really going to help the herbalist? I thought him too straight to twist to such a tangle."

"Rope will not help Pine Quill woo his maiden," Jo said softly. "He will try to put things right, the best way he can."

Ivy's laugh was cold and bright as a jay's. "Now, that I believe. How funny you sea people are, scurrying around as if it did some good to give water to the weak and protect the brittle from the wind!"

Brook said, "I think the people of the forest must have less mercy than the people of the merciless sea."

It was past noon when Rope and the wood spirit returned. Rope was grim; Ash's step was slow and labored.

"Incredible!" Ivy railed. "Sick as you are, you took it upon yourself to help the mad human. You are too kind for your own good, Ash. Look how it has weakened you!"

"Are you happy now?" Brook said bitterly. "Having wasted half a day?"

Rope frowned. "We found the Maid's Ease," he said slowly. "Took it back to his cottage. Ash held the herbalist while I gave it to his wife. I thought . . ." His eyes were troubled. "I thought others should know. They have no Witness here, so I took them to their neighbors. I told Lily the story and asked her to care for his wife. She took Rowan Berry inside. I followed her, to talk to her father. And then . . ." He glanced over at Ash. The spirit gazed down with eyes darker than a cedar's hollow heart.

Ivy's eyes gleamed. "And then?" she said, winding her arm around Ash's waist.

"I killed him," Ash said.

"I knew it! You have the soul of a gardener, Ash. Forever weeding. You cannot let nature take her course. Poor fellow." Ivy patted him softly on the back. "I shall take good care of you."

He laughed bitterly. "I don't doubt it!" He wrapped his long arms around himself. "So cold. So cold."

Rope did not tell of how Rowan Berry had cursed them for murdering her husband. He did not speak of the flies that drank his sweat as he and Ash dug a shallow grave. He did not show them the ring, Pine Quill's bramble ring, torn loose in the moment of his death. Rope had grabbed the ring of thorns, washed it at

Lily's well, and hid it at the bottom of his pouch. Not because he thought it was magical, or valuable. But it was important, somehow, to take something solid, something as real as wind or rain away from that dreamlike scene of madness and death.

They made supper quickly and ate it in silence.

Afterward Rope and Brook lay down and held one another against unquiet dreams. Ivy roamed noiselessly through the surrounding forest. Ash sat up, late into the night, staring at the fire.

Some presentiment kept Jo awake, listening to the old moon sing a song of bones and whispers. When brightness glimmered against her lids she opened her eyes.

Ash had thrust his long fingers into the embers. He sat, hunched above the rising flames, like a man staring at a secret treasure. Serpents of fire slid along his arms. A wind sprang up and a wave of flame broke over him, rolling across his shoulders and catching at his nose, eyelashes, ears. Hissing leaves curled and smoked upon his chest. He staggered to his feet and screamed. Huge and passionate, his cry scared the islanders to their feet. It was a roar of loneliness and torment and the pain of being alive.

The flames engulfed him. He jerked horribly, scattering the firewood, and fell to one knee. Sap dripped from his eyes and ran hissing from his fingertips.

Rope ran to the fire pit, seized a log, and clubbed Ash to the ground. Desperately he kicked dirt over the flaming giant, trying to smother the flames. But Ash swirled up in a shower of sparks and stinging smoke. Brook pulled Rope back from his smoldering corpse.

And still Jo sat, unmoving. She understood Ash as the humans never could. How right, how easy it would be, to give way to a spark eating you out from the inside.

How much better to be the flame than the shadow.

The fire was only soot and embers by the time Ivy returned. "I am sorry," Brook whispered. "I am so sorry."

Ivy shrugged. "It was going to happen."

"You are . . . very calm."

"The strong survive, the weak perish," Ivy said. "I am not too proud to drink the rain."

Seven's Line

"Get up. War waits for none of us."

Shale woke.

The man who had spoken squatted by another sleeper farther down the hillside. It was the morning after their escape from Delta. In the darkness someone moaned in pain.

Here was her adventure.

She smelled pine and chill sand and the sea. Her tunic was cold with dew. She wished the sun were up. Other sleepers lay bundled under the broken-backed shore pines. Stars still shone in a night-blue sky overhead. Only in the east was the sea rimmed with dawn.

Brook and Rope were gone. And the haunt.

"Delta lies in irons while you sleep." A man moved among the sleepers, waking each with a shake or a prod of his foot. He crouched for a moment by a pallet where a woman with a white kerchief knelt, spreading salve on a wounded man. The patient hissed through clenched teeth.

What was this island called? Thumbtip? Shale watched the shadow rouse his troops. Her skin felt tight over her hard cheekbones. Her shoulder still stung where she had caught a nail during the storm. Her legs and sides were bruised where woodlanders had kicked her.

When they had sailed from Delta's lagoon last night their shipmates had been full of relief and nervous laughter. Then the word spread that several Deltans had been hurt in the raid. One captured or killed. The laughter had died, and Shale knew she and Foam were being compared to a friend who would not be coming back.

She leaned over and shook Foam until he groaned and blinked. Someone had thrown a blanket over them; smoothest silk, embroidered with a knotwork border. Foam wrapped it more tightly around his shoulders and shivered. "Gorgeous. But whoever brought this along didn't know much about sleeping outside."

"Nor will he ever learn."

It was the commander, the man who had held Jo hostage mistaking her for Hazel Twist. Seven. He was pale for an islander and his eyes were the color of oak leaves. A long-handled sword was sheathed at his side. He wore woodlander pants and a sleeveless eelskin vest. The muscles in his bare arms were shockingly defined, as if they had been created not by the growth of flesh but by an act of will, and this was true, for he was a young man ardent, of high ideals, with a young man's belief that anything in this compromised world not worth paying for in blood was not worth having. He carried like a curse the hero's capacity for tragedy and terrible violence. Beholding Seven at that moment, Foam saw that some men were the tools of fate, and some were its weapons.

"Chain bought you this blanket with his life."

Foam said, "What can we do?"

"Die for the next man," Seven said. "There will be chances soon enough."

He walked away. Somewhere out of sight a thrush warbled a few notes, thought better of it, and fell silent. The darkness was paling.

Foam shivered and reached for the blanket, then stopped and let it be. His elaborately embroidered tunic sleeves were ripped; ribbons of cloth fluttered as he rubbed his arms to keep warm. "Spit. I hope I don't look like I feel." He glanced at Shale. "I hope you don't feel like you look! I wish Rope were here. Do you think they made it?"

"They made it."

"I suppose Jo could get them out of trouble, if she had to."

"Jo!"

"It wasn't such a bad plan," Foam said. "Taking the form of Twist was rather clever. If only—"

"Without telling us!"

"—she had told us."

Through the channel they could just see Spearpoint, the closest of Delta's three islands. "I would know if Brook were dead," Shale said.

"There were a lot of soldiers, Shale."

"I would know."

She climbed stiffly to her feet and walked a few steps toward the shore. The wind was out of the east, heading inland. "Probably making for the Arbor. I wonder how they will get off Delta? Steal a boat, I suppose."

"Or Jo might turn into a dolphin, and tow them off. Or become a boat herself!"

"She'd leak." Gingerly Shale bent down to touch her toes. Her straight black hair hung beside her cheek, tangling with her shark's tooth earring. Foam was hit with the reality of her. How alive, how *there* she was.

So often he felt so unreal—a crawl of white froth hissing across a wavetop and then gone. But Shale was as real as grass and shells. She kept herself always square to the winds of the world, while his sails luffed and his bow wavered with every breeze.

He grimaced at the image. There he was again, spinning his heart-knowing out into a messy cobweb of words. Shale touched her toes, groaned, then reached down to lay her palms flat on bare ground scattered with pine needles. She was not lovely, but he thought she was as beautiful as a sea bird, a flower or a flame.

Do I love her? Is that what I mean? He tried the words. Saying them in his mind sent a shiver down inside himself, a feeling very like fear. Could he dare to love a woman as strong as Shale? Because he wasn't up to her, he knew that. He would break around her like spume around a rock.

Love? Do I love her?

Sometimes, despite his unreality, he thought there was

something inside himself. But like a faint star it disappeared when he looked directly at it. And saddest to him that morning, he found that when he looked inside to see if he loved Shale, he could not tell.

"Someone's coming."

A man walked up from the shore toward them. He was tall and slender; his split black braid came almost to his waist. His eyes were grey and honest as stream-polished stone. "Do you like our dock?" he asked, gesturing at the barren beach.

Foam smiled. "It suits our boat."

The Deltan settled himself on a fallen log beside them. Grey hair threaded his beard and braid. "I am a singer. My name is Reed."

"Foam. This is Shale." Foam looked at the Deltan and smiled. "Well? Sing. How came Delta to be caught in such a net?"

"I cannot yet name this story's knot, for the tale has only begun." Reed looked out over the wide grey-backed sea. "It was ten days ago that we first saw the rafts. I was one of the first to see the strangers' fleet drifting down the Vein like leaves on a stream. Deltans gathered to marvel at the crudity of those little rafts, but they troubled me. Anyone coming to trade would have stopped at the shore and let us ferry them, I thought.

"Now, we islanders don't think much about war, but I had heard enough woodland stories in my travels and seen enough of their strange shadow-plays to know that soldiering is as natural to them as sailing is to us. So instead of trading breezes with the crowd on the dock, I promised a free night's song to anyone who would run me over to Spearpoint. I meant to find Seven.

"I had made fun of him, like everyone else: Craft the shipwright's crazy son, who spent seasons thrusting at imaginary foes on the Spearpoint beaches, or listening to the lessons of that exiled woodlander, Switch. He was training in a solitary place, and it took me long to find him. By the time we returned, Hazel Twist had seized the major docks and markets. The surprised citizens of the Foot had no chance of resisting an army so well-equipped and so skillfully led. By the time we had a fleet ready to leave

Spearpoint, the woodlanders had their fire-slings ready: terrible engines that hurled balls of burning pitch. We lost half our boats before we could beat back to safety, and all the time more rafts were landing on the Foot. Those willing to fight for Delta fled with Seven to the island of Mona, and thence to here.

"We meant to return the next day to scuttle all the boats we could find, before Hazel Twist could use them to move on the archipelago, but Fathom proved stronger than either side. We were pinned on Thumbtip by a terrific storm, and many boats were damaged."

"We weathered that little blow at sea," Shale said.

"That says much for your seacraft! It was a week before we had made repairs enough to risk coming in to Delta." Reed grinned. "You were an afterthought. I saw you marching down the street as I was sneaking back to the docks. Seven could hardly believe his luck. Twist—with only two guards around him!

" 'Don't forget there are soldiers in the streets,' someone whispered, but Seven would have none of it. 'Victory goes to the bold,' he said. 'Would the Gull Warrior turn down such a chance?' So off we went, tacking after you. But even as we plotted our ambush, more soldiers gathered. Seven was undaunted."

Reed paused, and shrugged. "You know what happened next. There were many soldiers, too many, and Twist was a haunt. Chain was killed and four others were hurt."

Foam shifted on his driftwood bench. "Your Seven has his share of, um, boldness."

"I would have done it." Shale stooped to lace up her boots. "It was worth chancing. Life is risk."

Reed nodded. "Perhaps Seven is too bold, but he is the only warrior we have. He was trained by a woodlander, but even among the forest people I have never seen his equal."

"No doubt, no doubt! But you don't leave the best swimmer to helm your boat, as we say on Clouds End."

Reed laughed. Behind them, someone began to beat on a hollow stump, and the singer slid off his log. "Breakfast! And after food, a council of war."

The fifty islanders on Thumbtip held their council where they had begun to build a makeshift barracks, sitting on the foundation stones or lying under the gnarled pines at the edge of the clearing. Foam and Shale introduced themselves, and were introduced in turn, though they remembered only a few names: Seven and his lady, Pond; Brace the carpenter, Glint the physician, scruffy Catch; elegant Brine and his sister Rose, heirs to one of Delta's largest merchant houses.

Seven sat on a big cedar stump by the fire pit. "How are the injured men?"

Glint was a small woman in her middle years. "They will live. Tusk has a bad cut and a broken wrist. Fin lost his left eye to the blue spray. I put him to sleep for the day. Tell me, what knowledge did we buy with their blood?"

Catch the longshoreman stirred and scratched the back of his neck with grimy fingernails. "That it's easier to scuttle ships than to build 'em."

"We sank all the big boats and most of the smaller ones," Seven said.

"Poor *Salamander* scuttled! Oh, well." Foam coughed delicately. "Shale and I would like to believe that at least some good came from your trip. We are both deeply in your debt for last night's timely rescue."

The elegant Deltan, Brine, flipped his braid behind his shoulders, avoiding Foam's eyes. "Islanders must hang together."

"Then I wish we had more Rope!" Foam muttered. More loudly he said, "We are two travellers from Clouds End, at the Mist's edge, and we like the hospitality on Thumbtip better than what we found in Delta."

Pond laughed. She was of middle height, with four long braids of dark brown hair that hung to the bottom of her back. Her tunic was the deep, luminous blue of the twilight sky. At her wrists were wide bracelets of knotted silver, and a silver torc was clasped around her throat. "But I am sure they would have loved to keep you. If I heard the story rightly, though, you were fairly on your way to freedom without us. Your gratitude does credit to your courtesy, easterner. Or your discretion."

"The woodlanders are building in Delta," Seven continued. "Twist is putting a wooden wall around the Foot. Traces of it on Spearpoint too. We also saw several rafts, tied to the lagoon dock on the Foot. They were stepped for a single mast with a small sail."

"Sorry-looking little boats," Catch muttered.

Brine shrugged, patting his braid more perfectly into place with a plump hand. "Such may be the only craft these forest people can sail."

"They're not good for much now, but if the woodlanders put in daggerboards they could make way," Seven said. "Only in good weather, I grant you, but they could fit eight men and a fire-sling on one of them. They would be slow, but they would do the job."

"Will the woodlanders think to add daggerboards?" Pond asked. "You've been in the forest, Reed."

The singer nodded. "All they have to do is pull up a dinghy to see how we build them. They are toolwise folk."

"So what do we do?" Glint asked.

Seven slipped his throwing knife from its arm-sheath and flipped it as he thought, toss-catch, toss-catch. "Switch would tell me to stop them now before they spread. Once they have a base beyond Delta, they can come at us from two directions. We can't let them take those rafts out of the lagoon."

Brine nodded slowly. "What if we sailed in under cover of darkness and burned the rafts?"

Pond frowned. "You would be seen as soon as you set the first one alight."

"Won't they have sentries down by the water?" Catch added. "And those fire-slings?"

Seven jammed his knife into the ground. He pulled it up, clotted with dirt, and wiped the blade off on his leggings. He sighed. "Consider this, then: we sail in fast and quiet for the lagoon dock. We lace the rafts with oil first and throw in a salvo of torches as soon as the alarm is raised, burning all the rafts at once. If the woodlanders spot us before we have finished, their own fire-slings will set the rafts ablaze."

Catch spat. "I ain't going back into the fire, friend."

Brine and Rose knelt on a square of sailcloth beneath one of the pines. They were both immaculate, wearing matching purple tunics with intricate gold embroidery fetched from their yacht that morning. Softly, Brine said, "Is that how you repay the people who rescued you?"

"The sweat ran down my arse-crack all day yesterday, building this barracks, Brine. I didn't see you humping rocks and I doubt your sister did enough work to get her armpits damp. I'd be quiet when it came to paying debts."

Rose colored and stared fixedly at the ground. "We were not raised to do your sort of work."

"What in Tool's Box are you good for?" Catch said, staring insolently at her. "Other than the obvious."

"Catch—" Seven said.

"I'm not sure I like this plan," Foam said.

The Deltans looked at him aslant, but he was following his thoughts and did not notice. "Too simple. It's just what I would expect If I were Hazel Twist."

Shale groaned. "You always make things too complicated."

"But so do the forest people! Hazel Twist has spent years think- ing about military strategy. Do you think he doesn't know that getting off Delta is the key to his invasion?"

Catch said, "Whoever goes back will end up cooked if we aren't careful."

Seven frowned and fed another twig to the fire. "We can't sit on Thumbtip forever, fearing to act because the enemy might out- guess us."

Glint grunted. "If you go ahead with this, then barracks- building will have to wait! I'll need help tomorrow, gathering herbs and making up medicine. If you sail to Delta, there will be more wounded."

"I can help," Shale said. "I often foraged for the Witness at home. There's bladderwrack on the beach, and I saw skullcap and crankweed on our way up from the shore, if you use those."

Glint nodded. "Elder leaves and yarrow and meadowsweet too, if you can find them."

"Rations are short here," Pond said, eyeing Foam and Shale. "As I am sure you noticed at breakfast. In Delta we go to the market to find our food. Could you teach us to live better off what Thumbtip offers?"

Foam grinned. "Why, Shale prefers her food with the dirt still on it!"

Reed stirred. "I too need a boat. I should carry the story of Delta's fall out of the other islands. With the Singer's help I may even send back some volunteers to swell your navy."

Seven nodded. "Good. We will need all the hands we can get."

Later that morning Shale gathered her detail of Deltans around an old stump and pointed to where a ring of mushrooms peeked through the grass. "These you can eat. See how the caps are small and round, not flat and floppy?" She picked a couple and gave them to her audience. The Deltans studied them suspiciously, wiping their hands after the sample had gone by, and Shale sighed inwardly. She shouldn't have shown them the bad ones first.

One of the mushrooms reached Pond. "Thank you," she said, popping it into her mouth. "Mm. These are better fresh."

Shale smiled gratefully. "I always thought so."

Rose edged forward. "What about this kind?"

Shale examined the high, peaked hood and wrinkled skin. "You can eat these, if you don't have anything to do for the next day." She grinned up at Rose. "Downing one of these is like swallowing Mist." Shale looked over her charges. "If you don't even recognize dreamers, what do they teach young women in Delta?"

Rose colored delicately. "Deportment, arithmetic, account-keeping, cooking, medicine. Everything that must be done on land with something other than strong arms and a weak head."

Women laughed.

"We do not go to the mainland picking mushrooms," Pond added dryly. "Most of us cannot even swim."

"You don't swim!"

Pond shrugged, embarrassed. "In Delta it is not good form for young women to get wet."

Shale's shark-tooth danced as she shook her head in amazement. "Is anything useful good form?"

Pond laughed. "Probably not. That is what makes it good form!"

"In the capital it is more useful to figure accounts than to recognize slugs," Rose said somewhat testily. Her eyes flitted up to give Shale one sly smile. "Although, if you could show me an edible slug, I would be much in your debt."

Shale sighed. She had never imagined she would be grateful for the afternoons she had wasted minding the children of Clouds End.

The next day was more of the same. While Foam went out fishing, Shale's crew left the wooded part of Thumbtip to scour the beach. "Now, the thing with clams is to walk along the shore until one squirts, and then *dig*," Shale explained. "There are three kinds you can eat. The most—" A jet of water clipped her on the ankle and she dropped, burrowing furiously and spraying sand onto Rose's legs. "Aha!" she cried, raising a shell triumphantly skyward. "See this red mark, like a ribbon tied around the back of the shell? These are good in spring, but by summer they become poisonous. If you're not sure, avoid them."

Rose squeaked as water spurted across her foot, then dropped and began to dig. She got her clam, but broke a nail doing it. "Hard luck," Shale drawled. "That's the wilderness for you."

Their second dinner was a good deal more filling than their first breakfast had been. After it was over, Seven announced that he, Brine, and Foam would captain the boats in the raid on Delta, each with three other crew.

"Brine!" Shale said.

"Shush!" Foam muttered, wincing. "If you must be rude, can you do it quietly?"

Shale didn't shush. "Seven's the leader, and you and I have sailed all our lives. But why Brine of all people?"

The plump Deltan glanced at her over the campfire. "Surprised?"

Shale grimaced at Rose. "Isn't sailing a bit too much like work for you?"

Brine's sister smiled without meeting Shale's eyes. "On the contrary. Boats are a way to avoid getting wet."

"Brine and Rose are racers," Pond explained. "You have to do something when your family is rich. Seven chose to be a warrior. Brine and Rose have been winning regattas for years." She smiled sweetly at Shale. "You see, there are some things we learn, even in the city."

Shale grinned and spat. "Suck an eel," she said.

Those chosen to sail to Delta gathered near Seven's tent at sunset. Here they listened to Brine detail every shoal and rock in Delta's lagoon. "Study the chart. Especially you, Foam. Remember, you will have to know this in the dark."

Foam stirred. "We should agree not to run for the same channel if things go badly. That way if the woodlanders start throwing fire we won't make one easy target."

"Also, about the fire," said a Deltan named Keel. "It burns hot and fast. Don't waste time trying to put it out! If you get hit, jump ship and make for shore."

"We will make our raid on the next cloudy night," Seven said. "If no clouds come soon, we will sail anyway, with the Gull Warrior's grace."

Foam winced, but Shale beckoned to him with an evil gleam in her eye.

Reed raised one eyebrow. "You want me to sing Seven as a Hero of Legend?"

"Like he just stepped out of the Mist," Shale said solemnly.

"It would help the rebellion!" Foam cried. "Everyone loves a hero, someone to look up to, to admire. People will rally the faster if great songs are sung of our leader."

Shale leaned forward. "A young man dedicates himself to his craft. He has an almost holy mission."

Foam's hands sketched greatness. "He seeks the revelation that comes from perfect self-knowledge! Strong, fast, graceful as a gull in flight! . . . Heroes of Legend are made not by their deeds, but by their singers," he prompted. "You know that."

"And he is amazing," Shale said. "You've seen him. You know."

"Oh, yes. Seven is an extraordinary man. I think he will seem less comic to you when you realize how hard he strives to achieve his ideals, and how close he comes." Reed's face softened into a smile. "But he does go on about the Gull Warrior, I admit. And if he gets more praise than he bargained for, it will not be more than he deserves."

"You'll do it, then?"

Reed nodded and went to finish packing.

Content, Foam looked up at the stars above the campfire, white-blue sequins in rich black velvet. "There's the Ship," he said. "The war hasn't scuttled her yet! Strange to come so far, and still see her up there."

Shale looked up. "I wonder who else is looking up at the Ship tonight?"

"Rope will blow like a walrus when he finds out it was fellow islanders that scuttled his precious *Salamander*."

Shale didn't laugh.

Foam reached out to give her hand a squeeze. "If they fared badly, you would know."

She was so tremendously alive, sitting there, just next to him, just touching. Her hand in his was small and hard.

Above their heads the stars were scattered with vast prodigality. "The world is so big," Foam said. The great sea murmured beyond the pines. And arching overhead, a second sea, midnight black, still greater than the first. We too, Foam thought, are points of light, and our campfires are stars, and something up there sees us, looking down, and wonders, and feels itself part of a great mystery.

Some time later they bedded down for the night. Shale was instantly asleep, but Foam lay staring up at the stars, greeting them like old friends: Tool's Box and the Ship, Kettle's Hook and a score of others. Each was motionless for as long as he stared at it—and then, when he glimpsed back later, each would have sailed on through its night journey. Emptying his mind, he fought sleep, staring up until at last he thought he had slowed himself to the pace of the wheeling world; thought he saw the majestic stars in the moments of their moving.

His eyes widened in triumph; focused against his will; he started; the sensation was gone, slipping away like water between his fingers. Perhaps he had never seen the stars move, perhaps it had been only the island shifting, turning slowly like a boat upon her anchors, rocked to sleep by unseen waves.

Rocked to sleep by unseen waves.

CHAPTER 12: THE RAID ON DELTA

As Reed sailed his dinghy eastward, taking Seven's story to Thistle and beyond, summer came maddeningly upon the islands. Three long days Seven's troops sweated in the hot sun, and three cloudless nights the moon waxed in a clear sky. Foam and Shale fished in the mornings, and foraged in the afternoons. They even pitched in to help the Deltans finish their barracks; apparently they didn't have building parties on Delta. "This is wonderful!" Foam gasped, fitting a foundation stone into place. "Apart from Brace, these people make me look halfway toolwise."

"Oh, you've always known how to do everything," Shale said briskly, running Brace's plane over what would become a rafter. "You were just lazy."

"So were you! How many times did you wriggle out of minding the kids!"

"True. But I learned early to make others mark what I did well. You made them mark what you didn't do at all."

"Mm. More fool I."

The barracks were finished in three days. At last they had a roof above their heads in case it rained. Now everyone prayed for rain.

At first Foam and Shale felt daunted by the Deltans, who seemed rather aloof, but Foam made friends quickly, and in a camp full of hungry city-dwellers, Shale's foraging skills made her instantly popular. She also struck up a friendship with Seven's fiancée. There was a line of steel in Pond that surprised Shale; she respected the way the Deltan could stay quiet and unruffled and yet mistress of a moment. For her part, Pond admired Shale's boldness. Pond also wanted to become one of Delta's Witnesses; she was impressed to learn that Shale was a Witness's daughter.

Along with Keel, the one Deltan fisherman in their camp, Foam and Shale each took a boat out in the early morning and again at nightfall to fish. The morale of Seven's troops was markedly the better for it.

Soon Foam and Shale were important people in the rebel camp, and their opinions were sought on many questions. "And why?" Foam said to Shale as they were going to bed one night. "Because we're backward barbarians, that's why."

"Lucky us."

When a fourth day dawned without cloud, Seven decided they could wait no longer. Their three swift four-man sloops sailed from the harbor at twilight, hoping to reach Spearpoint before the moon rose. Catching the landward breeze, they spread white wings and banked, graceful as gulls, heading for Delta.

Sunset drained like blood from the sky and dusk fell over the ocean. At the tiller of the *Arrow*, Brine glanced nervously from his sails to the horizon to the big jars of oil between his passengers' knees. "Be careful with your flints!"

On the thwarts Nest and Perch, old racing companions, laughed softly; but Rose's young face was drawn, and she did not smile.

Seven laid his sword in the bottom of the *Dolphin*. Belted at his side, it would get caught under the thwarts; sheathed on his back, it would snag when he tried to duck under the boom, an embarrassing lesson he had learned years before. "We are making good time."

"I have never raced the moon before," Shoal remarked, letting out his sheet a fraction. "She has the advantage of knowing the course."

"True enough," Seven replied, "but she does not know she is in a race."

Shoal shrugged. "Let us hope Hazel Twist, too, is feeling complacent."

"Pfaah!" Keel spat over the thwarts, looking at the oil pot between his knees with disgust. "This stuff stinks. We'll be dead from the smell before we get to Delta."

"Could be worse. We could have Sere on our tails," Foam remarked.

"Mm?"

"We were caught out in the Mist, see, up beyond Clouds End, and . . ." He paused to look at Keel and Bramble. "Nah. You wouldn't believe it."

"Even I don't believe that story," Shale said. "And I was there."

"Will they remember about the Middle Beach shoal?"

Rose's fine features were tense and there was a knot in her belly like at the start of a race, only far worse. "We will be lost if they forget about Middle Beach. If they ground, the noise will wake—"

"Tighten that sheet," Brine whispered. "We are too far ahead of the others. I hope the moon is kind enough to wait for them." His plump white hand rested on the tiller, light as a puff of cottonwood down. "They will remember."

Waves hissed and curled beneath his bow. For the sake of quieting his wash, Brine would have to slow down when he got to the lagoon, though every nerve would be screaming for speed.

They ran on into a lengthening darkness. Brine could no longer make out the hump of Spearpoint. But he had sailed these waters a hundred nights before. If he held the prow still, aiming for the Ship's stern lantern, the dark world would slide by him on every side until Delta's lagoon rushed around their flanks.

"And what about the Dagger? Will they remember the Dagger? And the Saw. Remember when we hit the Saw?"

"Rose!"

Waves slapped against the hull like children's hands. She wasn't looking at him. "What if they forget?" she whispered.

———

"The Mist churns into sea, the sea hardens into stone, then islands, then land. The land leaps into mountains and the mountains fade into clouds and Mist; for change is the way of the world.

"This is a story of the Mist-time, where all things have their truest shape and nothing is what it seems. It is a story of Clouds End, for I had it from my uncle, who had it from his father, who had it from one of the first settlers, who had it from the Singer one autumn night when the Mist rolled over Crabspit Bay.

"This story is a Round Turn and Two Half-Hitches, which is a good story for tying up your boat, or maybe fastening your dinner to your dreams."

"Scared?" Seven said. "Of course. But fear tells me that I am still alive. You will learn more about yourself tonight, I promise you, than you would in years on Delta. Everything has its own reward, even danger. Remember the story of Stonefinger's Thumbtip!"

"The stranger smiles, all friendly, and stamps her feet. She's got no braid, and her straight black hair hangs around her bony face, fluttering like rags of shadow in the breeze. Her eyes are deep as the night sky, and the hand she holds out to Clam is clear and cold as starshine.

" 'You got some sort of lie coming to pass the night away?'

"And the stranger looks at Clam, very serious, and says, 'There's no lie so big as the truth.' Then she looks back into the fire, and she whispers, 'There's no lie half so big as the truth.' Finally she mutters, 'Neighbor, there's no lie that can even see over the truth's kneecaps: that's how big it is.' And all this time there's a cloud of Mist bumbling around Clam's house like a big wad of cotton from a cottonwood tree, and the boards are warping, and the stove's turned yellow, and there are fish swimming in the chimney. The unwelcome visitor leans forward and she pins Clam against the back wall just with her eyeballs and says, 'I'll tell you a true story, neighbor, 'cause I can't tell any other kind. It was like this—' "

"But the Gull Warrior was as agile as Stonefinger was strong," Seven was saying. "He slid below the hollow rock and held his

breath until his lungs were bursting, swimming through lightless
caverns that only the sea had seen before."

"If they go right of the Foot, they must keep close to the Spearpoint bank, or they will ground on the shallows. And the current,
don't forget the current. You can still feel the Vein there . . ."

"Ever-crafty, always watching, the Warrior is never twice the
same. He feels each breath of wind, each tremor in the earth, each
ripple in the sea. He knows that in change lies his strength, and
that doom lies in becoming a man of stone."

"Spit." Shale swore suddenly in the gloom.
"Something wrong?"
"There was a better way to do this. We should have swung wide
around the outside edges of Delta's islands, then crept into the
lagoon from the bottom, using the Vein to push us. That way we
could have kept the sails furled until after the rafts were lit."
"Right you are," Foam murmured. "But we didn't. We had better take down the jibs before we enter the lagoon. We'll lose speed,
but we can't risk them luffing."
"If we abandon ship, that means swimming. I say we doff boots
now on the chance we have to dive."
"Good idea. Noses upwind, crew, and boots off."

"Dagger, Saw, Middle Beach . . ."
"Shut her up, Brine!"

"Spearpoint!" Shoal hissed.
"And there's the moon. She's going to make a race of it. Hear
that? Brine is taking in his jib. Wait just long enough to catch up
with him, and then do the same. Whisper time, my friends."

The moon was one third clear of the horizon when the *Arrow*
ghosted through the wide strait between Spearpoint and the Sock.
She was running slower without her jib, and slower still as Brine
tightened his sheet to keep her quite. He gave the Saw a wide
berth and risked a quick glance behind. Seven's boat was bending

nicely into line; Foam was hidden in the dark. So far, so good. Rose leaned back from the middle thwart, fingers like antennae on the sheet.

The *Dolphin* came even with the cluster of lights that marked Red Alley on the Sock. Seven edged to port, giving the Dagger extra room, to kill any chance of Foam running aground. The moon was mostly hidden behind Spearpoint now; all light came from torches and stars. A thousand pairs of eyes were watching them: hungry red stares from Delta, dispassionate white-blue scrutiny from the sky.

And, no surprise, the Deltans sailing an enormous circle around the Middle Beach shoal. "Looking out for us babies," Foam muttered. Tension was building in him like summer lightning.

They were almost at the docks. Shale lashed their sail and stood peering into the gloom ahead, holding the boom so the gooseneck wouldn't squeak against the mast.

Every eye was on the docks, searching for the fleet of rafts. It was surprisingly dark; the wall Twist had built around Delta blocked much of the city's torchlight.

Ah—the *Dolphin* had found a raft. Foam watched as Seven washed silently alongside. Someone leaned out, and Foam imagined the stealthy dribble of oil.

His own boat rocked, surprising a splash from the waves. He bit back a curse as Shale, still holding the boom, bent down and murmured something in Keel's ear.

Keel shook his head.

Foam let his boat peel softly back into the night. Dread clogged his lungs and he forced himself to take a deep breath.

Shale whispered again, fiercely.

Suddenly Keel nodded. He lowered his jar of oil gently overboard. His mate started to do the same.

The night groaned with the rending noise of wood grinding against wood, horribly loud. A voice called, and then another. Shouts hurried back from the dock.

Foam wrenched his prow to the *Dolphin's* stern; when Shale thought the moment right, she would let out the sail and they could follow Seven out of the lagoon. Not yet, though; Seven's crew were desperately splashing oil on a second raft, no longer trying to be silent.

A gong began beating above the docks. A flint clicked once, twice. A torch caught in Seven's boat and was hurled onto the nearest raft.

"Idiot!" Shale swore.

The huge grinding noises continued to port, where Brine's ship had vanished in the darkness. What had happened? Had he somehow smashed into the dock?

Oh. Oh, no.

"The ships," Foam breathed. "Fathom! The scuttled ships. They left them in the water."

Brine's crew grunted hysterically, trying to push clear of the wreckage, sobbing, no point in silence now, as the gong tolled and Foam could see as clearly as if he were there, the *Arrow's* keel trapped on the railing of some sunken Deltan yacht.

A glowing ball of fire arced from the shore and smashed into flames just ahead of Seven's mast. For one eternal moment he watched Shoal topple overboard, coated in resinous fire. Answering fire burst from the remaining oil jar. The man holding it shrieked, disappearing behind a shroud of roaring white flame.

A heavy rumble thundered from three places at once. It was loudest ahead and to starboard, but the tumbling, crashing sound rolled from the other side of the Foot, and, faintly, from behind them.

Seven's second oiler saved himself by jumping for the bow; a curtain of flame danced between him and his captain. "Sheet!" Seven roared, praying he could make the strait before he had to abandon ship. Another ball of fire came crackling overhead, and flames swept over an oiled raft. The heat was devouring. Seven pressed himself against his transom.

The rolling thunder ended in a series of terrific splashes.

The gong still hammered. A river of torches streamed down the hillside to the docks.

Shale let out their sail. Before her, Seven's blazing boat was now adrift. Streamers of flame ate away the *Dolphin*'s mainsail and licked up her mast.

Fire fountained from the docks and splashed into the *Arrow* just as she swung free of her obstruction.

Foam was gaining fast on Seven's burning boat; it had stopped dead in the water. Couldn't be the current, Foam thought, panicking. Too sudden.

The night was full of torches and the sound of running feet.

Hidden in darkness behind Seven and Brine, Foam had escaped the woodlanders' notice. But now the *Dolphin* was a blazing pyre. Foam yanked his tiller to the side as he saw Seven's boat jerk to a stop. Seconds later a ball of burning pitch ploughed into the water where their bow had been.

"Logjam!" Shale screamed. "They've jammed the channel! Swim for it!"

The inferno's roar deafened Seven; its heat lashed his face and hands. Sudden understanding broke over him. The woodlanders had rolled hundreds of logs into the channels to block their escape. The Vein's current was pushing the jam into the islander boats.

The *Arrow* was lost. The *Dolphin*'s crew was dead, or dying.

Hazel Twist had been waiting for him.

He vaulted backwards over the transom. Cold water blessed his burning face. He kicked down as light exploded above him and a globe of boiling pitch plunged into the sea. The knife strapped to the inside of his left arm wobbled, threatening to slide loose.

Shale hit the water first; Keel and Foam followed. The other oiler hesitated. Someone shouted, "Surrender! You will not be harmed!" and he cowered in the drifting ship, hating himself.

In the blackness beneath the waves Shale tried to use the Vein's current as a guide. A few more strokes underwater yet. She did not dare to be seen.

Light flared ahead of her and to the left; another fireball. She thought she saw a leg kicking away and turned to follow.

Just a few . . .

Her lungs screamed and her chest bucked, desperate for air. Without it her limbs turned to wood, then iron. She had been underwater forever.

Just a few more strokes.

Seven surfaced quietly. Two gulping breaths, then under again. His ship was wrapped in a shroud of flame. He was still too close, and the Spearpoint shore looked very far away. He angled toward it, away from the Foot. Pushed by the Vein's current, logs bobbed and ground ever closer, coming after him.

The swim was a long, dreamlike torture for Foam. Time after time he dove into the black water, and time after time he surfaced, gasping for breath, into a storm of sound: roaring flames, calls and orders, the beating gong. Away to the left, an endless scream. The Spearpoint shore seemed no closer. He thought he saw Shale once, her head bobbing up sleek as an otter's just as he was diving. And one time he saw Keel, eyes wide with fear, weirdly visible in the firelight. He had gotten off course and surfaced next to the burning hulk of Seven's ship. The first logs bumped slowly around him.

At last Seven felt the sea's floor rise beneath his feet.

Luck was against him. There were soldiers on Spearpoint too, though many fewer than on the Foot. He could see one, patrolling this strip of beach. Seven drifted tiredly, wondering how he could get out of the water fast enough to silence the sentry before he could raise the alarm. Wondering if Hazel Twist had thought of everything.

Heavy wooden gongbeats thudded through the night air. The

guard turned and began to walk back along the beach, peering out at the water. He did not carry a torch. Seven cursed silently. His master, Switch, had had eyes like an owl in the dark; probably a woodlander trait. Besides, Twist was smart. He would have told his men to avoid night blindness, and trust to their ears.

There was the throwing knife strapped to Seven's left arm. He was good with it, but only at short range. He would have to get close.

The sentinel was very near now. Seven dipped his head under-water. He was still too far out to risk anything. He counted slowly to ten, then let his head rise into the air. The guard was now fifteen paces to his left, almost at the promontory which marked the edge of this stretch of beach. Seven faded into shore, crouching double to keep his shoulders below the water line.

There was a ripple in the water to his right, and a faint gasp. Seven tensed.

The guard heard it too.

Seven crouched even lower, his knees against his chest, spreading his legs apart to resist the tide pushing him into shore. He slipped the knife from its sheath.

The sentry came forward, every step a lesson in caution. His feet ground small noises from the seashells and coarse sand.

Seven closed his eyes lest the torchlight from the buildings on the bluff spark a telltale reflection.

His nerves crawled as the footsteps approached, then hesitated. One step farther to the right. Then another.

Seven opened his eyes. The soldier was staring fixedly out at the dark sea. There was a soft plop, like something slipping below the surface. It might have been a fish.

Seven reminded himself that his arm would drip if he paused in his throw. He took a long, silent breath, then lifted his arm clear as he began to exhale, bringing the knife back to his ear. A line of drops pattered from his elbow. His arm lashed like a whip.

The guard turned at the sound of dripping water and caught the knife in his throat. His eyes bulged and he tried to scream. Air bubbled through the blood around the blade. He fell forward with his face at the water line, feet scrabbling against the shells. Gasping for air, he jerked the knife out. A fountain of blood followed his hands like a conjurer's scarf, and he lost consciousness.

Seven rose from the black water and waded into shore, listening for approaching guards. Quickly he searched his victim's body, trying not to look at his face.

"Seven?"

"Shale?"

She rose unsteadily from the water. "That swim was longer than I—"

He held up his hand.

Footsteps approached quickly from their left. A soft voice called, "Bone. Come here. I think someone is trying to land." The steps faded away again.

Seven met Shale's eyes, then slid Bone's sword from its scabbard. With discreet, confident steps he walked to their left: a friend coming to investigate.

Shale waited, tense as a hawser in a gale. She cleaned Seven's throwing knife on Bone's shirt and then walked around the promontory.

Seven was helping Foam out of the water. The corpse of another sentry lay leaking on the strand. Shale joined them. Wordlessly she held out Seven's knife. He nodded and strapped it back under his left arm.

At least he knew where they were. There was a path nearby; he had used it hundreds of times before, when this stretch of beach had been one of his early practice areas. He willed away exhaustion and led the others up the hill.

"Keel?" Foam breathed.

Shale shook her head.

Back on the Foot a gong still tolled. Buffeted by logs and current, three islander ships drifted on the black water, blazing furiously, floating pyres for their dead.

Hazel Twist woke to the sound of the gong. He was just pulling on his boots when Spear knocked on his bedroom door.

"Enter."

His subaltern strode in and bowed. "You are a genius, sir."

Hazel Twist coughed and sat slowly upright. "I'm a tired, middle-aged man, Lieutenant. Little more. They came?"

"They came and we caught them. It was magic."

Hazel Twist snorted. "I cannot share your wonder at the inevitable. Tell me as we go." Twist stood and patted his pockets absently, looking for his pipe. Misplaced. Oh, well. He would see to it later.

Ash Spear bowed him out the door. "They came in three ships, sir, though at first the men saw only two. Quiet as the wind. They are unearthly good sailors, I'll give them that."

"They would choose their best."

"Of course, sir. Happily, good sailing is no match for good generalship." Spear's jubilant voice billowed in the old warehouse. A couple of half-dressed sentries stopped chatting and snapped to attention as Twist walked by. "Rowan Cricket thought he saw something, but he wasn't sure. Then one of their boats started making a noise like a tree cracking in a storm. We figure he must have run over one of the ships they sank."

"That was lucky."

"We would have had them, anyway. We had two of them pinned right away. They were going for the rafts, just as you said they would. We got a direct hit on one with our first shot. By the time we cut the logs, both ships were burning badly."

"And the third?" They stepped out into the moonlight. The gong had ceased to sound.

"Abandoned, except for one man. Couldn't nerve himself to jump, so we offered quarter."

Twist nodded. "Good. How about the others?"

"We have patrols on all the beaches, sir. If they don't drown we'll have them by morning. From where they jumped it is not likely they could make it to any shore but the Foot, and we had men all over."

Twist grunted, unconvinced. "Do not count the bodies yet,

Spear. These islanders can swim like otters when they have to. Seven will be among them, Switch's famous islander pupil. How many prisoners so far?"

"Several of them drowned or burned. At the moment, we have four alive and in custody. We would have had a fifth, but we were unlucky. He was standing on the front of a burning ship and appeared ready to surrender, but when the other survivor dove off the back, the rock of the boat threw him overboard."

"And?"

"They were at the logs by then. He was knocked about pretty badly, and then rolled underwater."

Twist nodded. "So that leaves the one who did surrender, and . . . ?"

"Three others. They were in the boat that got hung up. They are badly burned. I told the surgeon to give them as much poppy as he deemed advisable."

Twist patted Spear on the shoulder. "You have done well. I was beginning to wonder if they would show up."

"I never doubted, sir."

Twist smiled. "Of course not."

Twist had seen badly burned people before, but the sight still sickened him. One islander twitched and gibbered, staring wildly up at the uncaring stars. The second was unconscious.

The third was a young woman in charred pathetic finery. A girl almost. She mumbled ceaselessly through cracked lips: "Dagger . . . swing wide . . . and . . . shoals. Shoals! On the Saw; new boat! Stay by the starboard bank," she whispered. "Stay close to Spearpoint!"

Twist looked to the surgeon. He shrugged and shook his head. Her clothes had been cut away, and the doctor sponged her crackled skin very lightly with cold water. She yelped as the sponge came up black with soot that had once been skin. "The Saw! The Dagger! Stay wide! Stay wide!"

Twist's eyes narrowed. He backed away and whispered briefly with his subordinates.

Red dawn bled into the eastern sky. Twist squatted on the sandy beach where the girl's cot had been placed, holding her unburnt hand. Nobody within sight was wearing woodlander clothes. "Rose?" he said quietly. He had asked the islander who surrendered for her name, so her parents could be notified.

"And a new hull! Remember?"

"Rose?"

She paused. ". . . right . . . right over the Middle Beach shoal."

"Rose, can you hear me?"

"New hull . . . Yes."

"Rose, we need your help. We need to move the base, but we're afraid of wrecking the boats. We don't want to run them aground. Do you understand me?"

"Watch out for the Dagger!" she cried.

Twist massaged her hand. Her skin was soft on top, rough on the palms from holding ship's line. "Can we get to Mona? Are there any shoals?" It was unlikely they would have made their camp on the island nearest to Delta.

Rose frowned, her mind wandering through a poppy haze. "Only the Comb Rocks," she whispered, frowning. "Is that right? Ask Brine. Brine will know. I'm so . . ." Her eyes wandered, losing focus.

Twist took his time. He knew she would die. The pain would fade, and her body would begin to heal. But then infection would set in, spreading like smoke under her fired skin. How barbaric the islanders were, to send their children to war. How tragic.

"Rose? What about the mainland? Are there any good harbors there?"

"Wh—?" She shifted restlessly, frowning.

"The mainland, Rose. Are there any good harbors nearby?"

". . . Pie Bay. Pie bay, piebay piebay." She slurred the words together like a child's song. Suddenly her eyes opened wide and looked beseechingly into his. "Where is Brine?"

"He is sick," Twist said. "He will be fine, but we cannot talk to him now. That is why we need your help."

She stared at Twist desperately, as if trying to remember who he was. He rubbed her palm gently with his thumb.

Her eyes blurred. She shook her head. "Watch out for the Tack, of course. Brine. I feel very strange."

Twist pictured the charts he had studied so often over the last weeks. The nearest good harbor would be Pie Bay; that put them on the south side of the gulf, and not far into the archipelago. So. They had opted to stay within striking distance of Delta. Reasonable. He closed his eyes until he could picture Comb Rock on the map. What was near the Tack, and had Comb Rock between it and Mona Island?

Thumbtip.

"Good," he whispered. "Very good. We needed your help, Rose. We will not forget." His throat tightened. His eyes were hot and ached. "You should get some sleep." His eldest daughter would be only three or four years younger than this woman. "Just sleep."

" 'Cave,' didn't you say, Seven? 'A cave where we can hide.' I would have called this a crack between two rocks."

"Shoal, Nest, Brine, Rose . . . Keel. Keel."

Shale curled into a rocky corner of Seven's hideout. She had never felt so exhausted. The swim to the Spearpoint shore had drained her utterly. She had always prided herself on her strength, but now her chest was hollow and she felt like crying from sheer rage at her own frailty.

"It will be a long day without water."

Foam looked up, shocked by her ragged voice. "If you think you hate it now, just wait until high tide."

Nobody laughed. The tiny cave was filled with the murmur of the sea and the cold hard smells of rock and water.

"Perch. Bluff. Nest. Shoal." The skin on Seven's face and hands felt stiff as cracked leather. Pain licked up his fingers as if they cupped a flame. "Keel. Perch."

"Shut up!" Shale told him roughly. "Do you think that helps?"

"It is owed." Seven's voice was heavy as stone. "They are dead and I might as well have killed them. I let Twist kill them."

"Then stop mewling and learn from him! Take Twist as your master. And get people who think like Twist to help you. Listen to Foam."

"Spare me," Foam said weakly.

"He has a toolish, slanted mind. Fathom knows it is not usually an advantage, but you must learn to be slanted, if you want to match wits with Hazel Twist."

Seven nodded slowly. "Very well. I shall learn." His iron voice brought Shale up short. She had lectured him as if he were a stupid younger brother, but now she caught a glimpse of the man who had driven himself for year after weary year, undeterred by pain or ridicule, toward a goal which earned him only scorn. "With luck, Twist will think I drowned. My father's house is on this island. We will go there when dark falls again."

"Why?"

"Food, for one thing. And a boat."

"A boat? I thought you scuttled all the boats."

"Around my house, there are always boats." Seven glanced down at his scorched eelskin vest and pants. "Did you ever wonder what Deltan child had parents so rich he could do anything he wanted? Even hire an exiled woodlander to teach him a skill the sea people despise?"

Foam shrugged. "We guessed your father was a big trader, or your mother was Delta's Witness."

"Would she had been. Then Pond would have been sure to be chosen for the profession. But it is not so. In Delta my father is far more important than any trader. He is the great craftsman of his time: he builds the best ships in the world."

"Wouldn't Stone love to talk to you," Shale said.

Foam looked around the shallow limestone crevice without enthusiasm. Water hissed and bubbled in a crack between his legs. "One question, Shale. Why did you get Keel to throw the oil overboard? What did you see that we didn't?"

Shale answered without looking at him, too tired to turn her head. "Not enough rafts. Two, three, four. If Twist was going to come across, he needed far more than that. So either he was not thinking of jumping from Delta, or the rest of the rafts were somewhere else, and these were the stragglers. Practice ones, probably. Either way, burning them wasn't going to make any difference. Lighting a torch only showed the woodlanders where we were."

"Which I did," Seven said.

Foam shook his head. "We had to do something. And we all missed things. I should have remembered those scuttled ships would be in the harbor. That was bad luck. If it hadn't been low tide, Brine might have gone right over the wreckage."

Seven hid his face between his burned hands. "It wouldn't have mattered. You were right. They were watching for us. As soon as the first torch was lit they would have pinned us down with their fire and their logs."

"That jam was clever," Shale said. "I didn't expect that. Probably all the timber left over from making the rafts. Any log too fat, or too skinny, or too warped."

The gritty smell of rock and water pressed against them, but heavier still was the knowledge that Hazel Twist had outsmarted them, and nine comrades had paid for it with their lives.

"We are going to get very thirsty," Foam said.

Craft turned restlessly on his soft mattress, wishing the nights would cool down. Between the gong and the raid and the fires burning he had barely slept. Something was squeezing his chest like the giant vise he used to bend ships' beams into shape.

He heard one of the guards downstairs cough, or perhaps sneeze. The leaf-eaters wouldn't keep quiet at night no matter how many times he complained. Not, he thought sourly, that prisoners often got their wishes.

It had been a long day, and the apprentices Commander Twist had sent along had been as stupid as always, and more inattentive than ever. The "walls" of the city had started coming down before dawn, to be loaded on to dollies and wheeled to the water's edge. Raft platforms, of course. He had guessed that from the start. Why else would you build a palisade wall in sections, and each section with a tiny little daggerboard slot, neat as neat?

Today, like most days, he'd had the bitter satisfaction of being right. The rafts were rolled into the water, pushed into formation, and roped together to make a giant floating quilt. They had stepped masts in them, and steered the whole contraption by big commands: all the sails on the left stay up, all the ones on the right stay down. That sort of thing. Clever, in its own way.

Not, of course, the same as a *boat*.

They were off by noon, headed out into the reach somewhere. It took little wit to guess who they were hunting. Not to judge by the extra guards downstairs.

As if summoned by the thought, his son's voice slid out of the gloom. "Father?"

The old man jumped.

His son stepped forward, a shadow pulling away from the darkness at the room's edge. "I need your help."

The old man belted his nightgown more tightly around his waist. "This is news? What about the guards?"

"I killed them. Listen, I need a boat."

"You killed . . ." The old man stumbled through the dark room, threw his arms (still very strong) around Seven, and then glared at him. "Well, boats, I can tell you, are not something we have in great stock right now. Someone knocked holes in them all."

There were two pale faces behind Seven, listening and pretending not to.

"I had to keep Twist from using them, did I not?"

"Twist? Use a six-yard sloop? With what crew?"

"Can we fight about it later? Right now I need a boat."

"There is one boat in the shed. I was building it for Commander Twist."

"For Twist!"

"Do you want the boat or don't you?"

Seven looked away. Nodded. "And we have to take you with us."

"Me! My whole life is in this yard! Don't talk such madness."

"There are four dead guards downstairs. Twist will know I have been here. He will know you helped me. There is no choice."

"Don't you tell me what I can and cannot do!" Craft remembered snapping at Beech Knot after lunch, slapping his clumsy fingers. Now stilled forever by his son. "However, I choose to go."

"Good choice."

"There is one other problem." Craft scratched at his greying beard. "I was building this boat for Commander Twist, you see. So I tacked the boards over-under, instead of under-over."

Seven sighed.

Craft glanced at Foam and Shale. "You see, a good boat is built so that when it gets wet, the planks swell up to make a tighter seam. Only, in this case, instead of swelling closer together, they are going to pull farther apart."

"Which means," Seven said, "wherever we are going, we had better get there fast."

CHAPTER 13: FOAM AND SHALE

The journey was horrible. For the first hour Seven and Craft bickered about how best to get to Mona. Then the sloop began taking on water. They bailed until their arms were wooden with exhaustion. "We might as well have swum," Foam groaned. They had almost given the ship up for dead when they saw Mona at last, a dark bulk against the paling East. Fifty lengths out they let the boat drown, and floundered in to shore a stone's throw from Mona's tiny dock.

They collapsed on the rough shingle and watched grey light spill over the world. Soaking wet and freezing cold, Foam huddled on the stony beach with his arms wrapped around his knees. "Dawn! And the sooner the day heats up, the better. I cannot remember when I was so tired. My chattering teeth are all that keeps me awake."

Shale laughed.

Seven squatted next to Craft. "Are you cold?"

"Of course I'm cold! What does it matter? Will you pull a blanket from a crab shell for me?"

Foam quirked his head to one side, smiling faintly at the sky. "The world is a giant eye, staring back at the stars. When it tires, it closes its lids—just as I am doing now—and gives way to dreams, which is why the night is so much more mysterious than the day."

Old Craft chuckled dryly, a long, thin sound like the stroke of a plane.

They turned at the sound of footsteps pattering on rock, then stumping on the wooden dock. "Back to work," Seven said, rising to his feet. "We need fire and shelter, and a boat to sail back to Pond and the others."

"If there are others," Shale said. "Twist may have taken Thumbtip from us, if what Craft says about a great fleet of rafts setting out is true."

"Pond and I agreed to meet on Hookfeather if Thumbtip fell. Those rafts are too slow to take Pond by surprise. If Twist headed for Thumbtip, she will have gotten the others away." Seven started walking for the jetty.

"You go ahead," Craft said. "The sun is beginning to warm me up. I will sit here and watch him rise."

Foam and Shale exchanged weary glances, heaved themselves up, aching in every muscle, and shambled after their leader.

A father and his son crouched by their boat; angular, square-jawed men, the son perhaps sixteen. He saw the strangers first, and tapped his father on the back. The older man stood slowly, leaving his painter secured. His braid did not have the full Deltan split, but broke into two plaits midway down his back. Calluses clung like barnacles to his big hands. His eyes lingered on Seven's scorched and sodden eelskins. "I am Cleat."

"My name is Seven. My companions and I—"

"Seven!" the boy said. "Is it true you led the attack against Delta? The singer said you were the greatest warrior in the history of the sea people. He said you fought ten men at once and won, and that you would defeat the Emperor's armies."

"The singer?"

Cleat squinted. "Reed of Delta passed through here four nights ago, telling many strange tales."

Seven held up his burned hands. "Do you see a hero before you?"

Father and son stood puzzled and silent.

Shale could stand it no longer. "Yes, you do! This is the man of whom Reed spoke."

"He is exhausted," Foam added, "for he has not slept. His clothes are cut and scorched and sodden, for he has been through sword and fire and water to bring us back from Delta alive. He is sick at heart, for the woodlanders have enslaved his people. He asks little of others, and much of himself; anything less than the defeat of the Empire is bitter to him. He is a mighty man, of a kind the sea's people seldom breed. Treat him with respect!"

Cleat scratched his beard. "And what does he have to say for himself? You have fine heralds, friend, but I would hear a word or two from your own lips."

"I would hear less from theirs, certainly. But we have not slept two hours in the last two days. We have barely eaten since the night before last. Show us a place we may rest, and there I will answer any questions."

"Oh, aye," Cleat said, nodding. "I forgot myself, to keep you standing so on the dock. Come. Welcome first, and questions after." He patted his son on the shoulder. "You must forgive us. It is a strange thing when a legend washes in from the Mist."

"Reed said you were the champion of the Gull Warrior himself!" Seven could have choked.

Cleat and Seven walked ahead, talking; Cleat's boy hung on the warrior's every word.

"You played that wind well," Foam said to Shale, lingering several paces back. "Taking the wheel from Seven, I mean."

"He is too embarrassed to sing himself. I was glad for your help, by the way. 'He has been through sword and fire and water to bring us back from Delta alive.' Very elegant, Foam. Very elegant."

"Am I not always?" Foam peered down at his shredded tunic and winced.

"I hope we can wrangle a boat from these people."

"Boat! I would be happy with a pair of boots. I am not cut out to be an adventurer."

"No? Even Rope is having adventures, Foam. Think how you would blush, to be stuck more deeply in the mud than him!"

Foam stumbled in to town, wondering if it were possible to sleep and eat at the same time. Shale walked back to fetch Seven's father.

Craft was examining a long trunk of bone-grey driftwood, rapping it with his large fist to see if it was still sound. He was a tall man, taller than his son, though not so broad. He had great wide hands with strong fingers and big knuckles.

Shale picked her way across the beach, a rubble of rocks and sharp-edged shells. "Boots!" she said enviously.

"Eh?"

She reached the log and sat on it, pointing at Craft's feet. "Boots. You have boots. Ours went down with our ship."

"You took 'em off before you went in, eh? That was clever. Seven didn't think of that."

"Not exactly."

"Mm. Nice length of wood, is it not? You could hollow it into a neat little coracle for some youngster. The wood is still sound, for all its wetting. Good sign. Can't build a boat from wood that's only sound when it's dry, eh!" Craft's face was sharp and his beard was like grey wire. "He is not much given to forethought, my Seven. That's his mother showing. She counselled him to stay out of the business. A mistake, I always said. Neither one of them could stomach the planning that goes into a boat. They wanted to ride each wave as it came. But it's the foresight that makes things possible, you see? It takes foresight to make a boat that will weather every wave."

"I suppose." Shale swung her feet in lazy circles as they hung over the edge of the log. Craft was not at all like the other wealthy Deltans. He met her eyes when he spoke, and did not hide his edges. "But I must admit I dive first too, and look for rocks after."

"He was always good with his hands. He made one or two neat little sloops before he was hooked on soldiering."

The first shafts of sunlight felt good on Shale's back. "You did not give him your blessing."

Craft shrugged, running a hand along the water-smoothed log.

"What you learn changes you. Can you take up the craft of killing without peril? I do not think so."

"Yet you let him study."

"Yes, we let him. It is the weak who are cruel. I saw the boy would be a willing soldier and a sulky shipwright. I would rather he felt strong enough to hold his hand, than feel weak and strike a fearful blow."

"A lucky choice, it looks now. More shipbuilder's foresight?"

"If I had seen the woodlanders coming, I would have told Switch to make him a general, not a warrior! Seven will learn, though. He will learn." Craft pulled himself up onto the other end of the log, and sat staring into the western sea, looking back to Spearpoint.

"He asks much of himself." Shale looked sideways at Seven's father. "I wonder where he got that from?"

Craft shifted on the log. He looked up and down the beach, and back at the lightly wooded ridge behind them. "A nice place, Mona. I often thought I would come here to rest for a fortnight or two, but I could never find the time."

"You won't be coming with us to find Pond and the others?"

"I am a shipwright, not a soldier." Craft snorted. "Besides, Seven wallows in this trough all sons sail through. He would rather the White Wolf bit his balls than take his father's advice. Oh, you say nothing, but you saw."

"We could use another shipwright with us."

Craft took a deep sniff of the early morning air. "I am not willing, at my age, to suffer his foolishness gladly. Best he learn to be a general by himself. He had better learn fast, though, and learn well. The first success will be the easiest. The woodlanders think us simple. That is an advantage we will have only once."

Lines of faint black smoke rose above the treetops as breakfast fires were lit in the village. Some time passed.

Shale struggled to stay awake. "Why the name Seven?"

Craft's eyes were hooded as he looked over the endless sea, and he spoke quietly, almost to himself. "He never said, but I think he wants to be the Seventh Wave."

"Why aren't you asleep?" Shale's head spun with weariness. "The sea is a lullaby to me this morning."

"Ha!" Craft chuckled, lean as cord and tough as leather. "I am old. Old! The old do not need so much sleep. When you sleep you dream, sorting through your life, trying to fit some things together and take other ones apart. Finding places to store what you might need again. But an old man's brain is already in order. He knows what he thinks and what he needs to remember, and he lets the rest go."

"It sounds wonderful!"

"Well, your joints creak and your teeth fall out, and that keeps you up at night too."

Shale laughed. "We should go up to the village. Get a nice breakfast." Fry some eggs, she thought. Or eel. Smoked eel . . .

Some time later she found she had been dozing.

She felt fragile and feverish with lack of sleep. Waves plashing on rock, boats creaking at the dock, the surf hissing across the sand—every little sound pressed into her as if she listened with her whole skin.

". . . at this captaining business," Craft was saying. "Would you do that?"

"Forgive me. What did you say?"

"I said I was hoping you would help him with this captaining business. The boy has a liking for danger. A bad quality for a soldier and a worse one in a general. If you could keep an eye on him for me, you would have my thanks. I ask as a father."

"I owe your son my life."

"With his mother gone, nobody else remembers him six months old, rocking on his tummy and falling on his nose." Craft's hands stilled on the driftwood bench. "*Pfeh*. Sentiment. The vice of the old."

"And what is the vice of the young?"

Craft laughed. "Stupidity," he said.

"Well, we got a boat," Seven muttered the next morning, tacking roughly leeward. "And paid dearly for it."

"*Eel*," Foam said. "I rather like this scarlet trim on her gunwales. A happy chance that a spare boat should have drifted into shore only a couple of days ago." He squinted out into the gulf around Delta. "I wonder where she came from."

Shale nudged Seven in the back of the leg, none too gently. "Wave to the nice people on the shore!"

"Drown the war, drown the boat, and drown Mona entire," Seven said, but he rose and stood gracefully in the stern, waving his thanks to the crowd. Their cheers carried faintly across the water. When the villagers were only a blur he sat down. "I hate this posing."

"We know, we know," Foam said soothingly. "Look at your father there, just behind the Witness. He wasn't clapping, was he? He knew you would prefer—Ooh!"

"Sorry!" Shale said. "Foot slipped while I was shifting position. Small boats, eh?"

"Curse these small boats," Foam growled. "Anyway, they gave you a place to sleep and food to eat; called you the spirit of the Gull Warrior; gifted you a boat—and all you had to do was tell a few stories!"

"Which we mostly did, anyway," Shale added. "You weren't much use. Too much squirming."

"Easy, Shale."

"No. She is right." Seven swung their bow to windward. "This is a war, not a duel. My real skills matter little now. I must lead. If the people believe me to be"—he grimaced—"a Hero of Legend, then so be it. I know the difference, and you know it too."

"On the contrary!" Foam cried. "To my mind you are the very image of a legend: a great man with a great bard. The Gull Warrior's great advantage is that the Singer tells his stories. No offense to Reed, but who can compete with that?"

"Hush!" Seven said uneasily. "I have no wish to anger the Heroes. I do not want to find myself tangled in this story Reed is making, like a fisherman fouled in his own lines. If people have to believe it to have hope, to give us boats and men, then so be it. But Reed's tales are not truth. Keel is. Keel and Shoal and Perch and Brine and Rose. The dead speak the only true stories of war."

Half a day later they found that Thumbtip had fallen. Well-organized soldiers moved along her beaches and a fire-sling looked out over the harbor where only a few days before the rebel ships had been anchored. Wearily, Seven turned his tiller and set course for Hookfeather.

The sun was setting by the time they arrived. Sentinels must have spotted them far out, for the whole rebel camp was waiting as they made their ship fast. Foam and Shale knew the Deltans were looking for friends and family who would not be coming back. They were hugged all around as they came ashore, but many of those waiting wept and would not meet their eyes.

Pond did her best to keep her voice calm, but relief showed in every line as she hugged Seven. When they broke their embrace, her hand quickly sought his. "Lookouts spotted Twist's raft army early, so—Your hands!"

"A little burned," Seven said softly. "It is nothing. Show us where we will sleep tonight."

Pond nodded and led them up a narrow path to a small clearing, gloomy and dim. A little red fire crawled over a few logs in the ash pit, throwing out sparse licks of heat and a welter of shadows. Cedars with drooping arms swayed sadly overhead. "We had more than enough time to make sail for here. But it galled me to see Twist's men take the very barracks we worked so hard to build." Pond shrugged at the meager foundations behind her. "We have begun again, but the going is slow. Such is all our tale. Now tell us yours."

Foam told the story of the raid to a somber audience, stopping more than once to blink and fight off sleep.

"I told that primping jigger Brine it would be his death," Catch muttered, stabbing the fire with a greenwood prod until it spat red sparks at him. "Idiot."

"At least he tried," Shale snapped.

Glint spread marigold ointment on Seven's burned hands and then wrapped them in a strip of bandage. "Quarrelling, are we? Good! Let us kill ourselves, and save the woodlanders the trouble!"

Brace the carpenter sighed. "The question is, what next?"

"Sleep!" Pond said quickly. "Sleep, until Seven and Shale and Foam have rested. Let us take our decisions tomorrow, when we are less weary. Nightfall always brings despair."

Foam nodded his agreement. "We have enough of that cargo in our holds already."

Foam's sleep was long and troubled by dreams of burning. It was almost noon before he awoke. After lunch Seven asked him to come explore the island. "If I remember right, there is a sandy beach just to the north of us. Not so long a walk."

Foam agreed, glad to avoid the hard work of barrack-building.

"They have made good progress here," Seven said as they walked. "Pond has them working well."

"They respect her."

"Who could not? She is a lady, Foam. A lady of Delta. I struggle to be worthy of her."

"Now that's a funny business, isn't it?" Foam smoothed his braids and straightened the ivory pins in them, fingers deft and thoughtless as the paws of a grooming cat. He frowned. "Trying to be worthy of someone. What does she respect? Should you be only what you are, or change yourself to be better—or at least more like her? Or would that make you seem false, or fawning?"

"These are abstract questions only," Seven said, smiling.

"Of course. Purest philosophy."

Their path now wandered along the top of a small ridge. A light wind blew through the poplars, whose leaves blurred to smears of moving green, covering and uncovering glints of a grey-blue sea. Seven stood a moment, looking down at the ocean. "I was lonely before I met her, but I did not know it. That was all that gave me the strength to endure it, I think. I no longer have the courage to live with my heart so empty."

He looked at Foam, who was also past twenty-five and unmarried and scorned by the good, sturdy, respectable people of the sea. "We are very much alike, you know. In another story, I would have been you."

Foam studied Seven's deep chest and arms corded with muscle. "I'd have to eat better, I think."

Seven laughed.

Later he said, "I love the smell of the islands. Trees and rocks and water all jumbled together. And the sound of the waves and the wind."

"Mm-hmm."

A pair of blazing ships staggered through a darkling bay in Seven's heart, burning. "Brine died for these islands."

He started down the fork in the path. "There it is. That sandy stretch there. Just where I remembered it."

"Have you been here often?"

"Betimes. Switch and I would come out and camp for a few days. I needed to practice where nobody would be scared by the sword."

Foam followed Seven down to the beach. He wore an extra pair of soft boots salvaged from Brine's yacht, but they were small and pinched. When he got near the water line he took them off and revelled at the feel of the heavy sand squishing between his toes.

Seven stood like a young god with the surf foaming around his ankles. "I should practice."

"Did Switch tell you how to fight men with sprayers?"

Seven grimaced. "I don't like those. A coward's weapon that takes no skill to use."

Foam squinted. "In other words, the only people who should be killers are people who really *want* to be killers."

Seven frowned. "Well . . . yes. It takes discipline to learn a skill, and discipline is the brother of self-control. With one of these sprayers, any man can kill on the whim of the moment. Or maim, which is worse."

"You prefer murder to mutilation?"

"There is a certain purity to it. No lingering on, useless and in pain. Either triumph or oblivion. It is a very clean distinction, don't you think? There is something better about that. More wholesome."

"Wholesome!"

Foam stepped back from the water line and lay on the warm, dry sand. "The story of your master, Switch, has always puzzled me. What was a woodlander doing in Delta?"

"He killed a Bronze. It was self-defense, so the penalty was exile rather than death."

Seven walked up from the water and lowered himself to the sand, stretching gently. "The remarkable thing about killing people, Foam, is that the more times you do it the easier it gets. Hard at first, of course." With his legs spread wide apart he reached for one toe, and laid the whole length of his torso easily along the leg.

Foam shuddered. "My tendons would snap like stretched seaweed if I did that."

Seven stared absently at the rain clouds building in the east. "The first time, I just stood there for the longest time. Then he raised his sprayer. I had never seen one before and I was frightened. I was not prepared for it. I lost my technique, I forgot to cut cleanly, I forgot to make it count. I swung wildly for his hand. Split it in half. There was a great deal of blood. I can remember feeling angry because there was blood on my sword. I always take particular care to keep it clean. And he was screaming and there were others coming up. He must have known I was going to kill him, but instead of defending himself he just kept staring at his hand and screaming. I have never been so afraid. Not afraid of him, you understand. Afraid of killing. I almost did not dare. But my second cut was better.

"That was a lesson I had nearly thrown my life away learning, so I paid close attention. The next time, I felt sick afterwards, but at the time I was very cool. The third time, when we rescued you and Shale, there were too many of them to think about anything. I was calm, calmer than I think I have ever been in my life. The louder the shouting got, the calmer I became. The woodlanders were going so *slowly*. Still, there were too many of them. They would have started spraying their own men from behind for the sake of getting me. My people were falling back to the boats, so I went after them. But by the time I killed the guards outside my father's place, I hardly felt their deaths at all."

He paused, looking at Foam, and shook his head. "No. That is a lie. I still felt the excitement and the risk. But the dread was gone. Like any other fear, the fear of killing a man goes away when you have done it a few times."

"I do not think I want to lose that fear," Foam said.

"Then I hope you won't," Seven said. "But I fear you will."

That afternoon Foam found Pond in a clearing just beyond the campsite, stripping leaves from a young elder bush. Her silver bracelets glinted between the elder's frothy white flowers. "Personal enemies?" he asked, as she tore off another handful of leaves. "Or was it a family quarrel?"

Pond laughed softly without looking up. "These poor things are too pliant to make good foes. Glint needs them. She boils elder leaves in a mix of fat and fish oil to make a salve that heals cuts and bruises. We ran out yesterday. Shale is down at the docks, if you are wondering, teaching the others how to gut fish." Pond grimaced prettily. "I volunteered to harvest elder."

"A mistake! Shale is a wonderful fish-gutter. Why, people all over the Edge sail to Clouds End just to watch her. She pops out the eyes with her thumbs like nobody—"

"Spare me! What do you want?"

Foam's grin faded. "Oh. Well. Actually, I—that is, I was wondering if . . . You see, I'm in need of a woman's opinion."

"Ah. An affair of the heart."

"How did you know?"

Pond plucked another handful of blade-shaped elder leaves. "Men rarely ask a woman's advice on anything else. Here, harvest with me."

"Perhaps I should just—"

"Careful not to snap off the twigs. They are delicate."

Foam joined her. They stood side by side, picking, as he became more and more certain that this was Not a Good Idea. "Ahem. Uh. Well. The, the, the fact of the case, of the matter, really, is that, that I have, have become rather—*fond*—no, fond is the wrong word . . . maybe—no, that isn't . . ."

"You have feelings for a woman," Pond said gravely.

"Y-e-e-s. Yes, I guess that is—Anyway, the problem is, I become quite idiotic when talking about this sort of thing."

Pond didn't meet his eyes. "Really?"

"Er—well. Anyway, there it is. I have these . . . feelings for this woman, but I'm not quite certain if she, that is, whether she is really aware of it. Them. The feelings, you understand. And I wonder, if I said something, would it, you know, seem *threatening?* Or would it, would it induce some, some response. Perhaps."

Pond suppressed a smile. Poor Foam was not even pretending to pick anymore, just weaving leaves together with nervous, nimble fingers. "You are not sure how she feels about you, and you are uncertain as to what you should say to her. Is that right?"

Foam nodded, feeling like an idiot, blushing hot and red up to his ears, five years older than his friends and stupid about everything that really mattered. "She's, she's rather an independent sort of person, you see. She could certainly cut a finer jib than myself, you understand. That's one of my—a problem. And yet, there have been some signs that she, you know, likes—I can't say, *has feelings*—that she likes me. I have, I think I could be good for, good to have. Around. For her . . . *Grr!*" Foam tore a twig off the bush. "Listen to me! This is unendurable." He turned to Pond. "Never mind. I shall retire to the Mist and dive for pearlweirds. If you will excuse me, I shall take my humiliation for a walk."

Pond nodded meekly. "I shall think on your words. And Foam, remember that women, too, find it difficult to remain poised in such situations."

"Not mine," he said grimly. "That's part of the problem."

Pond waved goodbye with a sprig of white flowers in her fingers.

"Work hard! Think of Delta! Be patient, and I expect you will hear something to clarify the situation."

Foam wanted to dip his face into a pool of cold water. There were a few other parts of him that could use the same treatment, he thought savagely.

Pond waited until he was safely out of sight and then, though she knew a real Witness wouldn't, she laughed until tears sprang to her eyes.

She cornered Shale during the bustle before dinner, stirring their biggest pot with a stripped branch. "Fish stew. Magnificent. And so wonderfully gutted!"

Shale looked at her warily. "Complaining?"

"Mm. On the contrary." Pond sniffed the rich stew, made aromatic with wild thyme. People were gathering in the half-built barracks as supper approached. Brace and a helper were shoring up a wall, squinting into the sunset. Seven was demonstrating a wristlock on Foam for a small group of interested Deltans; Foam smiled gamely until Seven turned his fingers a fraction, driving him to the ground. Catch loitered nearby, scratching his side and looking hungrily at the stew.

Pond lowered her voice. "You have a suitor."

Shale recoiled in horror. "Oh no! Is it someone odious?"

"Not at all."

"Worse and worse! What have I done to deserve this?"

"Perhaps you misheard. *Not* odious."

"I know, I know. That means I can't do something quick and painful to end the matter. Of course, why scruple . . . ?"

"Hard to do in good conscience," Pond said quickly.

Shale sighed. "I suppose."

"Ready yet?" Catch called to the cooks. Shale's scowl drove him back three paces. "N-nope," he stammered. "Not ready yet."

Shale slammed her wooden spoon around inside the big fuseware pot. "Where do they get the nerve!" she demanded. "Have I given anyone any encouragement? No. Have I been 'womanly'?

No. But does it matter? No! They decide to feel smitten without so much as a by-your-leave."

Pond wrinkled her brows. "I am beginning to think this suitor may be out of luck."

Shale sighed. "Is he intelligent?"

"Very."

"Handsome?"

Pond shrugged. "In a gawky kind of way."

"Funny?"

"Frequently."

"Impotent?"

Pond glanced up in surprise before she could catch herself. "I have no reason to believe so."

"Spit!" Shale swore. "For a moment he sounded like the perfect man."

Evening light hung gently in the sky, and the birds were settling. A gust of laughter came from the main camp beyond a stand of jack pines. Seven and his counsellors had slipped off to a small fire pit by his tent, though they had not yet taken a branch to be lit at the big central fire. Glint, Catch, Seven, and Pond sat together. Foam was also by the fire pit and Shale sat facing him, with her back against a young poplar.

"We should discuss strategy," Seven said when the dinner was finally ready.

"Oh, at least let us wait until our dinners settle," Foam said wearily. "If you can ever get Shale to stop eating."

"I wish Reed weren't gone," Catch said. "He always had a song or a story."

Suddenly Shale said, "I'll tell a story."

Foam grinned at the Deltans. "Listen up! She's a Witness's daughter, and can trim a story's sheets as well as any wisewoman."

Shale laughed, rapidly inventing the beginning of her tale. "This is a story of the Mist-time," she said, leaning forward and grinning at the company, "where everything is true and nothing is what it seems. It is a Rolling Hitch story, told of Queen Lianna's Court, and it goes like this . . ."

Shale's audience clapped softly in the gloom when she had finished.

"I've never heard you tell that one before," Foam said.

Shale laughed. "There are still a few things you don't know about me." Full dark had fallen as she stood up. "I need to stretch!"

"I'll get a branch from the big fire," Catch said.

Shapes had faded with the dusk, leaving only a play of voices in the night. Shale walked barefoot over leaves and roots and dirt. She felt as if she too had become less real, ghosting along the path to the shore. She was feeling her way as much as seeing it, following the empty places where the trees weren't. She slithered down a steep hill with one leg outstretched. At its bottom lay a slab of cooling stone; piles of weathered granite; the sound of the sea. She slid over the big curve of the first rock. Dried lichen flaked to powder beneath her fingertips.

Starshine glimmered on the water. Gulping fish jumped after invisible insects. A black wall had come in from the east, drowning those stars caught below the cloud line.

A peeved clam squirted at Shale. She laughed and splashed her hands in the cool water. She rose up with the sea foaming about her ankles and laughed again, big as the islands. Big as the sky. She rolled up her sleeves and washed the wood smoke from her arms. She bent down again and splashed water over her head, gasping with the shock of it, wringing the grime out of her hair, slicking her bangs back and grinning.

She crept back to camp, snuck behind Foam, dripped on him and snickered. "Ah—oo!" he squealed. "Quit that!"

"So—whose turn is it to tell a story now?"

"Talk turned serious while you were away."

"Despite Foam's best attempts to stop it," Seven added. "But we can't put it off any longer. Something must be done about Hazel Twist, and about Thumbtip. Come now, Foam. Teach me to think like a woodlander. How should I begin?"

"Couldn't we go to Thistle, or Mona, or one of the peopled islands? That way you wouldn't have to build a barracks, or if you did, there would be more people to help with the work."

"True, but that would make them military targets. I don't want to drag anyone unwillingly into the war. Not yet, anyway."

"Soon."

"I know."

Foam poked the fire into a steady blaze. "All right. Here's what I would do. First rule: fight to win. We have few men, few weapons, no experience. Twist can lose ten of his men for one of ours. We should *never*, ever, cross him unless we know we will win, and win decisively."

"But you said yourself the woodlanders are superior in numbers, weapons, and training," Seven reminded Foam. "So where does that leave us?"

"Not fighting."

"You think we should quit?" Catch said hopefully.

"Not at all. We should quit fighting pitched battles, certainly. But pitched battles are not the only way to wage a war."

Glint stirred. "I'm in favor. I'm too busy here as it is."

Foam nodded. "My next question is, What are our strengths? What do we do better than the woodlanders?"

"Sail," Pond said.

Seven nodded. "We have better boats, and we know these waters."

"Good. What else?"

Silence gathered in the clearing.

"Well," Foam said, "there's navigation too. You can count that as part of sailing, I guess. We know where we are, where we are going, and how to get there. If Hazel Twist tries to spread his forces through the islands, that should give us some advantages."

"Except for the fire-slings," Catch said. "I don't want burning pitch up my ass, thank you."

"There you go, thinking of battles again! Wherever Twist goes, we can get there first, warn the villagers and take them away. If the worst happens and his men fan out through the Inner Islands, we can at least stop them from picking off villages one by one.

The farther he goes, the more healthy, angry islanders will be banding together to resist him."

Seven nodded. "The farther Twist sails from Delta, the thinner he must spread his forces, and the more troops we will have on our side. But I don't want to lose the Inner Islands before we stop him."

"Neither do I. Still, I am more certain this war can be won than I was when I built this fire." Foam gestured with his poker so that the red tip danced in the darkness.

"You are right," Seven said. "By the Warrior, you're right. We can win this thing after all. Hazel Twist has failed to appreciate what lies before him."

Glint grunted. "I doubt that."

Foam shook his head. "That doesn't mean he can stop us. He will want to keep us small and keep us divided. He will want to strike soon."

"The key is that garrison on Thumbtip." Seven spoke quickly now, staring into the fire. "That is his jumping-off point. From there he can strike for Mona, and Thistle. He can find out which direction we headed and try to encircle us."

"Too late for that," Shale pointed out. "Even if we got caught unprepared here on Hookfeather, Reed is already spreading the word and rousing the people. They will be more watchful than Delta was. What happened to your Witness, anyway?"

"The Witnesses of Delta judge disputes and sign contracts; they cannot speak the future," Pond said wistfully.

"Don't they watch the Mist? Foam, we are surrounded by barbarians!"

Seven laughed. "Be gentle! Pond wants to fool one of our Witnesses into letting her apprentice. Remember that you are much closer to the Mist than we. Our omens come from the run of salmon or the tale of the wind, not the living mystery of the Mist-time."

"Food," Shale said.

Glint cocked her head. "What?"

"Food. Food. Even you Deltans can't catch a fish outside a marketplace. The woodlanders will trap what rabbits they can find and eat the berries they recognize. But the real food here comes from the sea. Fish, clams, crabs, scallops, oysters, mussels. If nothing else, we should be better fed."

"Won't they learn?" Catch asked. "After all, digging clams isn't so hard."

"It is perhaps harder to feed a large camp than men typically appreciate," Pond said. "They will learn, yes, but slowly."

"And make some mistakes too," Shale added. "If we're lucky, the first clam they eat will be a red ribbon."

"Brilliant!" Foam cried.

"What?"

"Brilliant! That's what we need to do. Poison their food! Change good clams for bad, crumble deadly mushrooms into their stew! Do you see it? We dare not fight them. But if half their troops were dead, and the other half sick as babies, we could take Thumbtip back with ease."

"Poison!" Glint spat.

Seven frowned. "Do you really want us to stoop to that?"

"I'm trying to save islander lives," Foam snapped. "If I fight, I will fight to win."

A log cracked open, freeing a cloud of red sparks to fly into the night. Seven sighed. "Ugly as the tales of war are, the real thing is uglier still."

"It's a beautiful plan," Foam continued. "It turns so nicely on our strengths. After all, we even know where the kitchen is in their barracks on Thumbtip, because we built it."

"How are we supposed to sneak through an armed camp with a bagful of spoiled clams?" Shale asked.

"Um. Well . . ."

"I don't mean to squash the idea. But before we make any decisions we'll have to go back to Thumbtip and have a look around."

"They will have guards," Seven reminded her.

"Mm. I just wanted to have a quiet look around, that's all. Are you up to another night sail? Foam and I would go alone, I'm sure, but we need someone who can find Thumbtip in the dark."

Foam cocked his head and stared up at the sky. "Not tonight!

One more glorious night of sleep, I beg you. I fear we may not get much in the days to come."

Shale lay on her back, restless, unready for sleep, looking up at the trembling poplar leaves and listening to their whispered stories of sun and soil.

Beside her, Foam's breathing was already long and regular, and his face had gone smooth with sleep. Shale grinned to herself in the darkness, flattered. She felt sorry for him. She did like him, actually. Which was a bit of a surprise. Since her Naming she had thought him more silly than attractive. But over the last weeks, she had come to value his silliness more highly, and the clever, abstract mind behind it.

But lovers!

When he had clutched at her during the storm, she had wanted only to get away. She was not proud of that. She was beginning to like Foam, like him very much, but she could not shake the feeling he would drag her down. He thrust this thing at her—she couldn't call it love. Where did it come from? She couldn't be his only friend, now that Rope was gone, and be his lover too. He could not ask her to make his life worthwhile.

Was she callous to feel this way? She felt guilty, guilty as she so often was that she could not give herself as people wanted. Could not be decorous for her sister Nanny, could not be a lover for Foam. The Witness's daughter and she could not even pledge herself to Clouds End.

No! She had to go. She had to journey and be happy and bring back wonders. That is what was given to her to do. If she lost her nerve, if she gave in to Foam now, or to anyone, then all the times she had refused to give herself were no longer part of a great plan to make good; it would all have been only selfishness after all.

Seven was lucky, so lucky. The woodlanders had saved him with their invasion. Suddenly all his years of folly and selfishness, all the times he refused to be what his father or his people wanted—all that had been made good.

Lucky, lucky bastard.

She stretched out again, very aware of her body as it slid beneath her tunic. How pleasant it was, to be well-fed and rested again, to be lying out under the stars on a warm night. She pulled a blanket over herself, just over the waist, up beneath her breasts. There.

They would be on some island, she imagined, seeing it in her mind's eye. No, Delta. Spearpoint. Seven's cave on Spearpoint, eluding pursuit. Shouting soldiers all around, rattling the bushes with their swords, calling to one another: dangerous fugitives, desperate rebels. The ones who . . . Hm. (Shale massaged her legs, just above the knee, relaxing, moving slowly upwards, letting her toes relax, her feet, her knees, her thighs, muscles softening under her fingertips.)

The worst moment: caught in Twist's room, poring over his secret charts, his special commands. Letters to the Emperor, detailing strategy, tucked inside a legging as they hear voices approaching, coming up the stairs of one of those great Deltan houses. He would have a big one for himself, of course. Foam freezes. Now, at the moment of crisis, she must lead.

The hunger in his eyes matching hers, clinched tight in their burrow while the enemy's soldiers surround them. The smell of rock, of water. She pulls him down on top of her, their bodies press together; she can feel that he wants her despite the danger. (The skin, higher up, strangely soft, even on her. All that walking, all her boyish ways, hasn't changed that. Still the soft swelling of flesh just below the hollow where the legs meet.)

Two sets of footsteps, maybe three. Twist and two bodyguards. No time to think and no weapons, of course. Not their style. In a room. What kind of room? Papers—lots of papers: charts, notes, reports, ship designs, notes on rafts, letters from the Emperor. A table where he works; pens, ink, so on. Lamps, a bed.

Paper! The door is closed but paper is piled high near the doorway. Foam looks to her for guidance. Swiftly, decisively, she glides to the door, drops the latch, grabs the lamp. She turns it upside down, pouring a wash of burning oil onto the papers. The footsteps have almost reached the foot of the stairs. Back now, to the window.

And after, steal a boat? a raft? and sail back to Hookfeather in triumph. A secret, glowing warm inside her belly.

Her tunic is already pushed up as he lies on top of her, her legs are spread, he cannot ignore the situation, though danger is everywhere. She locks his eyes with hers, pulls slowly up on his tunic; it brushes across her coiled hairs; he lifts himself, just enough to let the tunic slide free, incredulous. His blood rises too strongly to let caution stand in their way. He is free. His tip touches her (just lightly: so. Gentle as a finger, caressing her.) She reaches for him, holds him. Their eyes are still locked. His tip pushes lightly against her; he can't resist doing that much. Still she has not let him kiss her. Above, a soldier cries, "Be careful! Remember what happened to those sentries!"

Flames rise, crackling, dancing destruction over commands, reports, sightings, designs. A concerned murmur from behind the door; footsteps bounding up the last few stairs, rushing along the corridor. Crawling out the window of Twist's study, she swings a leg over the roof; hikes herself up. Splintering noises come from within. Foam's hands appear on the roof's edge; he swings, dangling in space for a dreadful moment, kicks himself once, twice, until she catches him and pulls him up. Below, the fire races through stacks of paper. Shouts of rage and garbled orders are gobbled up by the roaring flames. Someone runs off to sound the gong, but they are running now, leaping from rooftop to rooftop.

Smiling hungrily she pulls him in, letting him thrust, and kissing him, for the first time, hard. Footsteps: a soldier of the forest is standing on the rock directly above them as they couple in desperate silence.

And before: creeping up Twist's stairs. They came in a boat, of course; they have hidden it in Craft's house; they can return for it later, when the search has died down, after their rocking bodies are no longer joined, pushed down hard against the granite, the weight of him, the smell of rock, the sound of footsteps. The sea.

CHAPTER 14: LITTLE BOATS

After a blessed night of sleep, Shale took her students out the next morning to dig for clams. Most of what they found they left out in the sun to spoil.

Rain hissed into the darkness around Seven and Foam that night. After what seemed like an eternity waiting off Thumbtip, a hand reached up to the boat and gently rocked the rail. Shale gasped and pulled herself over the transom. "Give me my clothes! Warm night or not, I'm freezing."

Foam handed over tunic and leggings. Shale's nude body was almost invisible, but he felt a sudden surge of resentment that Seven should see it.

Shale pulled her tunic on and shivered. "That's better."

Foam eased the sail out and Seven turned the bow leeward, to let the boat pick up speed.

"No," Shale murmured. "Only go out far enough to talk."

Seven nodded and eased them out to the Tack. "Well?"

"Brr. Well, things are not as we left them."

Foam groaned. "Don't tell me they're being clever again."

"I'm afraid so. Remember how they hid the rafts on Delta?"

"I hate him," Seven said grimly. "I hate Hazel Twist."

Shale went on, unperturbed. "Our barracks now has a beautiful wall all around it. As tall as a tall man, with only two gates. I heard sentries."

"Bastards!" Foam pulled the sheet in more tightly, arms tense with frustration.

"So much for getting into the kitchen," Seven said. "Unless we want to storm the gates. Your news is not good."

"Outside the barracks there are two places with torches: one up above the sandy beach, toward the eastern end, and one near the harbor."

"Those will be the fire-slings," Foam said. "Positioned to get our boats should we try to land."

Foam nodded. "We need to take them first."

"Agreed. Did you find anything else, Shale?"

"Well, yes, actually. It was down on the sandy beach. I spent a lot of time pretending to be a log." She shivered. "I'm glad we waited until summer to have this war, I'll tell you. If the water had been cold on top of the rain, I don't think I would have made it back.

"Anyway, I floated in the surf until I was sure there was nobody around, and then I started up the beach. The tide was coming in, and I noticed that just above the water line the sand was terribly churned up. I felt it with my toes. Higher up the beach still, on the shore edge, the end of the churned area was marked by a ridge of wet sand."

"Someone was digging," Foam said.

"Exactly! Someone—or rather a lot of people—had been systematically digging along the beach. They had started on the western edge and worked their way east; it had only just started raining then, and you could tell that the piles of sand on the west were much dryer than the stuff over toward the middle. So my question was, What were they digging for? And I thought to myself, if I were from the forest, and had forty troops to use, maybe I would—"

"Clams!" Foam cried.

"—mine the beach for my food. I would pick an area and dig through it, brushing the sand off anything I found."

"They are a clever people," Seven said.

"But it gave me an idea. If Foam could take us in, I think there is a way we can use that store of clams I set out to rot this afternoon."

Foam whistled. "Of course! You're going to plant them there, to be mined tomorrow!"

Seven laughed. "Ingenious. But won't it be obvious? No, no, of course not."

"The tide's coming up," Shale finished. "Our footprints and our holes will be covered by morning. But when the tide ebbs tomorrow afternoon, and they go digging through the next section of beach, they should find a beautiful selection of red ribbons and bad bluebacks. The bluebacks shouldn't be gamy enough to be obvious, not after only one day, but they'll be spoiled, no doubt about it." She shivered. "Brr! Back in the water again! But this time I want Seven to come with me."

"Why him? I can plant clams as well as anyone, I think."

Shale patted Foam on the arm. "No offense. I'm not taking Seven along to dig holes. But the shells may rattle, or I might make a noise digging. If a sentry comes down to investigate, it seems wise to have Seven there to . . . be there."

"Fine," Foam growled. "Makes sense. Hey ho, Foam to the rescue."

Foam sailed as close in as he dared. Then Seven and Shale undressed, took the bag of clams, and slipped overboard, leaving him behind.

The boat rocked and the rain fell. Alone in the darkness Foam discovered a small bitter anger like a splinter in his heart. He had let himself be left behind again.

He was angry at himself, not Seven or Shale. He only got what he deserved. He worried his hurt, poking and prodding it like a scab, taking satisfaction from the pain. He had earned it—feckless Foam, Sharp's worthless son.

A gust of wind made the sails cough and he hauled the sheet tight. By the time the sails fell silent he had learned one other thing: the pain was not new. He had been living with it every idle day and every long night for many, many years. He had just, somehow, never noticed it before.

Stone always said, "Use your waist to pull nets, not your arms!" And Foam, like every other young man, had repeated it back to him a hundred times. And then one day he suddenly realized he only had to *use his waist* to pull.

So it was with this anger. He had been down before, and complained before, and felt bitter before. How many times had his own uselessness clouded his heart? How many times had he seen the slight in a young woman's eyes, or noticed that older men never came to him for help? How many times had he pointed out that the village built a ship for Rope, but not for him. "Just to make me mate!" he had cried, joking. "You were an afterthought, skipper." But the joke was on him and he knew it. You can only play the fool so long, Foam thought, before the fool is all that's left.

But only now, only tonight, drenched and shivering in the darkness off Thumbtip, had he seen that his self-disgust was a deadly wound, one that had maimed him for all his adult life.

By the time Shale and Seven returned, he was thoughtful and unusually quiet.

"You all right?" Shale asked, hurrying to pull on her tunic as Seven clambered into the boat.

"Mm-hmm."

"Got it done," she said brightly.

Foam said, "Good." He peeled slowly away from Thumbtip.

He knew she was worried by his silence, but he was too full inside to speak. Or too empty. The way his pain had stayed hidden while in full sight for so many years—that was a deep and subtle truth. The wonder of it rose in him. To think he could see no farther into himself than he saw into the dark, rain-filled night beyond their gunwales. "We are like little boats," he said at last.

Shale tried to find his eyes, but the night was dark. "What?"

"Little boats, bobbing along," Foam said. "Waving at one another and telling lies about all the marvelous places we have been. But the thing, the one thing we never do, is step out of our little boats, and dive down into the big black sea."

"To do that is to drown," Seven said softly.

Foam shrugged, and though he could not see the sails, he felt them fill as the sheet tugged against his fingertips. "Maybe. But at least you would have seen a little below the surface."

The next night the rain still fell, making a damp and miserable watch for the two woodlanders manning the fire-sling that guarded Thumbtip's southern shore. "I'm hungrier than Sere," Branch said moodily. "I should have had some of that soup, I suppose, but I'm so stinking tired of fish. If it was ever wet in its life, I don't want to eat it."

"I agree," Nut whispered.

Branch peered at his friend. "You're not yourself. You look white as a cloud, even by torchlight."

"That stew did not agree with me."

"Queasy?"

Nut nodded, wincing. "Cramps—in my gut. The rain. Cold. And the shot stinks."

"You could at least go upwind. Here, crawl around the other side of the sling."

Nut nodded again. "All right," he muttered. "Anything to keep—" A rush of bile soured his mouth. "Too late. I'm going down."

"I told you I thought I heard something down there. Might be a bear."

"On an island? Anyway," Nut said grimly, "if it's a bear, I'll throw up on it just the same."

"Better it than me, I guess. Sorry."

Nut swallowed hard and picked his way down the path, disappearing as soon as he stepped out of the torchlight.

The night was dark. Clouds throttled the moon. Branch could hear the murmur of the brooding sea below. Nut retched somewhere down the path. Branch started, suddenly glad he had skipped the stew. They were sending some rafts back to Delta tomorrow, Ash Spear had said. To report, get new supplies, and bring an extra sling, so they could leave these two permanently in place and have two more for the jump to Mona. He decided to volunteer for the trip back and rejoin the garrison on Delta.

Rain hissed and pattered against the tarp. Fear crackled across his chest as he heard Nut moan. Branch felt for his sword and checked his shot, each ball of pitch still wrapped in its covering of leaves, stinking of resin and gums, all kept dry under the tarp.

Wet leaves rustled in the darkness. "Nut? You there?" There was no answer.

"Damn fish," he muttered. He drew his sprayer; it trembled in time with his pulse as he crept down the muddy path. He stopped as he left the torchlight, waiting for his eyes to adjust, listening into the darkness.

Nut lay face-first on the path. "Are you all right?" Tension cramped Branch's chest. There was something wrong in the woods. Something else was out here with him. The cold rain was falling on something alien and full of hate for woodlanders. Was that the smell of blood, mixed with the rising stink of vomit? He laughed shakily. "Ah, stop faking you old fraud." He tried to grin and took a step backwards. He slipped and tried again. "You'll come up when you're good and ready," he called. Another step closer to the torches. And another.

A shadow leapt from a tremble of leaves and Branch threw himself up the hill. He yelled as a chunk of pain buried itself high in the back of his right thigh. The leg gave way and he slid back down the muddy slope. He could hear them breaking cover now. He clawed desperately, trying to drag himself up the path. "Murder!" he screamed.

An iron hand caught the point of his chin. Another gripped the back of his head. "Mur—"

Shale crept out of her hiding place to join Seven, standing above the limp corpse. She shivered violently, trying to forget the horrible crunching sound of the guard's neck snapping. "Come on," Seven said. "We have to get to the sling before they come to investigate."

She followed him up the hill. "This must be it." The stench of pitch and resin made her sick.

"Mm. A sliding cup. That must hold the shot," Seven muttered. "This winch here tightens it . . ."

"Come on, come on! Break it and go!"

"I want to turn it on the fort."

Stupidly Shale stared at the complicated machinery of grooved wood and wires, pulleys and escapements. Faint shouts echoed from farther in.

Seven's years in his father's workshop seemed to make the sling's operation less of a mystery to him. "Simple enough. Grab that end. No, not by the barrel. Get it at the base. Help me turn it around. Move!"

Grunting, they swung the heavy machine about. It was almost as high as Shale, fashioned from waxed ironwood that shook off the rain.

Seven scooped up a ball of shot and put it into the metal cup. "Stay back." He grabbed a torch and held it to the tarry ball. Dull flame gleamed over the surface, and vile purple smoke oozed from between glossy leaves. "Spit. Should have taken the leaves off." Seven twitched them away with his knife, and the flame blazed up. He pulled back on the latch. The cup rocketed forward, sending a gout of fire through the woods to land far short of the fort.

"Got the inclination wrong," Seven muttered. "Of course! They'd be shooting down. There must be a . . ."

The voices were suddenly clearer as a detachment of men came through the barracks' gates. Bits of burning tar ate into damp trees.

"No time for it," Seven muttered. He winched the cup furiously back into place. "Do what I did!"

Shale grabbed another ball of tar, stripped off its leaves, and dropped it in the cup. Seven handed her the torch and squatted at the front of the sling. Muscles bulging, he lifted the front end so that the barrel pointed over the tree line. Shale touched torch to pitch and then released the latch. The cup shot forward with a ringing twang, sending a bolt of fire arching high into the air.

They got off three more shots before the first line of soldiers came down the path toward them. Seven shoved the sling so its barrel pointed directly at them, and a bolt of streaming fire splashed over the front rank. Men threw themselves to the ground, screaming and beating at their flaming limbs.

"No fighting!" Shale yelled. She ran her torch over the rest of the shot. The balls of pitch roared up in a billow of foul smoke, lurid in the hissing rain.

Shale ran for the path to the beach. She tripped over the first dead guard and fell heavily. She scrambled to her feet, jumping the second corpse. Then down, racing over the stones, hopping as a sharp shell cut her foot, on to the sand with Seven's feet drumming behind her. Into the water, stroking out from land. She couldn't see their boat, but Foam would hear her splashing. There was no point in concealment now. Once they were fairly in the water, the forest people could never catch them.

She gasped in triumph, buoyed up by the cradling sea. She was its child; it would keep her safe.

The woodlanders had reached the shore. She turned and paddled lazily, hearing Seven stroke up to her. Gasping voices called weakly to one another on the beach. "Hit and run," she said. "And there's nothing they can do about it."

Foam sailed up and pulled them from the water. From the boat they could see fire-weirds dancing up from the barracks. "You got something!" Foam crowed. "When I saw the first stream of fire, I thought we were doomed. Then I realized it was going inland."

Seven nodded. "Light the lamps. Let the rest of the boats come up. We land at dawn."

"Two thirds of the men are sick. Seven are already dead."

Elm Plank nodded carefully, trying to ignore the first twinges of nausea. He hadn't eaten much soup. He might be lucky. "And Ash Spear?"

Plum Shoot shook his head. "He ate nothing but soup, and a lot of it. Trying to lead by example . . ."

"I see." Plank sighed. The barracks reeked of vomit and smoke. The air was thick with the groans of the sick and the burned. "Fire?"

"Controlled, sir. Mostly out. We lost two men when a roof collapsed. Three more incapacitated, chasing the assassins. And of course the guards on number two sling."

"And of course the guards." A spasm of agony twisted in Plank's gut. He badly wanted to lie down. "With Ash Spear dead, I am in charge. Obviously there is an attack planned. I judge us to be too weak to defend. I intend to take the rafts down and sail for Delta. Any objections?"

Someone heaved wretchedly and continuously behind them, coughing up food, bile, blood. "No, sir," Shoot said gravely.

Through the rest of the night the islanders watched the forest people take down their wall and cart their rafts to the long, sandy beach where they had mined for clams. The work was slow, for few soldiers were well enough to carry the heavy rafts. Last of all they moved the fire-sling from the beach down to their flotilla, and sailed away from Thumbtip.

Bleak grey light broke over the world.

It was a curious stand-off, as the rafts floated clumsily toward home. Seven held his people well out of fire-sling range. The islanders jeered their enemies for all the long time that dawn gave way to sunrise, and to morning.

Sitting in their boats, the victors had laughed and joked about Thumbtip's glorious recapture. Up close, the reality was far grimmer. A quarter of the barracks had burned down. The burned bodies of several forest soldiers lay trapped under smoldering beams.

"Just be glad we have a roof over our heads," Foam said, squinting to the east. "There's a squall coming."

Shale nodded. "It will catch those poor bastards before they get to Delta."

Seven looked over. "Fathom and the Warrior look after their own."

"Not so much work," Pond sighed, studying the sagging roof. "Brace can fix it."

"First we take care of these," Shale said, white-faced. She knelt by one of the corpses. Vomit had pooled beside his head.

"Don't look at it!" Foam said, laying a hand on Shale's shoulder. "Spit. It's bad enough without . . . dwelling."

"Don't touch me!" Shale jumped up and slapped his hand away. "Do you think you can just ignore this? Look! *Look at it!*" She jerked him toward the dead soldier on the floor. "See the blood in his vomit, Foam? See the place where the skin on his arm burned away and the meat's gone black? *We owe it to them to look.* That was us, Foam. We did that. You and I and Seven the Mighty Hero of Legend."

Seven stirred, and his face was hard. "Never fight if you don't fight to win."

Shale took a deep breath, feeling sick with anger. "Then I choose not to fight."

"Too late," Pond said, looking at the ground before Shale's feet. "What is done is done. Now we take responsibility for it, and go on."

Shale shook her head. "My mother is a Witness like you will never be. All you want is fine Deltan words to feel good by." She slammed out of the room, heading outside, into the gathering wind. "I'll take care of the bodies," she yelled.

Wind and rain moaned into the silence she left behind. At last Seven looked over at Foam. "I am sorry that you learned to kill."

Foam looked around the stinking barracks. "So am I," he said.

It didn't take him long to find Shale. She had a damaged raft the woodlanders had left behind and was trying to unhook it from the wall. They worked it free and dragged it down to the beach.

They used a sail to carry out the dead soldiers, then piled them on the raft and set the sail for open water. The funeral barge lurched away in the freshening wind, listing heavily. It would be lucky to leave eyesight without foundering.

Shale stood watching it with tears in her eyes.

"You did the best you could," Foam said.

She swallowed and nodded. After a while she said, "The sea will decide."

And later, "Sorry."

Foam nodded. They stood together as billows of rain swept over the grey ocean.

There was good fresh fish for dinner in a part of the barracks the fire had not touched. The islanders told more jokes and stories than they had for many nights, for they still lived, and the invaders had been driven back without the loss of a single man. In one corner a group of four friends played Islands with a ship's set. Other troops asked repeatedly for the tale of Shale's visit (dwelling on her nudity) and Seven's feats with the fire-sling (dwelling on his).

A slender woman with a braid wound through with wire of gold stood up after dinner and said, "Who would like to hear the story of Seven and his Band of Merry Islanders!" The crowd roared. Seven frowned. "Be a leader," Pond whispered, and he swallowed his embarrassment.

"Let's hear all about it," Catch yelled. "Do the rest of us get to go naked in the next part?"

"Listen and find out," the singer said.

Shale couldn't quite identify the storyteller. She reminded her a little bit of Brook, and a little bit of Jo, and a little bit of someone else she couldn't remember. "I can't think of her name," she admitted under her breath.

"Me neither," Foam whispered. "We'll ask after the story."

"Very well, then!" the singer cried. "Hear my words, for this is a story of the Mist-time (more or less), where everything is true, and nothing is what it seems.

"Now this is a One-Twist Ring story." From around her waist the singer took a belt of midnight silk, studded with clear stones. Twisting it once, she placed the ends together so they made a loop. "The thing about a one twist ring is that it seems to have two sides, but really it has only one. We are just at the twist, where the great stories turn to reveal the small ones beneath. As this story is yet only half over, I can only tell you the first part, one full circuit of the loop. Great stories give way to small ones; what happens here will end at home. This is the Tale of Seven. Listen well."

Outside-Inside

And then, to their surprise, the singer began to speak of Hazel Twist. His youth, his wit, his strategy, his courage. She spoke of his rise in the Empire, and his fair wife, Willow Blue. She spoke of the Fire that had come sweeping in from the edge of the forest, laying waste to the fair lands of Palm and Date.

Startled, the audience fell silent, glancing uncomfortably at one another. They strained to get a better look a better look at the storyteller, but she was far from the torches. Outside, the storm screamed and spat. Water dripped steadily through the leaking roof into the fire, and clouds of steam, smelling of smoke and blood, eddied through the kitchen and dining hall. Shale opened her mouth to whisper to Foam, to ask if he understood why the tale that was supposed to be of Seven was all of Hazel Twist. But however hard she tried to speak, Shale's words miscarried, dying stillborn on her tongue. She gazed at the singer—the *Singer!*— and her eyes widened in shock.

The Singer's eyes gleamed like embers and her voice was thin and desolate as the winter wind. "For the war-torches burn on both sides of the one-sided world. And every story has two sides, that are one. In every pair of twins, one must go into the Mist."

The Singer was wreathed in coils of mist, silver-sheened, electric. Her form began to ripple and flow. This story too will end at home. But the loop that ends by the hearthside will be deeper and more strange than the loop that brought you here." And it seemed to everyone in the hall as if she were somehow vanishing into her own words, into her own voice, until it was only the keening wind outside that whispered,

Great stories turn to small ones;
Bright fires fall to ash . . .

Jo's Line

CHAPTER 15: THE ARBOR

The morning after Ash had burned to death Brook and Rope lit their morning fire in a different place. Ivy wisely stayed away, foraging.

Brook was trying not to see Ash burning in her mind's eye, wondering if Shale were still alive. Jo was finishing off the remains of a rabbit.

"What now?" Rope said, jabbing the fire with a blackened branch.

"The same as always," Brook said. "We have a chore to do."

"We? We have a chore to do? What can we do, Brook? It's up to our haunt, isn't it?"

Jo licked her fingers and pointed daintily at Rope with the rabbit's thigh bone. "You do your part, Rope. I will do mine."

"You despise us, don't you? Well, I would like to hear what you have planned, Jo. I did my part dealing with the herbalist. I took him to his people. I made sure his wife was healed. But I never saw you cast your line. I never saw anything in your hold. You stood by and watched Ash burn while I tried to save him."

Jo's fingers tightened around the dead rabbit's thigh. "I don't like it when people are rude to me," she said softly. Her skin broke out in a sizzling blue sweat. The bone in her hand blackened. Melting marrow ran from its end. She flexed her fingers, and claws exploded from their soft flesh.

Rope swallowed. Brook cringed beside him.

Jo had lost all trace of humanity. Her hair was snakes of writhing silver, her talons scored the earth. Vast white wings unfurled from her shoulders and beat the air, driving up a cloud of ash and cinders. "I think you have forgotten what I am," she said. "I am not like the herbalist, Rope. I am not some guilt-addled human pretending inhumanity." She lifted her taloned hand. It was good to feel the wind in her blood. "You need not worry that I will fail in my part. Does the Emperor bleed? Then I will cut him. Does he drink? His cup can be poisoned. Does he sleep? Then I will breathe madness into his dreams. I am not of your kind, Rope. I really am a monster."

She gazed then at the islanders as they cowered before her. She saw them fumble for each other's hands, and she felt Brook's fear. Her twin was afraid. Afraid of her.

Jo's anger dwindled like a fire caught in a cold rain. She had ridden too much of the wind, played too often with the moon. She didn't want to be a haunt anymore.

"It is our story," Brook said quietly. "Yours and mine. Yours is the great part, Jo. The hero's part. And maybe I am only your shadow. But I think we are a sheet bend, you and I, big rope and little. That is a knot not easily untied."

"A sheet bend. But which is which?" Jo said. You are so much in me I almost cannot hear myself. Who leads and who follows?"

Brook hugged Jo's shoulder, feeling big enough to fill the hollowness inside the haunt's heart. "Perhaps it depends on the phase of the moon."

Jo looked almost normal again.

Rope grunted. "It's just—that whole thing with Ash. . . . And I believe in Chart, you know? Rope, biscuits, pepper. I like to be prepared."

"Do you think I do not hear the call of the flame? I am too close now to escape."

"What about Ivy?" Rope asked. "Won't the forest people notice how different she is?"

Jo shifted into the form of a woodlander, shorter than Brook and stocky, with curly brown hair and pale cheeks. "As for Ivy, she becomes more human every day she travels with you. You two really are very human, you know, and humanity is catching. Put a good set of clothes on her and wait. Before we reach the Arbor you will swear she was a Shrub or a Willow."

Brook said, "I have plans for Ivy."

Jo studied Rope. "Actually, you are more of a problem."

"Me?"

"Both of you. Too tall! And your faces: too weathered by wind and sun. To the woodlanders you will look older than you are."

"Old and ugly," Brook said.

"I didn't mean . . ." Jo looked at her helplessly. At last she inched around the fire. She reached out to touch Brook's hair, and now, absurdly, she was the scared one. She fought to smile as Brook flinched under her touch. "We will have to prune you."

"No."

Jo ignored Brook, unravelling her braid with nimble fingers. "They don't wear these here. We will have to tuck this into your clothing, and cut it short as soon as we can find a sharp knife." Brook's tense shoulders slowly relaxed, and Jo sighed with relief. Rope grinned and began picking at his knotted hair. Suddenly Jo felt like laughing. "Friends again?"

He nodded. "Always."

"And it has taken so long to grow back," Brook said in a plaintive voice.

Swiftly Jo undid the last knot that made Brook an islander. "Some day I will make you another," she said, gently combing Brook's hair with her fingers. "I promise."

When the haunt was done she said, "The Witness Knot as well."

"What?"

"Anyone could see that's not a woodlander bracelet. The Witness Knot must go."

"I will keep it hidden under my sleeve."

Rope cleared his throat. "It really does look odd. Good, of course. It looks good on you. But—"

"No."

Rope knew better than to pursue it.

Brook felt the knot like an anchor around her wrist, tying her to Clouds End. She stared with renewed suspicion at Jo. At her twin.

Twelve days later they spent their last night in the forest before reaching the Arbor. This close to the capital, sleeping on the ground was next to vagrancy, so they were forced to bed down in a tree, lying on planks wedged amongst the branches of a big sleeping oak.

Jo was out foraging. Brook settled herself in the corner of their platform. "The end of the road," she murmured.

"Spit!" Rope growled, peering around their tiny perch. "What if I fall and break my neck?"

"There's a railing. It's no worse than sleeping on a ship's deck."

"If the Pine country is run by the Pines," Rope said, "and the Cedar lands are held by the Cedars, who controls the Arbor?"

"The Bronze," Ivy said. "Bronzewoods are the greatest of trees. Their bark is gleaming gold and their leaves are scarlet-green. You will see them tomorrow."

Brook glanced at Ivy. "You must be looking forward to the Arbor. You will finally be able to cross."

Ivy shrugged. "I am in no haste. Crossing was Ash's quest. I am free of my roots and I mean to enjoy it."

"Tomorrow," Rope said. Suddenly his feet had never felt so sore. "Ugh! Almost there! It hurts to remember all that wilderness."

"In that case," Brook said wryly, "I advise you not to think about the trip back."

Dangling from the limbs around them, vegetable planters sprouted yellow-flowered squashes or okra or great purple cabbages. A light wind had come up at dusk, and the boughs beneath their platform swayed and creaked. A branch shivered as Ivy crept off to steal their breakfast.

"I don't like Ivy and Jo being gone at the same time," Rope said. "What do you suppose our haunt is up to?"

"I think our haunt is up to many things. Listen. Here we are, about to enter the Arbor. What is our job, if we want to save the islands?"

Rope frowned. "To keep Jo human, I guess. Isn't it?"

"I know, I know. I feel that all the time, like a weight." Evening was falling, and gloom pooled around the oaks. "But I have been wondering, Is that really our desire, or is it simply what Jo wants?"

"Hunh?"

"Think about it. From the first day she landed on Clouds End she has insisted that people go with her, stay with her, be with her, so she can be human. Is it because she wants to get to the Arbor, or because she longs to be human again?"

Slowly Rope nodded. "Or is it because she twinned you? She twinned you, and she . . . asked me for help on Shale's island." He colored, suddenly feeling Net like a web of pins and needles curled around his left wrist.

Brook felt her heart catch. What had happened there, between her lover and her twin? If he wouldn't tell her, she couldn't ask.

The haunt, the haunt was playing with them. Twisting them. "Why did I stop fighting Jo when I met her on Clouds End? Why did I make us rescue her from Sere on Shale's island?"

Around them the oaks and elms talked quietly together at the end of the day. Rope frowned. "You think this urge to keep Jo human comes from her?"

Brook shrugged. "I feel it as my own desire, but how can I know? Ivy said that she and Ash were called. She said Jo risked letting me be bound to the forest to draw them to us. Why would Jo do that? To get to the Arbor faster, I suppose. But perhaps there was another reason. With two wood spirits around, we worked even harder to make Jo one of us."

Rope laughed softly. "Like the time Foam got Shale to sneak up and scare us in the dark so you would let me hold you."

Brook looked up in surprise. "That was a plan? One of Foam's plans?"

Rope gulped. "Didn't I ever—? Ah. Um."

"Is anything I do ever my own idea?"

Rope changed the subject. "Remember, you can't believe

everything Ivy says. I wouldn't trust her farther than I could throw her."

"Mm," Brook said. Remembering Ivy's warning about Rope and Jo.

"You said you had a plan for Ivy. Now, whenever I turn around you are fixing her hair, or lending her clothes, or holding her hand. What is all that about?"

"I'm twinning her."

Rope blinked.

"You saw what she did to Ash. She leached the life out of him. That is her nature. With Ash gone, she is looking for another victim to suck dry. We needed her to guide us and find our food, so I dared not send her away. Instead, I offered myself as the victim. But I am tying her into a sheet bend. Surrounded by humans, walking out of the wildwood and into peopled lands, Ivy loses more and more of herself, and becomes less and less able to work her magic on us."

Leaves whispered overhead, veiling and revealing the stars. "I don't know," Rope said. "I would be afraid to mess about with magic."

Brook shrugged. She remembered Ivy's cool touch on her wrist, grinning as she talked of Ash's decline. In a voice so cold it startled Rope, she said, "I am not too proud to drink the rain."

The Arbor was a living city, carved into the flesh of vast bronze-wood trees. For hundreds of years they had grown, twining into each other, tended by squads of topiaries and legions of gardeners. Now they formed one great living mountain, pierced by slanting shafts of light, twisted into a gigantic maze of tunnels and ramps and archways. Overhead a red cloud hung, dust scuffed from the drought-stricken earth by countless feet treading the cracking paths around the capital.

Disguised as poor bumpkins from the Pine province, the islanders came at last into the Arbor, and wandered up through its labyrinth of branches. This is what it was for the children of the sea to step into the forest's beating heart: a wall of shifting copper, a sea of scarlet-green leaves, a throb and buzz, a heat; people like jewelled insects crawling through a jungle of their own making.

Except for the ground level, the city was a gloomy honeycomb of narrow passages with ceilings so low Rope had to walk permanently stooped. Occasionally they would turn a sudden corner and be dazzled by a shaft of sunlight falling through a light-well marked by a waist-high wall of shrubbery. These shafts of light angled through to the ground; far below, citizens of the Arbor with lacquered hair and enamelled jewelry passed gleaming through the light and then disappeared into the gloom beyond.

Branch after branch, tier after tier, and on each one, more people stopping or staring or talking or selling or simply bustling on. "All these people!" Brook said. "You can feel them behind the walls and under our feet. There could be anything; there could be murder on the other side of this wall, but we would never know." She fingered one of the glossy scarlet bronzewood leaves. "We could never understand."

"Come," Jo called. "I want to savor what the city has to offer. We draw ever closer to the Emperor, and tonight I must flutter to his flame!"

Anticipation burned in Jo like a fever, making her fey and giddy. Rope and Brook stuck together and said little, overawed by the vast, humming hive at the center of the forest. Ivy scampered everywhere, gawking at trinkets and exclaiming over the woodlanders' lacquered helmets and stylish clothes.

In a large clearing lit with many light-wells they mingled with the crowds. Ivy dashed over to peer greedily at a jeweller's table. Stomach growling, Rope loitered in front of the next stall, which sold cherries and blueberries, lettuce and yams, okra and green onions and carrots by the bundle. Not far from Brook a group of puppeteers lounged in front of a shop selling mulled drinks, talking to one another in tense, hushed voices, each carrying a leather puppet bag. One of them was tying up curtains of black cloth to make a hidden area in which they could prepare for their performance.

Jo turned her head. "Hear that?"

"Bells," Brook said. "Little bells, coming closer."

The jingling sound approached steadily from a side corridor from which people began to spill like flotsam pushed ahead of a wave. Finally a litter hove into view, carried on the backs of eight servants and garlanded with tiny brass cymbals that chinged and chimed at every step. The litter's open curtains and canopy were of gold silk, and its poles were scarlet. Behind it came a retinue of expensively coiffed men with purses and counting beads and parchments. Lastly came four swordsmen with shields and arm-plates. The servants all wore pants and shirts of golden silk with a scarlet slash cutting across the chest.

It was clear at once that they served no ordinary man. He did not recline in his litter, but sat cross-legged and straight-backed, glancing over the crowd with sharp, golden eyes. His face was lean. Everything about him suggested fierce drive and energy barely held in check.

"A Bronze," Jo whispered.

One of the puppeteers stepped before the litter and bowed until the back of his hand touched the ground. "Most worthy! Will you suffer to be entertained?"

"There is a performance you wish me to observe?" The Bronze examined the puppeteers impassively, but quick glances flew between the members of his retinue. Those carrying the litter shifted in place.

The puppeteer glanced up. "Not if you feel our little play would cause you discomfort."

The Bronze ignored another flutter from his retinue. "Of course not. Pray, proceed."

"How justly does the Arbor ring with the praise of your generosity!"

A little breeze of whispers gusted around the clearing.

As the puppeteers prepared, setting up their candles and their paper screens, Rope rejoined Brook and Jo. They could all feel tension building in the crowd. The marketplace babble had died away; conversations went on in whispers, and the speakers looked not at one another but at the clear space before the litter where the performance was to be.

The puppeteers had finished hanging black cloths in front of the drink shop so they could crouch behind them and perform without the sacred puppets being exposed to the eyes of the curious. They had chosen an area far from the nearest light-wells; when they lit their candles the paper screens were white panels glowing in the murk.

At last all was in readiness. "Behold!" one cried, and a shadow jumped upon the panel. At first the islanders took it for a stylized tree. Slowly the trunk split and the limbs dropped until the shadow took the shape of a man. From behind the black cloth a chiming stel intoned, deep, stately, ringing notes. "The father," a voice chanted. "When the wind blows, he lends his strength to stand against it. When the sun burns, he gifts his family with shade."

A second shadow jumped to the screen, much smaller this time and less certain in form, shifting and moving like a wind-blown bush. There was a sharp hiss of indrawn breath from the crowd around the islanders.

"The son." A snapping hand-drum skittered around the stel's steady rhythm. "Most precious and beloved of the father, he is yet young. He has the virtues of youth: passion and courage and high ideals. It is true he has not yet reached his mature growth and may still be swayed by the wind, but left alone he will grow into his greatness."

The retinue of gold-clad servants murmured angrily among themselves. One strode up to the palanquin and whispered urgently in his master's ear. For a moment the Bronze said nothing, examining the crowd. Woodlander eyes fled him like doves scattering at the hawk's approach. He dismissed his servant with a tiny shake of his head and let his gaze return to the puppet show.

A tambra now joined the hand-drum and the stel, playing a sweet melody that held a darkness in it, like the wind playing through the ashes of a cold fire. Bodies shifted in the crowd, rocking forward with excitement, as the shadow of a wolf padded onto the screen.

The hand-drum swirled and the tambra played as the son began to dance, ever so slowly, toward the wolf waiting on the panel's edge. The son's features blurred and shook; he staggered forward and then threw himself back under the father's arms, only to creep forth again, and always the tambra played its sweet, dark song.

The son's shadow became more wild, pulled in both directions, flying back and forth, swelling suddenly or shrinking to the size of a beetle. Suddenly the hand-drum surged and the panels rocked as the son leapt across the screen to crouch at the wolf's feet. But somehow, in the process, a fire had caught—perhaps a candle had fallen over—and a lick of flame began to creep up the paper screen where the son now stood, swollen so large that his outline had become badly blurred.

A gasp of shock went round the clearing. Even the Bronze started, thin lips tightening.

"Alas!" the puppeteer cried. "The son has caught a spark! He burns and the wolf burns with him! Alas! What can be done?"

Rope glanced around, waiting for someone to move. To his amazement nobody did. The line of flame was now licking hungrily up the side of the paper screen, searing the son and the wolf as well. Everywhere he looked, woodlanders stood as if paralyzed.

"Aren't these a useful lot?" he muttered to Brook. Striding into the cleared area, he lifted his waterskin and squirted the contents over the burning screen, soaking it down with the same methodical patience he would have used to wet a smoldering sail.

The tambra and hand-drum and stel faltered and fell silent.

The crowd watched in shocked silence. Rope began to blush, desperately wishing he wasn't the center of attention. He suddenly realized just how big he was, surrounded by this crowd of staring woodlanders, most of whom didn't come up past his shoulders.

The black cloth rustled and the head puppeteer crawled out from beneath it. He walked around to the front area and stared at his dripping screen like a man in a daze. Then he looked at the bearded stranger who towered over him. "You poured water on my screen!"

"Well, it was burning, wasn't it?"

The puppeteer gazed at him, dumbfounded.

Somewhere in the crowd someone giggled. A second person snickered across the clearing. Then a real chuckle broke out, and then another, and soon the whole crowd was helpless with laughter. They laughed until their faces turned red and they could not speak; they laughed until they wept. Secretaries in gold livery smirked and covered their faces with their hands. The litter shook on the shoulders of its porters. And above it all, even the Bronze's thin lips twitched, and his golden eyes gleamed.

Rope shuffled back into the crowd, miserably aware that he was far too huge to escape attention. "Let's get out of here."

Jo cackled.

Biting her lip to keep a straight face, Brook nodded, and they hurried for the nearest pathway out. Ivy trailed behind them, casting a last mournful glance at a table swathed in garish scarves.

Just when they thought they had left the whole incident behind, a trim young fellow caught up with them, breathing hard, and tapped Rope on the back. "Sir!" he cried.

"Spit," Rope groaned. The messenger was dressed in a livery of gold silk, with a scarlet slash across his chest.

The young man bowed deeply and then held out a leather pouch that bulged and clinked as if stuffed with seashells. "If it please you, my master sends this as a token of his gratitude, and bids me say that should you ever want for employment, you have only to present yourself to him at his home."

"Uh, oh, I don't think that—oof!"

Rope glared at Jo, who had thrown a wicked elbow into his side. "I mean, thanks," he said, taking the bag as if grasping a snake. "Oh, by the way, who is your master?"

Instead of answering, the young man blinked, barked with laughter, cast Rope an admiring glance, and trotted back the way he had come, shaking his head and chuckling all the way.

"You know, Rope, about trying not to be too obvious—" Brook began.

"Oh, shut up."

"Now, listen carefully," Jo said, hefting the leather pouch. She drew out a small disc of ironwood, elaborately etched with a metallic bronze dye. "This is money. You can trade it for food, clothing, or whatever else you want."

"Why?" Rope asked.

Jo shrugged. "It is the custom here. It is difficult to carry a deer from the forest to the market. So the hunter takes a token which represents the deer, and trades that instead."

"Who would be so stupid as to take the token?" Rope persisted. "You can't eat wood."

"Clearly. But you can trade it to the fruit vendor, in exchange for apples."

Rope snorted and shook his head. "This will only work as long as you can find people foolish enough to accept these tokens. What good are they, if you are out in the forest?"

"No good at all," Jo conceded, "but near the cities they are very useful indeed, for everyone has agreed, under the edict of the Emperor, to be fools together."

Brook said, "You mean you have no choice but to trade your real things for tokens?"

"Precisely."

They had entered another clearing. All around them shopkeepers extolled their goods: roasted nuts, dyed fabric, musical instruments, pipes and things to smoke in them. On their left an engraver displayed a selection of prints; to their right, two customers sat patiently in a beauty salon.

"I suppose it could work," Rope said, still pondering the woodlanders' odd trading system, "if everyone agreed to it at once. But it must change people, to deal with tokens instead of things."

Ivy studied the coins intently, rubbing them between her palms as if trying to warm her hands.

"Of course," Jo said. "There are men, and rich men too, who spend all their days collecting tokens—and won't buy things because it would mean giving the tokens up."

Rope laughed in amazement. "Money must be one of the Singer's inventions."

"Oh?"

" 'Things are truest, but nothing is what it appears to be,' " Rope said. "So a token becomes the essence of a deer, although it looks like a disc of hard, heavy wood. The Singer's power is to make her stories come true. I can think of no better example of her style than convincing everyone first to be fools together, and then creating men who gain power and wealth because they are greater fools than their fellows. Foam would love it here!"

"And Shale would hate it!" Brook added.

Shaking his head, Rope wandered over to inspect the engraver's table. A tall man with the distinctively overbred Cedar air about him, the engraver explained that he etched woodblock portraits of passers-by with strong acids, then sold them along with ink and printing instructions. To the side of his table were other etchings: trees, animals, children, and a framed poem:

Bronze-leaf   People-making multitudes   Clan-tight
        fire-warding   spirit-nurturing
                Fathering
                Empire
        in   the   reaching   into   a   deep
    Rooted   Arbor,   blue
                                              sky.

"Good work," Rope said.

The printmaker spread hands stained purple, black, and crimson. "Rarely are people satisfied, for I must use unfashionably strong lines," he complained, "and these are querulous times. Furthermore, the acid stinks, and the inks I require are from southern provinces now threatened by the Fire. I am seeking a new profession. Tell me, what do you do?"

"Sail, mostly. Fish some."

The printer eyed him askance. "Strange occupations! You must be one of the bargemen of Willow. It is said they prefer sleeping on the water to sleeping in trees! I am curious to know if this is true."

Rope gulped at his own stupidity. "Oh, the two are not really so different," he said quickly. "In one you are rocked by the water, and in the other you are swayed by the wind."

The printer nodded; acid had left white spatters on his sunken cheeks. "Aptly put! . . . How unfortunate that the tedious demands of sustenance force me to break off our conversation and attend to these uninteresting yet wealthy persons approaching my stall," he lamented, turning to face a gaggle of prospective customers with a smile.

Ivy stood dazzled before a clothier's rack. So many materials, so many colors! Crimson, topaz, lavender, marigold, sable: a drunkard's rainbow. Smiling, Brook joined her, exclaiming over the selection. Before she left, she pressed an ironwood coin into Ivy's hand. "You did well to get us here," she said warmly. "You deserve this."

Ivy's eyes lit up. She snatched up a pair of pink gloves and twisted a red-gold scarf around her neck. "Anything but greens and browns!" Soon she was decked in bright cloths, and her neck and wrists clattered with chunky woodland jewelry.

"The Arbor is nothing like Delta," Rope complained. "Too dark, too twisty, too cramped!" He halted at the door of a smoke shop and peered inside; pipes hung like strange fruit from the leafy walls within. "These people have many odd customs, but none stranger than these—pipes, you called them? You crush a plant, set it on fire, and then suck in the smoke! Toolishness! How dare they light fires in this drought?"

"Why did we land on Shale's island?" Brook replied. "Sometimes you want what isn't good for you."

"And where do we piss?" Rope asked. Several people turned and stared. "I mean, the whole city is so—*tended.*"

Brook found Ivy lingering at the door of a coiffurie. "Shall we go in?"

"Could we?"

Brook took her arm and laughed. "That's what the Arbor is about!"

There were two other customers already inside, a young woman getting her hair lacquered and an older man having a tattoo removed by a careful technician with a syringe of acid. The sour, burning smell reminded Brook of the clouds of blue vapor in Delta.

Her heart raced. She imagined Foam's dapper beard eaten away. Shale's sharp face pitted and burned.

An attendant approached them. Gleaming implements dangled from her belt: a slender wooden spatula, a set of coarse combs and fine brushes, two bulbous syringes, a pair of scissors, and a thin metal hook. "How may we serve you?"

Ivy looked questioningly at Brook.

"I think this lady would like her hair cut," Brook said.

Ivy's hand flew to hold her long hair, tucked into the back of her shirt. "Oh. I really don't think so."

The attendant nodded, considering. "You are right. Why bother cutting? These pretty provincial faces have their own sort of unpolished charm. Who would notice the enhancement?"

Ivy hesitated. "You think it would make a difference?"

The attendant shook her head. "Nothing that would be noticed in the provinces. You could tell, of course, but how many others would notice? Unless you intend to stay in the Arbor, of course."

Ivy studied the next customer's hair, which had been sculpted to a smooth bulb. Topiary, Brook thought.

"In the Arbor we have a way of taming living things," the attendant said, gesturing to one of the chairs. "Shall I show you how it is done?"

Only as the steel bit into Ivy's long hair did her eyes cloud and close. Long brown tresses slithered to the floor. All trace of the magic woodland spirit had gone, all mystery. In her place was a gawking country girl, weighed down under gaudy clothes and cheap jewelry. Above her head were paths made from branches, bound and twisted out of any shape of nature to serve the will of men.

Brook passed Ivy an extra store of money and left her wreathed in schemes and compliments. They promised to meet later, but when Brook caught up with Rope and Jo, she began walking briskly away from the clearing.

"I still need to piss," Rope said. "Where is Ivy?"

"I left her setting her hair," Brook said. "I do not think we will be seeing her again."

"Good riddance."

"Lost," Jo said. "She has strayed too far from her roots now. She will never get back." The haunt eyed Brook suspiciously. "Why did you encourage her? Did you know the Arbor would destroy her?"

"Perhaps we cared more for the islands than she did for the forest." With a voice as clean and pitiless as the sea, Brook said, "I am not too proud to fight for sunshine."

"Clever. Tell me, does it work on haunts too? Have you used me as you did her? Binding me to Clouds End as tightly as Ash would have tied me to his trees?"

"You were the one who called the wood spirits. If anyone had been lost to them, it would have been me."

"You were never in danger! I was waiting to capture them, to find out why they followed us."

"Or to make us take better care of you."

Jo's long nails bit into her palms. "So now, even when I save you it is for my own schemes."

"You are not like Ivy. We really are friends," Rope protested, blushing furiously.

People were staring at them. Brook grabbed Jo's arm and kept walking. "I will not beg forgiveness for trying to save my people." Turning down a narrow sideway, she met Jo's eyes. "Yes, we want you to help us. But that was what you wanted too. We did not mean you ill. If we befriended not the witch but the woman, can you blame us?"

They stood there a long moment, three foreigners in the forest's heart, while crowds of woodlanders hurried by, taking them for country simpletons. "I said once before that you were not simple," Jo said. "You know, Shandy told me I would give you back everything I had taken. She never knew how right she was."

Gently, implacably, Brook said, "I think she did."

"Excuse me?" Rope finally asked a passer-by. "How do you take a piss in this city?"

The stranger stopped with his head tilted to one side and one eyebrow quizzically raised. "Why, the same way you do it in the country, I believe."

They discovered where to relieve their bladders; they dared one another to get tattooed; they ate a succulent meal of wild pig and roasted nuts; they got lost wandering the mazy paths high above ground level and had to ask a smirking local how to get down again.

Then sunset came, and it was time to attempt the Palace.

A panicky kind of dread filled Brook's heart. When she spoke she tried to keep her voice light but inside she felt brittle as twigs burning. It was terribly hot. Her heart was racing and she couldn't get her breath. She did not want Jo to go.

But then, Brook told herself, she doesn't want to go either. But she has to. And you must not make it harder for her.

They walked down many twisting ramps until at last they had fallen to the lowest, darkest level. "Dry earth beneath my feet!" Rope said. "That is a comfort."

"Here is the rest of the money," Jo said abruptly. She closed Brook's hands around the leather pouch of coins.

Words jammed in Brook's throat. The iron resolve she had felt watching Ivy lose herself had utterly deserted her. She blushed; love made her awkward. "I want to say, say that—"

"Not now!" Jo snapped. "Not yet! I promise long goodbyes when the time comes." She strode toward the middle of the city, leaving Brook between tears and murder.

"Well," Rope said, clapping Brook on the back. "It could have been worse. It could have been me making a fool of myself."

"Your turn next time," Brook growled. "Don't let her get too far ahead."

There were no guards before the tunnel that led into the Palace grounds.

"I do not like the look of this at all," Jo said.

"Why would the guards all leave at sunset?"

"Because nobody would dare the grounds after dark," Rope guessed unhappily. "I don't like to think why."

The tunnel through the Inner Wall was dim and ominous, clogged with honeysuckle and lilac. "It's so hot," Brook muttered. She was ashamed to find how glad she was that it was Jo who had to go into that sinister perfumed darkness.

"Come on!" the haunt hissed. Brook's heart stopped. Jo strolled toward the archway. "I smell magic so thick I can hardly breathe. I may have to get to the Palace without shifting." She tapped a long fingernail on the sword at Rope's hip. "In which case, I will need your help."

"I can't use this, you know."

Jo shrugged. "You can keep someone busy for a moment while I run. What is the matter? Losing your nerve?"

Rope grunted. "Never had any."

"I thought the islands mattered to you."

"I didn't say we weren't coming. I just said I wasn't happy about it." He squinted up at the wall. "Trees!" He swore venomously. "All right. Let's go."

Jo waited until the lane was deserted, and then stepped into a blackness that smelled of lilacs. Rope followed, then Brook. Soon Jo and Rope were almost at a standstill: dark blots ahead of Brook, framed in weakly glowing blossoms. Trailing creepers twisted around Brook's neck and limbs. The air was hot and sweet, thick as honey. She tried to run forward but vines clutched at her. Rope's voice seemed faint and far away. She called out for him but his name died in her throat. Creepers crawled through her hair and clung as tight as Ivy's fingers around her wrist, leeching out her core. She was soil shaken from a plucked root.

Then Rope had drawn his sword and slashed away the fronds. Like snowflakes, white blossoms fell to the ground and were extinguished. A hot breeze broke open the cloying scent of honeysuckle. Brook gasped and stumbled from the tunnel. Rope sheathed his sword and held her close.

"I was drowning in flowers. I couldn't breathe." She hugged him convulsively, as if she could take from him what the vines had stolen. "I thought I was going to die."

Rope kissed the top of her head, giving her his strength. Looking over Brook's shoulder, he saw Jo standing in the moonlight, no longer a woman of the forest. Her flesh and hair were white as blossoms. Envy stood naked in her eyes.

"Charming," she said, brushing back her pale hair. It floated like cobwebs in the moonlight. A drowsing bee rose from amongst the strands; another followed, crawling over her shoulder and buzzing back into the honeysuckle. A shell bracelet clicked around her wrist, as it had when they met on Shale's island. Rope had never told Brook that Jo had offered herself to him. He had barely told himself how much he wanted her.

They stood at the edge of the Palace grounds. Behind them the glowing bronzewoods bled emberlight into the purple dusk. The Arbor's inner walls formed a six-sided court. At its heart stood the Palace, a drop of honey gleaming at the center of a comb. Light welled from its shuttered windows like tears through black lashes.

In the darkness between the Palace and the walls, strange shapes loomed, cut from the flesh of living trees. Above them hung a vast tipping egg. To their left, a swan with a serpent's head; to their right, yew had been formed into broken walls and toppled columns. "Living ruins," Jo said. "A strange mind crawls like a spider through this grass. Do you remember what the herbalist said? A certificate from Garden himself. I do not think I wish to meet the Gardener of the Palace grounds." She closed her eyes, and began to shift, flesh contracting, turning, arms folding into wings.

Magic made Brook dizzy, like a drug in her blood, as it had when Jo first landed on Clouds End and stole her form. How wild it was, she thought. How close to madness.

Jo's eyes snapped open and she staggered to the ground. Where her fingers touched, they burrowed into the earth. Her feathers wavered into leaves and her scream became only the hiss of wind in her branches.

Rope leapt forward and wrestled the haunt back into the archway. Her hands tore out of the earth trailing long white rootlets. Dirt dropped from between her toes and fingers. She clung to him in panic, listening for his humanity. Slowly, very slowly, her body lengthened, became softer and more solid, fleshed and covered with skin. She blinked. "Then again, perhaps I will walk," she gasped.

"What happened?"

The haunt shook her head. "There are strong enchantments here." She reached down, gently probing the soles of her feet with her fingers. "Someone, or something, has been working the Palace grounds for a very long time."

Perched on Rope's shoulder, Net swayed back and forth uneasily; ripples washed along his strands. He tingled as he brushed Rope's cheek.

Brook fingered her shell bracelet, needing to touch something shaped by the honest sea. "Then I guess we walk to the Palace together," she said. It was better to suggest it herself than to face her own cowardice when Rope volunteered.

Jo nodded. "I hoped you would not have to come this far, but I think you are right."

Holding his sword before him, Rope stepped into the gloom. The dry grass cracked and whispered beneath his boots. "Straight for the center?"

Jo was walking on his left. "We can try." She looked up at the giant egg, then to the ruined wall on their right.

"It's a maze," Brook said.

Beneath their feet the dry grass hissed and sparked. The waning moon rose over the edge of the Arbor. You will come back to me, Jo, it said.

No!

The old moon laughed.

A cat screamed in the dark. Rope turned and gasped, meeting the eyes of a man-high acorn with a rigid smile and two luminous hazel eyes.

"I can feel them watching me," Brook said.

Rope spotted a gap in the topiary and took several quick strides toward the Palace. Dread was pouring into him, passing through Net into the frail veins beneath his wrist, rising like water in a holed ship.

A dark shape loomed up before him. His heart seized up, clenched, beat wildly.

It was a vast topiary owl. Only clipped leaves and pruned branches, he told himself, nothing more. Huge, of course, but only an owl. With gaping black holes where its eyes should have been. Watching them cross like mice beneath its beak in the old moon's wicked light. Watching.

The fear had risen through Rope's body to his neck now; he held his head up, trying to breathe. The dry grass creaked and whispered underfoot. He sprinted ten steps and tripped over a tiny shrub, hitting the ground hard, bruising his thigh on the pommel of his sword. Gasping, he scrambled to his feet beneath the owl's talons.

But it was gone. There was only a tree now, only sprigs of yew. Footsteps crackled in the darkness behind him. "Rope?" Brook called. Her voice trembled with fear.

Only yew. As hard as he tried, looking at the tree before him, he could not see the owl. Only leaves. Nothing else. Strands of Net probed the air around his wrist, sipping fear from the hot night. Only yew.

"Rope?"

"I lost it when I got too close." Even as Rope spoke, the memory crumbled behind him. The owl had flown from the edge; there was no owl, there was only a tree, a carven tree.

He drew a deep breath and looked at Brook for the first time. Her bracelet clicked as she rubbed gently on his arm. "That feels good," he said at last.

Brook rubbed the bones of his wrist, the muscle and hair on top, the pale flesh, strangely vulnerable beneath. "Are you ready to walk again?"

He could see Jo glowing before them, kindled by moonlight. He took a first step toward her, then a second; each was easier. In a moment they were together. "Are we almost there?"

"I do not think so," Jo said grimly. "We have passed this pillar before, I think. We seem to be headed in the right direction, but then I lose sight of the Palace behind a hedge or sculpture, and when I pass out from behind the next wall of yew I am no closer than I was before."

"Just like the forest," Brook said. "You can never see more than three steps in front of your face."

Rope laughed. "Of course!"

"Of course what?"

"You can't see any better on the sea when it's dark, Bug. But we sail nevertheless."

"If you have an idea, I wish you would hurry up with it," Jo said.

Rope looked up into the hot night sky. "It has been too long since you were an islander, Jo. We may not be able to see the Palace all the time, but these hedges can't stop us from seeing the stars."

Brook tried to shake her fear long enough to think. "All we have to do is fix our course to the Palace by the stars . . ."

"And sail into it," Rope finished.

"Somewhat clever," Jo admitted. "You two are less stupid than you look."

"You flatter us," Rope said dryly. He looked carefully from the Palace to the constellations overhead. "Let us try going this way," he said, setting forth.

Following Rope's directions, they crept through the Imperial grounds, ears pricked for any sound, fear padding always just a step behind. Then they turned a last corner and stopped dead. Across a dried-up moat, a vast wall of bronzewoods towered over them, oozing dull red emberlight. They had reached the Palace.

"We can't let you do this," Rope said. "We can't let you go in there alone."

Jo shook her head. "If all goes well, let us say we will meet tomorrow at that inn we passed above the clearing where we saw the puppet play. The Bending Bough." Her eyes burned moonsilver as she looked up at the Palace where the Emperor waited. "You have done your part, Rope. All you humanly could. But this night is for monsters."

CHAPTER 16: GARDEN

Rope and Brook watched Jo walk toward the Palace. "We shouldn't have let her go," Rope said.

Drought fevered the midsummer night, and Brook was pierced by a sudden longing for a cool sea breeze, and the feel of a green wave lifting lazily under her as she drifted off the shore of Clouds End.

It would be a long time yet before she was home.

She reached for Rope's hand. It was hard to breathe in the hot night. Jo was a white shadow dwindling, walking away from them, walking away. And with every step, Brook's heart cried for her. And with every step, Brook's heart rejoiced. Her twin was gone.

"Come on," she said. "We have to get out of here. We don't have a wizard to save us anymore. If we are not out by daylight, there will be guards at the tunnels back into the Arbor."

Reluctantly Rope nodded. He squeezed her hand and turned to face the dark Palace grounds. Topiary sculptures loomed over walls of yew. "We came in from about there," he guessed, pointing. "All we have to do to get back is watch the stars and hold on to a straight line." They started off down a corridor of yew.

"This is a bad place to bring Net," Rope muttered. "It's like wrapping pure fear around your wrist."

Magic paced within Brook like a caged animal.

"This path is starting to bend," Rope said after a while.

"Bending quite a bit," he said some time later. He glanced unhappily at the stars. "We're veering badly. As soon as we come to a gap, try to strike left."

There were no gaps to the left. Only a smooth unbroken wall of yew curving into darkness. Brook faltered. "There is a gap on the right over here," she whispered. "We could try it and see if it leads to more open ground."

Rope shook his head. "No use starting all that. We could end up blundering around until morning. Let's just head back the way we came and try again."

They retraced their steps. The dry grass squeaked and whispered underfoot. Somewhere in the darkness an owl screamed. Brook reached to touch the Witness Knot on her left wrist, trying to calm down.

On they walked. Silence pressed around them, made bigger by the dry scrape of a cricket somewhere in the distance. The hedge had grown very tall; Brook could no longer see the lights of the Arbor in any direction. "We might as well be walking in the forest!" *I must keep talking,* she told herself. *I must think of something besides the fear.* "You know what I hated? Those days when we were up before the sun and I would walk through a spider web. I'd be slapping myself in the dark imagining this spider crawling around in my hair."

Rope did not answer. Yews towered overhead.

Brook wished she hadn't remembered the spiders.

Something fluttered by in the darkness and Brook gasped, heart hammering. *A bat,* she told herself. *Only a bat.* "Haven't we been walking a long time?"

Rope grunted.

"Shouldn't we have been back by now?"

"Yes."

The magic was crawling through Brook's blood. She felt it beating at her wrists and behind her eyes, as if her flesh could rupture at any moment and let the world pour through. In the darkness the dry cricket scraped, scraped. "We've been going around in circles."

"I can't tell!" Rope snapped. "The trees are too tall. I can't keep track of any stars."

They stopped. The darkness pooled around them. Walls of yew

towered far overhead. The cricket fell silent. Brook felt the faintest breath of wind on the back of her neck. An instant later an owl's scream drilled into her heart.

She ran. Pelting down an endless tunnel of gloom, plunging into the heart of the garden with her own ragged breathing roaring in her ears and Rope's footsteps pounding behind her.

Suddenly the corridor ended. They burst out into a small clearing and saw two monstrous figures running at them from out of a silver globe. Brook screamed and staggered to a halt. The strangers halted too.

"Reflections!" Rope gasped. "Just reflections, Brook."

Brook tried to catch her breath. "It's . . . It's a h-house!"

The silver globe was actually a cottage the size of Stone's house on Clouds End. As they watched, its walls rippled, shot through with sparks of color. "Fathom!" Rope breathed. "The whole thing is made of water!"

While their heartbeats slowed, they stood staring at the little house that sat like a drop of dew on the grass before them. Its mysterious interior was riotous with flowers. Gelid light oozed from their blossoms—orange, crimson, ocher, and magenta. Beside the cottage stood a shed; a collection of hoes, rakes, shears, trowels, and spades leaned against (or floated on) the liquid walls. "I think we've found the Emperor's gardener," Brook said.

Rope gulped. "Hooray."

Brook touched the Witness Knot and then walked toward the glowing cottage.

"What are you doing!"

"Sooner or later we have to get out of this garden," Brook said, coming up to the wavering doorway. "Whoever lives here will either help us get out, or turn us over to the Palace. Either way, we might as well settle it now. I am not going back into that maze for all the fish in the sea."

"Look at those flowers!" Rope said, trailing after Brook. "I want to reach in and eat them, like candy."

Tiny shapes flicked away from Brook's peering face. "Fish! Little fish swimming in the walls!" And indeed there were: guppies and goldfish, sprat and smelt, angelfish and striped jerries and tin-fish with leaf-shaped bodies and dull scales. Jiggers with tails like trembling blue cottonweed floated up toward the roof; miniature catfish with mustaches as big as their bodies prowled the floor-boards down below. Brook laughed with wonder.

"Net is going crazy!" Rope said. "He's crawling up and down my arm like a big green spider."

A lintel of pleached vines framed the doorway. Brook glanced back at Rope and knocked briskly, twice. They heard no sound, but jewelled fish scurried for cover as fat ripples spread from Brook's knuckles. A slowing swell washed through the whole humped house. Jumbles of flowerlight danced on the encircling yew.

A human form came wavering toward them. Then the cottage door popped open so quickly, a silver bubble bulged from its top pane and went drifting off into the darkness.

A wizened old man with eyes the color of grass stood in the archway. He had a long, weedy mustache which drooped to his waist and mingled with his unkempt hair. His skin was wrinkled, but his hands were supple and unspotted. His fingers were twice as long as they ought to be, and trailed off into long, soft white nails that looked suspiciously like roots. Scarlet bean-pods and cobalt bamboo leaves quarreled around the hem of his green robe. "You are late!" he observed. "Come in!"

The wobbling door stood open to admit them. Water dripped from its frame of vines. Brook stepped in. Rope ducked and fol-lowed.

The old man cinched the belt of his robe. "You may call me Garden. I have been expecting you, but I did not know exactly when you would come. That is the difficulty with these things, you know: precision. Nothing flowers exactly when you wish it!"

Plants were everywhere inside Garden's house. Large leafy plants rested on tables; small potted plants crowded the floor. Banks of flowers were stacked along the walls, blossoming beans clung to the furniture, and a pungent herbary dangled from the ceiling: sage and thyme, comfrey and marigold, chamomile and lemon balm and fennel that smelled like licorice.

Rope stared up in bewilderment. "How can you hang pots from a ceiling made of water?"

"Oh, that!" Garden waved his hand, accidentally slapping Brook with his trailing rootlets. "Once you get the roof to stay up, the rest is easy."

He led them into a room in which several shrubs had been sculpted into armchairs. "My studio," he said, gesturing vaguely at dozens of small paintings that bobbed on the water walls. "You will find it easier to sit in here." The floor was made of dirt, and the whole chamber smelled of fresh vegetables.

A tub of grey stones sat along the back wall. Suddenly Brook bent forward. "They're budding!" she gasped. And indeed, many of the stones had already burst into crystalline leaf.

"Ah, yes," Garden remarked, scratching his mustache unhappily. "One of my experiments. Someone told me that the mountain people keep rock gardens, so I thought I would try my hand at it. You don't have to water them much, but I still had a deuce of a time getting the things to grow." He shrugged regretfully. "I must not have the knack."

The islanders were speechless.

From under the biggest, fattest, most-worn chair peered a vivid scarlet flower. "Petal! Don't be bold! We have guests," Garden admonished, seating himself with a great creaking and crackling. "Please—make yourselves at home."

Brook laughed out loud. "I have no idea what you are going to do to us, but I am very tired. I would love to sit down."

Garden looked at her with ancient eyes. "Do to you? Let me assure you, young lady, I do not *do* anything. It is a point of particular pride." He shook his head. "No, it is an error of judgment, a misunderstanding of time, that leads people to think of 'doing' things. Things," he said, "do themselves."

The scarlet flower peeped from beneath Garden's chair. A neck like a rose stem skulked into view. Rope suddenly realized that Net was no longer wrapped around his forearm.

"Let me make one thing clear: I am *not* eccentric." Garden held up his left hand, looking ruefully at the long, trailing nails. "I fingerpaint. I took it up as a way of taking up fingers, if you see what I mean. If I don't keep them busy, the rascals go to root." He waggled his hand at them, making his long white fingers shiver. "I was afraid I might have to learn to paint with my toes as well, or perhaps play the tambra, but in the end I decided slippers were more convenient." And he propped up his feet on a stooping shrub, displaying a truly splendid pair of black velvet slippers, embroidered with living flowers that oozed candy-colored light.

Petal had now crept entirely into the open. At the base of her stem scuttled five fleshy roots, like the fingers of a pale hand. She slunk behind the trunk of Garden's chair, and then disappeared amongst the flowerpots against the far wall.

Rope wondered if Net could possibly be lurking around his leg.

"I should explain myself." Garden hastily pulled up his fingers, which had begun to burrow into the earthen floor. He chuckled, making his mustache shiver. "I am an arbormancer. In my groves mute Nature and I meet on an almost equal footing. I grow things here as my intuition prompts and look to see the world's patterns reflected in their branchings. Is the world changing more, or less, or staying the same? Are the seasons in balance? Is this world coming closer to the Smoke, or are the two drifting apart?"

Garden brooded upon them until Rope squirmed. "Well, which is it?"

Garden laughed. "You are direct, you islanders. When daunted, the people of the forest become only more polite and attentive and oblique. They search for hidden motives." He snorted. "Well, young man, the world is changing more, the seasons are not in balance, and the Smoke shows it."

Brook frowned. "Surely you have that the wrong way round. What happens here reflects what is happening in the Mist."

Garden shrugged. "I see no reason to give the Heroes priority. The world is a One Twist Ring: we affect the Mist, the Mist affects the real world. Stories from one get told in the other."

A wave skittered suddenly up the wall beside Brook, sending a school of flower-colored fish shooting to the ceiling. There was

a hissing, spitting noise, followed by several thumps and a pro-
tracted scrabble. A slim bean-planter bucked twice and then toppled heavily on its side, spilling out a pile of dirt and a tangle of
struggling vines. Net had a squeeze on Petal; she scraped his fibers
with her thorns.

"Net! Quit that!"

"Petal—don't be bold!"

Rope and Garden dove in and broke up the fight, but not before
Petal had given Rope a couple of good scratches.

Shaking his head, Garden brought out a pretty enamelled jar.
Petal cowered, laying her abject blossom on the old man's arm
and folding her thorns flat. "No no no!" the ancient wizard said.
"You were warned! A few hours of potting will teach you a lesson!"

Petal squirmed wildly, lashing her scarlet head in desperation.

Rope cleared his throat. "It was as much Net's fault—"

"Nonsense!" Garden cried, shaking his old head so his long
mustaches swept the ground. "Don't you go making apologies for
her, the little weed! I was there when she frightened the fish yesterday, wasn't I? I warned her then what the consequence of further boldness would be!" With a practiced hand he popped her
into her pot and scooped in handfuls of dirt from the overturned
bean-planter. "No: she must learn, and this will teach her!"

Petal stiffened, then swooned dramatically over the edge of her
blue-and-yellow prison. Garden looked at her affectionately. "Little fraud," he whispered.

She quivered with a moment's indignation, then remembered to
lie still.

"Too late! You have been unmasked. Now do your penance like
a good plant, with no sulking, and perhaps I will let you out early."
Petal squirmed with dejection, and then dangled listlessly over
the side of her pot.

Net, meanwhile, retreated up Rope's forearm.

"Interesting creature. You made it from the Mist, did you not?
There is a nice little One Twist Ring: a piece of Mist hardened
by a real-world person's story." Garden righted his planter and
tramped the remaining dirt into the earthen floor. "Pardon me! I

have been remiss. You must be hungry as well as tired."

He fed them cherry pie and green-onion cakes, washed down with glass after glass of celery water.

"Now," Garden said, dabbing at his mustache. "Where was I?" His fingers had begun to burrow into the ground; he grimaced with annoyance and pulled them up. "A great Fire rages perpetually on the southern borders of this country, sending up a Smoke that veils the Heroes' world. While your Mist has been moving away for as long as men can remember, our Fire is moving in.

"Over this long summer of drought, it has marched north as fast as a conquering army. The Palm lands are now only ash and memories. Parts of the Rubber and Teak holdings are gone as well, and still the flames speed north. The wind has aided them, and many have died fighting the blaze."

"I heard a story once," Brook said. "There was a Spark in it. The forest people made a bargain with Sere, I think, but the Spark stayed on behind . . ."

"Exactly!" Garden stroked his long, trailing mustache with his long, trailing fingers. "The Emperor believes that those who counsel moderation are wasting southern lives. He has flung his armies northward, to find a new home for his people. Fear drives him on, fear that the Fire will be too fast for him, fear that Bronze Cut and the moderates who have befriended his son will seize power and take the easy ways out, trying half-measures while the Fire marches on the capital."

"Is he right?"

"Who are you asking? Me? I can barely fingerpaint!" Garden shrugged. "Certainly the Fire is coming in. Will it overrun the Empire? Would it do so if the army were sent south, to fight it, instead of north, to flee from it? Can the people of the forest ever live apart from the trees? I do not know the answers to these questions. The Emperor thinks he does."

"So you think he's wrong," Rope ventured.

Garden shook his head. "No, no. I just don't care for the world he is making, right or not."

"We saw a play," Brook said slowly. "Earlier today. It was about a father and a son, and the son was drawn to a wolf who was like the Enchanter, and then they set the screen on fire. It seemed to be put on for the sake of this one Bronze."

Garden's trailing eyebrows rose. "Was he dressed all in gold silk, this Bronze, with a scarlet slash across the chest?"

"Yes! He seemed . . . He was like a storm-cloud that you know is full of lightning."

Garden nodded. "Bronze Cut! Young Hilt never could resist him." The old arbomancer gazed sadly out his silver walls toward the palace. "Like the people of the air, Bronzes are not born; they make themselves. Hilt is only a plain Rowan, but he is thought to be a key to his father's heart. Bronze Cut is the leader of a moderate faction within the Arbor. He has wooed Hilt with friendship and flattery, aiming to take the throne for himself when the Emperor can no longer hold it." Garden's face was grim. "I think this play was meant by the Emperor to send Bronze Cut his strongest rebuke, his deepest threat. He will kill the boy, to make it clear that none are safe who stand against him."

"Kill his own son!" Brook cried. "Then what we heard in Delta is true. The Emperor is mad."

"Mad? That I cannot judge. Certainly he is caught in a story bigger than himself—which may be all that madness is." Garden gazed shrewdly at Brook from under his dangling eyebrows. "Unless I miss my guess, you too are part of a larger story. Am I not right?"

As he spoke he reached out with his long white fingers and flipped up the cuff of Brook's shirt to reveal the blue Witness Knot coiled around her wrist.

"Oh, this," Brook said. "This is nothing! Just a—"

"A message!" Garden beamed. "Oh my. I do love messages. It has been so long since anyone bothered to send me one!"

"Are you a Witness?" Rope asked dubiously.

"Of a sort, of a sort!" Garden leaned forward, clasping his hands so that his long nails twined around themselves like sloppy wickerwork. "Clearly your Witness must have sent you to me in the hope that I could help you with some problem. I do not make any promises, of course. In fact, I can almost guarantee failure, because as I remarked before, I do not *do* anything. But I am pleased to be asked!"

"Er, we really appreciate that," Rope said, "but I think the message was meant for the Witness of Delta, actually. We were supposed to tell her about the woodlanders invading, but it was too late by the time we got there. Now we are here and we have done everything we can do, so—"

"I have been twinned," Brook said.

Garden sank slowly back into his chair. "Mm. Oh, dear." He reached out and patted her gently on the knee. "Yes, I expect that was it."

"I don't think so," Rope said. "Jo has done everything we ever asked of her. Rescued us in Delta—risked her life to face the Emperor! If she was going to do something bad to you, she could have done so long ago. I think she has earned our trust."

Brook's eyes never left Garden. "Can you help me?"

The old enchanter sighed and looked at Rope. "Of course it does no good always to believe the worst of people; that merely brings the worst to pass. But a twinning, now . . . A twinning is a serious thing. A knot not easily untied, as your people say."

Garden closed his green eyes and pondered. The ends of his long mustaches swayed gently with his breath, and the tips of his long white fingers twined amongst themselves as he thought.

At last he opened his eyes. "There are two kinds of story and two kinds of time. Think of a tree," he said. "Each year happens in Mist-time. The rain comes, the bud forms, leaves blossom and flower and fruit! Then autumn arrives, the leaves dry, and wither, and drop away. The story is done.

"But underground the tree's story goes on and on, year after year, following each new twisting root. Things of the Mist-time are stories of the leaf; things of the real world are stories of the root."

He reached out and tapped the Witness Knot. "Your Witness has made the heart of this design a one twist ring. That knot always has both a Mist-time story and a real-world story in it: the rise and fall of a leaf, for instance, and the root's slow, tangled, difficult tale.

"Now, as for your twin! There are two ways to untie a knot, even a one twist ring. One way is to follow it out, slowly unravelling every line to its end. The other way"—and here Garden looked gravely at Brook—"is to cut it."

"Cut it!" Rope cried. "You mean kill Jo? After all she has done for us?"

Garden shrugged. "I do not advise one way or the other—but yes. This is the way twin stories usually end. One survives—and one twin is killed, or thrown into the Mist."

Rope stared angrily from Garden to Brook.

Brook was afraid. She knew, as Rope could not, how great a risk she would take by letting Jo live. But something was flowing in her, something serene and strong and brave as Sage Creek when it made its jump over the bluff and ran past the houses of Clouds End.

"Jo did not kill me," Brook said at last. "She did not throw me into the Mist. She let me live, that first day." She shook her head. "I don't want to kill her." She smiled at Rope. "After all, that would be the story ending, and I have never believed in stories."

Rope sighed, relieved.

"Are you sure now?" Garden asked. "You will be taking a great risk if you choose to follow this knot out to its end."

"No, I am not sure," Brook admitted. "I am terrified. But I cannot kill her in cold blood. If that is the only way, I will not do it. If ours becomes a, a root story, I think I can be the stronger twin. I have Rope, and Shale, and Shandy and Clouds End to hold me."

Garden nodded. "Good. You must be grounded! Those of us the magic touches must put our roots down where we can. I took to trees; their crowns converse ever with the wind, but leaf, blossom, and bole are anchored firmly to the ground."

"Aren't you afraid of becoming too . . . treelike?"

The old man looked fretfully at his drooping fingers. "I am not hurrying the event! No, I relish my humanity. But as the years go by, and spring leads to autumn, and autumn to spring again, I shape the trees to my will. And year after year, I suppose, they shape me also to theirs. We grow alike as the years go by, as old husbands grow like their old wives. There is so much shared history, you understand. You make so many choices in your youth and they seem so free—but by the time you get to be older, each thing you do has the weight of your whole life behind it."

He looked up and smiled sleepily at them. "And so I sit here, weeding my little garden even while the Fire sweeps down on us. But you! You are young! You should be going now. Back to the Arbor, back to your island! It is time for you to leave leaf stories behind; yours is a root story now. A story of real life."

"So soon?" Rope said. "I was just getting used to all these marvels and adventures!"

Garden stood and shooed them through the house and out to his silver door. "Oh, I think you will find that real life has every bit as many marvels and adventures," he said. "But they are so big they can be easily overlooked."

He pressed an onion cake into Brook's hand and a poppy-seed biscuit into Rope's, and then pointed to the yew tunnel that had brought them to his house. "You will find that little path will lead you to the Arbor, and your home at last. Back to your roots."

As they walked away he waved, and his trailing white fingertips splashed gently on the surface of his silver house, sending ripples through the walls, and scattering the jumbled fish.

CHAPTER 17: THE SPARK

Drip.
Drip.
Drip.

It is good to drink.

The vast bronzewood Palace glowed like a dollop of bloody honey in the last hour before dawn. Jo did not look back at Rope and Brook as she walked toward it through grass dry and tangled as human hair. She crossed a band of tiny, sharp stones at the bottom of a desiccated moat. She whispered to herself, trying to drown out the world's thirsty voices.

Jo! I hear you, said the cracking earth. I smell the red water in you.

Not for you! My blood is my own.

She is ours, the wind said. It is not water you hear, parched mother. Tonight her veins crawl with creeping fire.

Jo shivered, feet barely feeling the dry earth, the wind blowing through her. What do you mean? she asked.

No more than usual, the stars remarked. The wind is a great liar. Pay attention at your peril.

But I am the wind's daughter.

Don't say we didn't warn you.

Loveless bitches! the moon cackled in her old crone's voice. Don't trust them, Jo. They pretend indifference to blunt the pain of their daily death. Already the sun is waking. Soon his eye will open and shrivel them like moths.

The stars replied with voices hard and cold as bells. It happens every day. Why get upset? And, we point out, it will happen to you.

Ha! You know as well as I the pleasure of his brand. The world longs for death; he has taught us to beg for it. I admit it! I pull death to my wrinkled dugs. Already the flames have licked me hollow, thrown all my self under their host of shadows.

Poor dear, the wind said. Pay no heed, small one. It's that time of the month, you know.

But the moon said, Jo knows me better.

it is good . . .

. . . to drink.

I must walk, thought Jo. She lifted clay-heavy feet and moved under the dying trees, under the Palace, to stand in the purple gloom beneath tangled bronzewood boughs. Her skin was slick and dry as scale. Her heart was a knot of blood. The fevered night had not sweated out one drop of dew. In the east the sky flinched at the sun's first touch, going grey with pain.

Drip.

Drip.

She stared at the hooked moon, gleaming like a splinter of bone above the West Tower.

You feel me.

Yes.

The moon cackled. What is your errand to the Emperor? What is your mission of mercy?

Jo grinned back. I go to pluck his sting, to take his Spark.

But why?

Because . . . Because I desire it.

You are not too meek to slay the sun, the ancient moon laughed. You are not too proud to drink his bright red rain.

Jo's nailed hands flexed into pinions, her feet hardened into talons and she scratched the baked dirt. She blinked at the burning moon with enormous eyes; left a whisper of red dust behind her and floated into the air, owl-formed, a flake of ash armored in moonlight.

A bat wheeled too close, tricked by the unkind wind. It jerked as her talons slid into its squeaking black body. Its black wings fluttered like dead leaves. Resting on a balcony of bronzewood to eat, she crushed its flesh in her beak, squeezing out its moisture, regretting every drop that fell into darkness.

I thirst! the old earth cried through cracking lips.

It was a small bat, and tough. Jo was not satisfied. In the distance, the wind whispered suave apologies to its next-of-kin.

Drip.

Jo sailed off the balcony, pressing the wind beneath her wings. She left the bat's corpse on the matted railing and circled up, flying at the moon. Far to the east, the sun burned away the darkness, leaving empty grey nothing in its place. Dawn fled before him, and the world cowered like a battered woman. The eastern stars shrieked thinly and went out.

A lone waver of birdsong, a lark's maimed hymn to the dawn:

Evil nests
In the green-gold branches;
He held murder to a candle, and it
Burned.

Declare yourself! the living Palace said. Are you fuel or flame? Only the Singer knows, Jo answered. Are you light or shadow?

Evil throws the only light within my halls, the Palace said. Evil is sticky; it crusts my leaves.

It is good, the earth sighed,

. . . to drink.

Jo landed on the parapet of the South Tower, hooking her claws through twigs like brittle bones. She felt the sap crawling beneath her toes. She flapped her wings and shrugged her shoulders, thrice. Her blood was thin and hot. She clacked her beak and hissed at the night. Do you hear that sound?

Drip.

Sound? the wind said politely. What sound?
The dripping. Drip. Drip. Drip. That sound.
From the room beneath her feet she heard the candles laugh. It is tallow, they said, nothing more. It is our white fat you hear dropping to the thirsty ground. It is our mighty labor to burn away the darkness; you hear our sweat.

Drip.
Drip.

I do not trust your laughter. I do not trust your fierce voices.
All things that move are cruel, the moon said. Jo, remember! Did I not tell you the sound of the flame is the sound of wind, the sound of wind that of water? If you want honest answers, speak to the stones and the stars!
What is good? Jo cried to the thirsting earth. What drips down to your parched throat?
What right has she to ask? the bats screamed. Is not murder its own reward?

I know nothing
    of guilt
    or innocence, the earth replied.
Everything
    draws its substance
    from me,
    Daughter of Air.

Even you.
You were born of me.
    Your cord was cut and tied:
    you are a knot of
    red water
    in a fine leather bag.

Drip.

It drips from me, said the corpse of the Emperor's son. My father solved the cunning puzzle of my life. With a single stroke below the jaw he cut through all my intricacies.

I am sorry.

Day is near, the moon said. Madness burns within the Palace, Jo. Will you flutter to that flame?

I made promises. I swore oaths. Help me!

Who is this *I*? A shape you took from an island girl.

Jo trembled, torn by twin desires. But at last she began to shift, small and smaller, a spider to walk between veined walls. I promised Brook, she said.

What burns in you? the moon sadly asked. Are you trying once more to be of the water? You will give back everything you have taken. Everything.

I promised, Jo whispered.

But the moon said only, When you are tired, Jo, come to me.

It was all Jo could do to spiderwalk through the Emperor's walls. The play of fear and desire and confusion was so strong within the Palace that no creeping thing could long hold to any purpose but to hide and madly sting when cornered.

Once inside, she took her human shape again.

Golden light, thick and dull as honey, welled from the bronze-woods into the Emperor's room. Certain stripped branches showed naked as beating veins in the walls and ceiling. Gulping candles in gold sockets projected from each of six walls. The Emperor's swing hung in the center of the room; each move sent a shudder through his six shadows. His dry fingers rustled in a bowl of roasted locusts. "I have been expecting you," he said.

His bony cheeks were hollow and his eyes were points of golden flame socketed in shadow. Where the light touched his skirts the satin glowed rich green, elsewhere midnight-black. He reached out with one foot and set himself softly rocking. The creaking swing was inexpressibly sad. With long bronze fingernails the Emperor shelled another locust, cracking the roasted carapace. "I knew they would send a woman as my death."

"I come at no one's sending but my own." *Believe that if you will,* the moon said from outside. *What of your island girl?*

"Do you not! Do you not indeed!" The Emperor crushed the locust shell between his fingers and dropped it into the bowl. "I believe Sere burns within me, and you are the shadow of that burning."

"You are fevered with madness."

The Emperor shook his head, swinging gently forth and back in the weak yellow candlelight. "The puppets themselves are sacred and unknowable. We are shadows cast by a little golden candle, White Lady. Shadows thrown upon a paper screen."

"Whose shadow am I, then?"

"Mine. You are the shadow I cast upon the world. It is men who serve a single master, and women who serve men. The habit of subservience runs strong within your sex. You are a play of shadows without shape." The swing creaked; ropes bit into the branches above. "Would you like something to eat?"

Jo shook her head. A bee tumbled from behind her ear and fell scrabbling to her shoulder.

The Emperor picked up another locust by its brittle wings. "But are men happier? No. Only in a position of greater certitude. It is Sere whose shadow I am—his light and his substance conjoin to create me. I too am caught up by inexorable forces. I too am a shadow on the screen we call The World As It Is."

The Emperor stilled his swing, and his gaunt face was as a mask of beaten bronze, chiselled in shapes of care, lit from behind by a leaping flame.

Jo! Jo, the candles called. Laughing, laughing. Will you fan the Fire, daughter of air? All flesh is wax—the wick and the burning are all that matters.

She forced her dry lips open. "Your puppet-play is illusion. I am not bound by its lines. The moon is in you, old man. You are longing for death."

The Emperor stirred his fingers slowly in the locust bowl; husks clicked and rustled. "You are only my shadow and a woman. The man who seizes his chance can twist his shadow to his own purpose. I must bend you to my will, as the sea must become the shadow of the wood."

"You woodlanders are all alike, using poetry to dignify your desires. There is no mystery in evil. You are no race of monsters."

"My duty is to my people!" the Emperor snapped. "Can you imagine I have not been tempted by compassion? Now, even now, with my clans succumbing to the Fire, I grieve for those islanders who must die . . . Yes. Death calls for me. I ache for dissolution. All things weary of life. All things long to surrender to the freedom of the clouds and stones."

"Silence waits at the end of every speech," Jo whispered. "Come. Come to me. I will teach you the secret that waits beneath the pines. I will show you what the Smoke knows in its circling."

He stood upright, angry hands clenched around the cables of his swing, staring at Jo. "You are evil," he said. "I should have known they would send me a beautiful death."

Bees crawled on Jo's moon-white flesh. Softly she said, "I spoke this hour with your son."

The Emperor shuddered. "What did he say?"

His grief was real. Not a flicker from behind the Smoke, but a father's anguish, and she took pity on him. "He knew only what the dead know. Red dust and silence."

"He will see his pyre today." The Emperor's voice was thin as paper, as flame. "Would you do me the honor of joining the ceremony? I would have my Death attend on his."

Jo stepped forward and laid a gentle hand on the Emperor's hard shoulder. Her touch was cool and soft as flowers. She knew then she would have to draw out the Spark that ate the Emperor hollow, the Spark that had cast a host of shadows over him and his son and his people. She must pluck it from him like a bee's sting that festered in his flesh. She winced, letting his heat surge into her body.

The hard candles blinked.

Stammering, the Emperor said, "My son had that arrogance that goes with being young. Knowing the portents as well as I, he sensed his danger, but still he gave his heart to Bronze Cut." The Emperor looked with wonder at his strong right hand. "Hilt did not know the terrible things old men can do." His fingers closed around the haft of his knife.

Jo's touch passed through him like ice water. He hissed and flinched beneath her hand. "Avoid introductions to Death! So fascinating an acquaintance must soon become a friend."

"Your shadow-play is over. I will show you winter's heart. I will teach you what the cold moon knows."

"But why?" the Emperor muttered, rocking back and forth with nervous energy. "Why do I not call the guards?" His shoulder beneath her fingers was taut as a straining hawser. Pride and despair were tearing him apart.

Jo fought back her fear, knowing she had to take his fire, dreading the terrible pain. "You called women formless, old man. The shadows of shadows. But it is you who are weak, to think that any human can be only one thing. I choose not to hold a single shape and I am strong, as strong as the wind that carves every mountain. As strong as the sea that drowns every fire."

The Emperor straightened and slapped her hand away. "Do not presume!"

Jo shook out her white mane, and a host of bees whirred into the air. "Shall I show you your shadow?" Hidden behind a veil of floating hair, her features blurred. When she looked up again she wore Hilt's face, blood leaking from his dead neck. "Is this what you desired?"

"Monster!" Gasping, he pulled out a long-handled dagger with a ruby hilt. Its point was sharp and flecked with fresh blood. Leaping to his feet, he jerked her head back with one hand in her hair. The dagger's bitter point slid against her stomach.

Jo heard the candles' hot voices, felt the shivering strength of the Emperor's arms, was surrounded by his scent: grief and withered leaves. His dry hands were spider-fingered. She *listened*, as a heart-drum drove pulses of burning pitch through his veins. She drew his Spark into herself, as a wind draws upon a flame.

He screamed and drove the knife home.

> Blood like venom, the
> cut of the Mist
> the
> burning

On fire   She said, *they die when they lose*
    Poison flooding in   *their*
                                     stings.

And she was shifting, shifting, wearing his mask, plucking his sting. She was him, two forks of one flame, two Emperors now, staring down as the knife slid in and out of her shifting flesh. They blazed up together into one great burning.

She twinned him then, from the grieving mask outside to the charred hollow place in his heart where the Spark raged. She sucked out that burning thing—call it madness? Genius? Destiny? Desire? She drew out the twist of flame that drove him to his enormities and swallowed it into herself through his knife and his rage and his burning eyes.

He would live on with his fires banked. But Jo screamed, covered in dying bees, as the Spark passed into her like desire: like freedom: like death.

CHAPTER 18: THE PYRE

By the time the sun was up, Rope and Brook had made it back to
the Bending Bough. Unable to sleep, they lay together on a grass-
stuffed mattress and waited for Jo.

Brook reached out to touch Rope's face. She felt the bristle of
his beard, then slid her hand down to his throat. His pulse made
her fingers tremble. She longed for Clouds End and the sea wind
and Shale's grin; she longed to touch Rope and be touched; and
all these things she felt inside herself like stones in a stream.

"Almost over," Rope said. "If Jo doesn't make it, I wonder if
the Emperor's soldiers will come for us."

"It won't be over, even if she succeeds. Jo twinned me. That
will not go away, whatever happens with the Emperor."

Rope scratched his beard. "Everyone thought my name should
be Rope, you know. You, Shale, Shandy. Except Foam. He suggested 'Walrus.' To make me see that 'Rope' wasn't so bad, I
guess."

"You don't like it?"

"It's so . . . dependable. Everyone thinks I'm too careful, too
slow, too something. But there are things I want as badly as you
or Shale or Foam, you know."

"Like?"

He rolled over and looked at her, and smiled, and stroked her
soft throat. Brook's skin prickled as if before a storm. His fingers
seemed heavy against the pulse in her throat. She thought of the
time they had kissed in the forest. Her hand flowed over his chest

and belly. The sounds of the Arbor—hawkers, couriers, countless conversations—struggled into their room, muffled and indistinct.

Creeping down Rope's arm, Net rose like a cobweb in a breeze, and then settled, a lace of silver reaching from Rope's wrist to Brook's throat.

The shock of Net's touch shivered away the walls between them. Brook flushed, feeling Rope's desire rush through her. They could have been one person, so clearly did she feel herself beneath his hand, chest rising and falling, skin drinking skin, one breath that shook in their chests, one heart that sent blood spinning through their bodies. Her hand ran over his shoulder, feeling bone and blocks of muscle as if they were her own.

Rope was part of her story. Rope and Shale and Clouds End too.

How stupid she had been! How blind. She had used her magic to peer into the Mist, instead of looking inside herself, where her real stories lay like bulbs in the dry earth. She touched the children within her, the one she had been and the ones she would bear. Across the world from home, stranded in this city of trees, she was branching, wrapping her arms around Rope, seeing her roots dig down deep into the soil of Clouds End. Seeing her life flower on a thousand branches.

She loosened the lacing on Rope's woodlander shirt. He pulled it over his head, muscular arms flexing and straightening. She slid her fingers up his chest, tracing the dark swirl of hair around his nipple. Then she sat up and pulled off her own shirt, feeling her heart kick as her breasts fell free. She met his eyes.

"We're not stopping this time," Rope said.

Brook's hands slid to her hips and pushed down her woodlander pants until the first curl of dark hair sprang free. "No." Naked, they felt for one another with thirsty hands. Brook shivered, pulling Rope's hand over her breast, dissolving in desire.

Outside, a waiting silence fell in the Arbor. There came a swirl of wind and a dimming sun. The air was electric. Heads turned upward. Eyes widened.

Then the city and sky sighed together and a soft rain began to fall. Cool on ten thousand uplifted faces, raindrops freckled the dusty leaves and touched life into dry smells. Laughter bubbled up throughout the Arbor. Children shouted and snapped their finger-drums. Someone somewhere beat a thin metal gong, sending out showers of bronze.

The rain came down in earnest, harder now, kicking up dust, hissing from the overcast sky, pattering through the Arbor's million branches.

Rope flinched as the first drop trickled through their roof and landed on his back. "Rain!" Brook cried. Joy flickered through her as pure as the sky, as quick as the glint of light on water. Her fingers slid up Rope's back and spilled down his arms. Drunk with touch, they kissed lips, shoulders, throats, flesh on flesh, skin sliding into skin like two streams running into a single river.

Brook was a channel, a streambed, and life was pouring though her, filling her up and spilling over her edges. She gasped and closed her eyes and came.

Rope trembled, entering. "Will you marry me?"

"Yes!"

"Will you marry me?"

"Yes!"

"Will you marry me?"

"Yes, yes, yes!"

Brook's body was sacred and real as the wind and the hilltop, as real as the trees and the stars. She was a stream and the nighttime. She was an island made from Mist and fire and sea. Her whole body was shaking and she cried warm tears as sweet as rain.

This was the morning of their last day in the Arbor.

Brook awoke to a bitter smell of burning.

Jo sat on the opposite bed with a cherry-wood pipe between her teeth. She was not an expert smoker, and her mouth pursed in an exaggerated pucker each time she inhaled. Her white hair coiled and writhed around her shoulders, but the breeze that slid into the room with her was not cool as of old, but a thin hot wind like unsatisfied desire. In the lamplight her narrow eyes winked like polished bronze.

Bronze. Silver no longer.

"You're back!"

Jo's mouth widened into a grin. The pipe trembled between her clenching teeth, and finally she coughed up ragged laughter. Smoke eddied surprisingly from her nose. "I got tired of watching you two sleep, so I bought this from a shop nearby." She held up a little wooden box lined with rubber. "Also twenty matches, free with the purchase. You use them to start small fires."

"*Mm?*" Rope grunted. "*Ng. Wha?*"

If she took my shape, no one would ever know, Brook thought. A cold shadow fell across her heart and the resolve she had felt in Garden's cottage failed her. "Jo's back," she said.

"She did it! By the Gull she did it!" Rope fumbled for the lamp above the bed, opening the flue to make a strong yellow light. "The Emperor is dead!"

Jo shook her head. "Not yet. But soon. The Spark has left him and he falls to ashes."

Brook scooped her clothes off the floor and wriggled into them. Rope blushed and reached for his pants. As soon as he got them on he bounded out of bed. "Wonderful!" he cried, grabbing Jo in a great bear hug. "A fair wind and a full hold it is, to find you back again."

Jo smiled but her face was haggard. "I am glad to see me too."

Brook said, "You must be very happy."

"Come on! Is that all you can manage! We did it! Or rather, Jo did it," Rope said generously. "Singers will honor your name for as many years as there are islands in the eastern sea. So tell us the story!"

"First we must be off. You two have slept the day away. The sun is setting now, and I have an obligation to fulfill. Hurry up!"

Rope scratched his side. "This is an itchy city," he announced. "I itch." He frowned. "Where are we going?"

"To a funeral," Jo said.

The Arbor hummed like a vine abuzz with bees. The Prince had been poisoned by a mistress, had committed suicide rather than face the Fire, had been killed by a jealous rival, had fallen from a balcony while intoxicated, had died (if you were very cautious) from natural causes, after a brief illness, after eating something that disagreed with him.

Rowan Hilt was dead, and the war against the sea people was over.

"It is . . . difficult to tell what happened between the Emperor and me," Jo said as they left the Bending Bough. "Everything true, everything important, lies between words. Or beyond them."

"A story of the Mist-time," Brook said softly. "Where things are most real and nothing is what it seems to be."

"I understand," Rope said, nodding. "One of those mysterious things."

Jo laughed. "Yes, most definitely. It was one of those mysterious things . . ." And she told them the story of her flight to the South Tower, and her meeting with the Emperor there. "He had murdered his son and it broke him. He was like a log that splits when you prod it, showing nothing inside but darkness and a burst of flame. He was not strong enough to contain a Hero. No human is. Sere had licked him hollow."

A troop of servants with torches hurried by, bowing quickly as the light sparkled on Jo's golden eyes. "So I released him."

"But you didn't kill him?"

"She took the Spark," Brook said.

"Mm. Yes. Your eyes have grown sharper." Jo looked at Brook then with a strange expression. Part curiosity. Part hunger. "I twinned him then, shifting even as he stabbed me. I shifted around his knife, drawing forth the fire that burned in him."

There was something autumnal in the air. It wasn't cold, but the wind seemed fresher and the sun had lost his sting. "A good day for a prince to reach his pyre," Jo said as they picked their way down to the Arbor's ground level.

"Why the long faces?" Rope said, studying the women. "The war is over!"

"Nothing is over," Brook said. Feeling Jo's emptiness beside her. "Nothing ever ends."

Rope spat. "I give up! We travel across the known world to get here, do the one thing we have been planning for months, and prepare to return home as heroes. And what do we get from you two? Gloom." He shook his head in disbelief. "Thank Fathom we didn't fail!"

Jo dipped her fingers into her tobacco pouch, lowering her voice as a trio of woodlanders in sumptuous mourning dress hurried by. "But were we right to succeed? Perhaps the war would have ended without our interference. Perhaps the Emperor was right, and I have condemned hundreds or thousands of innocent woodlanders to the Fire." She struck a match and breathed in the flame. "Hilt died, and I made his death pointless. Before it might have been a tragic necessity. Now it is only a horror."

"It was madness!" Rope cried.

"How can we know?" Brook said softly. "How can we know that the Emperor was wrong and we were right?"

A curl of smoke wavered around Jo's white face. "We cannot." She glanced at Rope. "Remember that puppet-play? Who is to say what happened after we left? Perhaps word went back to the Emperor that an agent of Bronze Cut had doused the flame and made a mockery of the Imperial message, sending a challenge to the throne. Perhaps that was what drove him to slide a length of steel along his son's throat."

"That is not fair," Brook said. "You can't blame Hilt's death on Rope."

"You are telling me what is fair!" Jo laughed. "I took the Spark. Was that what I wanted? I am of the air. Why should the people of the sea mean more to me than those of the forest? Was it really my idea to taste the Emperor's knife, to take his burning? Or did I do it only because I love you?"

"Wouldn't that be enough?"

Jo looked at her twin with gleaming golden eyes, feeling the Spark in her breast like a splinter of flame. "I fear the cost may be too great."

The funerary parade issued from the Palace at sunset. The air shook with the tolling of great bronze gongs, stately and inconsolable.

The Emperor led the procession, followed by a cadre of six noblewomen with proud, sorrowful faces. Behind them came a throng of servants bearing on their shoulders a vast tower of polished bamboo. Flowers had been wound into its every crevice, tongues of flame-blossom blue and yellow, black and indigo, violet, cinnamon, and dreadful gashes of red poppies and scarlet columbine. Atop this swaying tower Rowan Hilt's corpse rocked in a palanquin of thorns. From it rolled a scent of weeping honey.

It was full dark by the time Jo, Brook, and Rope joined the crowd of mourners at the city gate, heading south. They flowed midstream in a river of torches. Children ran by with sparklers flaring in their hands. The mute fire wardens put out a hundred blazes that leapt up around the parade. "This is crazy!" Rope said. "This morning's rain was only a spit on a campfire. It's still like tinder out here. They will burn down the whole forest!"

Next to them a woman with a lacquered helm turned from her companion. "The Emperor's son can be mourned no other way."

Jo bowed gracefully; a moment later Rope and Brook gathered their wits and did the same. "Our thanks," Jo said. "We have not been to the capital before, and our rituals are less elaborate."

The woman's partner, a middle-aged man with bone-grey hair, bowed his welcome. "Ash Splinter. The lady is Ash Bough. The sorrow we must witness is as intricate as the Imperial gardens."

A third woodlander joined the conversation, a portly young man with a secretive face. "Or perhaps we celebrate a painful joy as complex as roots stirring at the long-awaited touch of rain." He shrugged. "Maple Stem."

"Are you of that mind?" Ash Bough asked frigidly.

"The Emperor has called the army back to fight the fire. The cruelest cut makes way for the fairest blossom, so it is said."

Ash Splinter smiled without warmth. "And the aptest maxim makes way for silence."

Jo grinned, but Rope felt dull as a dogfish. He knew that

somehow they were talking about Hilt's death, but he was baffled
by the woodlanders' brittle smiles and slanted words.

They climbed a long flight of steps carved into a high mound
south of the city. The citizens of the Arbor ringed the howe with
murmurs manifold as the voice of the sea. Behind them the gongs
slowed like a dying heart that staggers and stops. In the center of
the hill's flat crown, lying atop its wooden tower, Hilt's body came
finally to rest.

"Switch!" hissed a voice from the darkness.

Ash Splinter and Ash Bough looked around in consternation.
Maple Stem bowed. "A pleasure," he murmured, backing into the
crowd. "I have a sudden wish to observe the sacred rights from
the other side of the hill."

"As do we," Ash Splinter remarked, taking Ash Bough's arm
and guiding her away.

"But we have not had a chance to give you our names!" Jo said
suddenly.

"Quite all right. Perhaps later—"

The haunt was implacable. "I would not dream of such dis-
courtesy." Ash Splinter paused and smiled with obvious annoyance, glancing ever so briefly at a lean man who approached from
a part of the hillside now oddly unpopulated.

"My name is Jo. Rope and Brook are my companions. I pray
you, will you suffer our company a little longer? We would doubt-
less benefit from your perceptive commentary on the mystery at
hand."

"We are but dilettantes," Ash Bough said quickly. "We would
never presume." She bowed with careful courtesy to the newcomer.
"Particularly when you have a chance to profit from the observa-
tions of so profound a sage as Bronze Switch." She took a step
backwards as she spoke. Ash Splinter had already vanished into
the gloom.

Switch was a slender man nearing the end of his prime. His
eyes were hollow and his face gaunt, as if years of hardship and
fierce passion had burned all excess away. His lidded eyes glowed
bronze. Something about him made Rope uneasy, a quality of hid-

den danger, as if fire would spray forth from those golden eyes if the woodlander ever chose to widen them.

The newcomer bowed to the departing Ash Bough and laughed. "I am anything but profound," he said. "You will not need my help. Island eyes are weak under leaf-shade, but when the Spark flies there will be light enough to see."

"How did you know we were islanders?" Jo said.

"I had occasion to stay in Delta for some years. I heard the sea in your voices."

The Palace mourners chanted around the funerary tower. A ring of musicians answered, playing a lament of curious savagery on tambras and chiming stels. One by one the Bronze women approached to lay gifts upon the funerary pyre: instruments, wreaths, lacquered bracelets and garments of silk, a kite, liquor and weapons and bottles of scent. A songbird in a wicker cage who poured out his heart as if knowing what was to come. Last of all came the Emperor, bearing a puppet within a paper cage, its shadow thrown by a gulping candle.

The crowd had drawn away, leaving the islanders alone with Bronze Switch. "Why do they burn the Emperor's son?" Rope asked. "It seems mad to make a fire after this drought."

"Perhaps it is, but fire is the only fit end for the noble. The Emperor's son could have no less." When Switch spoke again his words sheathed a sharp memory. "In the forest, I think, we know more of desire than do those who live by the cold damp sea. In a tree you see the record of a thousand lusts. Every leaf and twig is clawing at the sun; every root is seeking out the rain. We desire love, and wealth, and plenty, and the power to wither others, or make them grow. In our thirst for knowledge we trick the mute world into speaking her secrets. Desire drives us, and dares us to be great. And consumes us in the end."

Brook said, "But desire sometimes leads to evil."

Switch smiled unpleasantly. For the first time Rope noticed he had a sword at his side. "Of course. Every Spark calls up a host of shadows. For instance, I could kill you all. Here before these hundreds. You have no seconds and no clan."

Rope gripped the hilt of his notched sword.

"The Spark burns fiercest within a Bronze," Switch remarked. "Most of us do not survive. Some compulsion drives us into risk, or atrocity."

"Yet discipline is necessary," Jo said. The stranger turned to her and his eyes widened. She was no longer a woman, but a lean man, even taller than Switch.

"True," Switch said. "But discipline may slip. It has happened before. A Bronze has given in to impulse. Has slain several men and a woman too. For some slight offense, just enough reason to reduce the penalty from death to exile for five dreary years beside the mumbling sea. It has happened."

Jo nodded. Now she wore the Emperor's face. She reached out with a man's thin hand, fevered and dry as burning paper, to stroke Switch's cheek. Her curving bronze fingernails came to rest just below his jaw, where the great vein beat hot within his throat.

Switch's right hand was resting on the pommel of his sword, light as a mantis on a blade of grass. Awkwardly, Rope unsheathed his sword, knowing it would be no more use against this lean woodlander than it would against the sea.

Switch hooded his eyes. "Happily, discipline is the great virtue of the mature Bronze."

Jo's voice was a knife sliding from a metal sheath. "I think the Emperor's son would agree. Were he still alive."

Switch stood very still, not speaking. His life beat below the haunt's long nails.

The Prince's dirge stopped, leaving a great silence. A torch flared into life and passed its flame. One by one a ring of red fires sprang up around the funeral tower, gleaming like wolves' eyes. The crowd held its breath.

The firelight drained slowly from Jo's hand, leaving it white as salt. It dropped to her side. "I think we should flee the call of the flame."

"Perhaps that would be as well." Switch bowed crisply to Brook and Rope, but his eyes returned to the haunt as he backed away. "May you find whatever your heart desires."

Brook reached for Rope's hand. "I can tell a curse when I hear one."

After Switch had gone, the other woodlanders muttered and did not come near the islanders.

Standing alone before the funeral tower, the Emperor drew back his head and gave a long, shuddering cry that curled into the night like smoke, bitter with loss. A second time it came, and a third. Then three times the circle of torches wailed, shaking off sparks of grief, and three times all the citizens of the Arbor cried out, three roars hurled at the stars. And when the Prince had been mourned nine times, the torches leapt spinning into the air and the flowers exploded in a burst of flame.

Oils had been sprinkled on them, both the sweet and the bitter; swiftly were they devoured. Heat rolled from the burning tower. Higher the blaze rose, and higher still, until the thorns on the palanquin burst into spikes of flame, and Hilt's cage became a lace of fire. The night shook with hot thunder and a mad wind rushed amidst the burning flowers.

The Emperor stood alone before the blazing tower until a spar fell crashing to the ground. Then he took a pair of tongs and reached into the flames, pulling out embers from the fire and placing them in a brass box held by a waiting servant. Only when the box was full did he suffer an attendant, wincing in the blistering heat, to guide him from the hilltop. His people followed, looking back in fear and awe.

Brook watched the Emperor leave. One withered hand rested on the brass box. "I wonder what will happen to him?"

Jo's voice was like the wind in a broken tower. "He will be cold, I think. Cold as Ash was, now that the Spark has left him. It was the Spark that made all this, the murder and the madness and the war itself."

Behind them the pyre hissed and creaked, swaying drunkenly. Then, with a roar like the angry sea, the tower collapsed into itself, hurling a comet of flame at the heavens and spreading a cloud of stinging sparks over the fleeing onlookers. As people rushed around them Jo stopped and held Brook's eyes. "The great has become small, you see. I have the Spark now. Now all that was between the sea and the forest is between you and me."

It is the same story, Brook thought. But the leaves have fallen, and the tale will finish among the roots.

I wish I did not love her.

I wish I could end it with a single cut.

Seven's Line

CHAPTER 19: THE SHADOW WOOD

"Vanished." Shale shook her head at the darkening coast. Somewhere in the gloom Hazel Twist's troops were winding their way back home. "Gone as if the forest had swallowed them whole." Behind her on the middle thwarts Reed and Foam nodded, and in the stern Seven turned his head, steering by the feel of the tiller in his hand, looking back at the line of grim cedars silhouetted against the darkening sky.

They were returning from the mainland. Three months had passed since the recapture of Thumbtip; two weeks since Reed had returned with a little flotilla of starry-eyed volunteers from the Middle Islands. Seven had almost three hundred under his command now, most of whom sailed beside them tonight, glimmers of wash and snatches of laughter abeam.

They had much to celebrate, for after months of training it now seemed certain they would not have to go to war. The woodlanders had abandoned Delta, fleeing the empty sea for the shelter of the leaves. The islanders had sailed in to the first island that morning, leaving Glint with their wounded along with Pond to set the city right again. The rest had headed for the mainland to make sure the forest army had really gone. They had.

Now as the sun set, the sixty small ships of Seven's navy made a brave show, their sails humming with every twitch of breeze, their little lamps swaying like a crowd of fireflies rocking over the deep, heading for the greater lights of Delta's harbor, and home. But Seven's ship was strangely somber. The fresh landward wind whispered around her pennants and lines. Her spreading wash hissed out into the night. Seven shook his head. "This was not our victory."

"That makes it only greater," Foam said. "Glorious death is still death to me. We saw enough of war on Thumbtip for my taste."

"Like fencing with a shadow, this Hazel Twist. Why did he send his men to build those camps on the mainland shore?"

"To get them off safely, a few at a time," Foam said. "He never wanted a fight, not really. I think he was giving them something to do, something he could justify. He could tell the Emperor they were 'digging in' while they studied shipbuilding and sailor-craft. But taking the islands was a hopeless task and he knew it. He kept his men in order without ever risking them again to the open sea. After the squall that caught those who fled Thumbtip, I can't say I blame him."

Shale nodded. "I thought those signals from the mainland two nights ago were going to mean the start of a big attack, but they must have called the retreat instead. I wonder if Brook and Jo had anything to do with it?"

"Is my mood dark because there was no battle?" Seven said. "Am I that shallow? I do not believe so. I do not want more glory. And yet . . . We stopped Hazel Twist, but something else called him back. How can I be sure he will not return? My heart tells me we are not done with one another, he and I. I cannot shake his shadow from my thoughts."

"Then woe to him!" Reed said with a soft laugh. "And woe to all who stand before the Warrior's champion!"

"Hah! No more of that! With the woodlanders gone we need no more of that bilge. Chosen of the Gull Warrior! Was that your own idea, Reed, or did someone put you up to it?" Seven looked darkly at his lieutenants.

Foam fussed with the sheets. Shale gazed innocently up at the sky. "The stars are dimming. Fog's coming up."

Reed laughed again. "You must admit my singing did its business. Two thirds of your sailors heard my song, I think. And believe me, they did not leave Sealsbeard and Telltale to come to Delta's aid! They came because of you; because they wanted to stand shoulder to shoulder with the only hero the islands have produced in living memory."

"I did what you made me do. You with your songs and tales." The night air was turning damp. Seven pulled his cloak more tightly around his shoulders. He stared at his sword, lying sheathed before him with its butt on his bench and its tip on the aft thwart, like a narrow bridge over a dim gulf. "I do not like being smaller than my own story."

"Sometimes one is a ship, and words are the wind," Foam said. His voice was soft in the falling gloom. "No matter what touch you put to the tiller, the wrong words can blow you off course. If people say you are light, you come to believe them. A light thing is easily lifted, or moved aside."

"No one ever said you were light!" Shale said.

"No one ever built me a boat either, though they built one for Rope." Foam shrugged. "I do not blame them. I never watched narrowly for my own success. And then somehow I looked up and life was passing me by, and my playmates were no longer children, but no one believed I was a man. Including me."

Including you, he added to himself. The long summer he had spent with Shale was bittersweet to him. The campaign against the woodlanders had made them friends, but it had not made them lovers. Here, with Seven's army, he had grown greatly in her eyes, and in his own. Each dawn he felt more keenly how much he needed her in his life. Each sunset made them better friends, but nothing more. And if they could not be lovers now, in a new world where all the old rules were broken, how could he hope not to dwindle in her eyes when they returned at last to Clouds End, and home?

"Your people will know you for a man after this summer's work," Reed said. "You have been a captain of the islands. Everyone who knows of the war will know your name."

"Taste that!" Shale said. "We are storied in our own right, Foam."

"Great stories turn to small ones, and great fires fall to ash. This tale ends at the hearth, the Singer said. We won't be famous to anyone on Clouds End. This war will be only a story there."

"Night has come," Seven said.

The sun had set. Darkness rose from the east. The line of bobbing lights that was Seven's command grew ragged as they sailed out into the gulf; they seldom heard laughter anymore, or snatches of song. As Shale had predicted, a fog was rolling in from the sea. The air was chill and damp. Waves muttered at their prow and the quartering swell made the wooden spars creak and lift as every quiet roller went by. Coming from the darkness aft, Seven's low voice was like the voice of the wind itself. "I will tell you about stories," he said.

"It was just before my Naming that Switch came to Delta. We had seen no more than three or four woodlanders in living memory. He was a sensation, with his lordly manners and his steel. I already knew that I could never be a shipwright. Whatever I did, I had to do it as well as my father.

"I fell in love with Switch, with everything about him. He meant adventure, and courage, and excellence—and nothing about boats! I begged him to take me on, and begged my father to hire him. Looking back, I believe he thought the sea people soft. Not lazy, exactly. Untempered. As if nothing happened in our simple lives to test our mettle. Of course, brilliant as he was, Switch was from the forest; he could not understand the sea.

"A tragedy lay behind him; he had been exiled for killing a Bronze in self-defense. I spent more time with him than I think his own family could have done, from the age of twelve to sixteen, and yet I never knew anyone who seemed so alone. That hurt me then. I was a good pupil, but I could never blunt the edge of his loneliness. Perhaps the world was too strange for him, out from under the forest eaves. Or perhaps the woodlanders slipped past his guard when they cast him out so unjustly, and the part of him that dealt with other men was wounded and could not heal.

"All this by the side. Talking of stories and names, and how our stories drive us like the wind behind our sails, I remember now a story Switch told me once. I did not understand it at the time.

"I must have been fourteen when he told me the tale of the Shadow Wood. I had not done well in practice that morning (I forget why) and I was crying with rage at my own stupidity. 'Shh then, it is only a lesson,' Switch said.

" 'Not good enough!' I said. 'I want it so much, and I have tried so hard, for so long, and still I do it so badly.'

" 'What do you want then?'

" 'To be the greatest swordsman in the world,' I said.

"He laughed. 'A tidy little ambition! But how can that be? Have you forgotten me?'

" 'One day you will be old,' I said. And then, seeing him flinch, I said, 'When you step down, I do not want some forest bastard to take your place and his master to get the glory. Not only would I have failed, I would have wasted the teaching of the greatest master in the world.'

"He smiled then, in a curious way that had little to do with laughter. 'Let us rest for a time,' he said. 'I think you will make a reputation for yourself, Seven. But it is time I taught you wisdom as well as weaponry. There is fire in your heart and steel in your bones, but you are still an islander, and islanders are ignorant. While we rest I will tell you a story of my people, a story of reputations, and of a young man not unlike yourself, and of the gifts given by old men like me.'

"And so I sat down on the sandy beach, just a little up from where we swam ashore on Spearpoint—Remember, Shale?— Sweat was still streaming into my eyes, and my legs were trembling, but by the time his story was done my limbs were still, and my sweat had long turned as cold as the fog that gathers around us now."

This is a story of the Smoke, Switch said, *where the heat burns but the Spark is hidden.*

In the olden times at the roots of things, there was a king in the far south who ruled a land that has long been ashes and whose name no man remembers. Great stands of timber grew in the western highlands, teak and kore and ironwood, so they were never short of wood with which to build. In the eastern marshes his people tended vast groves of rubber trees and bamboo and sugar cane, whose blood could be turned to a thousand uses. In the north they grew food enough to feed three kingdoms: oranges and grapes and mangoes, quinces and pomegranates and tamarinds, figs and dates and almonds by the bushel.

But the king got nothing from the forest of the south, for it was cursed. The people called it the Shadow Wood, and would not venture beneath its eaves.

At last the king grew impatient. "The whole world envies our eastern marshes, our western highlands, our bounteous north. And yet the whole world laughs at us because we will not master the Shadow Wood. This is intolerable!" So he summoned his army and bade a hundred men go into the Shadow Wood and claim it for him. His armorers fitted them with spears and shields and his priests blessed them with prayers and incantations and the women of the capital were promised to them on their return.

On a morning bright with sunshine the hundred men set out. The smell of them was of fresh oil and leather and high resolve. The sound of them was of young men singing, fearless and full of joy. The sight of them was flashing eyes and steel and pennants snapping in the breeze.

But the hundred men marched under the shadow of the wood, and they did not come back.

So the king sent out two hundred men to look for them, but they did not come back.

So the king sent forth five hundred after them, but they did not come back.

So the king sent ten hundred men to find those who were lost, but they too vanished and were never seen again.

And every morning the shadows streamed forth from the Shadow Wood, and every evening they streamed back in, and joy left the kingdom, and silence came upon the armorers and the priests and the women of the capital, and fell heaviest of all upon the king himself. "So it is," he said at last. "We are not meant to have the Shadow Wood. Let that be an end to it."

But the next day a young man came to the capital. His walk was as graceful as a dancing girl's and his arms were as strong as a smith's. His step was jaunty and his spirits were high and the people who saw him in the street took one look at the long-handled steel that dangled by his side and knew he was destined for adventure.

The young man came to the palace in the morning and was granted an audience that very afternoon. "I am a student of this long-handled steel," he told the king, patting the sword by his side. "I know the Gull Warrior's secrets and I understand the Way of Stone. I have studied the Hundred Schools of Combat. I am looking to make a name for myself and I heard this might be the place. Is there anything really dangerous to do around here?"

And the king said, "Well, yes, as a matter of fact. Just to the south of us lies the Shadow Wood, which no man yet has ever claimed."

"Let me explore it!"

And the king said, "If you wish—but I cannot recommend the enterprise, for the rate of return has not been good."

But the young man said, "It was not I who went before," and hastened from the room.

Now he meant to plunge straight into the forest, but as he left the audience chamber a wrinkled hand plucked at his sleeve. The wrinkled hand was attached to a withered arm, and the withered arm led to the spindly body of an old man with a kindly eye. "Tarry a moment, young hero."

"I am afraid that is impossible, wizened ancient. I am off this very instant to explore the Shadow Wood."

"This I know," the old man said. "And I applaud your audacity!"

"Do not try to stay me with counsels of cowardice, wrinkled sage. My heart is set on this adventure."

"And credit it does you!" the old man exclaimed. "Listen but a moment further. I lost a brother to that evil wood many years ago, but my heart tells me he lives yet. If you see him, will you rescue him from the shadows?"

"But of course, aged petitioner! What else would a hero do?"

A corner of the old man's mouth twitched as if he meant to smile. "O most excellent youth! Let me grant you one thing more to help you in your quest, that you may surely bring my brother back."

"What aid do you offer, withered counsellor?"

The old man burrowed in a pocket and brought out a little silver box with one match inside and a tiny candle made of golden wax. "Only this. It is not much, but when all else fails, light the candle and you will see an answer to your problem."

"Many thanks, feeble grandfather!" With a deep bow and an elaborate flourish, the young man took his leave and headed for the city's southern gate, and the dark wood beyond.

He went far, far into the forest.

On the third morning of his journey he heard the sound of a great beast moving through the wood. Vast trees parted like grass before it, and it walked with a mountain's tread. The young man was tempted to use the golden candle, but instead he drew his long-handled steel, and turned to face an enormous wolf with limbs of rock and a muzzle of iron, towering taller than the tallest tree.

They fought from dawn until high noon, but the young man knew the Way of the Gull Warrior, who cuts and melts and is not struck, and at last he conquered his foe.

Several days later as the young man strode through a clearing in the early morning he closed his eyes and yawned, and as he did so he kicked over an anthill. From that hill poured forth a torrent of ants, each one the size of a wildcat. Again he thought of the golden candle, but instead he gripped his long-handled steel and fought for his life. All morning the battle raged, and all afternoon too, and the young man was worried and circled and chittered at by a thousand foes. But he knew the Way of Stone, that stands even before a thousand waves and is not moved, and when the setting sun ran like blood from a wound between the mountains of the west the last ant was vanquished, and the young man threw himself on the ground to sleep, ringed by a wall of his dead.

A week later the moon had died in the dark before dawn when the young man heard a mad gibbering that filled him with dread. This would be a good time for that golden candle, he thought, but it was dark, and he could not remember where last he'd put the precious thing. The gibbering grew madder, and louder, and closer, and finally the young man whirled, snatching out his long-handled steel. He found himself beset by a headless champion dressed all in slate-grey leather, wielding a terrible weapon: for this dark warrior used his own head as the ball of his mace. The head screamed and chattered as it swung through the air.

Then they fought a terrible battle, the like of which has not been seen since the last time the Fire ate away the world. Three mornings they strove together, and three afternoons, and three terrible nights, while the forest rang with the clash of steel on steel. But the young man knew the Hundred Schools, and at last the groaning mace fell silent.

When the final blow was struck, he hung gasping over the hilts of his long-handled steel, thinking about the darkness of the wood, and the length of the long march home, and the way his body cried for sleep. But only after he found the little golden candle and put it in a pocket just above his heart did he throw himself on the ground beside the headless champion. There he slept for a night and a day.

When at last he woke, he decided to strike for home. Surely I have done as much as one man could to claim this dark forest, he said to himself.

Finding his way back was more difficult than he had anticipated. It was dark, under the Shadow Wood. By day he could see no paths, and by night the stars were hidden.

Long he wandered, lost in shadows, until one evening as night was falling, he spied a light between the trees. With a cry of joy he followed it, arriving at last at a great house carved from the flesh of scores of trees. Gleams of lamplight slipped out from under the leafscreen like sly glimpses from hooded eyes.

Boldly the young man strode forward and knocked on the front door, a vast portal carved in a hollow trunk. The sound of his knocks boomed within the tree, fading slowly like the sound of a stone dropped in a deep well.

Suddenly the door swung open, and the young man started back in surprise. "By my long-handled steel!" he swore. "You must be the brother of the withered sage I met in the capital! Two men could not look more alike!"

A corner of the old man's mouth twitched for an instant, as if he meant to smile. "Why yes, I did have a brother in the capital once. But that was long ago."

The young man shook his head in wonder. "Had I not known about you, I would have said some strange enchantment had brought that wrinkled sage hither."

"Ahem," the old man said. "Be that as it may. You must be cold and weary, for the forest is dark and full of peril. Will you not come in?" And he held the yawning door wide.

For one long moment the young man paused, reluctant to cross the threshold. Am I to quail now? he rebuked himself. I who slew the wolf with limbs of stone, and the mound of ants, and the headless champion? As long as I have my long-handled steel, what harm can come to me?

With this thought in his heart he meant to stride forward, but his legs would not move. Only when he put his hand on the pocket just above his heart, and felt the silver box there, and the little golden candle, did he draw a deep breath and step inside.

"It is very dark in here," he said.

"You will get used to it in time." The old man began to climb a flight of steps carved into the tree's heart. These led up a great way to a walkway that ran between two trees, far above the ground. "Have no fear. There are rails on either side. So! I am surprised to see you here. Few travel even one way through the Shadow Wood. Did you then fail to encounter the Wolf Mountain?"

"I know the Way of the Gull Warrior, and so reduced that particular peak to rubble."

"And were you not seized by the Army of Thousands?"

"I was, but I know the Way of Stone, and I rebuked them with my long-handled steel."

"You were not vanquished by the Headless Champion?"

"You are perhaps unaware that I have studied the Hundred Schools," the young man replied. "Thus I was able to defeat that decapitated devil once and for all."

The old man rubbed his chin and shook his head in disbelief. "Truly, you must be a great hero."

Darkness whispered between the branches. As they walked from tree to tree, the planks creaked and swayed beneath their feet. The young man heard a stream murmur far, far below. He gripped the rails more tightly and hoped their journey was nearly at an end. "Tell me, doddering wise man, how came you to the heart of the Shadow Wood?"

The old man had reached a door in another vast tree. "You mean my brother did not tell you? When I was your age, I too was a great adventurer. I too won through to this place with my wits and a piece of steel with a handle just the length of your own."

Once again the young man paused, reluctant to enter the dark heart of another tree. "Then why are you still here? Surely a man who has scaled Wolf Mountain and turned back the Army of Thousands and defeated the Headless Champion could not lack the resolve to leave the forest?"

The old man had gone ahead, and his voice carried weirdly through the echoing gloom. "Who, me?" he said, with a strange little laugh. "Oh, I am a terrible coward. Why, I am afraid of my own shadow!"

"This will be your room," the old man said. The bed's curving headboard rested against the north wall of the tree; high on the south side a window notch flooded the guest room with moonlight. A spiral staircase wound up through the middle of the floor, vanishing into the ceiling.

"I shall only trouble you for a single night," the young man said. "On the morrow I will be fresh again, and with your directions

I should have little difficulty leaving this melancholy forest behind."

The old man said, "Just so. I shall be in the room below. Good night, and good luck!"

With this unsettling remark he vanished down the stairs, and the young man prepared to sleep. His every muscle burned and his every bone ached. His skin was a tapestry of bruises. He wanted nothing more than to crawl beneath the covers of his bed and snore the night away.

And yet he could not sleep.

The forest was in his room. The silken pillow felt like moss beneath his ear. The cloth coverlet felt like softest heather on his body; it smelled of wet leaves and blood and vixen. Outside, the secret trees whispered and bowed, and shadows crept around the corners of the room, rising and falling, slipping away at the edge of sight.

What had the old man said? He was afraid of his own shadow.

The young man found himself staring into the darkness, flinching at every creak of the wooden floor or crack of the wooden ceiling. Silver fell through the high window. Steeped in moonlight, the young man had the strangest feeling that his very essence was bleeding slowly from his pores, swirling out to the room's edge to be consumed by shadows.

Nonsense, he told himself. They were shadows, nothing more. Shadows could harm him no more than names called out by rude children. Shadows. That was all.

A muffled cry from the room below made him leap to his feet. Grabbing his long-handled steel, he rushed down the spiral stairs.

The old man's bed was empty. Quivering like an arrow in a target, the young man stood on the lowest stair, eyes wide and fixed on the creeping night. He saw nothing but moonlight and dim shapes and the shadows of tree limbs, crossing like ancient hands rubbed together in sinister amusement. The young man stepped toward the bed, walking like a dancer on the balls of his feet. His long-handled steel trembled, ever so slightly, in the hands that had held steady before the Headless Champion.

For a long moment he stood motionless beside the bed. Then with a great cry he flung back the coverlet.

The old man was gone. But underneath the blanket, hard-edged in the moonlight, lay his shadow.

The young man yelled and ran for the stairs. A flood of shadows poured after him. When he reached his own room he risked a quick glance back, but the moonlight showed the horrible truth: the shadows were following him. Somehow he knew that once drowned beneath that tide of darkness he too would never leave the darkling wood.

Up he raced, and up still farther, until he thought his heart would burst, pounding up stair after stair until he found himself in a tiny room with no more stairs to climb. It creaked, that treetop room, swaying in the murmuring wind, and the floor beneath his feet sloped first this way, then that.

He was desperate. He could flee no farther, but neither could he cut the darkness with his long-handled steel.

Then, at his wit's end, he remembered the old man's gift.

With shaking fingers he plucked the silver box from the pocket of his shirt, shook out the single match, and struck it on the bottom of his boot. He blinked in its sudden light and then held it to the tip of the tiny golden candle.

The candle spat and sparkled into life. The young man set it in the middle of the floor and then whirled with a great cry as the first shadow slid up the stairwell behind him. The young man lunged, jumping before the candle flame, and then struck into thin air.

The shadow hissed and writhed and died—for now the young man had a fine shadow too, and a long-handled darkness to wield against the night.

He stood against the shadows like a stone, lanced through their ranks like the Warrior and then melted away. He needed every trick he had learned from the Hundred Schools, for against him were ranged the shadows of the one hundred men the king had sent into the forest, and behind them the two hundred, and behind them the five hundred, and the thousand sent to search for the others.

But the young man was strong, and swift, and in the end the last shadow, stooped and wizened like an old man, turned and fled down the stairs. Curiously, this final shade rubbed his hands together, and the sound of the wind hissing through the branches outside was like the sound of distant laughter.

But the young man laughed too, for he was brave and a champion. Then he leaned upon his hilts, spent in every limb, and watched the golden candlelight sparkle down the length of his long-handled steel. He had turned back the tide. He was alone.

Almost. There was still a silver moon and a dark wood outside. The wind still whispered and a wild scent like wet leaves and vixen lay heavy in the air.

The young man glanced up at an unexpected movement. His eyes widened as a dark shape walked across the room.

His shadow, his own shadow leaned forward, glancing up at its master. And then with the smallest, softest sigh, it blew the little golden candle out.

And from deep within the darkness, the shadow laughed.

"And that is the story of the Shadow Wood," Seven finished softly, his voice like a thread of wind in the gloom. "Told to me by Switch of the forest people, as I have told it to you. You see, Reed, I too have learned the Hundred Schools, and I too have made myself in the image of the Gull Warrior. But I do not wish to be his champion. I do not wish to be my story's shadow."

Foam shifted on the middle thwart. "I do not believe you need to worry. Remember what the Singer said, the night we captured Thumbtip? She said that your story, which started out so much larger than life, would turn into a personal tale."

"Great stories turn to small ones," Shale said.

"My story . . . and Hazel Twist's. The thing we make together."

Shale shuddered. "Twinning stories are the worst. Remember those horrible ones Brook used to tell? And now . . ."

Fog still drifted in wavering white billows across the water. The lights of Delta were drawing steadily closer. It would not be long before they reached the lagoon. "I am not used to hearing fear in your voice," Reed said.

"A very good friend of Shale's has been twinned," Foam explained.

"Strange are the perils of living at the edge of the Mist! I am sorry."

Foam shook his head. "The funny thing is, the twin did not kill her. They both live still, she and the haunt. Or at least they did when we split up three months ago. We had even sailed to Delta together."

"Stranger still! But do not believe that it can last. I have told the Singer's stories for a score of years now, and the act of twinning is a terrible one. Your friend has a respite, not a peace. Sooner or later one twin will have to live in the sunlight, and the other be banished to the Mist, or the grave."

"What do you know?" Shale said. "You tell old stories to amuse ignorant Deltans. We live with the Mist. We salvage from it for our livelihood. Our island and our people are blessed with sight and wisdom to work it, to guard against it. Brook can look after herself."

Seven's ship rocked and creaked over the black water. The southern end of the Foot slid by their port bow, and the lights of Delta's harbor burned brightly before them. "Of course," Reed said softly. "I forgot my place. No doubt your friend will thrive in ways I cannot imagine."

But that was the end of storytelling, and the only words spoken for the rest of the trip were of sails, and lines, and docks.

"How quiet it seems!" Foam said as he tied their painter to a docking ring. "This morning all Delta was cheering. Are we old news so soon?"

Indeed, the crowded docks were strangely silent. Around them, the sixty other ships in Seven's flotilla were bumping up to the landing, their shivering crews laughing and looking forward to hot ale and warm beds. But the Deltans themselves were quiet, milling on the jetty, and the morning's joy had drained from their drawn faces.

It was Glint who approached them. They had left the physician in town to help Pond. The battered white bandage she used to wear around her neck had been replaced by an elegant silk kerchief. Her face was grim. The strong hands that had dressed their dying without a tremor now shook as she raised her arms and clasped Seven to her breast.

He stiffened and pulled back, holding her shoulders. "What is it?"

Foam and Shale stood nearby. Fog curled and smoked across the harbor behind them, and the night breeze blew chill.

"Pond," Glint said.

Seven stood as if turned to stone.

"We think it was cutthroats, deserters from the forest army. She had finished arranging the berths and wanted to see her parents. I never thought to send anyone with her. Delta was saved! Twist had gone, and I thought . . ." Her voice caught. "When she didn't come back we asked directions to her house. Rich place, off on its own. You know it."

Glint closed her eyes. When she opened them again she had herself under control. She might have been telling one of her patients that he had the canker and had little time to live, plain and steady and compassionate. "They must have slipped over while Twist was marching down to the lee docks. They had taken the place apart. Pond was in the dining room. At least she never saw her parents. I found their bodies in the back room."

Still Seven stood unmoving.

"She is dead," Glint said.

Silence spread like nightfall over the returning navy. In all that great crowded space were only the sounds of boats creaking and rocking; sails luffing softly in the gentle breeze; the endless dark mutter of the sea.

Seven turned and walked back to his docking ring.

"What are you doing?"

His cunning fingers slipped Foam's knot and he pulled the painter free. "First I will find her killers. Then I will find Hazel Twist. Reed, Glint—take care of Pond for me. Burn her. Like Brine and Rose and all the others." He cocked his head for a moment, getting the lie of the wind. "She hated the cold."

"You are mad with grief," Foam said softly. "You cannot go, Seven. There is nothing to be done. The war is over. Grieve for Pond here. She would want it so."

"I look like a woodlander. I can talk like a woodlander. I lived and ate and breathed with one for years," Seven said. "I know where they went back into the forest. I know the country around the edge of the bay. They have only a day's start."

"What would you do if you found them? Even you cannot slay a whole army."

Seven laughed. "Oh, I shall be patient," he said. "Hazel Twist has taught me something about patience. I am not a slow pupil. Not when learning how to kill."

"This is madness." Shale strode forward to grab Seven.

She screamed and stopped short, staggering off balance. Where a moment before Seven had been squatting with his back turned, now he crouched before her. His knife pricked her neck. "Never touch me," he said. "If you take one step closer, I will kill you. I swear it."

There was a blackness in his voice and his strong killer's hands. Shale backed away. A puff of wind came up, stirring a clamor from the boats. Like daggers of flame, their tiny lanterns danced in Seven's eyes.

Delta watched as the hero of the islands climbed into his boat. He used his sheathed sword to push away from the dock. Then he set his sail and slid smoothly out into the night, heading into the darkness under the shadow of the wood.

CHAPTER 20: WILLOW

"In the end I think it was inevitable," Hazel Twist said one night that autumn, sipping his brandy from a pearwood goblet. "The Emperor had lived too long with the certainty of his own doom."

Alder Shade rocked slowly in the swing next to Twist's, sucking on a black briar pipe. Rowan Spark prowled around the talking room, threading between the tree trunks. He ducked to avoid a lantern hung from the ceiling branches. An ivy of shadows wound through the room, thrown by the lantern's weak yellow light.

Spark grimaced. "What kind of man could do it that way?"

"A Bronze, of course."

"Live coals," Shade rumbled. "Taken from his son's pyre. They say the stewards tried to stop him after the first, but the Emperor held them off with a sword. He used tongs to pick them out of the brazier and popped them down like baked locusts. His tongue looked like a hank of black leather."

"Shade, while I would be more than happy to refill your drink," Twist remarked, rising and walking to the cabinet where he kept his liquor, "I note without approbation your tendency to linger on the gruesome."

"Apologies," Shade murmured, holding out his goblet. Pipe smoke eddied from his nose and mouth. "But you must admit the method was unorthodox. I wonder why he chose to forgo the customary Thirsting."

"How it must have burned!" Spark said. He glanced at the

hanging lanterns and shuddered. "Six days faster anyway."

Hazel Twist decided not to refill his own glass. "The Emperor and his son lost between one moonrise and the next, leaving Bronze Cut with undisputed power. He has been lucky with the rain. It looks to be a clement fall." Twist returned to his swing and settled comfortably within its mesh. The three men fell silent, pondering the future of their nation. Normally Twist was fond of such speculations, but Rowan Hilt's murder and the Emperor's grisly suicide had turned such thoughts bitter.

At length Twist stirred. "The reason the Emperor's death is so shocking, I believe, is that it was so personal, so apolitical an act." He fingered his goblet of brandy, turning it slowly before his eyes. The talking-room was fragrant with the smell of damp willow-wood and alcohol. Rain pattered on the ceiling and ran down the tree trunks, disappearing below the plank floor. "Our state, after all, is like a Power to us. The clans, the whole community of our people, have a history and momentum that seems as great as that of the forest itself, or the mountains, or the sea.

"But something like this reminds us that our laws and customs, our history and our politics, are not ruled by processes as sure and immutable as those by which the mountains are created and consumed. To eat fire!" He shook his head. "That is the act of a single man, torn by anguish." He sipped his brandy again, feeling it burn across his palate. "We empathize, of course. We cannot help but imagine the sensation, and we recoil. But more than that, we are reminded that the whole delicate human web within which we exist can be rent by sudden emotions. In the end we are all at the mercy of our passions, and the passions of others."

"You will not catch me eating coals," Spark said.

Twist watched a moth flutter drunkenly around the nearest lantern. "And we are reminded that we too have such passions. We are forced to acknowledge our enormous capacity for cruelty. We must admit to ourselves the wild urge for self-destruction. The Spark smolders, as the old story says. It longs to be free."

Shade stirred. "To talk of such things, Hazel Twist, may be to speak truths which are more wisely left unsaid."

Twist smiled. "Such is the folly of wisdom!"

"—Did you hear that?" Spark said.

Rain pattered insistently on the roof; dripped down the tree trunks; vanished into darkness. Branches creaked in the warm wind and their leaves sighed, weeping. "Hear what?" Twist said.

"That. A—grunt, maybe. I thought I heard something moving outside, and then a sort of a . . . grunt." The others listened. "No," Spark said at last. "Nothing now."

"A dead branch falling," Shade suggested.

"Or a raccoon."

Spark shrugged. "Something."

Shade covered his pipe bowl with two fingers, drew deeply, held the smoke inside, and then breathed slowly out, letting it trickle from his lungs. "It is very pleasant to be here, Twist, for the autumn rains. I even took some pleasure from the ferry ride, though we Alders are not fond of boats."

"Boats! Do not talk to us of boats!" Spark had been one of Twist's junior commanders during the war. "I shall never think twice about crossing this little creek again. Not after daring the sea."

"Was it really so bad?" Shade asked.

Twist said, "He was caught out in a gale with only a raft beneath him. Three-quarters of the men were drowned." His subtle Hazel eyes looked at something far away that caused him pain. He shook his small head. "It was always madness, trying to take the islands. We were not meant for the sea. It is a great Power, greater perhaps than the forest. Certainly it bears no love for us. We refused Fathom's offer when he came to the Tree, remember, and with good reason."

"Well, I still think you have it rather nice here," Shade said, returning to his earlier theme. "It was wise of you, I think, to avoid the Arbor."

"Unsuccessful generals are rarely made welcome by the State," Twist said dryly. "And it is beautiful, here in Willow. I am well content to live in my wife's house and watch my children grow."

Shade looked up. "There it was."

"What?"

"Spark's animal. Only it wasn't outside this time, it was from somewhere back toward the rest of the house." Rain fell into the uncomfortable silence. "Not in the house, of course," Shade added. "On the roof, I meant. Or perhaps at the base of one of the trees."

"It seems strange to me that I should be the only one not to hear this noise. It casts a shadow on my heart." Twist rose and placed his empty goblet on the sideboard. "Gentlemen, if you will excuse me, I shall make a quick survey of the house. No doubt Blue is sleepless again tonight, or one of the children is roaming. My apologies."

"Go on! While you are gone, Shade and I shall swap stories that only bachelors should hear!"

Twist smiled. "I doubt you can say anything I have not heard from my wife."

Blue's family had left the walkway from the talking-room to the rest of the mansion unpanelled; a corridor of trimmed willows was the only roof. Rain dripped from the leafy canopy, sweet and warm as blood; trailing outer branches swept in a green waterfall down either side. It was very dark, beneath tree and cloud. One hooded lantern rocked in the breeze, dripping light like golden oil on the willow creepers and the slick planking.

As he walked, Twist let his hand rest lightly on the rail, feeling the smooth wet wood slide beneath his palm. He appreciated its strength, tamed from the raw power of the living trees. As alien, really, as the mountains or the sea.

The wind wove cloud and wood together in the troubled night. Raindrops broke into willows' tears.

Twist hurried to the other end of the walkway. He had become a city-dweller, a householder. Even in the army his rank had always bought protection from the outside. Now Nature pressed itself against him: vivid, vulgar, seething with mysteries.

He was glad to reach the mansion proper. This part of the house was large and utilitarian; first built before the days when the Willows had been great, it was not designed to hang among the trees. The talking-room had been an elegant afterthought of Blue's grandmother, inspired by her many rings in the Arbor.

All was quiet. Silently Twist padded to the girls' room. Every-thing in order. He checked on Jay next. The boy was sprawled on his back with his teeth showing, a sure sign he was not faking sleep; awake it would have been beneath his dignity to let his mouth hang open.

Dread was building in Hazel Twist, as if each reassuring sign hid a more terrible calamity. He found himself hesitating on the threshold of his own bedroom, one hand on his sword hilt. He cursed himself for an aging fool and stepped inside.

Blue lay on the bed, still as death, with her wavy blond hair tumbled about her shoulders. He darted to her side and felt for the vein at her throat, then sighed with relief to feel the strong, steady pulse beating there. Her chest rose as she turned to his touch, still half-asleep. "What?"

Twist laughed softly at himself. "I love you," he said. He knelt and kissed her on the neck.

Weak with sleep she cradled his head in the hollow of her shoulder. "Coming t'bed soon?"

"Very soon. I will show our guests safely to their rooms and then return."

"Mm? M-hmm . . ."

He kissed her again and rose to his feet, feeling happy and foolish. It was the wind that did it, he told himself. The wind in the trees. And him with forty-three rings under the eaves of the forest. We never escape from our fear of the Outside.

Of course it was the talk about the Emperor's suicide that had made him uneasy.

He heard the first yell as he stepped onto the walkway. Spark was shouting for servants, and a voice he did not recognize howled his name like a curse. The wet planks bucked beneath him like waves as he raced back to his friends.

The talking-room was bright after the darkness outside. Spark and Shade crouched with their backs to Twist. Before them stood a stranger, a tall man in tattered clothes. He held a long-handled sword before him. The steel was beaded with rain. In an islander's voice he said, "Greetings, Hazel Twist."

"Why have you come here?"

"You can't threaten three people," Shade growled. "You're a madman, and you're bluffing."

"Am I? What do you think, Hazel Twist? What do you think, Rowan Spark?" The stranger smiled unpleasantly. "Do you think I am bluffing? Or does your fear whisper that you have known me before? What about Bone? Do you think that Bone would recognize me? Of course Bone is dead now," he explained to Shade. "I killed him long ago. A knife through the throat. No matter how many men I kill, I can still remember every detail of every murder. Do not make me remember you."

"You bastard!" Spark swore. He drew his sword.

The islander smiled.

Hazel Twist grabbed his friend. "Spark! Stay back. This must be Seven, you fool."

Spark blanched.

"Seven?" Shade asked.

Twist studied the islander, seeing him in the flesh at last. "He led the Deltans against us. This is the famous pupil about whom Bronze Switch tells such extraordinary stories."

Shade looked at Seven with wonder and new fear in his eyes.

"My master was not a Bronze; he killed one. That is why he was exiled."

"Is that what he told you?" Twist shrugged. "If you are not a Bronze, the penalty for killing one is death. There are no exceptions. Bronze Switch killed three men and a woman over an imagined slight and was sent from the Empire to acquire self-discipline."

"You lie."

"Why would I?"

"You are a woodlander. You do not need a reason to lie."

Twist's eyebrows rose. "Perhaps you might consider Bronze Switch in just that light."

"There were four guards outside my father's house. I killed them as easily as a man kills ants." Seven's eyes were as empty as the sea. "I was always good with my hands."

Hazel Twist prayed that Blue was awake, that she was taking

the children, that they were creeping from the other end of the house, into the rain, that they were gone, that she would not be sleeping, sprawled on her back with her long hair wound around her throat. The islander stood before him like a shadow, a creature of the rain and the night and the wood's wild heart. "What do you want?"

Even now Seven's hand was easy around the hilt of his sword. "She was to be a Witness, Hazel Twist. She went to visit her parents when we came back to Delta. They lived out from the city. It was a beautiful house, Hazel Twist. At sunset you could watch the seals playing down in the cove. Her father told stories of Delta in his grandfather's time."

"Who was she, Seven?"

"They mutilated her parents, Hazel Twist. What do you think they did to her? She was a beautiful woman, Hazel Twist. Do you think they raped her before she died or afterwards?"

"I am sorry," Twist said.

"We too grieve for your loss," Shade rumbled quietly. "But why come here? No one in this room was there that day, I'm sure."

Seven nodded. "True. True enough. But a general is responsible for his men. Am I not right, Hazel Twist? And these men were of the forest. I strangled them both. It took me a long time to find them. They fled west, up the Vein and into the grasslands."

"We had left the islands long before," Twist said. "You know that."

"They were deserters. They thought they would be pirates, brigands, robbers. They had learned that the people of the islands were harmless. Defenseless. It was their time under your command that taught them that, Hazel Twist."

"You can't hold that against him!" Spark said. "It is madness!"

"I burn, Hazel Twist. The pain eats me from inside." Seven's sword point was unwavering. Rain dripped sadly down the tree trunks. "I caught them and I throttled them both. I held the second one in my arms and watched the terror in his eyes as he kicked out his life. But when it was over, the pain had not gone away." Darkness pressed against the circle of lantern-light. The room swayed sadly, rocked in the willows' arms. Seven's face was deep in shadow. His voice mingled with the pattering rain and the creaking wood. "The pain remained. Do you know why?"

"Because it did not bring her back."

"Shut up! Don't ever talk about her. No. The pain remained because I had not gotten to its roots. I had not seen deeply enough. Had it not been for the war, those two never would have come. I would never have sailed to the mainland that day. I would have been there. The hurt remained because I had taken my revenge on followers, not leaders."

Seven looked at the wet blade of his sword. "I am tired of killing," he said. "So tired." He looked at Spark and Shade. "Do not make me kill you."

"What are you going to do?" Spark demanded.

"First I will kill Hazel Twist. Then I will kill the Emperor. The Emperor will have better guards; I have left him for last."

"You cannot kill the Emperor," Twist said.

"I do not care how many guards he has. You must know that. I have to kill him. For her. There is so much pain in me, Hazel Twist. I know it is her. She is asking me why I have not avenged her yet. She is uneasy, Hazel Twist. She is a lady. She is ashamed, to be found cut and beaten and raped."

"You misunderstand me. I know you can kill. But the Emperor is beyond your reach."

Seven's fingers tightened. "Dead?"

Twist nodded. "By his own hand. He too felt a pain inside, Seven. He swallowed blazing coals until he died."

Seven cursed.

"The man who ordered the war is gone," Shade said. "Give up your quarrel with the dead."

"The man who waged that war still stands before me."

"We were only doing what we were told!" Spark cried.

Seven laughed. "That is ever the excuse with you forest people, is it not? 'I was only doing what I was told' 'It was not my responsibility' 'It was the Emperor's command.' Islanders do not allow others to make their choices for them. Every man must answer for his own deeds." He spat. "That for your excuses."

Twist said, "Every man must answer for his own deeds—but the acts of the men are blamed on their commander? The commander they had deserted?"

Shade and Spark stood motionless. Seven paused, staring at Twist as if trying to see him among shadows. The sword was heavy in his hand; the tip drooped. "Words," he said at last. "You made it possible for them to act. Vengeance is just."

"I am not Stonefinger," Twist said. "I am a man. A man who was your enemy only for a while, and only by accident. I too lost friends in the war. My best lieutenant you, with your high ideals, poisoned and then burned alive while he lay dying, too weak to roll out from under a falling beam."

"I am sick of your words!" Seven shouted. The sword snapped up. "I am going to kill you now, Hazel Twist. I have let you talk too long."

"Stand!" Twist said. "Stand and listen, you fool. You learned everything you know about war from me, and by the Fire you will not stop learning now!"

Shade and Spark gripped their swords more tightly and licked their lips. Fear crushed their chests with terrible strength. Shade knew from Switch's stories and the way Spark stood, unnaturally pale and nervous, that the first touch of steel on steel would mean their deaths.

Seven hesitated.

"You want to hurt me?" Twist demanded. "Then come here. How old are you, Seven? Twenty-three? Twenty-four? Follow me across the walkway, into the house where my children lie sleeping. You can cut their throats, if you want to hurt me. I have cared for them these eighteen rings. How long did you love your lady, Seven?"

Twist dropped his sword. It clattered at his feet. "We can go farther, to the next room. If you want me to hurt as you hurt, there is always Blue. She is the moving center of my world, Seven. Rape her. Cut her throat. Strangle her in bed. She is blond. You don't see many fair-haired women in the islands, do you, Seven?"

"Twist!" Spark gasped. "What are you saying?"

"This does not concern you, Spark. Put down your weapons, both of you. Do you think it makes any difference to him whether you have them or not?"

"I hate you," Seven said.

"Rape her," Twist said. "She is past forty now. It may not be such a pleasure to a young man like yourself. But it will hurt, Seven. It will be twenty-two rings of life you steal from me, and all the years ahead."

"I do not want . . . My quarrel is with you."

Rain pattered on the roof. Outside, the creaking willows wept.

"Come now. Even you must see that killing me will destroy my family. As you have been destroyed."

"Why did you say that, about Stonefinger?"

"Those clothes suit you very well, you know. Your build, your features—you could be a woodlander. Tell me, is your hearing keener than your fellows? Do you see better in the dark? How could you see Bone to throw your knife, without him seeing you?"

"Do not mock me."

"I will do anything I want to my assassin," Twist said. Inside he was dizzy with fear. Had he gone too far? How hard could he push? He had to keep control, keep control, take the moment away from Seven, force him to see what he was doing, force him to know the people he had come to kill.

Blue. Lying in bed with her blond hair around her throat. He would give anything, gladly give his life, so long as she woke up again.

Twist put his hands on his friends' shoulders. "Put down your weapons." Two more swords clattered to the floor, scarring the polished planking. "Do not act in his shadow-play. I am no man of weapons. This is no duel between Stonefinger and your Gull Warrior. This is an execution. Let it proceed as such."

"I thought you would have the courage to fight."

"Why?" Twist asked. "What would be the point? Why should I waste my time? To make you feel more just? Come," he said, turning for the door. "We were going to kill my wife."

"Be quiet!" Seven was shaking. "When will you learn to be quiet!"

Twist fought his fear, trying to think. The pain had dragged Seven so far down into darkness. So many nights dreaming of revenge. It would be a miracle if Twist could force him to see the light. "What? You insist on only killing me? It will cause me less pain, and of course I appreciate the courtesy."

"I hate you."

"I know."

"You know. You know," Seven said. "You always know." He smashed the nearest lantern, spilling liquid fire onto the floor. Nobody dared to move. "It hurts," he said softly, raising his sword. "It hurts too much."

PART THREE
The Twins' Loop

CHAPTER 21: THE WEDDING

Shale waited impatiently on the dock of Clouds End, hugging herself against a cold wind that cut the sea into chop. She squinted
at the sloop beating up from Trickfoot. The sky was scoured blue,
the sun a hard white ball falling swiftly into the west.

"*Crafty*," she muttered, recognizing the narwhal bone bowsprit.

Bass edged his boat into the dock and tossed her the painter.
Shale whipped a round turn and two half hitches around a docking
ring. "Mom spotted you from her tower. What brings you here?"

Bass laughed. "A very special cargo. Brought all the way from
the palace of the forest people, if you believe it."

Brook walked slowly out from behind the cabin roof. "Hey,
stranger. Remember me?"

Shale cut loose with a yell they could hear on the Harp. She
grabbed the *Crafty*'s gunwale and pulled herself aboard. With
another earsplitting whoop she swung Brook off the deck in a huge
bear hug.

"Oof! No!" Brook gasped.

Shale put her down.

Brook winced and glanced down at her swelling tummy. "Sorry.
It's just that—"

"No. No! You didn't!"

Brook smiled. "I did."

"You didn't! A baby! Disgusting!"

Rope finished furling the sail and stepped over. "Good to see
you again," he said, smiling and bracing himself.

Shale turned. "Were you responsible for this?" she demanded, pointing at Brook's belly.

Rope's smile faded. "Well . . . Oof!"

Shale swung him off the deck too. "Caught you off guard!" she crowed. "Swap's Spit! Do you still have a face in there, or is it all beard?"

"*Ungggh*," Rope said, trying to catch his breath.

And behind Rope hovered Jo, half-smiling, with downcast eyes. Shale stalked over to look her up and down. "Well, haunt, you did it." She clasped Jo gravely, and gravely hugged her. "I cannot tell you how much it meant to the islanders when Twist's army fell back. And how much it means to me, that you brought our goslings home."

"What happened the night we split up?" Brook asked. "We heard a few details from a singer named Reed when we were passing through Delta, but we want the whole story!"

Shale laughed. "Let's get out of the wind and take you inside. Food first, tall tales later!"

"Food!" Rope said fervently. "Hot, and lots of it. With extra plum wine for my cousin Bass here for bringing us home on such a filthy day."

"It was no trouble," said the black-haired young man from Trickfoot. "What else is family for?"

The whole village of Clouds End, including Swallow's four-month-old, crammed into the meeting hall that winter night, bringing out vast stores of food and friendliness. The cold wind whistling outside only made the great fire cheerier, and the conversation louder, and the food tastier. At first they were wary of Jo, but the twin did not seem to have harmed Brook, and as the evening went on and the wine flowed, they forgot to be afraid of her.

Brook and Rope were besieged. Everyone in the village took turns touching Brook's tummy as if they'd never seen a pregnant woman before. Especially her foster-mother, Otter, whose eyes brimmed with joyful tears all night long.

Not once but many times the travellers had to explain that they had gone to the heart of the forest. Some were skeptical, but old Stick was quick to believe. "We are made for adventure, us Clouds Enders. Comes from breathing the Mist, y'see. Remember, my grandfather came out here—"

"Only one year after the island was discovered," the villagers chorused.

"—and that's the stock we come from! Fisherman-explorers, like Swap and Chart after him."

Shandy hollered for attention and proposed the first of many toasts in honor of Brook, of Rope, of Bass, of the Gull Warrior, of Jo, of Foam and Shale, of the weather, and, of course, in honor of Clouds End itself. Which was really, as Brook muttered sleepily at the end of the evening, what it had all been about in the first place.

It was a marvelous homecoming, the sort of feast where everyone gives you as much as you can eat of everything you like the best, and then won't let you help with the cleaning up. It lasted through the night and into the morrow, and dawn was breaking when the last villagers tottered home to bed.

"We had a Building when Shale and I returned," Foam explained as he and Rope put out the next morning. "The *Walrus* isn't the craft the old *Salamander* was, perhaps, but she's a sturdy tub."

Rope glowered. "*Walrus*, eh?"

"An excellent name, I thought. Shale did the knotwork on it. We have two holds, one for fish and another for dry cargo in case we want to do some real trading."

The two men sailed east, skirting the shoals between Clouds End and Shale's island, until Foam's tiny stock of patience ran out. "Well? Talk! I got some of the story last night, but I need more."

"What do you want to know?"

"Everything! Every impression, every incident, every person you met, what you ate for each meal, and the trees you passed, individually named and in the order you passed them, please."

The sun was out, but the day was still cold. Rope had borrowed fishing gear from Stone: heavy, hooded tunic, mitts, and sealhide boots with an extra fur lining. "It feels very good to see. The forest has no horizon. You would not believe how you come to miss that."

"So how did you get to the mainland? Stole a boat? Or did Jo turn into a dolphin and carry you there?"

"We stole a one-master."

"Wasn't named *Eel*, was she?"

"That was it! How did you know?"

Foam laughed delightedly. "Lucky guess! Oh, if Seven only knew!" The breeze freshened, and the mainsail pennant snapped briskly overhead. "What about the rest of the story? I see marvels in your face. You are older than you were."

Rope smiled and squatted with his back against the mainmast. "It is very odd. When you tell a story, the important things are what happens. You know, Chart went here, and this is what he saw, and this is what he did, and then he came back. Our tale was stopping the war. But the things that mattered to me were very small. Private things."

Foam glanced at him. "Great fires fall to ash, and great stories turn to small ones," he said. "Soon to be a husband and a father, heh? I envy you. I always thought it would work out between you two."

"Yes. I suppose it will."

"Do I detect a note of reluctance?"

Rope looked up at the mainsail pennant snapping in the breeze. Above it, a single gull wheeled in the vaulted sky. "I know, now more than ever, that I do not want to live without her. But there are risks, when your life gets tangled up with someone else. Just taking care of a boat is big enough. To be a husband now, or a father! It makes you think. Those are heavy responsibilities."

"You are the most responsible person I know," Foam said simply. "I cannot imagine a better father."

"I don't know," Rope said. "I thought I was over my dad going into the Mist, but ever since we found out Brook was pregnant, I have been trying to imagine what kind of father I will be. But when I look inside myself, there is no father there. Only a hollow space."

Foam grunted. "You can have mine."

"And now it seems like that missing part of me has meant a lot, after all. Maybe my caution is only fear of going away like my father did. And the secret is, I want to. A tiny part of me wants to go into the Mist and find out what he left us for. I know that isn't reasonable. I know he probably did not choose to leave. But there is this three-year-old in me who does not believe it. That thinks he left me for the Mist. And that child still makes many of my choices."

Foam glanced curiously at his friend.

Rope smiled, trying to shake away the doubts clouding his heart. "What about you? Your summer was exciting, from what we heard."

"Exciting? There was excitement, all right. It's the exciting parts you try to forget."

Foam cleated the jib for a starboard tack. "The main thing about the war, for me, was finding something I was good at. Strategy, as it turns out. Thinking of ways for Seven to kill people."

"And keep your people from being killed."

Foam shrugged, accepting the correction. "Some things seem easier, now that I have been important. I can skipper my own boat. Not that I don't know which of us is the better sailor!"

Rope waved one mitt impatiently.

"Pull that sheet in a little. There, that's good. And I fell in love," Foam said. The sun broke into dazzles on the cold waves.

"Anyone I know?"

"Who would have thought it?"

Rope pulled the sheet in even tighter, tense with wind, taming it. "Did anything happen?"

"No." Foam shook his head and laughed. "Remember all the times we used to talk about them? Women, I mean."

"We weren't anchored to the subject."

"Well, you were not. You didn't need to be. I found it endlessly fascinating. The point is, we surely didn't know anything, did we? I mean, there was a great deal I think someone should have told us, because we certainly were stupid."

"Yes," Rope said. "We certainly were."

Foam eased the tiller a little closer to the wind. "I always used to think, girl of your dreams, the hesitant courtship, will you marry me? The Responsibilities of Adulthood and Happily Ever After. But the girl of my dreams was not thinking the same things at all."

"Women are smarter," Rope said. "They talk about important things while we are talking about . . . I don't know. Fish, I suppose." He grunted, easing out the sheet. "Another thing like that," he said suddenly, taking off his left mitt. A chilly grey tendril tested the air briefly before withdrawing to the warmth of Rope's sleeve. "Remember Net?"

"Well, hello! Who could forget!"

"Now take him, for example. I guess it's silly, but secretly I always imagined he would be important. Like a magic sword. Something central to my story."

"And he isn't?"

Rope laughed. "Sure. The way my boat is important. He hangs around my wrist. He plays with Brook."

"Well, then!"

"Is that it?"

"Maybe." Foam shrugged. "You made Net, Rope. He is part of your story. Not Jo's, Not Sere's, and certainly not the Emperor's. Great stories turn to small ones. What matters to you aren't always the big things. They are wee and private. My guess is that Net will turn out to mean a lot that way, as the years go by."

"Hmmm." Rope ducked as the boom swung overhead. "Ever kill a man?"

"More or less."

"I'm sorry."

Foam looked away from his friend. "Me too."

Shandy handed Brook a cup of peppermint tea. "Well, it seems you handled your haunt well enough. Did you get some help from the Witness of Delta?"

"Never had a chance to look for her. We did meet the Arbor's Witness, more or less."

Shandy's eyebrows rose.

"He said that Jo and I were part of a one twist ring," Brook said slowly. "The story of the war and the Emperor and all that is still happening, only now it's between Jo and me somehow. Do you understand that?"

Shandy nodded thoughtfully. "I believe so. I have often thought the Singer's stories were like whales. You may only notice them when they jump—the war was a jump—but they are there afterwards too, running beneath the water." She saw Brook shiver. "Did this Witness give you any advice about Jo?"

Brook took a sip of tea. "Mm. He told me I could either cut the knot between us, or follow it out."

Shandy grunted. "You and Jo both still seem to be breathing."

"If this is a story of the real world, a root story, I think I can be stronger than Jo. I have you and Rope and Clouds End. . . . But Jo took the Spark when she stopped the Emperor, and it's eating her up inside. Her eyes have turned golden—had you noticed? And all the way home she was nervy. Fey. She smokes all the time now, like a woodlander. I feel sorry for her."

"After she twinned you!"

"I know, I know it sounds strange. But we are each shadows of the other, and a part of me cares very much for her. She saved the islands, remember. And while she was in the Palace, taking the Emperor's Spark into herself, Rope and I were safe in a room far away, making this." Brook patted her tummy.

"I was wondering about that."

Brook laughed. "Just so you know, we agreed to get married before we, um, you know."

"Ah, yes," Shandy said. "I know about that sex stuff. Moss told me about it once. Sounded nasty."

Brook giggled into her tea.

The Witness grinned, wrapping her hands around her own cup of tea, blessing the warmth that soothed her old joints. "Just remember that this story is not yet over, Brook. 'Haunts get what they want.' Jo does not strike me as the sort to go quietly into the Mist."

"I know. But I can't worry about her all the time. I have to live my life." Brook looked around at Shandy's dim, cluttered house, rich with the smell of beeswax and cut timber. "I love this place. I love Otter's house. I love this island. I love the people on it. It is home. I never knew how much it meant to me."

Shandy laughed. "Well, you were young. Young people are stupid and vigorous. Old people are lazy and smart."

Brook took a sip of tea. "I feel smarter," she admitted, rising to tend the fire, "but I don't feel lazy. I feel stronger than I have in my life."

"Children will take care of that, I promise you. Children and other things." A comfortable silence grew between them. "Well," Shandy said at last, tugging on her blue shell earring. "It's less than a week to midwinter. If you want a proper wedding you will either have to get married in five days, or wait three more months for spring."

"Five days it is, then."

"It might be easier to wait."

"I want to do it now," Brook said. "Spring is a false time to wed. Too many promises. Winter is best, cold winter. Then the days just get warmer and warmer."

Shale went first, picking her way down the steep path to Crabspit Beach. "So what was it like, the Arbor?"

Brook came more sedately after, holding onto the jack pines that flanked the path. "These trees are so small! They would barely be shrubs in the forest."

"Were there very many people?"

"Thousands! More than I want to meet again in the rest of my life." They were getting near the shore; the air smelled of cold sand and seashells. "You would hate it. It's very cramped. Lots of tiny rooms, packed together. No matter where you are, someone is right next to you."

"Like here," Shale said dryly.

"Well . . ."

"I think I would like it." Shale stepped on to the beach, grinding shells into the damp sand beneath her feet. "Do they smoke there? The soldiers did. You could smell their pipe smoke in the dark."

Brook stepped down to the shore. "Sounds like you had a busy summer."

Shale nodded. Her hood was down despite the cold and her black hair fluttered free. "I guess I should say how terrible the war was—and it was—but it was exciting too. We sailed everywhere in the Inner Islands. There wasn't much killing, after the first few weeks. Just dodge and counterdodge. I think Twist was stalling, waiting to be called home."

Brook joined Shale, feeling the damp chill begin to seep through her boot soles. "Rocks! Rocks to trip over, instead of roots. Bliss."

"Did you say they smoked?" Shale asked.

"Hmm? Oh, yes. Tremendously. Even Jo took up the habit."

"Really! Has she got any matches?"

"Probably. Why?"

"Aren't they wonderful? I envied the forest soldiers their matches, I can tell you. I want to show some to Mom. Then I shall sail to the Arbor and trade for them."

"You want to—! But what would you trade?"

"I don't know. Eelskin, I suppose. Ivory. We must have something here the forest people want."

Brook walked down the shingle, listening to the familiar soggy crunch of sand beneath her feet and the cry of faroff gulls. "You amaze me. I never want to leave Clouds End again."

Shale laughed. "I want to go everywhere and see everything! Twice."

"It is important to have roots."

"I have them, I have them!" Shale cried. "It's all I can do to keep from tripping over them with every step! I have only gotten the first taste of what it's like to be free, Bug. I want more."

Brook walked back up the strand, and slipped her hand into Shale's pocket. "Well, don't go yet," she said. "I am going to need you here for at least another five days."

"Oh, no." Shale shook her head sorrowfully. The fog from their breath curled up between them. "You mean to be a responsible adult. I can just tell. Can't you put it off until spring?" Brook shook her head, and Shale sighed. "You never did waste time once you made a decision."

They watched the pale sun melt like a snowflake into the sea. Shale's hard hand curled around Brook's. "War I can handle. Motherhood . . . too scary. But you! You will be fine."

"Do you think so?"

"Absolutely. You can have my babies, too."

Brook laughed. They walked down the shingle together. "Don't you ever want to have children?"

Shale shrugged. "Now? No. If I had a child, I might change my mind. I'm working very hard at not having one." The surf lapped against the strand. Birds were going to roost in the shore pines and the cottonwoods. "I did have an offer."

"For children?"

"Well, for love. It comes to the same thing in the end."

Brook laughed and peered down at her tummy. "I am in no position to call you cynical."

"Hunh! Well, Foam is charming, and expressive, and he makes me laugh. Besides, put two scared people together long enough among strangers and they are bound to think about sex."

"You too?"

Shale kicked at an upturned shell, sending it clattering among its fellows. "I'm human, aren't I?"

"You are fooling yourself if you think it was no more than that. People really do love, you know. That's not just a story."

"But I don't love him. Not like that."

"Do you think you will always feel this way?"

Shale looked over, scowling comically. "If I change my mind, I will rescue a handsome prince from captivity and settle down to raise mobs of tiny pink babies. Satisfied?"

"Satisfied." Brook huddled beneath her hood. "Shale?"

"Mm?"

"I'm scared." She stared out at the darkening waves. Cold and deep.

"The pain?"

Brook shook her head. "Not the pain so much. Scared I won't be able to have the baby. Isn't that stupid? Scared I won't be good enough and it will be born dead, or crippled. Sometimes I can't believe I could give birth to something that wasn't broken. And I have these dreams. Terrible dreams."

Shale hugged her friend. "Shh," she whispered. "Everyone has those dreams, Bug. You know that."

Brook nodded wordlessly.

"It will be perfect. You'll see. A wonderful howling red blob for me to pick up and fling around when you're not watching."

And Brook looked back at her, smiling, with tears standing in her eyes. "Am I going to die?"

"Yes. But not yet. Not until we are old and wise and wrinkled together."

Brook laughed, then shivered. "Let's go back. If I stay out in this cold much longer, I won't make it through the night."

The next few days were a blur of preparation. The villagers held a building party to make Rope and Brook a house. Shandy decided to put Jo up until the ceremony was over, though she sent her daughters away while the haunt was in her house.

Finch, who had been enjoying an unaccustomed freedom for the last six months, suddenly remembered what it was like to have an older sister, and found that older sisters getting married are the very most time-consuming kind. Making food and sewing took up every moment that wasn't spent eating or running errands. The only consolation, as she told Otter, was that Brook had gotten nicer since she had been away. She was practically considerate about the drudgery she was inflicting on Finch, and made noises about some kind of reward.

Finch didn't put much faith in these promises, but it was nice to be appreciated.

The wedding day dawned clear and cold. The ground was hard with frost; the grass looked made of metal and squeaked underfoot. As the light broadened, Brook and Rope returned from their wedding walks, and the meadow filled with villagers slapping themselves, grinning sleepily, and remarking that at least it wouldn't rain. They were dressed in their best winter wear, sealskin tunics edged with heavy braid. Shale's hood was fringed with shark's teeth, and Foam was resplendent. He had added a shoulder-cape plated with mother-of-pearl that shimmered as he moved. Snippets of conversation eddied around the small meadow as Clouds End prepared for a happy, holy event.

Jo looked at Stick and shuddered. "What are you doing out on so chill a morning, old man?"

Stick cackled. "My grandfather came out the year this island was discovered. Haunts are not the only ones to brave the Mist! Begging your pardon, White Lady. He was here for the first wedding on Clouds End, and our family will be here for the last."

"It will be your funeral if you stand too long in this cold."

The old man grinned. "I reckon I'll be here for that too."

Sweetpea walked by and smiled. "Brr! Too cold for an old woman."

Beside her, Otter sighed. "Mother, you are not old."

"Hah!" Sweetpea grunted, pushing a coil of white vapor into the morning air. "You just don't want to be middle-aged."

Rope stood near Shandy's brazier with Brook, happy and scared at once. "You look nervous," Brook whispered. "Want to back out?"

"No, it's just that Net has crawled inside my shirt to keep warm. What if he crawls down into my—"

"Hey!" Shandy bawled.

The slanting morning sun struck sparks of color from the glistening snow. A big blue shell hung from Shandy's ear, and her sealskin jacket bulked over layers of blue skirts. Skirts, sleeves, and jacket were covered in empty pockets.

"Women and men of Clouds End, it is cold! And yet this cold keeps a secret we come to celebrate with a very special ceremony." The heat from Shandy's brazier lapped against her shins, and she reminded herself, as she did at every wedding, not to kick over the cup she had set beside it. For the first time, she looked at the couple before her. Rope first, impossibly straight-backed, nervous, excited, rather pleased; then Brook, smiling and radiant. "Brook and Rope, I stand here with your friends and family, the birds and the beasts, the sea and the sky, to Witness your union.

"For every force that pulls you apart from the world, from each other, and from yourselves, there are others pushing you together. I want to remind you now of those things.

"We stand here on midwinter day, when the sun is weak and the darkness strong. But the day of death has a secret, a secret it will tell tomorrow, and every day for many months. Beyond death there is life again. You know times of joy cannot last, but remember that despair is fleeting too. Trough follows wave; they are but aspects of the same sea, a moving pattern of low and high, dark and light, joy and sorrow."

She made a signal and the Rolling Hitch began to form, children inside, elders outside. Brook walked to the left of the knot, where little Pebble solemnly presented her with a crab shell she had discovered by the docks. At the other end of the Rolling Hitch old Stick winked and pressed a long ivory comb into Rope's hands. "Two days' whittling, but many years' use, I hope!" Rope grinned and walked the Rolling Hitch, passing Brook at the midpoint, receiving whispered congratulations while the Witness spoke on.

"As you walk the Rolling Hitch, you make a towline, attaching yourselves to the powers of the world. The Powers surround us and hold us from extinction. The sun gives way to the moon, the sea creates the land, the land creates the mountains, the mountains vanish into cloud, and the clouds themselves end in Mist and sea. Change tears us apart and makes us anew. Feel the world. Look up into the endless sky. Listen to the sea. Feel the rock beneath your feet."

The islanders' breath had begun to fill the meadow with a clean white mist.

Brook and Rope had reached the ends of the knot. "You are a part of the world, as much as the tree or the otter or the sea itself. All things mingle and mix. When your problems seem the worst, remember that change is forever and forever renewed. You have tied yourselves to the world with a Rolling Hitch; feel its power pass to you as blood passes down the birthcord from a mother to her child." Gravely the couple gave the Witness their gifts and gravely she put comb and crab shell into pockets on the hem of her lowest skirt.

Then with a wave, Shandy dissolved the Rolling Hitch, and the Sheet Bend began to form. It was a much more solid knot, including even Jo. "When we are married, we are knotted together, but our ends are still single lines. When we are lonely, we must remember that our mates are not our only company. There is a power in the friendship of others that is smaller, sharper, and warmer than the company of the wind and sea. This power too you can use. Walk the Sheet Bend now, tying yourselves to your fellows. We celebrate you each."

At one end Sweetpea folded her arms around Brook, eyes bright with tears, and then gave her a honey cake, still warm from the griddle. Across the knot Stone gripped Rope's arm and smiled through his thick beard, holding up a shiny brass fishhook. "Good for a few meals, I hope."

"We could have used this in the forest," Rope said, remembering a rabbit-bone hook and a meager breakfast.

A murmur went along the human corridors as each villager blessed Brook and Rope in turn.

Shandy smiled, feeling the sun on her face and the stone beneath her feet, feeling the energy of the wedding being gathered, tested, pulled tight into knots that secured them all. "You have walked the Sheet Bend," she called. "You are tied to your village." She popped the honey cake in a skirt pocket and let the brass hook dangle from a pocket on her sleeve.

"And now, the wedding knot. The Reef celebrates a third kind of power, the power that two people have together." This time they started back to back. Foam hugged Rope, meeting Shale's eyes as she clasped Brook. "Top this!" he murmured. The crowd gasped as he pulled a shimmering arm band from his pouch. "Mistwood. I scraped it off the hulls and spread it on a round stone. I used my dad's engraver to carve it just as it was setting." The arm band shimmered pearl and silver. As they watched, the lines of knot-work seemed to writhe and flow into new designs.

Shale grunted. "I fear my gift is less spectacular." She held up a wad of leather and shook it out. "How does this thing work again . . . ?"

"It's a leather bag with a soft lining," Foam said, puzzled.

"That lining was a horror to sew, I'll tell you." Shale's gift had two holes cut in the bottom and a set of straps dangling from the top. "You can wear it either on your front or back."

Brook laughed and cried at once. "It's for carrying my baby!"

Shale grinned. "No excuses now! This way you can walk across the grasslands with me and bring your kid along."

A river of joy spilled from Brook's heart as she walked the Reef Knot, passing Foam and Shale, Otter, Jo, Finch, Nanny, and all the others; standing before Shandy as they had begun, surrounded by those they loved the most.

Shandy sized them up when they returned. "So what did you find on the marriage walk?"

Brook glanced over at Rope and laughed. "Let me go first." She drew a long white feather from her pouch and held it aloft. The villagers looked and then sighed, for clearly the feather had been touched by the Mist. It seemed to shine from within, and though there was no wind, it tugged and fluttered as if being blown to the east.

Shandy nodded. "A powerful sign. You have always had the Sight within you."

(And in the crowd Jo smiled; for Brook had discovered the present Jo had left for her to find.)

Shandy took the feather from Brook and tucked it in her left breast pocket. Then she turned to Rope. "And you? What did you find on the shore on your wedding day's dawn?"

Rope blushed and coughed and mumbled, reaching into his bag. "This is all I saw," he said sheepishly.

"A boot!" Shandy cried, holding it aloft. "A child's boot!" Shale sniggered, and then Foam laughed, and then Stone chuckled, and soon the whole crowd was rocking with mirth. Shandy dangled the little leather boot above her head. "Has anyone lost a boot?" No answer. Shandy frowned. "Is it a good boot?"

"A fine boot!" Foam called.

"Is it a fit boot?"

"A fit boot!" the crowd replied.

"Is it a wedding boot?"

"A wedding boot!" they roared.

"Very well!" The Witness grinned and stuffed the little boot into her right breast pocket. Then she bent and raised the cup that had been waiting by her brazier. "The world has seen you apart. It now sees you one." She gave the cup to Brook, who sipped cold water from it and passed it back. Shandy gave it to Rope.

"Your people have seen you apart. They now see you one." And the villagers stepped forward, forming a dense ring of warm bodies, a magic circle of smoking breath.

Shandy took the cup back from Rope. "You see one another apart." She poured the water onto the glowing coals in her brazier, and a great cloud of steam hissed into the cold air. "Now you are one!" The mist cleared slowly, and the dark shadow at its heart was Brook and Rope, twinned in a long embrace.

It lasted a good while, that first married kiss, until at last old Stick grumbled, "Well, of course they'll keep at it—it's the only way to stay warm!"

Rope and Brook broke apart amidst roars of laughter. "Food and drink in the meeting hall!" Shandy cried.

It was a giant feast and a happy time, for Brook and Rope had each other, and their home, and Clouds End had them too. All the travellers who had sailed for Delta so many months before had returned, and for one night even the haunt was made to feel welcome. Wine flowed, and honey cakes were eaten, and the islanders swapped songs and stories all through the day, keeping their boats in the harbor and their fires burning bright.

CHAPTER 22: THE BIRTH

Rope woke slowly on the last day of winter, following the fragrance of roasting mushrooms out of his dreams. He opened his bleary eyes and returned Brook's smile with a sleepy grin of his own. "Unh," he grunted. "Smells good. Rope want."

Brook broke a duck's egg into the skillet. It sent white tentacles creeping over the mushrooms and hissed in surprise at what it found. "Awake at last!" She started to get up from her stool before the fire, stared at her distended stomach, and thought better of it. "You can get your good morning kiss over here."

Rope threw back his blankets and stood on the cold matting, shivering as he reached for his heavy tunic. Once dressed, he knelt behind Brook and kissed her neck until she giggled.

"I know it isn't for another month, but this is getting too huge," Brook said, patting her tummy.

Rope peered hungrily into the hissing skillet, tickling Brook's neck with his beard. "Is that about ready?"

"Ah. Ahhh."

Rope frowned. "Is that a No?"

Brook smiled faintly, listening to something deep within herself. Pain flickered in her face, pain and concentration. "Rope. Don't worry now, but I think you should ask Shandy to drop by."

"Why? Are you sick?" Brook stared at him as if he were very, very stupid. "Oh," he said. And then, "Oh! You mean now? To-day?"

Brook laid a hand on his shoulder. "Go out the door," she said. "Turn left. Go to Shandy's house. Knock."

"Yes, right. Knock. Yes."

"Rope?"

"Yes? What? What?"

"Be calm."

Rope leapt to his feet and ran to the door. "Calm. Absolutely. Shandy. Yes. Right!"

"I'll never forgive Brook for getting married," Shale swore as she and Foam walked down to the dock. "My sister has been trimming my sails for days. 'When are you going to find a nice man?' 'I do so look forward to having a niece!' 'Isn't it lovely, dear little Brook married at last.' Aaarrrggh!"

Foam flipped up the hood of his tunic and kept his hands in his pockets. "Is she still riding you for spending too much time on the boat?"

Shale laughed. "On the contrary, Nanny now approves. She has decided it is the only way I will spend time with a nice, eligible young man. You have become quite a favorite."

The low sun came out of a dazzle of white vapor to the east. Ships creaked and rocked against the dock. Some were already out fishing, black against the horizon, their winch arms out like insect legs. "The joke is on her," Foam said.

Shale stepped on to the wooden dock, making for the *Walrus*. "It's so relentless, that's what gets me."

"At least there is some benefit to spending time with me."

Shale squatted by the painter. "I like spending time with you, all right?"

"Of course! Who could not?" Nimbly Foam hopped on board. He would have to watch himself. Nobody found self-pity attractive. "Off we go! Wind is light and from the east. Jump aboard. Shake out the sheets and draw up the anchor! Today we sail into Adventure."

"Besides which, Brook tells me hardly anything about their trip. Pumping those two for stories is like milking trout."

Foam ran up the mainsail. "I know, I know."

"Do you think they will be all right if something goes wrong?"

"With the baby?" Foam sighed. "I think so. But it would be hard." He used an oar to shove them off the dock and then set his sail to catch the light landward breeze. He worked his way north along the island's leeward coast. Double-Eagle's twin peaks loomed to port; the Harp was a tiny blot of green ahead. "The sea is too big. You look out on these little islands, tiny fragile little things. You remember all the terrible things that happen."

"Good things, too."

"Of course. But the big things, they're mostly bad. The raid on Delta. Shoal burning like a torch. Brine gone, and Rose. Pond murdered. And who knows what happened to Hazel Twist? Did Seven get to him, or did our Hero of Legend just disappear?"

Shale shook her head. "Seven would never give up."

Foam watched ahead for shoals. "Brook's parents drowning. Rope's father disappearing into the Mist. Brook being twinned. Jo taking the Spark."

"Whatever that means."

"You know what I thought of, when I heard that? I thought of the little golden candle in the story Seven told. The Shadow Wood."

Shale shivered. "Of course the bad things seem big, because you don't pay attention to the good ones. A good meal, or lying in the sun. When you make up lists like this, life always seems terrible. People usually dwell on the bad things because it makes them feel grand."

"I don't do things to feel grand."

"Well, you hardly do anything at all," Shale joked. "You don't count."

Foam touched the tiller, taking them a little out from land. "Perhaps it is easy to see the good in life when you refuse to take anybody's pain, Shale. That's fair, I suppose. You have the right to keep yourself off any shoals you see." Anger burned in Foam, anger at Shale and anger at himself and all his stupid months of hoping that somehow they could be more than friends. "But somewhere we let you get the idea that it was all right to hurt people. We said, 'Oh well, that's just Shale. You know her.' It isn't good enough anymore. I am tired of you hurting people, Shale. I am tired of you hurting me."

"I was making a joke. Just a—"

"Find something funnier." Foam's hands were tight on the wheel. Shale hadn't trimmed the sheets when he turned out, and the sails were beginning to luff, snapping in the landward breeze. "Part of growing up is thinking about other people, Shale. Until you start doing that, you will always be the oldest child on this island."

Shale trimmed the sheet, then knelt and threw a round turn and two half-hitches around a cleat. She turned to look at him, hurting. "I'm sorry."

Creaking, the *Walrus* heeled to port as she passed the north end of Clouds End and her bow came into a quartering breeze. Shale stood a long time silent. Her eyes were glistening. She drew in a long breath and turned to look abeam, blinking. She brushed a single tear angrily from her cheek. "Is this what you wanted?"

"No."

Shale stepped aft and stopped near the trapdoor of their dry-cargo hold. "Think Stone will let us go to the mainland this year?"

"Probably not."

She nodded, still not looking at him. "Maybe next year." She watched the pale spring sunshine glinting on the water. Then her eyes closed, squeezing out more tears. She grabbed the ship's rail while a long, shuddering breath shook her body. "Doesn't anyone understand? Do you think I am nothing more than selfish? Doesn't anyone see I am doing it for all of you? I am Shandy's daughter. I know my duty. And my friends give me so much, so much more than I deserve. And I am not worthy. But I am trying, you see. Trying so hard to make something worth giving back. To give the world as a gift to Clouds End."

She stopped. Tears rolled down her face, and dropped into the sea. "Of course. Of course some of it is selfish. But doesn't anyone understand how much of my life is for you all?"

Propping the wheel, Foam walked to her side, reached out and held her shoulder. He felt the distance between them, no thicker than the cloth of her tunic beneath his fingers. Gently he touched her, sad and vulnerable, riding the gently rolling deck of the *Walrus* as if standing on dry land. Softly, he said, "I'm sorry. You always seem so strong."

"What a virtue!" Shale cried, laughing unhappily. "To be so strong my friends fear me."

Shale, invincible Shale, suddenly so vulnerable. "Your friends love you."

"They love me and they fear me," Shale said, looking over the port rail. "Like the sea."

"Shale," Foam muttered, blinking bashfully over the wheel. "I . . . I . . . I have never told this to anyone, but . . . Well, I was the one who hung those mackerel in the meeting hall for your Naming ceremony." He risked a sheepish glance at her.

"I thought it was you!"

"And, and . . . and that day on the ship, when you came on board naked? I peeked."

Shale blushed, half laughing, half crying. "Was it awful?"

"It was the most wonderful thing that ever happened to me. Well, one of the most wonderful things. Certainly one of the five most wonderful things. No question."

Shale cleated the jib sheet and then took Foam's free hand and held it tightly in her own.

Gravely, Foam said, "Do you want to hear my deepest, darkest secret? You have to promise not to tell."

"I promise."

Foam leaned close to her. His lips brushed her shark-tooth and he felt the tear-tracks on her cheeks. "I love Shale," he said. He looked into her tearful grey-green eyes. "Now remember, you promised not to tell. If she found out, I would just die."

Shale laughed and blinked. "Are you sure?" she whispered. "I think Shale might want to hear that just now." And then she started crying all over again.

———

Nanny was waiting for them when they returned. Shale gawked, astonished, as her prim sister threw herself down on her knees to lash their painter to the dock. "Nanny! What in all the oceans . . . ?"

Nanny looked up, eyes sparkling.

Foam looked at Shale. Shale looked at Foam.

"Brook!" And then Shale leapt over the ship's rail, thudded onto the dock and raced up the meadow path for the village.

Late that afternoon the birthing room was warm. Shale had the fire blazing.

"Relax," Rope murmured. He rubbed Brook's naked lower back, massaging it as he had for the last hour.

Brook smiled faintly and took another sip of honey-sweetened tea from Shale. "Sorry. You aren't any of those things I called you."

"Happens to everyone," Shandy said briskly. "When the hard contractions hit you think you'll never make it."

"It's not me," Brook said. She gasped. "It's not me anymore. Too strong!"

A bowl of vinegar water was on the floor beside Shandy; she had her small arm well inside Brook's vagina, running her fingers lightly over the cervix. "Hand-span and widening," she said gently. "I can feel the baby's head against the opening, smooth as a pearl. You are doing just fine, Brook. Just fine."

Brook groaned, convulsed by another contraction that seemed to go on forever. Finally she relaxed, smiling like a dozing child.

Rope hovered miserably near the bed. Shandy and Shale and even Brook seemed to feel some touch of holiness about the business, but for him labor had been nothing but Brook suffering through hours and hours of terrible pain while he stood powerless to help. "Is she all right?"

Shandy slid her hand from the birthing canal and washed up. "She is fine. In fact, you can take a break now, if you need a rest. This is the last calm. The contractions are just as hard, but she is through the worst of it, where they come in waves one after another. Now she can catch her breath."

Bliss stole over Brook. "She is so beautiful," Shale murmured.

Her mother nodded, smiling with tired eyes. All her daughter's toughness was melting away before the power and mystery of birth. "It's the last moment of peace before the struggle," she said. "For some women there comes a time when whatever makes you *you* goes away, like a stream losing itself in the sea. I thought I was dying, my first time."

The Witness grinned. "Keep giving her sips of tea with lots of honey, Rope. She will need all the strength she can get." Shandy took a swig herself. "For that matter, so do I. Oh, getting old," she said. "Getting old."

Outside, the new moon was rising.

And on the ceiling, in a dim corner above the bed, a bone-white moth held motionless, peering down on Brook with shining golden eyes.

Some time later Brook grunted explosively, hands hooked under her own knees, bearing down.

"Oh, Brook. Oh, honey."

"Keep bracing her!" Shandy snapped. "I can feel the baby's head." She stroked the inside of Brook's vagina, pressing out the knots of tension. "Does that feel good?" she asked, massaging the lips.

"Yes-Unh!" Brook nodded, grunting again and bearing down.

Shandy's fingers moved up. "There?"

Brook winced and shook her head. "Too! Too intense," she gasped. "Rope?"

"I'm here, love! I'm here."

"Rope?" Another contraction shook her, and the baby's head slid against Shandy's fingers with a gush of blood.

"It's coming," Shale breathed. "It's coming."

Brook grunted again and bore down.

"Hold it and push!" Shandy cried. "Push!"

"Rope!"

The white moth fluttered to the head of the bed. Its golden eyes caught the gleam of the bedside lamp as Brook brought forth a child.

Brook reached for her baby, only to be ambushed by a great contraction. She groaned from the bottom of her being. Shandy looked up sharply. "Baby's small but shapely. It's a little girl."

Brook smiled and gasped. Her face was drawn with exhaustion. She had never been farther from the Mist, never felt more grounded and purposeful. Her body was being wrung out like a rag and the pain was unbearable, and still no destiny, no story woven behind the Mist could matter compared to this. "Shale—hold baby! One—more!"

Another head slid into view at the lip of Brook's vagina. "Now we know why you decided to start early," Shandy said.

Brook groaned again, and a second head emerged, red and crumpled. Shandy ran her finger quickly around the baby's mouth, clearing out the mucus.

And then, just as Brook closed her eyes and gasped for one last shove, and the others watched the second baby being born, the moth fluttered up from the head of the bed, lurching like a leaf in the wind. It fluttered to the child already in Shale's arms and stopped to cling, as if by chance, on the little girl's face so that white wings fell across her eyes.

The second babe came easier, sliding out in two long pushes. "One girl, one boy," Shandy said, rapidly checking them. "Both little but in perfect shape. Just as they ought to be." She slapped the infants and let their cords blanch before cutting them. Brook fell back in Rope's arms with her children mewling at her breast.

"You did it." He kissed her sweat-damp neck. Brook gazed back at him, a look of blind relief, barely recognizing him, so happy that it was over, so happy she had her babies.

Shandy was studying Brook's vagina for tears. Shale leapt across the room to fetch more water and clean cloth.

Nobody saw the tiny white moth. Nobody watched it flutter toward the little boy. And nobody even noticed when Net, curled around Rope's wrist, lashed out and flicked the moth away before it could touch the little boy's face.

The next instant all eyes were on the children. As they would be, in one way or another, for many years to come.

Brook and Shandy were drowning in exhaustion. Even Rope felt utterly drained. Speechless and profoundly grateful, he swaddled his children and watched Shale begin the messy process of cleaning up. Shandy sponged the tiny tears in Brook's vagina.

Then the old midwife collapsed into a kitchen chair. Shale stoked the fire, finished the cleaning, and passed over a crock of honey. Shandy and Brook, both half-dozing, ate it with their fingers. Rope placed the two snugly wrapped babies in Brook's limp arms. "They're so tiny!" he marvelled.

"Beautiful," Brook sighed.

Shale went to refill the waterskin. Spring came with her when she returned, pattering warmly against the roof and walls. A wild, fresh breeze blew away the stale air. "It's raining," she said.

CHAPTER 23: JO'S CALL

A time of real-world stories followed, though neither Brook nor Jo ever forgot the Mist.

That spring kindled into summer and was consumed by fall. Brook had no other children; Boots and Feather were her two. Rain-soaked winters came—three, five, seven of them—each blessed with a few magical days of snow. Seven times the grey days closed in, leaving Brook quiet and withdrawn, and seven times her heart lightened with the twins' birthday and the first glint of spring sunshine on Sage Creek.

Finch married a bitter young man named Shallot, to Brook's dismay, and Nanny married too, a fellow from the Harp. She had two babies in two years, which Shale thought indecent. Shallot's friend Scrape drowned, caught out in a spring storm. Old Stick became the first person to spend a night on Shale's island, a source of profound satisfaction to him until the day he died, shortly before the twins' fifth birthday.

Shale and Foam began trading regularly to the mainland, making at least one trip every season, and a second if spring came early or fall late. Foam had hoped that something would happen after he told Shale that he loved her, but nothing did. For a while she was wary and avoided him, but soon she needed someone to sail with her to the mainland, and he volunteered, and they became even closer friends. But Shale wanted neither marriage nor children, and Foam wanted no other woman. So there it stayed.

It was a good time for Rope and Brook, though raising twins turned out to be much harder than walking to the Arbor.

As for Jo, the haunt came and went. She would vanish from the island for months at a time. Then one day she would be back, knocking on Rope's door to ask for shelter for a night or a month. As the years went by, she spent more and more time with them. Finally Shandy suggested they build her a house. Brook didn't like the idea of the haunt making herself a home on Clouds End, but as the alternative was having Jo stay in her house for months at a time, she gave in.

In time the villagers began to think of Jo as their particular haunt, another bit of flotsam the Mist had tossed out for them to salvage. When Foam and Shale went to the mainland they always brought her back tobacco, and she became one of the landmarks of Clouds End, a white-haired woman wreathed in smoke as if she smoldered inside.

Brook's children seemed to like her, though, especially little Feather. She and Jo would chatter for hours about the shapes of clouds or the doings of beetles. Brook had to admit that Jo was a great help. And yet, every time she saw the haunt with her daughter, a shadow came over her heart. She never left them alone together.

Jo's visits were difficult for Rope and Brook. Just when it seemed they had spent all their lives raising children on Clouds End, Jo would show up, and the narrow eyes now burning gold in her salt-white face would make them remember that once upon a time they had been part of something wondrous and strange. She reminded Brook too much of the magical story she had abandoned, and reminded Rope of how dull ordinary life could be.

Though none of them ever said it, all three felt in their hearts that their story had not yet come to an end.

The twins were sail and rudder to the same boat, Shandy thought. Whenever the one was hurt (as happened sometimes to Boots) or upset (which happened frequently with Feather), the other knew at once. Yet you could hardly imagine two children more different. Boots was dark and chunky and patient, while little Feather was fairer than any islander the Witness had ever seen.

Out by Sage Creek, making baskets on a chilly day in early spring, Shandy watched Brook with her children. Boots was working on one of the knot puzzles Rope made for him; little Feather was showing her mother a spider's web.

"Well?" Shandy asked. "Is the spider hungry?"

"Feather says so." Brook stroked her daughter's neck. "What do you think, Boots?"

Boots didn't bother to look up. "Who cares how hungry a bug is?"

"He is just as hungry as you!" Feather said hotly. "A spider's hunger is as big as a whale's, you know."

Boots paused to think this over. "That's true."

"Feather might have a touch of the Mist," Shandy said quietly as Brook left her children to come back to weaving baskets.

"I know."

"Most likely she will grow up just fine, but there is a chance—just a chance—she might choose to be one of the people of the air. Are you prepared for that?"

Feather was peering into the eddy, reaching out to prod a floating stick back into the stream. Please don't take her, Brook prayed. Please, Jo. Please don't take my child. "Many children talk to animals at this age," she said.

Shandy shrugged. "Where was I? Oh. I remember. Stories. We have talked much of medicine of late, and island history, but we seldom talk of stories. Never, now that I think of it."

Brook knotted her twigs together. "Tell me more about the whale. You were twelve, did you say?"

"That's history. Stories, real stories, are what I meant."

"What is the point?" Brook said. "Stories are not true. They are not real. They are about this wonderful place, the Mist. Everything is exciting there and everything has a reason and everything works out. So you get . . . discontented with the real world. You start thinking it's boring, because it isn't filled with magic like the Mist is. You start thinking heroic deeds are all that matter. You forget the value of the little things, family things. Making dinner. Looking at the stars. Talking with your children." Brook felt a sudden, passionate love for Feather and Boots. They seemed so fragile.

Boots, scowling, had managed to untangle one part of his puzzle knot. "Life is not made of toy puzzles," Brook said. "Nothing ends so easily."

Shandy lashed an end-knot in her basket and looked up. "That was a shower from a clear sky." The Witness scratched her grey hair. "What you say is true—but it is not the whole truth. Some stories are too simple. I agree. But some are good, and we need those ones."

"Why? Why not stick to what is real?"

"Don't fall in the water, honey," Shandy called. Feather, who had been steering her twig-boat through the dangerous rapids, frowned, teetered, and stepped back with a sigh.

"Think of a chart," Shandy said. "A drawing on a flat piece of paper. It can't really show you how big a mountain looks when you get close to it, or how it changes as you sail by. It can't show you rocks at low tide and high tide both. It can't show you the stars above at the same time as the sea below. But we have charts anyway, and they are very useful.

"Stories—good stories—are like charts. They warn you of certain dangers. They teach you lessons you could otherwise learn only by making terrible mistakes."

"I suppose you are right," Brook said at last. "But I still think most stories hurt more than they help."

"Then make better ones," Shandy said. "How the young snivel! They always seem so outraged that life is not perfect. If you find a chart is wrong, you correct it. You don't swear off all charts forever." She gestured at the children. "Make stories you want them to hear. Make stories where talking and sunsets and rain and families are just as important as slaying monsters or tricking heroes."

Brook laughed. "Very well. I think I will."

Boots looked up, bored with his puzzle. Feather had wandered far up the length of the creek, until she was almost lost in the shadow of a copse of trees. "Hey!" he shouted. "Come play with me!"

The tiny blond figure stopped and turned, and then came pattering back.

Spring was late coming that year, and though the sun often shone, the days were still cool. Shandy's back had persuaded her to let Brook take care of the herb garden. There was an ache along the witness's spine that never went away, and a new brittleness in her joints. Her fingertips were losing some of their touch; she often had Brook do the more delicate parts of birthing. And while Shandy's Sight was sharper than ever, her vision was beginning to cloud.

"Young Twig's apprenticing to Sharp," Moss said one night as they settled into bed. "Now we know for certain Foam will not take his father's place."

Shandy snorted. "You know Sharp. He needs someone he can boss around."

Moss chuckled, lying back with his hands behind his head. "I remember how you used to look up to Sage," he said. "Back when we were first courting. You thought she was the most wonderful woman. I remember you said once you wanted to grow old just like her: wise and kind and serene." He rolled over on his side, looking down at his wife's dim face. "Well, you are old, anyway."

Shandy jabbed him in the ribs with her elbow.

"Oof! And wise, too. Arguably wise."

"You don't think I am kind?"

Moss checked his ribs. "Would you settle for spiny?"

"Serene?"

Moss kissed her cheek. "Wise, now. Wise enough to know yourself."

They lay in silence. At last Shandy sat up in bed. "I am old," she said bitterly.

"You are beautiful."

"I am old. I am old."

Moss held her as tenderly as he would his grandchildren, wrapping his arms around her thin shoulders. "I know what you're doing," she said at last. "After all these years I know what you are hinting."

"I figured you would."

The darkness pressed in on Shandy like the darkness of death. She didn't fear it anymore, mostly. Only sometimes, late at night, when she felt her own heartbeat, or thunder rolled over her island, or the Mist coiled like a snake in her blood. She felt the tickle of her husband's beard against her cheek. Her old cheek.

(Under the bed, a white mouse scratched once and then held still. Listening.)

Shandy was calmer now. "I think I would like to see the Harp again," she said. "Or Trickfoot or Double-Eagle."

Moss gave her shoulder a squeeze.

"You will come with me, won't you?"

Moss kissed the top of her head, nestled below his chin. "I will."

"But you're right. I need an apprentice. And it will help ground Brook. For a long time Jo was trying to be one of us, you know. Trying to fit in. But she has been getting thinner lately. More desperate. If she sees Brook apprenticing . . ."

"If Jo was going to kill Brook, she could have done it long ago."

Shandy grunted. "Jo is changing. Besides, she might not kill her. Might just cut her loose. Throw her into the Mist. Who would know? We would wake up one morning, notice that Jo had not been around for a while, but there would be Brook, just as always—"

Moss said, "Like now, you mean. Jo has been gone since midwinter."

Shandy shivered, staring at the ceiling. "Who would ever know?"

(The white mouse crept through a crack in the floorboards, out into the night. So little time left.

So little time.)

Later that night Brook's eyes flew open. A beam of silver from the full moon had come sliding through the shutters to ring her like a bell, blowing away her sleep as a fresh wind blows away fog.

The night was alive with sounds. Not the muted, muffled noises of the forest but island notes, each one crisp, however faint. Rope lay with his back to her in the big bed, breathing gently. She heard the sheets slide on his chest with every breath. Heard the children turning in the next room. A breeze whispered outside and made the moored ships rock and creak and bump against the dock.

From out of the darkness a voice of laughing silver said, Come with me!

A second shock ran down into Brook's heart, stronger than the first.

She lifted her sheet and slipped out of bed, quietly quietly crossing the room to where her sandals stood beside the door. Silent as a spider. She was not afraid of waking Rope or the children, not exactly. A certain magic had enfolded her. The night had called to her and her alone; her family would not wake. No, she was quiet because it was right to be silent. This was a secret she did not want to share. A spell she did not want to break.

Outside, the night was warm. To the west, tattered clouds split on blades of starshine. In the east, a bright moon paled the sky. A warm wind streamed over Clouds End, over the bare-branched aspens and elms, spilling down from the Ridge to wash through the village. The stone houses were unreal in the moonlight, giant toys strewn at the bottom of the meadow.

Brook had not stopped to make her braid; for once her hair blew free, shifting and sliding around her shoulders, long tresses black in the dim light. The strangeness of it made her dizzy. What would it be like to wear it so always? Scandalous! Laughter streamed up within her, bubbles rising through dark water, but she made no sound. Wind and moonlight were in her like wine.

The village slept as if enspelled. Quietly quietly she took the meadow path over the Ridge and down to Crabspit Beach, the fated place where she had first met Jo.

The haunt stood waiting for her at the water line. With each wave, white foam frothed up around her feet; hissed; died. Seeing Brook, she cocked her head and bowed. Her mouth a thin-lipped desperate smile. "Sister."

Brook nodded back. Each wave broke at many places on the shore, many times, so that Brook heard first the nearby crash, then a patter of smaller crashes from left and right, like echoes. She stood next to Jo. Before them, a path of wavering silver light led into the Mist.

And the moon, the singing moon!

As a child, Brook had listened to Shandy's stories, where marvel piled on marvel until she shook with wonder. But she was always looking forward, forward, looking to grow up, to be a woman. And the older she grew, the more stories she heard, and like autumn, they turned old, so slowly she never saw it happen, until by the time she was Named she had almost forgotten what the shock of wonder was like.

For a time sex held a power almost as strong. The awareness of a man's body! So intense it was like touching, though he sat across a table or on a different thwart. But sex was sharp and exciting, like danger; not the deep, round, wave-billow of wonder that took you from yourself.

Tonight the moon poured wonder around her and into her until she felt it spilling from her eyes, until she lifted on its wave. Beholding the moon, its silver song, she knew she could be witness to its utter mystery, if only she let herself go. If only she let herself dissolve into the warm wind and the silver night. And she thought her heart would break with moonlight, and she knew she would give anything, anything to get there, to cross into that other place she had always secretly known, the secret continent of stories and marvels and dreams.

"Please come with me," Jo said. "There is a flame in my heart that casts a host of shadows. Do not let me burn." And she held out her hand.

Brook took it, and Jo stepped forward onto the silver path that led across the sea to the Mist. The haunt rocked gently as each wave went by beneath her feet. Fragments of light spun out from her dimpled footprints, glinting for an instant, then swallowed in shadows. Jo's eyes were dancing points of gold. "The path is not hard to walk, as long as you don't look down."

Brook followed, dark hair swirling and mingling with Jo's white, letting herself be lifted by a wave of wonder. Melting on the warm flood of night.

Don't look down, Brook thought. Don't look down. And there was so much else to look at, stars and twists of cloud, moonlight, and far ahead, tall crested waves ghosting through the night. A hundred things to watch, without thinking about the cold black sea beneath her feet.

"Why don't you want me to look down?"

"Don't leave me." Jo gripped her wrist a little tighter. "This might be our last chance."

But Brook was not trying to stop, was not thinking of her husband, her children. Asleep at home, they were in another world. They did not matter, not here. Not now. And she would come back and see them again. Some time. She stared fixedly ahead, forcing her eyes to look only at the silver path.

But the thing was, she was walking on water. And she knew she could not do that. Jo, maybe—Jo was a haunt. But Brook— her flesh was not of that kind.

"It can be!" Jo cried.

They were very far from shore now.

It was the sea beneath Brook's feet, the cold sea. Deeper than mountains, colder than stars, blacker than midnight. Their god, if Clouds End had a god.

She saw Blossom's face, bobbing in the seaweed.

Jo's fingers were like steel around Brook's wrist, holding her up.

Brook's heart was pounding. She could not walk on water. She could not walk over the bodies of the dead. Walking over Blossom, seaweed tangled in her hair; walking over Scrape who vanished in a spring storm. Walking over her parents, their drifting drowned bodies rolling face down in the darkness. Looking away from her.

Brook screamed and fell in, choking on black water. Desperately she struck out for the shore. She thrashed through the freezing surf and finally crawled out onto the rocks at the Talon. There she sat, head slumped between her knees, helplessly shivering and gasping for air. Seawater dripped from her long hair. Dread and wonder drained from her.

Well.

It was only her island. Her island at night.

She turned at a gleam of light. Jo had built a fire on the rocks above the beach. Her twin looked cold, so terribly white and thin and cold sitting there in the moonlight. The fire was small. Brook could barely hear the flames.

Jo looked at her. Then she hunched over the fire and rested her hands upon the orange embers. Rivulets of flame crawled up her arms, writhing around her as they had writhed around Ash so many years before. Then, as Brook watched, her whole body caught, hissing and crackling, until the haunt was only a paper-thin sheet of bending fire.

"No!"

Quickly Jo dimmed, pulling her hands from the fire. She walked slowly back toward the village, toward her little house.

Brook watched her go.

When the haunt had faded into the night, Brook reached for her shell bracelet and clenched her hand around it. She had been willing to go. She had been willing to leave her husband and her children and her island to walk into the Mist. Whether that was Jo's spell or her own desire, the moon's touch had woken something in her that would not easily go back to sleep.

Her story was close now, swirling around her like the Mist rolling in around an island. The distance between her and Jo was very small.

Slowly she stood and walked home. She hung her nightgown on a peg to dry and put her sandals by the door. Rope mumbled when she crawled into bed, but she curled up without answering and hugged him very tight. She was crying. It took her a long time to get warm, and only then did she fall asleep.

In the morning she made breakfast. Feather had already gone outside and Rope was not yet up. Boots, dawdling at the door, grunted in surprise and picked up one of her damp sandals, stained with salt. He frowned, then looked up at her in sudden alarm.

Brook smiled falsely and put an egg in to fry.

It was the first time she had ever lied to one of her children.

The same morning, Shandy was sipping a cup of peppermint tea when Shale crept to the kitchen table. Her daughter looked to the back of the room, where Moss lay humped under a quilt on the big bed.

Shandy grunted. "Don't worry about waking your father. He could sleep through a hurricane."

"The weather has turned fine again. Swap's Breeze is blowing." Shale had chopped her hair off extra short as she did every year to celebrate the end of winter.

"Mm-hmm." Shandy sipped her tea. "When I was your age I wanted to be Trader so badly. I wanted to go so many places. But of course no one would dream of letting a woman do the job, and anyway the Trader has to stay close to his home island. Besides, Beam was still in his prime then. But even years later, when I had done my vigil and become Witness, I was terribly jealous when he took Stone on. Reliable, Stone is. But adventurous? And here I was, bursting with curiosity, and no longer allowed to even paddle out from shore in a rowboat. Unless I gave up being Witness, of course."

"You wanted to leave Clouds End?"

"Like flowers want sun, some days."

"I had no idea." Shale sipped her tea. "I know, I know: nothing new there."

Shandy breathed the vapors that curled from her cup, and took a long swallow, tasting mint and warm honey. "I need you to go to Delta for me. Stone will have trades for you to make, but I'm going to send an extra lot of pearlweirds with you, because the thing I need is rather special. . . ."

Later that spring Brook came home from the herb garden one day to find her children watching Rope grill a large bass over the fire. "Cooking again! What a lucky wife I am."

Rope turned his fillet over with an expert's touch, gently, so the white meat didn't flake to pieces. "Shale and Foam are back," he said, as if just happening to remember it.

"Already! But it's still four days to the full moon!"

"Fair winds and hard work, I suppose." Rope stared at his fish, inspecting the char lines. "They must have had some pretty important reason for going, don't you think?"

"Any visit to Delta is important."

"We helped unload the boat," Boots said.

"Anything exciting in the cargo?"

Rope just kept staring at the fish, while his smile got wider and wider. "Fuseware, flour, cloth. Jo's tobacco. Matches," he added. "That sort of thing."

Brook glared at him. Swinging around, she said, "Children—"

"Uh-uh!" Feather shook her small blond head. "We won't tell!"

Boots nodded solemnly. "Nope. Not us."

Later that week, Brook met Finch and Shallot on her way to Shandy's place. Immediately Brook could see her sister was furious. The earrings Shallot had given her when courting, stacks of tiny purple shells, chattered bitterly with each short, angry stride.

Shallot stopped, smiled, and bowed very politely to Brook. "I always knew one of you would amount to something."

Brook stopped, speechless. Finch threw her a look of mingled rage and misery, and then walked on before Brook could think of anything to say.

At last the midsummer bonfire was lit, sending a host of cheery orange sparks up to join the stars. When the old songs had been sung, Shandy shooed the villagers back from the meadow to the meeting hall despite the balmy weather. "Brook, would you mind taking my brazier back home and putting it away while we get things started?" she said evenly.

Brook knew better than to argue. She forced herself to walk to Shandy's house as if nothing were happening. And I will to another as you have to me, she thought to herself. Was that right? Yes, it was. And I will to another, as you have to me.

The hall was curiously quiet when she returned. Warm yellow light leaked from its shutters. Solemnity gathered in the night air. Brook hovered on the threshold, gathered herself, and then went in.

Shandy sat at the head of the table. An empty chair was beside her. In front of it, gleaming on the tabletop, was a ceremonial brazier of burnished copper. Brook approached it slowly, marvelling at how new and radiant it seemed after years of minding Shandy's worn old thing. "Oh, it's beautiful!"

Coming closer, she saw the Witness had engraved the brazier with a band of knots, scores of them in a subtle braid, graceful and intricate as ivy. Brook let her fingers brush the metal; power dilated through her as it had when she first touched Net, as if those knots had trapped the Mist itself. "It's beautiful."

Slowly Shandy rose to stand before the village. "Brook, I offer you apprenticeship as Witness of Clouds End. If you accept, I give you this brazier in token, as Sage gave mine to me."

Brook said, "And I will to another, as you have to me."

Shandy clapped her on the shoulders. "Then let us eat!" The room burst into a roar of cheers and congratulations.

Shandy pulled out Brook's chair and leaned down to her ear as the tumult of well-wishes rained down. Solemnly, she said, "Were you surprised?"

Brook nodded, every bit as grave, smiling as if her heart would break. "Astonished."

It was a long night and a merry feast, and everyone congratulated themselves on having found a fine young woman to apprentice to the Witness.

Everyone except Jo. The wine she drank was bitter on her tongue, and every laugh was like a match struck and held against her skin. All night long Brook became deeper and sounder and realer while Jo withered, thin and brittle as a leaf. A leaf tumbling down Sage Creek, spilling into the sea and drifting away, drifting ever farther away from Clouds End and into the Mist.

Jo waited for a day when Brook was out delivering a baby, and the twins were with Swallow and her children. She stopped by Brook's house early and invited Rope to go berrying on the North Point. The villagers rarely went there, for the point was cluttered with brambles. Still, summer had ripened and the blackberries were ready. There were huckleberries too, hidden under lacy grey leaves, and bright blue mountain grape.

"Ever since this spring, Brook has had these days when she founders for no reason at all. Does she want to be unhappy?" Rope said. He had found a run of mountain grape. Pluck, twist, pop: another handful of berries like soft pebbles in his fist, then down into the pouch at his waist.

Beside him Jo shrugged. "Brook was seven when her parents drowned, remember. Fostered out to Clouds End, new people, new houses." Her white fingers slowed, fell still. "So lonely. And the ribbons she wound in her hair the day they sent her from the Harp still smelled like her mother. Otter threw them out a few years later. Cleaning. And Brook never said a word, but crept out to the Talon and cried as if her heart would break."

The haunt's hair had turned to brown, and dark eyes glistened in her face. A bracelet of blue shells wound around her wrist. "You should not do that," Rope said.

"I must. The sea is hard, harder than stone. And the Mist is harder still."

"Jo, are you all right? About the Spark, and all?"

"What do you care? You have your life."

Rope touched Jo's shoulder with an awkward hand. "I care."

The haunt said nothing.

Words failed Rope. How could they thank her? In saving the

islands she had taken a hurt that was slowly killing her; anyone could see that in her frayed laughter, her fire-eaten eyes. But Brook and Shandy and the other villagers did not want to save her. They were only waiting for her to die.

There was no way to say this, of course. Not to the haunt who had twinned his wife. Now Jo would die and Brook would be Witness as she had always wanted. Rope shrugged, angry at his helplessness, and held out a handful of berries. "Hungry yet?"

Jo laughed and touched his hand. "Thank you."

His heart caught. Her hand on his was soft as flower-flesh. "Ah well, let us see, what have we got here?" he said, reaching into his pouch. "Ow! Spit!" He snatched his hand back, spilling blue berries, and sucked on his fingers, swearing softly.

"Thorn?" Jo clucked sympathetically and took his hand. "Hm. Thorn," she said. She bent her head and her lips brushed Rope's fingers.

The pain faded, but a different kind of fire raced into him. Jo stilled, holding his hand while her chest rose and fell with three long breaths, breasts just brushing his forearm. Rope remembered the time they had met on Shale's island; remembered what she had offered him there. Remembered her nude body, glistening, and the honeysuckle smell that came from her. She could be his. He could be a partner in her story, not just an afterthought thrown in by the Singer, a dull islander set there to show off her brilliance.

Jo's eyes held no guile, only loneliness and gratitude. She had sacrificed much to save them all and asked nothing in return.

All these thoughts flashed through his mind as her shirt slid against his forearm. Net, flushed red, coiled around his wrist.

Rope took a deep breath, despising himself. He was a coward. He was wrong, wrong, to turn down this moment. But he was who he was. "Maybe we should be getting back." He had not meant to whisper.

"Unfair," Jo said. She held his wrist, touching him through Net's scarlet mesh, and then so much of what she was poured into him, a great wave of loneliness and anger, and beneath it all a leaping flame.

Desire twisted through him and he reached for her. He knew, he knew that it was wrong, he knew he would regret it, he knew he should think, he should stop, he should look away from her fierce eyes and her anguish. He knew he was tying a knot he could never undo.

But all those thoughts were far away, distant voices calling from beyond a wall of fire, and he really didn't care what they said.

Afterwards, when the sun was slanting toward the west and he had made her go, he sat alone in the dim green gloom. If only he had not jabbed his finger. If only Net had not been around his wrist. If only he had been stronger. He reached into his pouch to find what had pricked him, and gingerly drew out Pine Quill's ring of thorns.

He closed his eyes.

His fist tightened around the bramble ring and he squeezed as if to crush it, squeezing and squeezing until blood leaked between his fingers, staring at his hand, remembering Pine Quill. Wondering how he could ever have done something he knew to be so wrong.

That night Brook shifted in her bed, floating up from the depths of an uneasy sleep. Rain pattered softly outside. Something had disturbed her. It was Rope settling into bed. He lay with his back to her. She murmured his name. She had not been easy to get along with since Jo had called her in the spring. A cold wind was blowing through her life. But Rope was so warm. She wanted to make up for it. Warm and solid. Dependable.

She snuggled up to the small of his back. Slid an arm around his waist, molding herself softly to him; her mind swam with night-thoughts, dream-fragments slipping away, elusive as fish diving below cold rocks.

Cold. There was a gap between her belly and his back. She grunted softly and wriggled closer. He flinched. She had been dreaming of water (always water, always the sea and ships. Always her dreams had been of strange voyages, uncertain crossings: storms, alien islands whose people she somehow knew. Walking on water. You can never look down, she remembered. You have to step softly and you can never look down.)

His flesh had fled from her again. She came further awake. His back was stiff. The arm that held her hand made no hollow for her; it lay like a dead thing, a wooden limb. She remembered how quiet he had been at dinner. How quiet. The last of her dreams fled.

A faint glow from the little lamp they left in the children's room was the only light. She rubbed her hand in small circles on his chest. "What's wrong?"

Silence.

Brook propped herself up on her elbow. "Are you angry?" She felt her face take on an expression of quiet concern, but inside she felt sick. Something terrible was about to happen. She killed the thought, blacked it out, refused to give power to the dropping darkness of the wooden rafters, their old sad dusty scent.

Rope did not answer. Outside, rain pattered against the roof, trickled down into darkness and spilled into Sage Creek. A ship turned slowly about its painter, creaking. The wind told sad stories to the sodden leaves; their lament like the sound of the sea. In all these sounds Rope was overcome by silence, wrapped in it. Webs of silence wove around him.

Brook's hand faltered, stopped, an intruder against his chest. "Have I made you angry?"

"No." He lay on his side with his back still to her. "There is something I have to tell you."

"I know I'm not always easy to live with."

"I have to tell you."

"I will try to be more cheerful. I don't know what it is. Something happened this spring, and now it seems so easy for clouds to block the sun. Even when I was little, I was sad if I could not see the sun. On the third day of cloudy weather I would always, my father would have to—"

And Rope, lying stiffly in their bed, felt the old sad smell of the stone walls creep into his chest. His lungs felt musty and hollow. His heart was a dried thing, locked in an old box.

"And the rain. The rain makes me sad," Brook whispered. Silence pressed down on her, closing her throat, closing her chest. Her heartbeat was big in the sudden emptiness of her body. It shook her with every pulse.

Rope, staring into the darkness, said, "Jo and I went to find berries. In the berry patch on the North Point." It was as if someone else were saying the words. They could not be coming from him. "We made love."

Now Brook's arm was wooden too. It lay stiff against his chest. They were two puppets lying together on the ground. The parts where they touched were dead. And Brook said, "Thank you, Rope. That must have been very hard for you to say."

Oh his back was stiff as wood beside her, stiff as a locust's husk. He had ceased to struggle against the silence. He had nothing to say.

And Brook, looking into the darkness now, not looking at the man that once belonged to her, said, "You are right to hate me. I deserve it."

"Don't!" He turned over suddenly and grabbed her by the shoulders. "Don't do this. Please. Don't." He forgot himself long enough to meet her eyes and crumbled like a moth in a puff of flame. "I'm sorry."

"Please don't shake me."

Rope sagged. Net left his wrist, crawling to Brook's arm. Twined there, gripping her fiercely. "She was so lonely. Whatever happened with the Emperor . . . she is burning from the inside, you know. She didn't—"

"How dare you say these things to me."

"I am sorry. I am so sorry."

"Sorry? Sorry for what? Sorry Jo is beautiful? Sorry you had a chance to fuck her? Nothing for you to feel sorry for." She was talking now, she couldn't help it. "It is so strange how you go along, and you have a very steady idea of the world. You tell yourself you are ready for change, but you aren't. And then the world drops out from under you. You're falling and there is nothing to stand on, you're drowning and you can't see which way is up. You feel ready for the worst, but what actually goes, the support that goes, is something you never thought to question." She swallowed. "And it's as if you were dead. Something in you dies. You are a stone in a shell. A little stone, rattling in a shell. Your body." She looked at herself and cried out with hatred. She threw herself down on the bed, and covered her face with her hands.

They lay rigid, barely breathing, while outside the sad rain fell. "I'm sorry," Brook whispered. Her voice was muffled; she moved her hands away from her face, put them at her sides. "That was thoughtless of me. I must have sounded very bitter. I am sorry."

Rope strained against the silence. "Brook?" He felt like a thief, touching her name. "I don't know what happened. I know, I know I am not a good person. This proves that to me. But I love you. I love you." He was crying. "I feel like I had this beautiful thing, this magical thing, and I just threw it away. Just being careless. And it can't ever be unbroken."

"None of that." Brook took his hand, steadied herself. "There has been enough of that sort of talk. Most of it by me." She stroked his hand, not feeling it. "Do you still love me?"

"Yes! Yes I do, if you could see how much—"

"Do you still want to be married?"

"Yes. Please."

"Well. The knot is not cut then, is it? It just took a turn I didn't expect. That's all." She would not let herself hear the sad hiss of the falling rain. An emptiness bit her heart; she would not feel it.

Net crept down her arm and bound their hands together. "There," Brook said, snuffling with laughter. "He has his own opinions about all this."

Rope did not speak, remembering Jo's touch singing through Net and the heat of her desire. He felt the little Mist-creature around his wrist and hated it.

They held one another, rocking before the dying fire.

Rope said, "At the time, I didn't feel bad, you know. It was so clear to me that I loved you, first and always."

Brook nodded. "And Jo was lonely, and in pain. She is out there now, alone. In the darkness." An owl hooted from up on the Ridge. "She has a house but no home to go to, no family. She is lucky she could find a friend. You were her last chance. Her last root."

"I have put a scar on myself that I will feel until my dying day."

Brook only shook her head. "Shh. You cannot see the future. The world is too strange a place for that. Just lie still. We are together now. That is enough." And later she said, "We are all, all so human."

Rope grew gradually still within her arms, staring with open eyes at the darkness, head cradled in her lap.

"I will have to ask you not to sleep with her again."

Rope flinched. "Of course. I will never—"

"I realize I should not be upset. After all, why is sex any different than talking from your heart, or holding hands, or working a fishing boat with someone? You spent days alone with Foam and I was never this jealous. But this hurts me." (Did you like it? Did she make you feel good? Was she better than me? Of course, of course she was. Brook crushed the questions down. She could not ask, she would never ask them.)

"I love you," Rope said, clasping her hand in his.

Brook flinched at his touch.

She was still awake when the rain slowed and stopped. Still awake when grey light crept into the room.

She imagined Jo, lying asleep in her little house. Lying as Brook had seen her lie so often on their way to the Arbor and back. Asleep, the haunt seemed much smaller. Too small to twin an emperor! Too small to hack away the lines that held Brook to the world. Her white wrists were thin and her long fingers not even so strong as Shale's. Often she lay on her back with her head lolling to one side, and her long white throat seemed as fragile as a girl's.

Across the room Brook could see the little oil stove where she did her cooking. Rope's sword hung above it on the wall, a trophy from their journey. It had come a long way with them, that sword. Taken from Cherry Gall after he'd been killed by Seven the night they fled from Delta.

Jo so fey on the way back, prowling the camp like a restless animal, smoking and pacing until she dropped with exhaustion. So still, so still, lying beside the fire. So many times Brook thought she had stopped breathing, and her own heart raced. Then at last the haunt's chest would rise.

It had come a long way with them, that sword.

Beside her, the man who had fathered her children, who had walked the marriage knots with her, lay still, pretending to sleep.

There are two ways to untie a knot, Brook thought. Rope beside her. The sword in its leather sheath hanging on the wall. You can follow it out to its end, past all the bitter twists, past all the loops that wring your heart.

So still Jo was, so small asleep. Hardly more than a girl.

Or you can cut it.

Rope stirred and pillowed his head on his arm, looking up at her. "What are you thinking?"

"Nothing," Brook said.

CHAPTER 25: THE STORY OF THE SEVENTH WAVE

Some weeks later, near summer's end, Rope woke early. In the east the sky was grey as ashes. He thought to get some water from the creek for tea, thought to bustle about the business of breakfast. Then he looked at Brook sleeping beside him and shame froze him.

Every day now was a journey across a sheet of rotten ice. With a look, a word, the world gave way beneath him and he was plunged in misery. Solid, dependable Rope—and he had betrayed her. He remembered Jo's warm back curved beneath him as he thrust, and then Brook—her wooden limbs, her broken voice. Guilt gripped his heart, and he did not even have the right to resent it. Worthless, he had thrown away the only worthwhile thing he had.

He had fallen from Jo's life. Brook did not allow the haunt to come to their house or talk to the children. Rope did not dare meet Jo's eyes if they passed in the village. He and Jo had been a Clove-Hitch story: one easily pulled apart.

He would never be Trader, of course. He would be (he tasted the thought) the Witness's husband, like genial Moss. Someone to organize picnics and gather gossip for Brook to weave into the ongoing story of Clouds End. Anchored here unless he was willing to sail away without her. He had been left standing on the dock, while Brook sank her roots into the island, and Jo drifted out to sea.

He felt a tingle around his left wrist. Net poked a sleepy grey frond out into the morning air, shivered and withdrew. A moment later he crept forth again and inched along Rope's left hand. He reared like a caterpillar, swaying with the faint breeze that crept through the shutter. He was pinking up now. He began to reach out toward Rope's right hand, cautious as a cat putting paw to water. Farther and farther he leaned, clamping ever more tightly around Rope's left thumb, so that the tingling intensified, running like warm water along the inside of Rope's wrist.

The rising sun's first dart caught Net a glancing blow, knocking him gold. He flailed wildly for Rope's right hand, just managing to wrap one frond around his master's thumb. Now the warmth circled Rope's chest, running down each arm and jumping across to the opposite hand. The wind came up outside, and Net swayed between his thumbs like a lace of sunshine.

Clouds End stretched and sighed as if glad of the sun's warmth. The morning birdsong began in earnest. A pair of squirrels went dashing over the roof. The dawn wind swept down from the morning sky and shook out a few early leaves.

For the first time in many weeks Rope felt at peace. He was not past his guilt or his shame; soon the day would begin with all its memories. But he had looked out through his shuttered window and glimpsed the sky and remembered, if only for a moment, that the world was a great mystery. He was a husband and a sailor and a father. His home was all around him, and beyond it the sea and the sky and stars. He remembered what Garden had said: that the real world was full of marvels and adventures so big they were easy to overlook.

And Rope thought then that life too was a series of waves made by the wind, and the wind was the Singer's voice, and each life was part of a great story. And when he was unhappy and confused, it was good to remember that sea and sky were still there, far greater than his problems, and the story he was in was their story too.

A small rivulet had been diverted from the fat end of Teardrop Pond to water the herb garden. Here the soft air was all about plants. It glowed green, with banks of vivid flowers; it smelled of cilantro and clover; it was full of the sound of growing. Sunlight, which elsewhere dashed spangles off the sea, or fell in pale stripes through wooden shutters, seemed in the garden to well down from the leaf tips, smooth and gold as honey.

Rope had come here with Feather and Boots and his two best friends. "Go ahead and play," he said to his children. "I mean to talk a while with Foam and Shale."

Feather raced off. Boots went more slowly, trudging by the little stream and frowning into its depths.

"They're good kids," Foam said, stretching out on the grass with his back propped against an old aspen. There was something like longing in his eyes as he watched Boots stump downstream.

Foam was in his thirties now. He kept a decent braid in back, but the top of his head was bald, tanned and freckled, and when his eyebrows lifted in surprise, wrinkles spread improbably over his pate. The first threads of white were showing in his braid.

He is getting older, Rope thought. We all are.

Shale might be getting older too, but it didn't show as much; with every passing year she just looked more and more like herself. "I like Feather," she said. "She's got a spark or two in her."

Rope hunkered down beside Foam. He thought of Jo, with her silver eyes burning gold, loneliness searing her inside. Blown apart by the breeze. He prayed Feather would not become one of the people of the air. "Once you have tasted things, tasted the bigger world, one island can seem cramped. Always the same place, the same friends, the same people."

"You sound like me!" Shale grinned.

You could not say he and Jo had been lovers. Love was not what they had shared. Sometimes he thought he had been a terrible person; other times, their lovemaking seemed one tiny knot in a braid too big for him to understand. "We are never really part of the story, are we? I mean, a story is a wave, and we are drops of water. The wave picks us up, and then drops us, and then moves on. All we can do is watch it. But sometimes I want so badly to ride the wave. I want to be part of something important."

"If you don't think having a wife and family is important, you are stupider than you look," Foam said sharply.

"I know, I know."

Boots was still studying the stream. Farther away, Feather held a conversation with a clump of scarlet valerian.

"It should mean something to you, Rope. To marry the woman you love and have a family." Foam put his hand over his heart and sighed at Shale. "I would trade!"

Shale swatted him on the leg.

Wind brushed through the aspens, making their trailing leaves rustle like tresses of thick green hair. Foam cocked his head sideways and watched Rope moodily knotting stems of grass. "Isn't it surprising, the way things work out? I used to go looking for mysteries, but I have come to learn that the most mysterious things of all are happening under my own nose."

Shale wrinkled her nose. "Oh, now you sound like Brook. It is all very well to say, 'Look how wonderful ordinary life is!' But sometimes ordinary life is dull. If I did not get restless, if I did not want something more, I would be washing poop out of my child's clothes instead of sailing to the mainland. You and Brook may do fine, staring awestruck at beetles, but there is nothing wrong with wanting something special and different. Where would we be if Seven had been willing to do just what his father did?"

"And the years go by," Rope said. He remembered Garden, with his fingers rooting to the ground. "The years go by with all their decisions. And the older you are, the more it seems as if each new choice has already been made by all the other choices you made before." The first branches grope out as they will; the last fill in where they must.

Foam sighed. "You sound low, my friend. You sound like a man feeling trapped, a man who feels the rest of his life is already told. I do not believe it! Life is strange, stranger than you can know."

"Your life, maybe. You get to go places."

"You are sailing into fatherhood. I would trade in all my trips for that one voyage."

Rope forced the bitterness from his voice and changed the subject. "Which reminds me, how was your latest journey?"

Foam's hands strewed miracles. "Marvelous! We sailed through another blank place on Stone's charts; Shale loves doing that. And we traded our pearlweirds for enough matches to keep Clouds End supplied for years, and leave plenty left over."

"You have become quite the mariners."

Foam laughed. "Who would have thought it? But with Brook staying on Clouds End so much, and Shale chasing everywhere but—I tell you, I have seen a good deal more of Fathom's kingdom than I care to. Of course I know who is still the better sailor."

Rope said, "I think we all know who the better sailor is now."

Boots studied the shallow stream. A small trout held itself against the current, wavering. It slipped backwards and then held, slipped and held, until it found shelter under a chunk of granite. Boots intended to build a dam. He wondered where best to put it.

Across the stream, Feather chatted with a tall scarlet poppy.

Boots reached carefully into the stream and pulled out a large grey stone. He wondered if it was happier wet or dry. Wet would be cool, but he thought stones didn't mind cool so much. On the whole, the rock seemed happiest underwater. There it glistened, smooth to the touch and less heavy.

"The poppy said I would be a queen!" Feather announced. A fat bumblebee buzzed into the flower, humming a small work song as he tramped through its pollen.

Boots shifted downstream, beyond the granite. "No she didn't."

"You can be emperor," Feather allowed. "That's almost as good."

A wide place where the water was slow and shallow, or a narrow place where it was deeper and more swift? He settled on the shallow; in his experience, rocks in rapids shifted from where you placed them. "She didn't say that either."

"Did too!"

"Did not."

"Well, if you're so smart, what did she say?" Feather demanded, pouting. She was very pretty generally, but pouting made her look like a small blond fish with lips.

Boots placed his first stone symbolically in the middle; he would work out to the banks from there. "She said that it was good to drink the sun."

Feather's eyes went round. "How did you know?"

Boots looked up at her, rather puzzled. "Because that's what she said."

"You never said you could hear things!"

Boots shrugged. "You never lied before."

Methodically, he began to search for his next rock. His sister's astonishment gave way to distraction as the east wind hid some secrets under a lilac bush for her to find. Boots paid no heed. He had more important things on his mind.

Summer gave way to autumn, and a whirl of early snow brought down the last leaves.

Life was different for Brook now. For seven years she had lived her life in the real-world, letting her magic sleep. But the call that had brought her down to the beach to meet Jo that moonlit night in spring had woken it at last. She had tried to harness her gift, apprenticing to be the Witness of Clouds End, but she was aware now, all the time, of the Mist running beneath the world like blood under skin.

Shandy's foretelling had been true. Jo was getting desperate. Now she had struck at Brook's heart. Was Jo clinging to Rope, clinging to anything that might keep her from fading into the Mist? Or was she also trying to cut Brook loose? Brook tried not to give in to despair or self-hatred, tried not to take out her hurt on Rope or the children, but not since her parents died had she been asked to ride a wave so dark and deep.

Some days Brook's fear came back, a sudden cold shadow that fell over her heart as she worked in the herb garden, or watched her children racing around the meadow. How delicate, how fragile the world seemed that year! As if her life were made of Mist, and one strong breeze could blow it all away. Some nights were the darkest of her life; yet when she was happy the joy was nearly unbearable. Walking a knife-edge between the real world and the Mist, she had never been so alive.

Shandy was talking about sending her on her Witness vigil at midwinter, but Brook had a hard task ahead of her first: making up stories that ought to be told. When the elm above Teardrop had lost almost all its leaves, she was ready to try one on the children.

"This is the story of the Seventh Wave," Brook said. "It is a story of the Mist-time, where everything is true and nothing is what it seems."

The children she was minding sat on the mossy rocks above Crabspit. To the east a wall of purple cloud was building. A circle of small faces stared up at her, none more solemn than Feather's. Boots was frowning at his fingers.

"This is a Sheet-Bend story. Now, as you know, in a sheet bend the big rope and the little rope are all looped together, so you can't talk about one without mentioning the other, until you get to the end and pull them both tight."

Little Rope, Big Rope

The Mist churns into sea, the sea hardens into stone, then islands, then land. The land leaps into mountains and the mountains fade into clouds and Mist; for change is the way of the world.

In the beginning there was Mist over all the waters of the world. But at last the sea churned the Mist into Delta, the first island. Of course you've all heard lots of stories about the people who lived there then. Well, this is the second or maybe first story there ever was about Tool and Swap and Wit and Kettle, and the only story that tells about Stand.

Now, Wit wandered around the island asking questions of everything and listening to the answers through her Big Blue Shell, so she was happy. And Tool gathered Mist and sticks and oyster shells to make strange new toys, so he was happy. And Kettle found clams to boil and eels to bake, fish to stew and snakes to fry—

("Yuck!" went all the children, happily wrinkling their noses and sticking out their tongues.)

—so *she* was happy. And Stand had dolphins to race and squid to wrestle, so *he* was happy.

But Swap was bored. He was always wanting to make trades and go new places and see strange things. But since there weren't any other islands yet, and he couldn't have gone to them if there had been, he got very bored. He spent most of the day wandering around the beach and peering out at the sea, hoping something exciting would happen.

Which is why he was the first to notice the Bump.

It was a special sort of day—rather like this one—and he felt sure something exciting would happen. Up until now the sea had always been perfectly flat, and the wind completely calm. But now a breeze pulled on his braid like a naughty child, and there was a Bump on the sea's broad back.

It wasn't a big Bump, not yet, and it was far to the east. Still, there had never been a Bump before.

Well! Swap rushed around the island until he found Wit on her hands and knees, listening to a spider make pretty compliments to the passing flies. "Wit! Wit! There's a Bump!" he yelled.

Wit jumped into the air and almost fell down again; with her Big Blue Shell held close to her ear, Swap's voice was *very* loud. "Bump!" she snapped. "You've had a bump on the head, I think— charging around yelling in people's ears."

"No, really! There is a Bump on the sea!" And he dragged her down to the beach so she could see the Bump for herself. It was there all right, and it was getting bigger and closer and closer and bigger.

"What do you think it means?" asked Stand, who had noticed the Bump while he was swimming.

"You've been wrestling squids again," Wit said, frowning. She could see the sucker marks all over his big strong arms and wide brown back.

"We were just playing."

Wit scowled once at him, and twice at the sea. "I would surely like to know what that Bump is all about," she said.

Tool was the next to join them on the beach. He had the tummies of four dead jellyfish strapped under each arm and a hat the size of a sail strapped under his chin. "I was sitting at the top of the Tall Tree wondering if I should try my Flying Gear when I saw this Bump. What is it all about?"

The others shook their heads.

Then Kettle came down to the beach to look for clams, and she too stayed to look at the Bump.

"I say," Tool said. "Isn't it getting bigger?"

"Closer too," said Wit.

"It's coming right for us," said Swap. And suddenly he didn't care so much about exciting things after all.

As they watched, the Bump got taller, and wider, and bluer, and greener. It rolled over the ocean toward them, and its top was white with foam. It was very close now, and it made a sound like thunder growling.

Wit said, "I'm not sure I like this."

And Tool said, "I wonder what it is."

And Kettle said, "Maybe we should eat *now*."

And Swap said, "I wish it would go away."

And Stand said nothing at all, but dove into the water and swam out to meet it.

But the Bump picked him up and hurled him back onto the island and then rushed over the rest of them.

Do you know what it was?

(The village children looked at one another, frowning, trying to remember if they had ever heard this story before. Boots glanced back at the storm-clouds to the east and then turned to meet his mother's eyes. "It was a wave.")

It was a wave!

It was the first wave that had ever been. It rushed over the island

and it gobbled up Kettle's fire and it broke Tool's toys and it swept away Swap's beautiful collection of shells and stones and it made them all very wet and angry and out of breath. Worst of all, Stand was hurt, and lay groaning on the hard stone where the wave had thrown him.

Wit was stuffed full of seawater and scraped from falling on the stones and madder than she had ever been in her whole life. While the others stumbled around in a daze wondering what had happened, she shook her fist at the departing wave and yelled "WHY?" at the top of her lungs. But when she held up her Big Blue Shell, all she heard was the sound of the water and the rock, just like you do when you're standing on the beach. And this was the first time the world had refused to answer her questions. Then she grew very thoughtful, and a little bit scared.

(The trees on the Ridge conferred, lamenting what the cold wind told them. Far to the east, a shadow crept over the water.)

Big Rope, Little Rope

Swap wasn't nearly so happy when he saw the second Bump as he had been the first time. He hurried back to tell the others, and they huddled together on the highest part of the island. Tool used his seaweed ropes to tie everyone to a tree so they wouldn't be washed away, all except Stand, who said it was beneath his dignity.

The wave was every bit as blue and green and wet and sputtery the second time. As soon as it was past and Wit could catch her breath, she called out "WHERE IS IT COMING FROM?"

And the wave said, "From the sea."

It was Tool who saw the third wave, sitting at the top of the Tall Tree and looking through a bubble of Mist that let him see faraway things as if they were near.

"This is becoming a nuisance," Kettle muttered, for the waves always doused her fires, and she hated having to light them again.

This time, as Kettle scraped the sand out of her pots and searched for firewood, Wit cried "WHO IS IT COMING FOR?" to the wave's broad back.

"You," it said.

"I don't know why you keep asking these silly questions," Stand said to Wit as the fourth wave approached. "We know what it is now. We won't be fooled again."

Wit only frowned. "There is something coming," she said.

Stand scoffed. "When?"

"We will see." After the fourth wave passed she cried, "WHEN WILL IT HAPPEN?"

"The Seventh Wave," the sea's voice said.

"Now look here," Tool said, taking Wit aside when the fifth wave came into view. "We need to be more exact about this Thing coming. Is it just another wave, or something different? Is it made of fire or fur or feathers? Is it longer than a stone or colder than an eel? Can it fit through a crab's nose? How many bubbles does it weigh?" He wrinkled his nose at her and looked terribly superior. "In short, we need *precision*, Wit."

So as Wit watched the fifth wave roll by from her seat in Tool's Tall Tree she called, "WHAT IS IT?"

And the wave said, "Death."

(Even Pebble, who was almost old enough to mind herself, felt uneasy with the storm coming up behind their backs. Feather shivered in the cooling wind. Wordless, Boots reached out to hold his sister's hand.)

Everyone on the island was feeling very nervous. "Soup," Kettle counselled. "Lots of good hot soup. That will help drive off any sickness that might be coming."

"I have been working on something that might help," Swap said. "I hollowed out a tree with the knife that Tool gave me. When the wave comes, the wood will float and we can all be safe inside."

"Flying's the answer," Tool said sagely, squeezing the jellyfish tummies under his arms. "We will be safe in the sky."

But Stand said, "Why are you all cringing? We should meet this thing head on! If we let it master us now, it will master us forever."

Then they all fell to arguing, until Wit said, "I can see the sixth wave." Then they were quiet. Wit grabbed hold of her Big Blue Shell. "I will learn what I can learn."

When the sixth wave went by she called, "HOW CAN WE BE SAFE?"

But the wave said, "You cannot."

From the moment she saw the Seventh Wave, Wit felt as fragile as an eggshell. "Hurry!" she cried, running to find the others. "It is coming at last!"

"Run to the log!" Swap said.

He and Wit went to crouch within his hollow log. At first Kettle wanted to stay by her fire, for she had put in an especially yummy snake to boil. But as the wave got nearer and taller and blacker, she decided she could always boil snake another day.

But even after they got Kettle to come into the hollow tree, they could not make Tool or Stand join them. "Flying!" Tool yelled. "It's the only wise alternative!" He had clambered to the very top of the tallest tree, and hung there as it swayed in the rising wind, clutching his jellyfish tummies.

As for Stand, he prowled the shore getting angrier and angrier. "Are we always to run from this thing?" he cried. "Is Tool not clever? Is Wit not wise? Am I not strong? I will fight this Death, whatever it is, and teach it that an islander must have respect!"

Wit coaxed and Swap wheedled and Kettle cried, but they could not make Stand come into the hollow tree.

The Seventh Wave got taller and darker and wider and colder, until the wind before it bent the treetops almost to the ground, and its roar was like a thousand thunders, and the black crest of it gobbled up the sun. But still Stand waited on the shore, shaking his mighty fist and yelling at the storm.

Then the great wave fell upon Delta. It lifted up the hollow tree and flung it like a toy so that those inside were battered and bruised and breathless, and Wit was thrown out and had to cling to the stern and Kettle was tossed overboard and had to grab on to her pot. But Swap was safe inside his hollow piece of wood, and that is how the first boat came to be.

As they floated, dazed above the black water, they saw Tool drifting by, coughing and spluttering. He never was brave enough to jump from his tree and fly, but the puffy jellyfish tummies he clutched under his arms had pulled him up to the surface after the great wave buried his tree.

Swap pulled them all into his little boat, and pumped their backs until they spat out all the sea they had swallowed.

Then something else floated by. "Stand!" Kettle cried.

But Stand was dead.

Because the Seventh Wave cared nothing for his strength or his swimming or his anger. It had not even noticed he was there. It fell upon him like a thunderbolt and killed him dead.

Tears streamed down Wit's face as she looked at Stand's broken body and she felt her heart would break. "WHY!!"

But though she held her Big Blue Shell to her ear and listened as hard as she could, the world never answered.

"That's a sad story," Pebble said.

Brook nodded. "Yes, but it's a true one. And Wit and Tool and Kettle and Swap lived past the Seventh Wave, and you all know stories about their adventures. We have much nicer boats now than Swap did then, and nobody has to eat fried snakes anymore. As long as you respect the world, and know its strength, you can have lots of adventures too."

The children nodded, round-eyed.

"Next time I will tell a funny story," Brook said, suddenly feeling awful. Her stupid story had been too grim. It made her heart ache to see the children looking up at her, their little faces so uncertain. Maybe they were better off believing only good things.

"You can't sail if you don't know where the rocks are," Boots said solemnly.

Brook looked up at him, startled and grateful.

Then she saw someone walking across the rocks to join them. It was Jo. The children scooted to the side to let the haunt through. She smiled, white hair billowing and snapping before her face, blown by the wind rising from the east.

A whip of Mist cracked in Brook's blood.

Jo was gaunt, thin and fierce as lightning. Fire sparked behind her eyes. "Did I miss the story?" she said, reaching down to stroke Feather's hair with her long white fingers.

"Don't touch her."

Jo's eyes were two golden flames. "You should give me something, Brook. It would not take much to make me happy."

Out on the sea, ships hurried home, disappearing around the Talon on their way to the leeward docks. Their sails cracked in the gusting wind.

Feather's blond braid lashed around her small face in the rising breeze. "Storm's coming," she said.

The last of the fishing boats were in and their sails were down. Rope, Stone, Seal, and Sharp pulled the smaller sloops up the shingle and carried them into the boathouse. Moss and Foam went from boat to boat with the older children, fitting each with extra floats to keep their hulls from slamming against the dock.

The swell was running high. The dock creaked and groaned with each tall green roller. Halyards and hawsers thrummed in the wind. "A real spring gale!" Rope yelled.

"Yep." Stone followed close behind, hoping they could get three more boats up before the storm hit.

The first peals of thunder broke overhead, crashing over the island like gigantic waves. Shandy jumped up from the table, staring at the shutters.

Moss stamped in, slamming the door. Rain dripped from his

beard as he put a long arm around her. "It's only the thunder, old woman."

Shandy snorted.

"You never did like storms much," Moss chuckled. "I always liked the show."

Shandy paced, stumping grimly from one end of the room to the other, freezing at each flash of lightning, holding her breath until the thunder exploded overhead. "I made Brook promise you the house after I am gone, Witness Tower or no."

"You aren't going anywhere in a hurry," Moss said, taking off his dripping tunic and hanging it on the mantel to dry.

"When she needs to do a Watching, she can ask your permission. That's all there is to it. I am not going to see you moved out of your own home"—lightning ripped the sky and the clouds roared in agony—"just for Witnessing," Shandy whispered.

Moss came to stand behind her. "Brook would never throw me out." He slid his hands around his wife's stomach and held her close. "You know that."

"By Wit's Ear she won't."

The gale fell on Clouds End, rattling at Shandy's windows as if trying to tear her home apart. She felt Moss, big and safe behind her.

"It got dark so fast," she said.

CHAPTER 26: THE TWO HEROES

Two days later on a morning grim with rain, Rope's cousin Bass beat around the Talon to bring them a visitor. It was Seven.

Foam was puttering around the dock when they landed. Seven helped Bass furl his sails and hopped out of the boat. He gripped Foam by the shoulders. "Well met, Lieutenant."

"Astonishment! Amazement! Wonder! You look good," Foam said. But Seven was older, far older than he had been. The smooth, clear expression Foam had known was gone. The Deltan was tough and wind-tanned. Thirst and privation had carved deep lines around his mouth and eyes and his smile was hard. He wore pants and a shirt like a woodlander. "What brings you to Clouds End?"

"You do!" Seven laughed again. "I have set my sail for the Mist. I thought I would stop by and see you on my way. Come help me unload my gear while Bass visits with his family. I had no wish to sail out to the edge of the world alone, so I have been crewing on any ship who would take me through the whole summer. It was many moons before I found any who had even heard of Clouds End."

Foam clambered aboard.

"My father told me you have dined with him in Delta a time or two," Seven said.

"Well, you know Shale. It was her idea to start trading to the mainland. She is the wind in our sails."

"Trading with the forest people."

"The war is over," Foam said.

"And the dead stay dead."

Seven had a woodlander sword belted at his side. It swung in time with his strides.

"Long trip?" Foam asked.

Seven shrugged, pulling open the cargo hatch. "Hm. Plains, mountains. Even trekked through the great Northern Desert for a while. A long voyage. Of course, every voyage is long when you have no harbor to come home to."

"Whatever happened to the man who wanted to save the islands? The patriot? I never thought General Seven cared about things out of sight of the sea." Foam went down the narrow ladder into Bass's small cargo hold. He collected a load of winter gear stowed behind a tall fuseware vase with a silver plug.

Seven came down to the hold, crowding Foam into the bulkhead as he bundled up a mound of clothes and blankets. It was very dark belowdeck, and the wind cried softly over the hatchway. "Back then I had more to care about."

"I am sorry about Pond."

Seven shrugged. "It is the way of the world. But you can never surrender. You keep fighting." As he started up the ladder his body blocked the hatchway, and the light failed.

He was waiting when Foam climbed out of the hold. "Actually, you touch on the reason for my trip. After years of wandering I thought to myself that if there was one place where the dead could be brought back to life, it would be in the Mist."

"Seven—"

"Do I disturb you?"

"No. No, of course not."

Seven hopped nimbly from the boat. "I thought I would take Pond to the Mist to see what could be done. Stonefinger is said to have power over death. And who knows what the Singer could do?"

"She has been dead for years, Seven."

"I know. I brought her ashes. Easy to carry that way. I doubt she minds much." Seven turned and gave Foam a hand out of the boat. "She is in that fancy bottle, the one with the silver top.

Whatever you do, don't pour that into the lamps some dark night!"
He was still laughing as he stepped off the dock and started for
the village.

The east wind sobbed, pulling an endless stream of tears from
the clouds as another storm gathered overhead.

By the next day all traces of the storm had gone and the sky no
longer leaked. Mountains of puffy white cloud towered overhead,
ceaselessly refashioned by the wind.

Seven prowled through Clouds End, watching the villagers re-
pairing the damage the storm had done. Foam was fixing boats;
Shale straddled her mother's roof, plugging leaks. Brook he found
working in the herb garden with Finch and Swallow. "And of
course all the time he acts as if the rain were my fault," Finch
was saying.

Swallow laughed. "I won't see Seal for a week! Not while his
precious boat needs nursing."

The ivory comb that Stick had whittled for Brook's wedding
gleamed cloud-white as she smiled up at Seven. After meeting
him the day before, she had decided that all the things Foam and
Shale had said over the years were true. He was meant to be a
legend. The Mist was in him; you needed no magic to see that.
"Good morning, honored guest."

"Good? You people seem not to understand what has happened
to you. Can't you see how much work there is? Work just to get
back to where you were three days ago."

Brook looked down at the mud where her garden had been.
Springs of chamomile huddled with chastened yellow heads, giving off a sweet, bruised smell.

"Two ships sunk, most of the others damaged, the dock skewed,
the gardens wiped out." Seven squatted down beside a clump of
muddy rue. "The sea is cruel."

Brook caught a curious glance from Finch and shook her head
ever so slightly, wondering why Seven had to make the hard job
of being happy harder. "I guess this would be a disaster on Delta.
Here on Clouds End the sea keeps us in our place."

"Or floods us out of it!" Swallow said.

Brook tended another sprig of rue. "It rains on us, and we do not always care to get wet. But at least the rain is real. Few of the doings of men are." Once she would have said that making love would count, but the thought of Rope and Jo together stilled the words on her tongue. She shrugged and glanced at Swallow. "We women have an advantage over you, Seven: I was never as close to the world as when I had the twins." Swallow nodded.

The memory of birthing whispered through Brook and she shivered. The unbelievable pain, wave after wave of it. What she most remembered now was the panic-stricken struggle to stay afloat, to remember that each contraction would pass. Battling not to give in, not to drown in craziness and fear and agony. Much like life, really. The trick was to remember that things came in waves. To keep your head above water and know that some day the pain would be over. She thought of her children. The pain would be over and joy would take its place. "That is something very special."

"Killing," Seven said.

The women looked up, startled. "What?"

Seven stared down the length of Sage Creek. His eyes were tired, his clothes worn. A very different man, Brook thought, from the dashing warrior she had first glimpsed in Delta many years before. "Killing," Seven repeated. "The moment you kill someone. At the instant you murder a man you are completely aware, completely part of the real world. The guilt and dread come later, but the moment itself . . ."

"I cannot speak to that," Brook said.

Seven laughed. "Death is real. It cannot be ignored. You cannot ignore the rush toward death. It is in everything. It is in you."

"In labor, just before I started to push, I thought I was going to die," Swallow said.

Seven stood up. "Perhaps you are right, you easterners. Perhaps the storm is real, and your houses are illusions. But I am of Delta." He shook his head. "You are wrong to give up, to cringe before the storm." He forded the shallow stream, stepping lightly from rock to rock.

"What are you going to do?" Brook asked.

"Wait until your ships are mended," Seven said. "And then I shall build a boat."

Three days later, on a secluded beach at the north end of the island, Seven opened like a flower to the sun, long-sword whistling through the mid-morning air. He faded back; slid forward, slow as a drop of water rolling from an icicle; exploded into a whorl of moving steel; came up; poised; still as a crane, meeting the gaze of a snow-white woman with golden eyes.

"The morning to you," he said politely, standing with one knee raised to the top of his chest. Toe pointed. Motionless.

It was early autumn, and cold. "Am I interrupting you?" Jo asked.

Seven furled, spun down to the ground, rose like a tide and fell like a flood—stood calmly before her and bowed. "Not at all."

Jo nodded sardonically, studying Seven for signs of intelligence. "You wear woodlander clothes. I am surprised."

"The style of the islands is a good one and very comfortable. But my friend Shale has also made herself some woodland gear; shirts and pants are more convenient if you want to run or stretch." Seven paused, pulling on a sealskin tunic. "And your name?"

"Jo. I fear our first meeting was rather confused. You thought I was—"

"Hazel Twist! And then you turned into a gull and flew away. You are the haunt of whom Foam and Shale spoke. And it is you we have to thank for stopping the woodlander invasion."

Jo laughed. "And you are the man who held the forest people at bay. So now the war's two heroes meet in a place where the war itself was never more than a rumor."

"It was known out there, lady," Seven said, pointing into the east. "Out where the Gull Warrior ranges."

"You are from Delta. Tell me: on the night we left the Arbor, we met a woodlander who said he had spent some years in your city. His name was Bronze Switch. Did you know him?"

Seven sheathed his sword with curious slowness. "Bronze? Bronze Switch?" Jo nodded.

The surf was a shiver along the cold shore. There were no trees nearby. The beach smelled of seaweed and shells. The greatest warrior of the sea people stood for a long moment, listening to the waves heap and fall and run hissing over the sand. The same sound he had heard all his life, while time took away the people he loved. While time slowly took away everything he had.

"I met him," Seven said at last. "Bronze Switch. But I did not know him."

"There you are," Rope said, later on that chilly afternoon. "I've been looking for you."

Jo sat far over Teardrop Pond, on the elm's long arm. "How brave of you! I doubt your wife would approve."

"I haven't seen you for a long time. I wanted to know if you were all right."

Jo ran her hand along the rough grey bark. "Don't the trees look different without their leaves? So empty." She stared up through the scraggly branches to the vacant blue sky. "I wonder if Seven would take me with him."

Rope sat on a boulder near the creek's mouth. The scrub pines to the west made the clearing dim and gloomy. His hands were stiff in the chill and his fingernails were tinged blue. His breath smoked when he breathed. "Did it mean anything to you, what we did?"

Jo sat twirling her feet idly above the black water. "Do you really want an answer?"

Rope picked a twig off the ground. Leaning forward, he painted flowing patterns on the water. A jackdaw croaked, fluttering in the bare branches of the elm. Rope's twig stilled, its ripples drowned. "Because when I think back on it, I sometimes wonder if I was really there." He glanced up at pale Jo, sitting over the black pond. Her hair whispered around her face like drifting snow. "For a very long time I hated myself for it. For betraying her. But I could live with that, in a way, because at least it was something I did. It was my story."

Jo said nothing. The jackdaw croaked and cocked its head. Watched. Listened.

"But sometimes I wonder if it wasn't between you two all the time. Was I ever really part of it? Or was I just a baited hook?"

The cold wind blew through Jo's heart. She laughed to let it out. "Did it matter to you?"

Rope coughed, and steam coiled from his mouth. The cold made his fingers hard and stiff as leather. He refused to look around to see if anyone was listening. "Yes," he said steadily. "It meant something to me. I wanted to be close to you. I desired you. You are beautiful, you make yourself beautiful, I do not apologize for desiring you. But I also wanted to be close. You were in pain."

"Pity! So that is what I felt between my legs that day. How noble."

"I have already said I desired you. I said that."

"You did," Jo said sadly. "And you did pity me."

A deeper, colder blue was creeping from the east. The pond was black with the elm's hard shadows. The jackdaw croaked and sailed into the dim copse beyond. There would be frost in the morning. "What do you want me to say?" Jo asked. "Should I say that I love you, that I need you more than Brook, that you should leave her? Or should I say it meant nothing, that there is no guilt, that Brook and I, we settled it between ourselves."

"I don't know."

Rope stood up. The cold was getting to him faster than it once had. "I don't know what I want you to say." He stepped over the creek and walked slowly around the pond's rim. "The truth, I suppose."

"What if I do not know it?"

"Did I make a mistake?"

"By staying with Brook?"

"Mm."

Jo looked away. "Do not ask me to say that."

"You are both movers. I get stuck. I don't move very much, so

I get friends who do." Rope stopped, leaning against the trunk of the elm, resting one arm along Jo's branch. "I have learned some things I did not want to know."

"That must be hard."

"You even sound like her." Rope smiled in frustration. "May I come up?"

Jo looked back along the branch. "Do you think that would be wise?"

"May I come up?"

Jo looked out over Teardrop to where Sage Creek slipped silently between the darkening trees. "All right."

The branch shuddered as Rope inched sideways and settled himself beside the haunt. They sat together over Teardrop Pond. The setting sun withdrew its warmth and left the world to blue-black shadows.

He put his cold hand over hers. "Don't leave without telling me."

She nodded. Wind played between the bare branches of the elm. And the wind pulled her story from her, whispering her life at last to Rope and Teardrop and the hard shadows. A flood of old sorrow poured from her; she was draining into the cold dusk. "I don't remember much about my parents," she said. "Except that they never wanted children.

"I was born on Mona. My parents were not cruel, they never beat me, but I was lit from the last spark of their passion. However hard I looked, I never saw any sign of love between them.

"I grew up without friends; the only child born within two years of me was trapped under a dock and drowned when I was three. So my only playmate was my sister.

"She was very pretty and terribly bold and she had a voice like silver bells. She was not really my sister. She came out of the fog when the light was still grey. We met at my secret cave. When we played, we did what she wanted: naughty things I would never have dared on my own. No matter how often I got in trouble, she never got caught. She never let a grown-up see her. She whispered at other children only once or twice, to scare them.

"You should not think I saw her every day. Most times I just crouched by myself in the secret cave, hoping she would come, listening to voices approach and fade away. As I grew older she played with me less and less. Finally she would only come on foggy mornings when the moon was new.

"The last time she came to the secret cave I was eleven years old. I had just bled for the first time, so my Naming was only days away. She would not play with me but stood at the edge of the Mist shaking her head. I thought she hated me for bleeding and I was horribly ashamed. I cried because I was so lonely. So terribly lonely. I begged her not to go.

"Then she crossed her arms and said, If you want to play, come with me."

The sorrow spilled out, leaving Jo empty. She was crying; she was crying, but she no more felt her tears than a statue felt the rain. "So I went. Into the Mist. Only there I lost my way and wandered into the Gull Warrior, and forgot my secret sister, and forgot my name, and forgot myself." A sob shook her empty body. "And there I will return."

Rope looked at her in grief and wonder. The day had given way to cold twilight. He had to do something. Stop staring and do something. He squeezed her white hand and put his arm around her shoulder.

Jo glanced up at him, startled, gold eyes flaring. "I did not ask."

"I know."

She reached to touch his hand. "Anything I take from Brook I have to give back."

"You are taking nothing," Rope said. "This is mine to give."

When two weeks had passed and the ships had been mended, Seven asked Stone for permission to use the boathouse.

He worked each day, all day. He no longer went down to the sandy beach to train. He shaped the timber with his adz and plane, bent it in the steambox, and tacked his boat together, piece by piece.

Stone was no fool. When he heard that the son of Delta's most famous shipwright was building a boat in his yard, he asked if Seven would let the villagers watch. So the men of Clouds End cut back on their fishing and gathered each day in the boathouse, asking polite questions and helping Seven when he needed a spar cut, or a plank planed.

Although they always observed a respectful distance, there was something soothing in their company. Seven found himself looking forward to each day's work. Not that he meant to give up his voyage. Not that his heart did not ache. But at least when he woke in the morning he knew there would be something awaiting him besides his ghosts.

Foam and Shale dropped by at least once a day to watch and talk about old times, when no other islanders were around. "Getting on," Foam said one afternoon, surveying the work.

"Yes," Seven said. His ship was shaped like a leaf, with a strong oak hull.

"Why willow-wood for the deck and rails?" Shale asked.

Seven's hands fell still. "For his wife."

"Wife?"

Seven's eyes were colder than the grey sea, his voice more empty. "I heard her screaming for days afterward. Weeks. And the children."

"You need not tell us anything," Foam said.

"He just would not stop talking. It was pouring rain; I could not think for the sound of it." Seven blinked and shrugged. "I put my sword through his throat just to shut him up."

The boathouse smelled of wood. Wet spars, aging timbers, fresh sawdust, curls of planed wood they would gather at the end of the day for kindling. Seven heard again the sad sound of rain. "Someone had to be blamed, you see. So I found someone to be responsible. Someone wise and loving. Someone who meant everything to someone else. And once I found him, he started talking, trying to make me go away, twisting me around. But I was stupid. I could not let him do that to me. Not again." The old pain squeezed at Seven's chest. "I should have listened. But I thought I had already learned everything he had to teach me. So I killed him. I killed him for Pond. And do you know what I had then?"

Foam shook his head.

"Two dead people."

Shale looked away.

Foam said, "Seven, if it means anything—"

"Don't," Seven said. "My sins are between me and my dead."

He launched his ship on the last day of autumn. The villagers watched from the rocks. Foam and Shale walked out to the end of the dock carrying a large bag between them.

"Morning," Seven said, squinting over the rails. His hull was smooth and bare, without the usual knotwork carving.

Shale scowled. "Going without us."

"Yep."

"Nice ship," Foam remarked. "Got a name for her yet?"

"Not yet. I will by the time I return."

"Speaking of returning," Foam said, "we wondered if you were taking adequate precautions. We though we should help out." He and Shale lifted the large bag over the rails and set it on the foredeck.

"Where am I supposed to stow it?"

"In your cabin, I guess." Shale shrugged. "In that bag you will find plenty of rope and a deal of biscuits."

"More pepper than you could use in a lifetime," Foam added.

Seven studied the bag. "If you don't leave soon, I think I risk crying."

"We would never tell," Foam said.

Shale nodded. "Promise."

The Deltan eased his slender ship out of the harbor, turned her nose eastward, and sailed into the rising sun. Some time later Foam and Shale walked back up the dock. If Seven wept they never told of it to any soul.

CHAPTER 27: THE TWINS' STORY

One month later the last of the jerries had run. The fish barrels were full, the gardens dead, and the harvest feast would soon mark the start of the hungry part of the year.

Sweetpea was complaining more frequently of arthritis. Shallot had left Finch. Gone to visit relations on Trickfoot, he said, but nobody expected to see him again. Finch left her empty home and brought her baby to live with Brook and Rope, severely testing the twins' patience. They did not for an instant believe they had ever been so much trouble.

The harvest feast was delicious, as always. "Here we are stuffing ourselves because we know food will be scarce by spring," Jo said sardonically to Rope. "Much like erecting a funeral pyre in a drought-stricken forest, is it not?"

"Mm." Rope was remembering Jo taking the shape of the Emperor, running her nails along Bronze Switch's throat. Remembering the puppet play they had seen in the Arbor. Wondering if he had put out Rowan Hilt's life when he doused the fire eating the puppeteers' paper screen.

Skinny, energetic Twig boasted to the other children about his grandfather Stick, now dead two years: the first person to spend a night on Shale's island. Shandy told a story of Queen Lianna, and Foam contributed one of the Gull Warrior's less likely adventures. "Anyone else?" Shandy said, wiping tears of laughter from her eyes when Foam had done.

"We have a story!" Feather cried.

Brook smiled at her daughter. "I think Shandy wanted a grown-up story."

Boots frowned. "It is a grown-up story. I mean, we're kids, but the story is for grown-ups."

Brook glanced at Shandy, who smiled, shrugged, and gave in. "All right. Who will tell it?"

"Me," Feather said.

Boots nodded.

"Ahem!" Feather glared around the room, waiting for silence. Parents quieted children who didn't see why they had to hush for a mere kid.

"What kind of a story is it?" Foam asked.

Feather glanced quickly at Boots. "One Twist Ring," he muttered. "Second half of one, anyway."

Brook could not help glancing at Jo. Their eyes met and held for the space of a long heartbeat. They were two halves of a one twist ring, Garden had said. Two shadows of a single flame.

Feather said:

"This is a story of the real world, where everything is true, and nothing is what it seems to be."

Inside-Outside

After Seven stowed the bag Foam and Shale had given him, there was barely enough room to lie down inside his tiny cabin.

As he sailed he thought about old Craft, his father, still making ships back in Delta. Craft would be pleased with this boat. She handled well, swift and sure as a gull in flight.

He was eager to plunge into the Mist before his fear could grow. He thought often about Chart, the greatest explorer of all time, with his endless supply of rope and biscuits and pepper. He thought about Foam and Shale. And Pond.

The Mist came over him at twilight. Moonlit clouds swallowed the sky, luminous grey. The Mist began to thicken, taking shape. Fear rose in him. He knew it would work the Mist, but he couldn't stop it surging from his wrists and ankles. Fear trickled like grey fog from under his tongue.

The first ghost he saw was that of Bone, the sentry he had slain on the beach after swimming away from the disastrous raid on Delta. Then came Ash Spear, sick and burning. The four soldiers he had killed in his father's house. Hazel Twist, steel in his throat. Brine. Rose. Shoal screaming as pale flames danced above his shrivelling skin. Two bandits with black tongues.

Pond.

He threw himself into his tiny cabin and pulled the hatch closed. He huddled in the darkness, surrounded by willow-wood, locked in a floating coffin.

The casket began to rock, dipping and plunging amidst the waves. The swell was growing. He heard the wind's cry and the willow's tears. What kept him sane was the smell of pepper, overpowering in the tiny crawl space. Pepper and biscuit.

A knock crashed above his head. "Who floats in the hollow log?" roared a hurricane voice.

"Seven. Who are you?"

And the waves cried, "Fathom!"

Then there came a great storm upon the sea.

Feather pursed her lips and glared at a restless child in the crowd, who swiftly fell silent. "That's better," Feather sniffed.

She dropped her voice down. " 'I will set you free on one condition,' Fathom said. 'From time to time I may be angered, or playful, or simply bored, and I will drown you beneath cold waters.'

" 'One moment! I must consider your offer,' Seven said. For, you see, he meant to learn the secret of the sea. So lying there in the dark, barely able to move in his tiny cabin, he took the extra rope his friends had given him, and wove it into a slipknot. And when the knot was ready he called out, 'Very well! I am of the sea. I accept your offer.'

"So then Fathom lifted up the hatch and tore back the planks above the cabin and said, 'Now you are free!' But before he could do anything else, Seven, who was the mightiest warrior of all the islanders, leapt up and dropped the slipknot over his head.

" 'What do you want?' Fathom cried. 'How dare you?'

" 'I dare anything,' Seven replied. 'And I want to know the secret of the sea.'

" 'Ha! No mortal can force my secrets from me!' Fathom cried. They wrestled then for nine or maybe eight hours, and even though Seven was the mightiest warrior of all the islanders, he grew very weary. But his slipknot held fast and the more Fathom struggled, the tighter the knot closed, until finally he had to stay still just to breathe, and a calm fell over the sea.

" 'Very well,' Fathom whispered. 'You have bested me. What do you want?'

"And again Seven said, 'The secret of the sea.'

" 'And if I tell you, will you let me go?'

" 'If you promise to tell the truth, and not to hurt me after I set you free.'

"Fathom was very angry, and his face turned as purple as a storm-cloud, but 'Very well,' he said. 'I have no choice. The secret of the sea is this: to stand is to lose. Ride the wave, or drown beneath it.'

" 'That's it?' Seven said.

" 'That's it.'

"So Seven took the slipknot off Fathom's neck, and the Hero left in a very bad temper. And Seven said, 'It is good to have plenty of rope,' as he stored it back in his tiny cabin.

"He sailed on through the Mist for nine or maybe eight days. Sometimes his ghosts went away for a while, but usually there were some with him, and he had to learn to get along with them as well as he could. He could even look at them, if he had to, but he could not bring himself to listen to their voices.

"One day, as he sailed on through the Mist, he saw a spark on the horizon. It leapt from wavetop to wavetop, running like fire toward him. Before he could think to do anything, he saw Sere standing before him, a flat dancing figure like a shadow of flame.

'Hello!' Sere cried, with a voice like a hungry volcano. 'You are Seven. Fathom told me about you.' And he reached out with jerky arms to devour a passing porpoise.

"Seven said, 'Could we carry on this conversation at a slightly greater distance? You are burning a hole in my boat.'

" 'Oh. Sorry about that.' Swaying and dancing, Sere held out his own right hand and gobbled it up with a crackling laugh. 'You have something here that belongs to me!'

" 'I do?' Seven said, feeling his right hand begin to burn. Fire danced over the fingers he had taught so well to kill.

" 'Mmm, yes. The ashes of your dead love.' And then Seven realized that Fathom was getting his revenge by sending Sere to take away the thing that meant the most to him in the whole world. Now his heart too began to burn with his love for Pond who was dead.

"But he could hardly try to wrestle with Sere as he had with Fathom. So he said, 'One moment. I keep the ashes in my hold.' He reached into his tiny cabin, pulled up the casket of pepper that Foam and Shale had given him, and gave it to Sere. For he knew as well as you do that Sere has eaten far too much to have any sense left of taste or smell.

"Well, Sere opened the lid and found the casket full of tiny black grains like ash. 'My thanks,' he said cheerfully. 'I expected you to be more troublesome, after what you did to old Fathom.' He winked at Seven and sniggered.

"Seven bowed deeply, feeling again the hungers that had driven him to practice, and love, and kill. 'You made me,' he said. 'The good and the bad together.'

"The flaming puppet danced and grinned, feinting as if to eat the masts, and then darting suddenly away. 'I have done worse.'

"Seven sailed for nine or eight more long days, not knowing what he waited for and not sure if he would like it when he found it."

Feather stopped to cough and take a sip of water.

"Then one morning his boat began to rise. He was on a pinnacle of rock, growing like a mountain from the sea. Oh no! he thought.

I shall be stranded in the air, and never sail out of the Mist and back to the islands! What shall I do?"

Seven saw then that he was held in the palm of an old man, enormously tall. His massive feet were bare and grey, his legs carved into stiffly moving muscle. His chest was hidden in a mat of curling white hair that blended with his beard and the hair on his head, and all this hair was wonderfully fine, finer than cottonwood down, tremulously wavering.

"Mountains turn to cloud," Seven said.

"Hello," Stonefinger said, in a voice as soft as fog.

Seven bowed deeply. "It is said that stone lasts forever and its master has power over death." He was a cloud inside; dread left him drifting, unanchored. He took his life in his hands. "Can you give my beloved back to me?"

Stonefinger shook his sad, cloudy head. "No," he said. Ocean waves curled about his knees.

Never give up, Seven told himself. Never give up. But something inside him pulled into tatters, mist shredded by the wind.

Stonefinger sighed, a long, gusty breath, and shook his head. "I grieve for you." His eyes and mouth were obscured by drifting coils of hair. A bar of sunlight shone through him, leaving a circle of misty gold on his brow.

"Will you do nothing for me?"

"Death is sudden and reckless and unpredictable. It has all the qualities of the sea. Had you noticed?"

Stonefinger flipped his fingers in the cold sea and ripples raced from them, quickly created, quickly gone. "Death is closest to the people of the sea. They stand impossibly upon it, walking on water until the inevitable happens, and they slip." He took his fingers from the sea and dried them on his beard. The hairs writhed and drifted like the spines of a white sea anemone. "I have often wondered how you bear it. To live in a world that is always changing, held above the sea's grasp only by shelves of stone that could be flooded in an instant. Such is the perilous existence of the people of the sea, for the sea is their god and the Gull Warrior their champion, that evil spirit who destroys all I create."

Seven tensed, but Stonefinger ignored him. "It is only now that I am old, older than old, that I begin to feel a need for change, a need to let go. Some time, in another eon or so when I have gathered all I can from the stone which is my first love, I will surrender, and drift where the wind directs. Then, perhaps, I will visit the sea and learn the secrets that it kills to teach."

Stonefinger considered. "You islanders must be a very wise people, for you must learn in fourscore years what I have not yet mastered in a long age of the world."

"I do not feel wise," Seven said. "I feel only pain."

"I grieve I cannot give you back your loved one. You have made a hero's journey. I will offer you this, that I have never before offered to any people but my own. Stand with me on the mountain's peak. Perhaps you will find wisdom there, of a sort, and relief from pain."

Then Stonefinger lifted up Seven's boat far, far above the sea, while Seven clung to his mast and looked out in wonder. "Stand," Stonefinger said. "Stand and look upon the world."

Islands of white cloud hung down from the deeps of the sky, changeful as rivers, solid as mountains. Seven stood, blinking, as Stonefinger held him up to the dawn of the world, looking east to the crawling sea. Looking south, grasslands gave way to forest, and eventually to a ribbon of fire below a pall of smoke. In the north, the grass was splintered by rivers. Then a barren place, and beyond that a desert at the fingertips of vision, where a web of dancing ice rose hard and white above the land.

To the west, towering mountains, immeasurably vast, crested at last into a spume of cloud. A stone hymn rose through Seven, ringing against the sky.

Feel

the

grandeur
of
the
living
world!

Feel
it
turn
beneath
your
feet.

Feel
it
swing
above
your
head.

It
is
vaster,
older,
kinder,
crueler.

"Does it fear nothing?" Seven whispered.

Time.

Wind-toothed
time
it
fears.

"But it keeps fighting." Seven felt something revive within himself. Bereft and destroyed and directionless, his indomitable will still breathed. "It keeps fighting."

But the mountain said:

Perhaps.

Perhaps
the
sea
struggles,
or
the
ice.

The
stone
endures.

Only
endures . . .

until
the
forest
is
desert.

Until
the
sun
goes
out.

Until
the
fire
freezes.

Until
the
earth
is
mist.

Until
clouds
end.

Dazed and frightened, Seven clutched for his rails. Through a rift in the cloud overhead he could see the stars growing closer. "Spit!" he whispered. He was humbled by the stone's voice, but he could not endure. He was of the sea: he must struggle, or perish.

Then he thought of the bag Foam and Shale had given him. "It worked for Chart," he muttered. "It can work for me."

Feverishly he grabbed the extra biscuits, crushing them in his strong hands. He threw crumbs on the deck and on the ground and down the maintain's sides, all the time fearing he had gone too high for rescue.

Then a speck, a dot, a fly—a bird flew out from behind the moon's silver face. It drifted down to him as gently as a snowflake and landed on his transom. It was a gull.

Shrieking, it gobbled bits of biscuits.

As if that first quarrelsome cry had been a long-awaited signal, other gulls began to scream, wheeling and screeching above the boat. Seven threw biscuit crumbs madly into the air. The more gulls there were, the more tightly they pressed together, fighting, banking, carving the air with incredible grace. A form began to emerge, building from the gulls as Seven's ghosts had built from the Mist. . . .

"The Gull Warrior!" Feather cried. Several children cheered; the rest had fallen asleep. Behind Feather, a small fire hummed quietly to itself, a little song of sparks and embers. Outside the sun had long since set, and the winter moon had begun to rise.

"And then the Gull Warrior chopped at the mountain, pecking and slashing and biting and beating it back down to size, as he always did when Stonefinger tried to grow too tall. At last he had that mountain pecked right down below the surface of the water, and Seven wisely shipped his oars and pulled away as fast as he could.

"The two Heroes fell to fighting. They battled for seven or maybe six days, and in the end the Gull Warrior was victorious. Spotting

a weakness in Stonefinger's defense, he aimed a mighty blow and
shivered the stone man to splinters."

It was over. Bits of shattered rock rained from the sky. More
than one piece bounced off Seven's shrouds and onto his deck.
He reached out and touched a fragment. Red marble. Still warm.

He remembered what Stonefinger had said, about the evil Gull
Warrior destroying everything he tried to build. He was not sure
what he should be feeling. Even Sere who was allied with the forest
people had treated him better than Fathom.

"Quite the show, eh?" said a sweet, weary voice by his elbow.

Seven jumped almost out of his skin. "Singer!" he whispered.

"And you are Seven. We have met." She reached out and picked
up a fragment of warm red marble. "He does explode nicely." She
held the piece of stone up to her lips and breathed on it. Then
she held it in her hands and started rubbing it and stretching it
and molding it this way and that.

"Hey! I can talk. You must not be telling a story."

"But I am, right now, even as we speak, everywhere the wind
blows. You are in the story, you see." And all the while she spoke,
she was shaping the stone into the form of a small man made of
rock.

The figurine was larger now. It moved fitfully in the Singer's
hand. "This is a fine boat you have here," she said. "I appreciate
good work. I see you brought along plenty of rope, lots of biscuits,
and a good supply of pepper." The Singer nodded approvingly.
"Always wise." The figurine in her hand was now—Seven could
not explain this—the size of a normal man, even though Seven
and the Singer were still sitting on the foredeck of his small boat,
and the figure still fit comfortably between the Singer's palms.

"You are making Stonefinger again."

The Singer nodded. "I need him to keep things exciting."

"Is that all the Warrior's struggles are to you? A trifle? An
amusement?"

The Singer gazed at Seven then with her ancient eyes. For the first time he beheld a strength and a will more terrible than his own. "Fathom does not rage nor does Sere burn with more passion than I tell my stories."

He could not bear to meet her eyes.

The Singer considered. "A ship like this, a ship with character—it needs a good name." She rose, and placed Stonefinger in the water. The man of the mountains waved peevishly and sank below the water. "May I suggest *Clouds End*—port of leave and call. You must sail there twice from different sides that are, after all, the same, to make a proper one twist ring."

She stepped over the side of the boat to stand, rocking gently on the waves. "I would love to stay and talk," she said, "only, I am telling a story right now, this instant, even as we speak." Seven saw lines of weariness around her eyes. "Wherever the wind blows, I am telling stories to the grass and to the clouds. It is a great labor. Too great, I sometimes feel. But there is no use complaining. One must persist. To give up is also to lose. But then," she said, gliding away in long, smooth strides, "you knew that all along, didn't you?"

Seven sat a long time in the Mist after the Singer had gone, thinking of how he had become a man of stone. How he had held stiff before Pond's death and let himself be broken. And he thought of the Gull Warrior, ceaselessly circling, dodging, feinting. Patient and fierce and playful.

There was a balance, then, between struggle and despair. The balance that let the Warrior ride the wind. The balance every islander knew who dared the waves in a well-built boat, poised between the unreachable sky and the unfathomable sea.

At last Seven took the silver-stoppered bottle and opened it and shook Pond's ashes overboard, weeping. Then he cleaned off his deck, and shook out his sail to catch the wind, and turned his white-winged ship for home.

When the story was over, a daunting silence hung in the meeting hall.

"Never give up," Jo said.

Everyone was staring at Feather. "Um, that's all," she said, in a small, meek voice.

Brook touched her daughter's hand. "Where did you hear that story?"

Feather looked at her brother for support. Boots shrugged. "The wind told us," he said.

CHAPTER 28: WHERE ALL THINGS ARE TRUE

On midwinter morning, eight years to the day after Brook's wedding, a single white gull beat up from Clouds End, heading east. As it rose, the low roar of the waves faded; the patient thoughts of the old stone went dumb as well. The gull was free, as free as the air and as alone. Voice after voice fell mute as she pulled away from the world, away from its pain and blood and fire—flying back into the soft white breath of morning.

The wind blew through her ribs, touching the secret places in her heart. It poured through a growing emptiness and set her whole body helplessly singing; and a silver voice whispered, Come with me.

But Jo said, Not yet.

Brook too had left Clouds End, sailing for the last time from its shores to make her vigil on Shale's island, her final act before becoming Witness.

She sat on a large rock in the middle of the stream she had named after old Stick, watching the water sweep endlessly toward her. It was deep here but clear, running over clean stone. Splinters of sunshine glinted on the surface. Farther down, coin-colored fish darted out from the banks or held themselves against the current for many heartbeats before sliding back into the shadow of her rock.

She loved running water. After all, she had taken a stream's name for her own: Brook. There was much of herself here. So she had chosen this place to wait for the island's name.

Shandy expected her to find the name, of course. That was why she had been sent here for her first Witnessing. So she waited, wondering if the Singer would find her again.

But the more Brook thought about the Singer and Sere and Heroes and the Mist, the less they meant to her. The island was not some story; it was itself: leafless birch-limbs and the cool winter sun on her back and the smell of cold water. She had been here all day, listening to the wind hiss through barren branches. Sometimes the water seemed not to be pouring toward her at all, but to be still, and it was she who moved, sailing upstream, while just below her dangling feet foam curled out from a stone prow.

A tangle of twigs slid toward, by, behind her, wet-brown and slowly spinning, out of sight, gone. They had broken from their roots to go on a great journey that would carry them beyond all trees, beyond all grass and stone and sand, into the endless sea.

And Brook thought about desire, and anger, and fear, and joy— sliding by her one after the other, ripples in the river of her life. Downstream, her parents drifted in the ocean. Far upstream, grandchildren, or perhaps new friends, were already floating in-exorably down on her. And it seemed her whole story was like this: a ceaseless shifting, a stream woven of uncountable waves.

Her backside ached from being in one position too long, and she stirred, smiling at herself. Well then, if life was a stream, there were good sturdy rocks in it too. Rope. Her children. Shale. Clouds End itself! Wind. The sea. These were her safe places, her stepping stones across the stream of life.

Stones in the stream. "Islands," she whispered. She remembered Boots, his tireless dam-building. What were islands but rocks in the water? The world was a great stream, a play of un-certain waves studded with these stones. And her people stepped from one rock to the next, walking their mighty journey upstream to the source, the last mystery. Into the Mist.

"Stepping Stone," she announced to the trees and the rock and the bubbling water. "Your name is Stepping Stone. Do not forget!"

The gull found Brook as midwinter night was falling. It drifted like a snowflake from the darkening sky to land beside her little campfire. Jo stretched; blurred; shook her head until her face widened and her feathers gave way to silky hair. Fingers wriggled from an outstretched wing.

Across the campfire, Brook sat with her brazier on one side and her little ceremonial knife on the other. Weakness shivered through her, bringing back the memory of the long-ago morning Jo had first landed on the shore of Clouds End and changed her life forever. She remembered how hurt she had been to understand for the first time that she might not want to see the story waiting for her in the Mist.

It occurred to Brook that she was very much alone.

"Hello," she said.

"Sister." Jo cocked her head to the side. "Have you named the island?"

"Stepping Stone."

"That's good."

"Not part of the Sere and Warrior story, but—"

Jo snapped with laughter. "It is our story. We can name it what we want."

Night sounds were building: the roar of the cold surf, always more solemn after the sun went down; the tiny campfire, hiss, crackle. A coal popped open and a shower of sparks burst from its heart.

"What do you want from me?"

"Are you so busy you have no time for talk?"

"No, I—"

"Just talk." The haunt seemed tired and frail, as frail as one of the paper screens from a woodlander puppet show—so dreadfully thin, Brook felt she could tear at any moment and reveal the fire behind.

"Do you love me?" Jo said.

Fifteen heartbeats. Twenty.

"You do. You do love me."

"Sometimes, it's as if we are lovers," Brook whispered. "And sometimes it's as if we are fighting to the death."

The fire had left Jo's eyes for the first time since she took the Spark. In the moonlight they gleamed silver again. "I am in you," Jo said. "No one will ever know you as I do, Brook. Not Shandy, not Rope, not your kinsmen nor your children. I am closer to you than you are to yourself. I can see what you never dare to look at. And I love you."

Brook reached up and brushed Jo's white cheek with her hand. "I know."

"Do not become Witness, Brook. It is all I can do now to hold on. You have a family and a life and a village around you and I have nothing. But at least we share the magic. Even if I am the ugly sister, the one nobody wants, I know we are still somehow the same. But if you chain even your magic, sinking it down into the rocks of Clouds End, then you take away the last thing that keeps us together." Beneath Brook's hand Jo's skin was cool and soft as blossoms; so precious. So precious. "I love you, Brook. At least let me do that."

And Brook ached to go with Jo, to stop fighting her and walk a path of moonlight over the black sea. But her hand fell as she remembered the sad sound of rain, Rope confessing, the world dropping out from under her. Remembered how it felt to learn she was as worthless as she had always feared. "Rope loves me too. But you both betrayed me."

"Why can you forgive him but not me?"

"I forgive him because I have to," Brook said. "You are right. You are like me." The moment when she and Jo could have been friends was passing, passing. Gone. She hated herself for destroying it. "I guess I expected better from myself."

The campfire's flickering red light held the two women close together, surrounded by a vast sighing darkness.

Jo turned away. She took one of the sticks Brook had gathered and tossed it on the fire. When she looked back, a gold flush had crept over her eyes. "Cold out tonight, isn't it? Remember Ash?"

Brook watched fire crawl up the new log, licking black blisters onto its skin.

"The world is not always kind," Jo said. She pulled out one of her bootlaces. "What is this one?" she said, tying a knot around the end of a stick.

"A round turn and two half-hitches."

"It has been too long since I practiced."

Jo undid the knot. Brook hunched closer to the fire. "Shale taught me that one. Actually she taught me all of them."

"The night is cold," Jo said.

"We always stopped everything and played outside when it snowed," Brook said. "Once it started early in the morning and Shale hid on my roof until I came out to play and then dumped a huge pile on me as I stepped out the door."

Jo laughed. She twisted her bootlace round, down, up through the hole . . .

"Around the tree," Brook prompted.

"And down the hole again. And that is a . . . bowline?"

"Mm-hmm."

The fire cracked and a dance of sparks flew out. Red light played over Jo's face. "I am burning."

Brook shifted in the darkness. "Are you sure you want to share your secrets with me?"

"Who else is there? You at least can understand."

Jo's hair drifted around her shoulders like smoke. Red-gold light flickered in her eyes. "When I twinned you I took on so much of the sea. Then I took the Emperor's shape, and took the Spark that was burning him up inside. And now . . ." Shocked, Brook saw that Jo was crying. Crying! Gold tears gathered in her eyes and rolled one by one down her face, falling into shadow. "Air, sea, and fire struggle within me. They are tearing me apart, Brook. They are tearing me apart."

Jo waited until her voice stopped shaking. "Have you ever seen a spark fall on a piece of paper, Brook? It makes a little hole, a little black hole with a faint red rim. And every time the wind blows through the hole, it eats away its edges. It makes this hollow space. And the larger the space gets, the colder and emptier it is, and the more air comes through, and the more the fire burns. The more you want it to burn." She picked apart the bowline, head bowed as if she were speaking to the knot. "So there is this hollow place, you see, where the wind blows through. And it is always growing bigger."

Jo took the two ends of her bootlace and laid them side by side. "Is your story finished?"

Desperately Jo began to plait the two strands together. "This is . . . ?"

"A reef knot."

"What is it for?"

"To join . . ." Brook stopped, looking into the fire. "To join two ropes of equal strength."

Jo said, "Did I do it right?"

"Yes." Brook turned away from Jo and looked into the darkness. "But it's only string."

A long heartbeat later Jo said, "You are hard, Brook." Her eyes were drying, drying. Dry. Dry as cracked earth. Dry as dead grass.

Brook's eyes were caught by the fire's ceaseless weaving. "I am not a very strong person." She felt contemptible; she hated herself for her weakness, her envy. Her fear. "You have beauty. Knowledge. Magic. You can see where I am blind. You have everything I ever wanted."

"Except roots."

"You are tired." Brook searched through her pack and dug out a strip of smoked bass. "Have this. I took plenty. There is water in the cup there; I got it from the stream."

"Thank you," Jo said. The fish she did not touch, but she gulped the water gratefully. Her hand when Brook touched it, taking back the cup, was as dry as paper and fiercely hot.

"When Ash killed himself, I could feel why he did it, feel the hunger. The release. But the pain!" Jo drank a second cup of water more slowly. "But at least he wanted to burn. Brook, I have been fighting it for eight years now. Eight years while the Spark ate me hollow."

"I am sorry."

"You should be! You and all the sea people. I leeched fire from the Emperor, and the forest troops pulled back. But I got nothing for it."

Brook said, "We are grateful."

"No, you are not." Jo drained the cup. "You are happy it was done, but you do not care about me."

Brook said, "Sometimes great things can be asked only of the great."

The haunt laughed. "Yes! Yes, that is me: a grand character in the story of the islands. A Hero of Legend." Night had come, and the little campfire hid Jo's face in shaking shadows. "Ask Seven how nice a thing that is to be. Do you think it matters more to him that Delta honors his name or that Pond is dead?"

"More water?"

"Please."

Brook poured out the last of the water and passed it back over the little fire.

"It is your anniversary tonight. Eight years now you have been married to Rope. Did you like the feather I left for you to find on your wedding day?"

"You left that?"

The haunt's hand was a dim blur as she took the cup. "I did not stop the Emperor for the islands, Brook. I did not do it for the Warrior, not in the end. I did it for the people I loved."

"Rope, for instance."

"Of course I loved him! I had to, Brook. I had no choice. As long as you loved him, then I must as well." Jo looked away into the darkness, blinking back tears. When she faced Brook again the gold in her eyes had faded. It was only the fire, reflected in brown eyes.

Only the fire. "Did you never understand? I told you from the beginning. Haunts never die. Sooner or later we all get caught, knotted in a sheet bend with something stronger than ourselves. You were that thing, Brook. You are the candle and I am the shadow you cast."

"Me? You were the one with the magic! With the beauty and

, every chance you could."

"Of course I fought you! The fish fights the hook, too. I was fighting for my life, Brook. Fighting to be something more than your shadow."

Down the beach behind them the surf hissed and mumbled. The sea's breath was salt and seaweed and cold sand. Darkness lapped around their little circle of firelight.

"That night last spring," Brook said. "You called me out to see the moon."

Jo nodded. "I heard Shandy talking—Oh yes, I never left Clouds End, not all the times you thought I was gone. I was a mouse under your floor, an owl in the woods. You were my family, you villagers. And though you did not want me—none of the villagers and you least of all—I could never leave you. You were all the very little I had.

"I heard Shandy talking. I knew she was planning to make you her apprentice. I knew you would become even stronger then. And all this time the Spark was eating me away, and the hole in my heart was getting bigger, and the wind blew through. And you, you were like Ivy," Jo said. "You would never help me. You were content to see me drift into the Mist. You were not too proud to drink the rain."

"I am sorry," Brook said, and she meant it. Jo, poor Jo, was a broken thing, an empty sorrow that could not be filled. She alone could have been the haunt's friend. And she had walked away.

Jo's face had lost its edges: the great hooked nose, the bony eyebrows, the narrow eyes, all blurred, softened, settled into features much less harsh. An islander face. "I did not want you to be her apprentice. Shandy! She could give you one island; I could give you wind-rhymes and starsong, the dolphin's chat and the owl's cry, the stones and the sea! I was jealous, I suppose."

"There is more to it than that," Brook said. "You did not sleep with Rope for my good. I nearly drowned when you took me on that path of moonlight."

Jo nodded. "I wanted you to come with me into the Mist. The Spark has almost hollowed me out; unless I pass it on, I will be consumed, and lose myself for good." She drank the last of the water. Set the cup down. "It is lonely in the Mist, Brook. So lonely.

"I was lost there for a long time before I met you. I had a friend there once. She still speaks to me sometimes. But I am too old to play with anymore even when the moon is young. When she is full, she blinds me. When she is old, she laughs at me."

Jo's voice was softer now, full of longing. "We could have had great fun, on the other side! The things I would have shown you!"

"Once I might have come. But not now. There are too many things to hold me to the world."

Jo said, "I have been thinking about that."

And she turned a shell bracelet around her wrist. Click. Crack.

Brown. Her hair is brown now, Brook thought, feeling her heart jump unsteadily. And her eyes are dark brown, too. And her face is my face.

No one will ever know.

And Jo, looking into the fire, said, "You know what happens in twin stories, Brook. There are terrible truths in stories." Reflected flames danced in her eyes. "Give her to me, Brook."

"Give who?"

"I left the feather for you to find."

"No!" Not Feather, not her little girl. Hunched over a spider web, blond braid carelessly thrown behind, all grass and mud and laughter. "Please, Jo, not this. You cannot ask this of me."

"Give me the child and I will leave Clouds End forever, I swear it. What is not offered will be taken," Jo whispered. "Do not make me ask for more, Brook."

"No." Brook's mouth was dry. Slowly, slowly, her hand slid through the shadows at her side, reaching for her little copper knife. "I could have killed you," she said. "I could have left you here for Sere eight years ago, as Shale wanted me to. I could have killed you after we left the Arbor, but I chose to let you live."

"You would not kill me, but you were willing to let me burn. You with your husband and your family and your home, you were great enough to let me come and beg for scraps." Jo stopped. "I sound angry. I would have done the same. Oh, Brook, I would never kill you," Jo said softly. "I could never do that. Never do that. A sting is all, a little sting. You'll barely feel it." And now the nails on Jo's hands were long and golden, as if made of beaten bronze. When she shook her head, her brown hair began to spark and glow.

The Emperor had stabbed her, Brook remembered. And she had lived. She had plucked the Spark from him and now she meant to give it to Brook.

And Jo said, "You always knew a story waited for you, Brook. You always knew you were meant to take a great journey in the Mist. You knew that the day I met you. Last spring you felt it call you from behind the moon."

"They will know."

Jo shook her head. "The real things do not care: the sea and the stone. They do not care if either of us lives or dies."

Panic was rising, filling Brook up like water, drowning her. "They do on Clouds End! The rocks know my footprints and the trees know the touch of my hand and Sage Creek has whispered my name as it ran out of Teardrop, not yours. They will know! You think they won't tell the difference? Rope will know. Net! Net is of the Mist. Net will know."

Hanging in four braids behind her neck, Jo's brown hair swung softly as she shook her head. "Do you really not understand? Brook's story will go on. Brook's story will go on and Jo's will end. One twin always goes into the Mist. Jo swallowed fire and Brook was the lucky one." As she spoke, a bee tumbled from behind her ear and hung around her shoulder, buzzing. Another one followed, then another.

"Feather and Boots! My babies will know it isn't me! Shandy will make you give it back, give everything back . . ." Brook's voice broke.

"You have always known, Brook." Jo looked at her with soft brown eyes that were terribly her own. "I am your seventh wave."

"It isn't fair!" Brook cried. She was sick with fear. Her insides had been turned to Mist; she was fog swirling in a shell of skin. "You didn't carry those babies. You didn't scream to give them birth. You never woke up in the middle of the night and stumbled through the darkness to feed them."

"Don't cry, Brook! Don't cry." There were tears in Jo's eyes. "I would die before I let anything happen to them, I swear it. No one can love them as much as their mother, don't you see?"

Little Feather with her blond hair flying. Boots, hunched over a puzzle, frowning his serious frown.

With a cry, Brook grabbed her copper brazier and hurled it at Jo, scattering the campfire embers and throwing a gout of sparks into the air. Then she was running for her life.

She staggered wildly down the sloping dune toward the beach, boots crunching through pebbles, driftwood, crab shells. There were no footsteps behind her, no human sound but her ragged breathing.

Onto the beach. Sand sucked at her feet and she ran as if in a nightmare, so slowly, every step a torture, angling for the boat she had sailed here from Clouds End. The little ceremonial knife was slick in her sweaty hand.

Where was Jo? Had she stunned her twin? Clipped her with a lucky hit when she threw the brazier? She risked a glance backwards but saw nothing.

The cold night sky glittered with a million stars. Her heart was racing and her gasps were huge in her ears. Crashing and hissing, waves broke in the darkness. Creeping froth glimmered in the starshine just ahead. She was almost at the waterline.

Good. Good. She had time, she had a little time. She reached the harder sand and ran faster, throwing up a spatter of spray with every splashing step. If only she could make the boat.

Lacing up Boots's heavy winter coat.

She felt the faintest puff of wind on the back of her neck, and her heart froze. An owl's scream exploded behind her head; talons pierced her shoulder like nails.

She stumbled into the sea and turned to see Jo behind her.

The haunt's hair sparked and shone. Veins of fire pulsed in her throat and dripped like burning tears from her eyes. The sea bubbled at her feet, sending a great cloud of steam up around them both, and her voice was like a hiss of wind rustling over burning paper. "The world has seen us apart," she said. "Now it sees us one."

Fixing Feather's braid.

Brook gripped the little copper knife, feeling the Mist burning in her heart. "I'll kill you," she said.

This is a story of the real world, of Mist and stone and starshine, that is also the tale of two women.

Two women? the Witness asked.

And the wind, who tells all stories, even this one, even now, said, Brook.

It was the early evening of a clear winter day when Brook's boat rounded the Talon and coasted home. A group of villagers were waiting on the dock: Sweetpea, Otter, Stone. Shale and Foam. Shandy.

Shale caught the painter with a grin and tied it to the docking ring with a round turn and two half-hitches. "Guess we'll have to call you Witness from now on!"

"Never called me that," Shandy grumbled, smiling.

Big Stone, beard now wholly white, held out an arm to help her from the boat. "I suppose we are equals now, foster-daughter. You may stay up as late as you like."

Brook walked down the dock. The others remained behind, watching her. "She has been crying," Shale said. "In Fathom's name, what does she have to grieve for?"

Shandy watched Brook step off the dock and onto the island she would never leave now, until death, or a new Witness, or the end of the world released her. "Herself," she said.

Brook walked alone. Here was the shore where she had seen Jo for the first time, and their lives had been knotted together. Climbing up the shingle, she came to the place where her twin had built a fire and thrust her arms into its red heart after Brook failed to follow her behind the moon. And here was the path through the meadow, where they had walked together so long ago, Jo treading on the wild flowers and making them squeak the day she first came to the village. Higher still, the Ridge with its stand of bare-branched poplars. There was a big elm up there that they had both sat upon, and below its hanging arm the cool green water of Tear-drop Pond. She would swim there in summer, and in autumn the falling leaves would spin slowly to the south, caught up in the pull of Sage Creek.

The stream that had given Brook her name leapt boldly over the bluffs and bounded through the rocky channel below. Then it slowed, passing the herb garden and the meadow, Sweetpea's house and Shandy's. Then down to the docks, where their little boats creaked and rocked on the back of a sea vaster than mountains and colder than stars and deeper than the sky.

And there it passed, that one little stream, out of Clouds End forever, and was lost.

And she went on to her house, and there was yellow light, and fire within; and the evening meal was ready, and she was expected. And Rope drew her in, and set her in her chair, and put little Feather upon her lap.

Brook drew a deep breath. "Well, I'm back," she said.

ACKNOWLEDGMENTS

A large book owes many debts. Thanks most of all to Christine, my love, and to Philip Freeman, to whom this book owes its theo-geology and much else besides. Thanks to White Dwarf Books and to Sean Russell, chief among the many writers whose generosity and support has meant much to me. To this day I am amazed by my agent, Martha Millard, and my editor, Susan Allison, who cope so gracefully with my frustrating tendency to turn in books utterly unlike one another. Lastly, I want to acknowledge a debt that can never be paid to J. R. R. Tolkien. He might not have liked this book, but neither it nor my career would have happened without him.